Meet your Match

Meet your Match

kandi steiner

Published by Kandi Steiner, LLC
Edited by Elaine York/Allusion Publishing, www.allusionpublishing.com
Cover Design by Staci Hart
Formatting by Elaine York/Allusion Publishing,
www.allusionpublishing.com

To the ones who run despite the rain,
who jump without fear of falling,
who open their hearts when the world says it's foolish to do so,
and who are just crazy enough to believe in love.

This one's for you.

Chapter 1

The Most Heinous Vase Ever Created

Maven

"It smells like rich assholes in here."

I wrinkled my nose to hammer that point home, and my best friend let out a soft laugh before sipping from the glass of champagne she held daintily between her fingertips. The diamonds on her warm brown wrist glittered under the chandelier, but as impressive as her jewelry was, it didn't hold a candle to the long, black, starlight-like dress hugging her curves and draping down to the floor in romantic sweeps of shimmering fabric.

"And you know that because you've had your nose buried in a rich asshole a time or two in your life?"

"Don't even have to get that far to sniff one out. Just being in the same room suffices."

The room we were *currently* in was of the ballroom variety, with elegant chandeliers, pristine marble floors, and a majestic, vaulted ceiling painted like an Italian chapel. It was one of the most historic buildings in Ybor; an old social club transformed into an upscale party for tonight's event.

When we walked up the grand staircase earlier, I was entranced by the lush gold and blood red tones. The way they mixed with the expensive wooden trim transported me back in time, as if we were attending an 18th century royal affair.

Tampa's rich and famous filled the lavish space, dressed to the nines in tuxedos and gowns that cost more than everything I currently owned put together. The only reason I was able to dress to fit in was because of Livia, who had a flair for designer clothes even before she was the highest-paid dentist in the state.

Mostly because her *dentistry* didn't just consist of filling cavities and routine cleanings — although, she'd argue she did plenty of that, too — but rather handling the absolutely brutal mouth trauma suffered by professional hockey players.

She'd been ecstatic for the chance to get me out of what she referred to as my "hippie clothes." I much preferred the flowy fabric of my Free People dresses to the form-fitting mermaid number Livia had strapped me into tonight. Although, the gorgeous yellow tone of it was my favorite. It complemented my rich, creamy brown complexion beautifully, and I'd styled my hair back in a sleek ponytail so all attention stayed on the dress.

Livia folded one arm over her middle, balancing the elbow of the other on her wrist and tilting the champagne flute to her lips again. "What exactly is the scent?"

"Dirty money, designer leather, and Bond No. 9," I said easily. "With a hint of that particular fragrance that you only find in the lobbies of million-dollar condos."

"Does my condo lobby smell?"

"It's the most pungent one in Tampa."

Her coral-painted lips curved into a saccharine smile, one that told me she took that as a compliment.

"Well, good thing you're only here to report on the event and how much these rich assholes raise for charity tonight," she said. "Wouldn't want you to catch the stench."

She elbowed me with the joke, and I smiled, pulling my phone from my clutch and switching it to cinema video mode before I took some close-up shots of the elaborate centerpiece glittering on the cocktail table we were standing at.

When I had that clip, I tucked my phone away and wrapped my hands around the camera hanging from my neck. I adjusted a few settings before taking a photograph of the table, then of Livia as she winked and tipped back the last of her champagne.

Outside of this event, when people saw us together, we didn't fit. Livia was born and raised in Long Island, New York — and her parents had the vacation house in the Hamptons to prove it. I was from the opposite side of the tracks, a humble upbringing in a suburb inland from Tampa Bay. She was also four years older than me, graduating with her doctoral degree when I had just barely clinched my bachelor's.

Still, from the moment we met, there had been an understanding between us. It was the kind you only found in someone who saw you for who you are and didn't expect you to be anyone or anything else. It was rare, and special, and something I never took for granted — especially since finding any kind of connection like that with the *opposite* sex seemed futile at this point.

Livia Young was the best thing to come out of the most traumatic relationship of my life.

As if she could sense where my head was going, Livia gently touched my shoulder. "You good?"

I ignored the twinge in my stomach when I responded. "Good. You want a picture with any of these prissy athletes?" I teased, holding up my camera.

Livia smiled at me like she knew something I didn't, shaking her head with a small smile on her lips.

I didn't mean to be so judgmental when it came to these types of events, but my upbringing made it hard to do so. Add in the events of my adult dating life, and you could say I had yet to be proven wrong.

My parents were nonconformists, through and through. They'd met while serving in AmeriCorps and proceeded to dedicate their lives to working in the communities they lived in. I was brought up on little, with a constant reminder to be grateful for all that we had. And I was — truly. Gratitude ran through me like a rushing river at having parents who cared for me, who were so selfless and kind, who filled our home with love.

It wasn't until *I* fell in love with a silver-spoon-fed athlete in college that I grew to resent those who were more well off than we were.

I blinked, deciding not to dwell on him, or anything else in the past, tonight. This evening signified the beginning of a new chapter for me, one I would make the most of.

This was my first event as the newest addition to the Tampa Bae Babes.

Despite the rather cheesy name, the TBBs were well known throughout the city for their social channels, and for the most listened-to podcast in the Bay. They covered everything from where to shop, dine, and stay, to interviewing the most influential players in the city — whether their game be politics, medicine, science, history, real estate, or pop culture.

After working tirelessly building my own online brand in the city, I was now the newest member of the team, with my specialty centering around Tampa Bay sports – which was hilarious, considering I'd rather read the dictionary front to back ten times than watch a single baseball game.

It wasn't my end goal. For me, that would always be covering what really mattered in Tampa Bay and our communities – the people giving back, every day, quietly and selflessly and without recognition.

But for now, this was my way in, and I was happy to take it.

"I need a refill," Livia said, waving her empty flute in illustration. "And I should also probably make an appearance at the VIP tables. Our general manager loves to show me off like a prized pig."

"You *do* make a very pretty pig," I cooed, running my fingers through a strand of her silky straight hair with a doting expression.

She swatted my hand away with a roll of her eyes. "Be right back."

"I'm going to get some shots of the silent auction items," I said. "Meet you there?"

Livia nodded, and then she was splitting the crowd of people like Moses split the sea, every head turning to watch her as she passed.

I took my time ambling over to the tables of items up for bid, mentally planning out the video and photo content I'd put together of the night. I made sure to take multiple video angles and transition options, knowing I wouldn't be able to come back and re-do any of them later. My parents often laughed at my job – not because they were mean, but because they genuinely didn't understand it. Not many did.

You tell someone your job is in social media, and the first reaction is almost *always* a staunch laugh.

But as confused as I was about where my life would go next, I loved what I did. I especially loved that I'd built an audience online who cared about the same things I did, who wanted to meet the game changers in their community who were the unsung heroes. I'd built a loyal following on that mission — one I wanted to take to greater heights with the Tampa Bae Babes.

But first, I had to do my time as the sports girl.

When I made it to the tables, I held my phone steady and walked slowly down the line of items up for bid. The Gibson Gala was hosted by the athletic teams in the Bay, a rare coming together of our hockey, baseball, and football teams as they raised money to benefit the many charities they supported. As such, most of the items were sports-related, everything from signed balls, pucks, and jerseys to suite tickets and player experiences.

I wished I found it impressive, that I could look at the outrageous bids already scribbled on the books in front of each item and find it awe-inspiring. Instead, I fought the urge to roll my eyes at every person in the room who felt so generous just by attending this event, never knowing what it really felt like to give back, to be face to face with those in need and extend a hand out to help them.

When I came to a rather ugly and oversized vase that stood out from the sports memorabilia surrounding it, I paused, frowning and letting my eyes assess it. It was oddly shaped, the mouth of it warped like a watch in a Dalí painting, and the body was misshapen like it had been melted instead of carved to perfection. It looked like a pottery piece made by a child trying their hand at it for the first time, the whole thing devoid of color and a proper finish. It was just a gray, weeping heap of clay posing as something of value.

"Fan of art?"

"Is that what this is supposed to be?" I asked before even looking at the person behind the low, smooth voice that asked me the question. When I glanced back over my shoulder to place a smile with my joke, it fell flat at the sight of Vince Tanev.

I didn't have to be even mildly interested in hockey to recognize our hotshot rookie, the one who had been taking the city by storm since he burst into headlines this preseason. He caught everyone's attention with all the goals and assists he racked up early in the regular season soon after, and he held that attention with his activities off the ice — namely partying, stumbling into his condo with three girls on each arm, and becoming known for randomly showing up in popular shops and restaurants, hanging out with fans like he was a regular person.

Which he *was*, I reminded myself, as I let my smile slip farther off my face.

I knew him not only because of all that, but because he was frequently spotlighted in the local news for being a community hero. But from what I could tell, the events were all a public relations sham, and he was all too happy to pretend like he gave a shit long enough to have his picture snapped before he was back to being a playboy.

Vince Cool.

Tampa had bestowed the affectionate nickname upon him, inspired by Snoopy's alter ego *Joe Cool,* and the rest of the nation had been quick to jump on board. He was hot, young, cocky, and, worst of all, the kind of player who backed up his shit-talking effortlessly.

Because he just kept getting better and better with every fucking game.

I didn't have to study him long to note that his usually messy hair was tamed tonight, styled in a sleek wave that accented the lines and edges of his handsome face. Those cheekbones were enough to make a poet dedicate their life's work to him. Coupled with his thick lashes and lips that always remained in a rich boy pout, Vince was impossible not to find delectable. Those attracted to the male variety went especially apeshit over the little scar on his right eyebrow, the one that gave that pretty face just enough edge to make you wonder if he'd tie you up in bed.

He was stoic and severe, the kind of man who exuded power without ever having to say a single word.

His pouty lips crooked just a little at the corner the longer I stared at him, especially when my eyes flicked to the column of his white throat exposed by the top two buttons of his dress shirt being carelessly left unfastened. No neck had a right to be that hot.

Finally, I met his gaze, his hazel eyes simmering the longer we stared at each other. I couldn't tell if they were more green or gold, the two colors battling for dominance as his lips quirked up a bit higher.

My smile flattened as I turned back to the vase, and Vince sidled up beside me, his posture confident and relaxed as he slid his hands into the pockets of his slacks.

He was at least a foot taller than me even in my heels, so I stood a bit straighter, holding my chin high.

"It *is* quite hideous," he said.

That made me relax marginally, because at least we agreed on one thing. "And yet, some rich prick is going to make an outrageous bid on it and pat themselves on the back all the way home."

"Why does bidding on an ugly vase make them a prick?"

"Because they think being charitable means throwing their inheritance money at some absurd piece of *art*," I spat that part with a laugh. "And suddenly now they rest easier at night, feeling like God's gift to mankind."

Vince tilted his head a bit. "Well, I suppose that's better than using their money on blow and hookers, right?"

"Oh, I'm sure they get plenty of that, too."

"A lot of charities depend on financial support from events like this."

"Sure," I snapped without meaning to, my teeth grinding a bit. Livia had given me the tough love only a best friend can many times and told me I have the tendency to come off as a bitch to people who don't know me well – especially when we got on the topic of the state of the world.

But that was the infuriating truth, wasn't it? Any woman who wasn't smiling and laughing and being amicably pleasant was a bitch.

I wore the insult with pride.

"And a lot of the people here will donate *maybe* one percent of what they make in a year and brag to all their friends about how *involved* they are in the community."

Vince angled himself toward me then, and I met his gaze with my chin still held high.

"So anyone who doesn't dedicate their life and finances to activism is just a shit human, huh? You must be a perfect little angel – a modern day Mother Theresa."

"At the very least, I don't do community events for PR stunts," I shot back, folding my arms over my chest. That called attention to the camera still strapped around my neck, and Vince arched a brow.

"Right. You just cover the *stunt* and pretend to be above it all."

"Aw, were you expecting me to fall at your feet and fawn over how amazing you are like the rest of your doting paparazzi?" I asked with my bottom lip poked out. "That's so cute. Go ahead." I held up my phone and pretended like I was recording. "Tell me about all the charity work you do, and I'll pretend you do it because you *want* to and not because it looks good for the team."

His eyes were hazel stone where they watched me, the corner of his mouth crooking like he wanted to smile. But his jaw was tight, brows in a hard line, like I was an opponent skating out onto his home ice.

"I guess you have me all figured out."

"Wait, this is a perfect shot," I continued, tucking my phone away and grabbing my camera, instead. "Tampa's Hotshot Rookie and The Most Heinous Vase Ever Created."

His lips *did* quirk up a bit at that, just a smidge, just enough for me to feel supremely satisfied when I snapped a photo of him standing in front of the auction table with his hands still resting easily in his pockets.

When I dropped the camera to hang around my neck once more, we were in a standoff, both of us watching the other. I wore a smirk that matched his. At least, until his eyes broke contact with my own and raked slowly down my body. He didn't even pretend to be ashamed, just took in the deep V of my neckline with appreciation, his brow arching more when he noted the high slit of the dress that revealed a sliver of my upper thigh.

My neck burned furiously under his gaze, but not half as hot as my temper, and I was ready to lay into him when an arm looped through mine from behind.

"Sorry," Livia said. "Got tied up telling gruesome stories to the crowd our GM was entertaining. Oh, I see you've met Tanny Boy."

Vince turned his attention to my best friend, a wide smile spreading on his face. It was so different from the sly smirks he'd been giving me all night it nearly knocked the breath out of me.

"Hey, Livvy," he greeted, leaning in to kiss the side of each of her cheeks. It brought him a little too close to me, considering Livia still had her arm threaded through mine. "Long time no see."

"That's a good thing for you," she mused. "Take care of those veneers and avoid another puck to the jaw, and we can keep our time together in more fun settings like this one."

He flashed his teeth again, and I found myself wondering which ones were real.

"Ah, but I miss your chair," he said, and his eyes appraised her just the same way they had me. "You know we look forward to having a tooth knocked out knowing it means a trip to your office."

I was tempted to scoff, but Livia seemed used to the blatant flirt. She only rolled her eyes and waved him off with a smile.

"Sorry to interrupt," a slight voice said, and then we all turned to a young girl with cheeks as pink as a rose. She wore a simple black cocktail dress and a golden name tag that told me she was a volunteer working the event. "But are you Mr. Tanev?"

"The very one," he said.

With a shy smile, the girl gestured toward the vase behind where Vince stood. "Perfect, thank you for coming over. I'm so sorry to disrupt your night."

"Not a disruption at all. In fact, it's been the highlight so far," he said, and his eyes caught on mine before he followed to where the girl was leading him to the table.

"If you can just sign that photograph we placed there beside your artwork, we'll frame that and include it as part of the bidding package."

I frowned, trying to make sense of what she said as she handed a Sharpie to the rookie.

"It would be my pleasure," he said, and after scrawling his signature out on the photograph of him in a sweaty celebration after a goal, he dropped the marker to the table and turned back toward where Livia and I stood. "Although, I don't expect you'll get much for such an ugly thing."

His eyes were on me with those words, and I tried with all my might not to swallow or back down from his gaze.

"Oh, I'm sure you're wrong," the volunteer said. "It's not often a pro athlete also has an artistic inclination. This is the kind of work that a collector would be proud to display."

"You made that?" Livia asked, her eyes wide and impressed. "It's beautiful." She shook her head, appraising the piece further. "Save some talent for the rest of us, why don't you?"

I rolled my eyes, which made Vince smirk in victory.

The volunteer went right back to whatever it was she was doing behind the tables, and Vince kept his eyes fixed on me long enough to make me look away.

When I finally did, he adjusted the cuff links on his wrists before nodding at Livia. "Better get back to it," he said. "Enjoy your evening, ladies."

He didn't so much as glance at me again before he was striding through the crowd, and where the seas had parted for Livia, the opposite was true for Vince. He was magnetic, calling to every person he passed without saying a single word. He didn't get farther than a few feet before a group was enveloping him, pulling out their phones for pictures. And as soon as he'd break free from them, there was a girl or two or three tugging on his arm and vying for his attention next.

"I can't imagine the life he lives," Livia said with a curious smile.

"I can," I bit back. "The carefully curated kind."

"Okay, grumpy. Not everyone is evil until proven a saint," she mused, laughing. Then, she tugged me toward the stage. "Come on. Let's find our table before the speeches start."

I let her lead the way, schooling a few breaths to shake off how flustered that stupid man had made me.

Adding insult to injury, the vase went for ten-thousand dollars by the end of the night.

Chapter 2

A Real Piece of Work

Vince

A calm energy ran through my veins as I taped up my sticks the morning after the gala, but there was something razor sharp beneath it.

It was only our second home game of the regular season, and while a win felt great no matter where we earned it, there was something special about one in our barn. If we were going to be taken seriously as competitors in the Eastern Conference, we needed a dub tonight against the Toronto Titans. They were leading the conference and coming off a Stanley Cup win last season.

If there was ever a time to prove Tampa was back in the game, tonight was it.

I wasn't too worried. Coach sensed as much at the gala last night, and he warned me not to get too cocky. But it wasn't cockiness.

Well — not *entirely*, at least.

I just saw things exactly as they were.

Our lines were stacked with veterans. Our defense was focused. Our goalie was the best in the league. We were running efficiently, and we'd studied tape so long my eyes had crossed.

Plus, we had me.

They could call it cocky if they wanted, but I was the missing piece for Tampa — a strong right winger on the first line with the tenacity this team had been missing. I bulldozed my way into rookie camp after graduating Michigan in the spring, and I hadn't let up since. Coming straight into the NHL after college wasn't an opportunity I was going to waste, and I didn't care if I had to ruffle some feathers in order to keep my spot here.

My teammates loved to give me shit, to remind me I was just a rook and that I'd be humbled as the season progressed.

But that hadn't happened yet.

I felt the win tonight. It was ours. Home ice just felt better, we had won three games in a row, and having the support of our fans always ticked the energy up a notch.

Although, the Tampa fans were restless after nearly a decade of half-baked seasons — and I didn't blame them. The Ospreys had only made it to the playoffs twice in that time, and had choked in the first round on both appearances.

But again — that was before me.

I finished taping my sticks just in time for my headphones to be flicked off my head by the hand of Jaxson Brittain, a defenseman who was quickly becoming one of my favorite to work with. He was only a couple years older than I was, a Canadian known for battling in the corners and being quick on the ice. We'd struck up a friendship easily when I came to the show.

"Let's skate, Pigeon."

I smirked at the nickname, another for *rookie* that the veterans loved to pin me with. Then, I was up and following him out of the locker room and onto the ice.

The energy was loud and boisterous as teammate after teammate joined us, the music thumping and chirps sounding off in every direction. A morning skate was just a way to get the nerves out, to warm up and prepare for the game later in the evening. It always felt like settling in for me, that first glide across the ice, first tap of my stick against the puck, first shot on the open goal. My muscles revved to life like a race car engine, firing up for the challenge ahead, while my mind floated up into a focused kind of fog only game day could bring.

After a while of just skating around and shooting pucks into an open net, our goaltender finished his stretches and took his place in front of the goal.

Will Perry — or *Daddy P* as we called him — was an absolute weapon, and he was the sole reason I had celebrated when I found out Tampa was going to be my team. Our lines needed work, and our defense could be stronger, but Daddy P was steady and strong, easily one of the best in the league, if not *the* best. He was as fierce a goalie as he was a father to his daughter. Shockingly, his wife had passed away unexpectedly before the kid was even a year old.

I'd never lived through something like that, but I could tell it had carved Will Perry into an unbreakable stone wall — which was exactly what we needed in a goaltender.

There was a challenge in his eyes as he snapped his mask into place, as if to say *give it your best shot, fuckers.*

He barely crouched into position before we all did just that.

Puck after puck flew toward the net, with no less than ten seconds in-between but usually no more than that, either. It was a race to see who could score on him first, or if any of us could do it at *all.*

I'd won this little game the last four morning skates in a row, and I had no intention of relinquishing my title today.

I missed the first two attempts, but the rest of the team didn't fare any better. And on my third shot, the puck flew high and fast into the top right corner of the net.

"Hello!" I screamed, gloved hands flying into the air along with my stick as I celebrated the win to the tune of a dozen groaning teammates. "Top cheese, baby!"

"Lucky shot, Pigeon," Will grumbled, peeling off his mask.

"Aww, did your lovely lady locks block your view, Daddy P?"

He ran a hand back through his long hair before shaking the sweat off. "Jealous of the flow?"

"That flow didn't help you block the cheese. Maybe you should call your mom after practice, have her teach you couponing so you learn how to save."

Laughs rumbled around the rink, and even Will smirked.

"Someone needs to humble your ass, Tanny Boy," Jaxson said, skating up to me before sliding to a halt and sending ice up over my shins.

"And is that someone supposed to be you, Brittzy?"

"Please," Carter Fabri said, skating a circle around us before he lazily shoveled a puck down the ice. "Brittzy couldn't humble anyone with those bendy ankles."

"Nize it, Fabio. My left nut dangles better than you," Jaxson fired back, and then he was chasing Carter down the ice, catching up to him easily and stealing the puck away with ease.

Carter was a rookie, too, but I was worried about him being sent back down to the AHL before the season ended. He was good, but he wasn't *great*, and as much as I loved partying with him, he wasn't the center we needed to bring the Cup home. Still, I hoped he'd at least stick around until the team threw our rookie party, because the sonofabitch was goofy as hell and always made for an epic night out.

I felt focused and ready by the time morning skate came to a close, players making their way off the ice one by one to head home. We didn't have to report back until five. Getting ready for a game was a little different for all of us, but it almost always included a nap, and I was looking forward to mine as I skated toward the locker room.

I was almost to the boards when I noticed our dentist, Livia Young, talking to Coach at the mouth of the tunnel.

The sight of her conjured up one of her friend from last night, and something between annoyance and intrigue sparked in my chest.

I didn't even know the girl's name, but I knew one thing for sure — she was a judgmental, snobby princess. She'd had her nose so high in the air last night I was surprised she didn't bruise it on the ceiling.

Still, she was a striking little brat, and something about the way she razzed me made me want to bend her over my knee and spank an apology right out of her sweet ass.

Maybe she was right. Maybe it was because I *was* used to being fawned over, to every woman I came into contact with swooning into a puddle on the floor. Or maybe it was because a knockout in a yellow dress tilting her chin up at me in defiance made my chest spark with a challenge.

And I *loved* a challenge.

Whatever the reason, I hadn't forgotten about our interaction. And I was curious to know more about the golden-eyed girl who'd called me a prick.

"Does it make me a masochist that I pray for a puck to the teeth every game just so I can be on a table underneath that woman?"

I chuckled at the comment from Carter as he skated by, his eyes on Livia, and he waggled his brows at me before hopping the boards.

"Looking good, Dr. Young," he said as he passed her and Coach McCabe. "Loved your dress last night."

While Coach gave my teammate a flat look, Livia just rolled her eyes and smiled. She had to be used to it by now. You didn't get away with being the team dentist and looking the way *she* did without getting comments like that daily.

"If only you hit on the puck as hard as you do our dentist, nineteen," Coach said, clapping his shoulder and walking back to the locker room.

Livia turned to me just as I hopped over the boards, and I sidled up beside her, leaning against the glass. "You've got the patience of a saint."

"It'll be the day I *stop* getting hit on that I'll be upset," she said with a dazzling smile. "Have fun last night?"

A flash of her friend hit me again with those words, her golden eyes and freckle-covered brown skin. I wasn't the least bit ashamed of how I'd seen that ponytail pulled tight at the back of her head and wondered what it would feel like to wrap it around my fist and take control of her like a wild bull.

I would probably be haunted by that curve-hugging yellow dress for months, and annoyed by her quick-to-pass judgement for another few after that.

"More than your sidekick, I imagine."

"Maven?" Livia asked with a soft laugh. "Ah, her bark is worse than her bite."

"I think I was victim to both last night," I mused. "She's a real piece of work."

"That's not her typical scene," Livia said in way of defense.

"No shit."

At that, Livia tilted her head, eyes narrowing as she studied me. "Interesting that you're still thinking about her this morning."

"Well, I haven't been insulted so many times in a ten-minute period since rookie camp, so let's just say she left an impression."

Livia tongued her cheek for a moment before she straightened. "I need to get going. Got an afternoon full of patients before tonight." She paused. "Maven King is her full name, by the way. You should look her up."

"With all my free time," I joked.

She just smirked and wiggled her fingers at me before disappearing down the tunnel, and I hung back for a moment before making my way inside, too.

ত ত ত

Later that night, when I slipped inside my Maserati parked in the player lot, still high off our second home game win and far too keyed up to even think about sleep, I couldn't help myself.

I pulled up Instagram and typed in *Maven King*.

Chapter 3

Opportunity of a Lifetime

Maven

I walked into the office on Thursday with my eyes glued to my phone screen, where a dozen Instagram notifications stared back at my dumbstruck face.

I'd woken up to find that Vince fucking Tanev had followed me.

He'd also liked six of my photos.

I couldn't wrap my head around how he'd found out my name, let alone why he would have had the balls to follow me *and* to not even try to hide the fact that he'd scrolled through my profile.

One of the photos he'd liked was my most recent, me and Livia in our gowns at the gala with champagne flutes tipped to our lips.

But he'd also liked one of me in my hammock that I posted last month, and one of me with my parents when we'd done beach cleanup in the spring, and one from my meditation retreat last fall.

The motherfucker had *stalked* me, and hadn't even been the least bit ashamed. It was like he wanted me to know.

I was still blinking in half-confusion, half-irritation at his audacity when I swung into my office. My heels click-clacked on the marble floor, and I slung my purse over the hook on the back of my door before flopping down into my chair.

My mouth was a little dry as I clicked on his profile.

Vince Tanev

41

your friendly Tampa Bay Ospreys ice king

also known as Vince Cool or Tanny Boy

I snorted at the *ice king* reference, tapping my thumb on his most recent photograph. It was a professional one I assumed was taken by someone who worked for the team, and it showed him celebrating a goal at their away game earlier in the week.

Clicking out of it, I scrolled past photo after photo of him on the ice, broken up only by him in well-tailored suits showing up to the game, or hanging out with his teammates at the bars they loved to frequent after a win.

I paused when I saw one of him posing with a youth hockey team, clicking to view it bigger. Then, I swiped through the carousel of images showing him skating with the young players and signing sticks and pucks.

"Real genuine," I mumbled under my breath.

It was almost disappointing, how much his profile confirmed exactly what I'd assumed about him. He was just another cocky playboy athlete with no concept of the real world.

Just like my ex.

James Baldridge had swept me off my feet so quickly it was dizzying. We were in our junior year of college, both drunk at a party when we stumbled into each other. The connection was instant, the sex was hot, and we couldn't get enough of one another.

The more time we spent together, the more we started falling.

We were soul mates — at least, that's what it felt like.

But we were complete opposites — him from a well-off family who spent their summers in the Hamptons with Livia's, and me from a family of hippies who spent our summers tending to our garden. He was well known on campus, the best golfer on the university team and one of the best in the nation. He would go on to play in the PGA Tour, and no one doubted it — not then, not ever in his life.

Meanwhile, I was aimless, getting a communications major with no idea how I would use it. He had aspirations for a future in professional golf, while I was content to waste a day at the beach or volunteering at a local animal shelter.

But that was what I loved most about James. He made me feel safe to be exactly who I was, made me feel like he loved me for me. It was such a refreshing change from all the losers I'd hooked up with in high school and the first couple years of college. James didn't play games. James showed me what a healthy relationship was. James was end game.

I didn't realize just how much we didn't mix — not until I was on his arm at his brother's wedding.

I was underdressed, unimpressive, and so far from welcome it was painful. I could still close my eyes and feel those judgmental stares from every corner of the venue, how they assessed me and found me wanting.

The only thing that got me through that experience was knowing James loved me, regardless of my status. We were already talking about having a wedding of our own. We were solid. I believed everything he said to me when he swore it didn't matter that we were different, that our families were different.

He loved me for me, and we were strong enough to weather any storm.

Except the very next weekend after his brother's wedding, he broke up with me — and his parents made sure I understood why.

It had been two years, and still, my chest stung with the reminder of that heartbreak, of how I'd held fast to every memory of our relationship, and sobbed for a week straight before I finally shoved it all into a box.

I still had that box, though.

I wasn't sure I'd ever be able to let go of it, of *him*, entirely.

I was vaguely aware that it wasn't fair to judge an entire class or system by the action of one jerk and his family, but since no one had yet to prove me wrong, I was steadfast in my beliefs.

And Vince Tanev was of the James Baldridge variety — *that* I was sure of.

I scrolled all the way to the top of his profile again, tapping on the little arrow that would take me back to my feed.

Except my nail hit the edge of my phone case, and my thumb dropped down on his profile picture instead — therefore, pulling up his latest story.

"Shit," I cursed, clicking out of it before I even saw what it was. Panic zipped through me with mortification right on its heels.

And then I laughed out loud at myself, because the likelihood that *Vince Cool* ever looked at who viewed his stories was nonexistent.

But what if he did?

"Good morning, gorgeous."

I jumped a little at the knock that came on my doorframe with those words, locking my phone screen and tossing it on my desk. Reya didn't seem to notice as she slid inside the office with Camilla on her heels.

Reya and Camilla were the founders of Tampa Bae Babes. Both Cuban-American and born and raised in the area, it had started as nothing more than two best friends posting about the places they loved around the Bay. Reya had long brown hair, wide brown eyes, an athletic, petite body, and the kind of calm and inviting smile that could make you confess all your secrets. Camilla, on the other hand, was tall and slender like a model, with short hair angled at her chin, sharp facial features, and gray eyes that sparked with her goofy grin. Where Reya was calm and serene, Camilla was loud and enigmatic, the two of them together making the perfect storm.

Somewhere along the way, they'd become the number one source for locals and tourists, alike.

They went from only running an Instagram, to having real estate on every social channel imaginable, including TikToks that went viral without them trying, a YouTube channel with more views than any other Tampa-based outlet, and the podcast, which had crested half-a-million listeners at the end of last year.

Everyone knew the Babes. They weren't just gorgeous, but funny and smart, too. They were like celebrities when they ventured out on the town, and one visit from them could catapult a local business overnight.

One area they were lacking in, however, was community wellness, which was a big reason why they'd pulled me on to work for them. Of course, they were also lacking in the sports arena, and according to their business strategy, that ranked higher.

"We have the opportunity of a lifetime for you," Camilla said, clapping her hands like she was going to burst at the seams while she waited for Reya to tell me what this *opportunity* was.

"Your coverage of the Gibson Gala is our highest performing content of the week. The owners of *all three teams* have reached out to tell us how much they appreciated us being there," Reya said. "They've had numerous sponsorship offers roll in, and they're tickled pink."

"That's great," I mused.

"*And*," Camilla added with one finger pointed into the air. "The general manager of the Ospreys loved the attention we brought to their philanthropic efforts, particularly that delicious photograph of Vince Tanev and his handmade vase that raised ten-thousand dollars."

I'd never fought so hard not to roll my eyes in my life.

"He loved it *so* much," Reya continued. "That he asked if we had any ideas to drum up excitement now that the season is underway. We have four back-to-back home games in early November, and he wants to pack the stands."

"We pitched an idea off the cuff," Camilla said, and my head whipped between the two trying to keep up.

"Thinking no *way* would he go for it," Reya added.

"But he *did!*"

Camilla and Reya bounced excitedly, and I just blinked before a little laugh puffed out of me. I leaned forward, resting my elbows on my desk. "Go on, spit it out."

"We have a Tampa Bae Babes exclusive, something never done before." Camilla spread her hands over the space between us as if she was painting a picture. "One Month with Tampa's Hotshot Rookie – Vince Cool."

I hoped I kept my features schooled when those words tumbled out of my boss's mouth, that I didn't blink too much and she couldn't hear how tight my throat was with my next smile.

"Okay..." I said carefully.

"It's all-access," Reya said. "Twenty-four-seven coverage. We're going to set up dedicated profiles on our major-hitting platforms. Think daily Reels and TikToks, exclusive sit-down interviews and days in the life on YouTube, podcast specials, stories, tweet updates."

Camilla cut in. "And *you* will be the main face of it all."

"Me?" I squeaked.

She nodded enthusiastically. "They *loved* you at the gala. Unsurprisingly. I mean, you're gorgeous, and smart, and the content you created was top notch."

"They've agreed to give us a closer look than any local news outlet has had before," Reya continued. "You'll be at the games, home and away, in the locker room, at practices, at his home, out at the bars, all of it." She waved her hands excitedly. "We're going to have every resident of Tampa Bay foaming at the mouth."

"Probably half the country, too, because that man is *fine,*" Camilla added, fanning herself with a smile.

"Are we sure this is the right move for us?" I asked, hoping I sounded like a smart partner offering a strategic question rather than the panicking mess I actually was on the inside.

"It's a *dream* move," Camilla answered easily. "This was our goal, to get a strong foothold in the sports arena.

There's a rabid female fanbase here in Tampa that is going to lose their minds."

"It'll also bring in a higher population of male viewers," Reya added. "Which we need. Desperately."

I knew I didn't have a leg to stand on when it came to arguing with them. They were right. On paper, this *was* the opportunity of a lifetime.

But Vince Tanev was a playboy and a prick, and I wanted this assignment about as badly as I wanted my arm chewed off by rats.

"What about focusing more on the people the Ospreys highlight at each game as their community heroes?" I tried, pathetically. "They choose someone from the Bay each game who's doing real work to give back. Let's take it beyond getting a check and a two-minute spotlight at the game. What if we could really use our platform to elevate their community efforts?"

My beautiful bosses blinked at me, then at each other, before Reya offered me a sweet, sympathetic smile.

"Look, we hear you. We know that's your goal, and it's one of ours, too."

"But this is *huge*," Camilla cut in. "Like, unheard of."

"And, honestly, it's the perfect segue," Reya added. "Vince Tanev is known for being charitable and spending time in the community. You can showcase that and shine light on how involved the Ospreys are."

I suffocated the groan I wanted to unleash at that. Even if I did point out the fact that all players did that shit for public relations purposes, it wouldn't change their minds.

This was my assignment, whether I liked it or not.

It had been a dream come true when I was pulled onto the TBB team. I was the only one outside of the founders to have a front-facing role. Sure, we had assistants and administrators, researchers and media buyers, account managers and creative directors, but I was a *Babe*.

I was making more money than I ever dreamed of — doing something that I loved — with the opportunity to have my own segment inciting the change I'd always hoped to.

I loved this job.

And if this little segment was part of the journey to get me where I really wanted to be, then so be it.

"Okay," I said on an exhale.

The girls squealed in delight, and then I was yanked up out of my chair and wrapped in a hug by both of them. I laughed and hugged them back.

"This is going to be so *fun*," Camilla exclaimed.

"Yeah," I agreed. "The funnest."

"Just wait until we tell you what the Ospreys are paying for this," Reya said, waggling her brows. "You're going to be living the sweet life during this assignment. They're footing the bill for *everything*. I'm talking lavish hotels, a condo in the same building as his, a per diem so high you could eat at Michelin Star restaurants for every meal..."

She ambled on, but her voice went fuzzy in my ears. My eyes flicked to my phone, thinking about the bizarre notifications I'd scrolled through that morning.

I wondered how Vince Tanev would respond to the news.

But not as much as I wondered how I was going to survive a month up close and personal with the cockiest sonofabitch I'd ever met.

And the hottest one, too.

Chapter 4

Distraction with a Capital D

Vince

"You're serious."

It wasn't a question so much as a statement of mild disbelief. I arched a brow at Coach McCabe, who seemed about as pleased as Daddy P after someone managed to score on him, before I turned my attention back to our general manager.

Richard Bancroft was a joyful man, soft around the waist with pale white skin, ginger hair, and rosy-red cheeks. He always wore a smile like he'd just found out his only daughter was getting married, and he was also known for pitching some of the stupidest ideas with that grin firmly in place.

He was known by staff and players alike as Dick, which was the nickname he gave himself back in college. Of course, depending on what he'd wrangled the team into that week, the players might have used it in a more callous way than he intended.

"It's brilliant!" he said, and I wasn't sure if he was trying to sell me on that statement or my coach, who still wore an unamused frown and his arms folded over his chest.

Where Dick was soft and cheery, Coach Shane McCabe was lean, tall, and severe. At thirty-eight, he was the second-youngest coach in the league, and one look at the guy told you he had a chip on his shoulder and a point to prove. He was the kind of coach a player dreamed of working with, one who was stern and took no shit, but also didn't ride your balls too hard.

"Just *think* of the buzz it'll stir up," Dick continued. "You're the hottest news this team has had since 2004, kid. And if we didn't use that to our advantage to fill those seats," he added, pointing in the direction of the rink. "Then we'd be fools."

"It's a distraction," Coach said from his corner.

"It's a *goldmine*," Dick argued, and the rare look of severity that overtook him as he looked pointedly at Coach told me this wasn't up for debate.

The Tampa Bae Babes was going to do an exclusive, a month walking in my shoes in the height of my first season with the Ospreys.

And that feisty little snoot from the gala was the one who'd be in charge of the piece.

Maven King.

I smirked a little at the thought of her, that same mixture of curiosity and indignation flaring in my chest. To say I'd been surprised when I'd looked her up would have been a vast understatement.

I didn't know what I expected to find, but it wasn't a bohemian flower child who had fifty-thousand followers and a love for being barefoot in her parents' garden. After seeing her all dolled up in a gown with diamonds glittering on her earlobes, it had been a shock to see her in her natural habitat — earth-toned flowing fabrics, foundation-free skin, and natural, curly hair.

The images of her with her family were a stark contrast of the ones I had with my own. My parents both came from money, their grandparents smart with their investments. We had what I'd heard referred to as generational wealth, the kind that meant we really never had to want for anything.

I wasn't too proud to admit growing up in that atmosphere had spoiled me a bit. I liked designer clothes, exotic cars, expensive restaurants, and luxury travel experiences. I didn't know what it was like to check the price tag on something before I bought it — even before I got the nice signing bonus as a rookie with the Ospreys.

Still, my parents both had careers, even though they didn't technically need them to provide for themselves, and they brought me and my sister up with the same expectation. I was thankful for their support when I told them hockey was my dream.

I was well aware that not every kid had the opportunity to play an expensive sport, let alone have their parents at almost every game.

I'd spent more time than I'd ever admit scrolling through Maven's pictures and wondering what her childhood was like, smiling a little more with each new discovery I made at who she was now. And seeing a post about her parents and their philanthropic nature, along with the dozens of photos and videos of her out in the community with them, I, at least, had a little context to put with the attitude she'd given me at the gala.

I also found it quite amusing, to hit the little heart button on a few of her photos and have the satisfaction of knowing she'd likely blow a gasket when she got the notifications.

Even as intriguing as I found her, I agreed with Coach on this one. Having *anyone* follow me around would be a nuisance. But having *her*?

Distraction with a capital D.

But if this was part of the path I needed to take to impress my GM and inch my way closer to the Calder Memorial Trophy, then I wasn't about to argue. I wanted to be rookie of the year, and sometimes that meant doing stupid shit I didn't want to in order to make the bosses happy.

The way Dick was behaving, I didn't think I had much of a choice, anyway.

"Whatever I can do to help the team, I'll do it," I finally said.

"Atta boy!" Dick beamed, hopping out of his chair as I rose to stand, too. He shook my hand and clapped me on the shoulder as I shared a wary glance with Coach. "Everyone who counted Tampa out years ago is about to eat their words."

"Yes, sir," I agreed when we pulled back.

Richard and Coach talked for a few minutes before we were excused, and Coach let out a sigh once we were out of the front office suite and in the elevator heading down to the team's domain.

"I'm sorry," he said. "I'm sure you can see there was no talking him out of that one."

"It's fine," I assured him. "Besides, maybe he's onto something. A little good press can't hurt, right?"

Coach lifted a brow. "As long as it stays good."

I smirked, drawing a little halo around my head that made Coach relax a little on a laugh.

"I'm supposed to have a call with the..." He paused, scrunching his nose. "What do we call her? Reporter? Influencer?" He shook his head. "Regardless, we're touching base this afternoon. Bancroft is eager to get her in here and get started, so I imagine we can expect her at practice in the morning. I hope she settles in quickly because we head to Boston tomorrow night."

"Oh, good," I said as we stepped off the elevator and made our way toward the locker room. "She'll be here just in time for me to smoke the Beavers."

"For *us* to smoke them," he corrected.

"Right," I said with a wink.

Coach just shook his head, blowing his whistle when we made it back to the ice. I had to pause to change into my skates again while he called everyone together to run over our drills for the day.

"In trouble already, Pidge?" Jaxson asked when I skated out.

"Nope. Just stepping in as Tampa's shiny new toy."

He cocked a brow.

"Some reporter is going to follow me around for a month," I said nonchalantly. Then, I lowered my voice so Coach wouldn't grill my ass for interrupting his practice. "Remember the girl in the yellow dress at the gala?"

"Like any of us could forget."

"She's the one."

"Proposing already?" He smirked.

I flattened my lips. "She's the reporter, the one who's doing the piece."

Both of his brows shot up at that. "You mean *she's* going to be the one following you around?"

I nodded.

"What all does this entail, exactly? Like just here at the rink?"

"Everything," I said. "Practice, travel, home games and away games, too. My life on the road. My life here in the city."

"Like... twenty-four seven?"

"Apparently."

A shit-eating grin curled on Jaxson's face. "Interesting."

I just nodded with a smile of my own.

Interesting, indeed.

Chapter 5

Take Your Best Shot

Maven

Nothing annoyed me more than the fact that I was shaking like a leaf when I stepped onto the elevator the first morning of my new assignment. The lovely gentleman from the front desk had personally escorted me on, holding the door for me before pushing the button for Vince's floor once I was inside. When the doors closed again, I blew out a frustrated breath.

I'd barely slept, my mind racing with the kind of anxiety only an unknown assignment with very high expectations could bring. Reya and Camilla were depending on me to hit this out of the park, and I couldn't let anything distract me.

Least of all, the pouty-lipped rich boy I was assigned to cover.

My eyes snagged on my reflection in the elevator mirrors, and I felt a little better that at least I *looked* put together.

Colorful palazzo pants hugged my flat stomach and narrow hips before flowing down my legs, the rich oranges and purples and turquoise designs weaving together in the most gorgeous way. I'd paired a delicate white top with it, the straps thin and stretching over my collarbone, and just a sliver of my stomach showing.

My ink black hair was in its natural state, the curls airy and shaped around my face with the perfect volume, despite Florida's humidity doing its damndest to make it frizz. I had what I called a five-minute makeup routine that mostly consisted of tinted moisturizer, brow gel, and mascara, but I'd run a shiny gloss over my lips and added my favorite gold hoops to my ears as a final touch.

I looked calm, confident, and beautiful.

I just needed that to permeate a few layers deeper so I *felt* all those things, too.

I could almost see my parents and their confused expressions in my mind, the look they gave me when I told them I was going to college instead of into the Peace Corps, the one they gave me when I graduated and told them I was going to focus on building my brand on social media, the one they gave me most recently when I told them I was the newest addition to the Babes.

They watched me like they had no clue what the hell I was doing with my life.

Sadly, they weren't wrong.

I was in a strange predicament — walking into a literal dream job with my stomach churning. I felt torn, like two halves of a fragile paper heart. Because although I was making more money than I'd ever known I could earn on my own *and* I loved the work I did, I felt almost... guilty.

Like it wasn't enough.

Like *I* wasn't enough.

What was I doing to better the world, to help people, to make a difference?

Add in the fact that my new subject had a particularly unsettling effect on me, and you could say I was having a little meltdown in that elegant elevator thrusting me toward my impending doom.

"Get it together, Maven," I coached myself, shaking out my wrists. The bangles on the left one made a tinkling sound as I did. "You are a bad ass, independent woman who can do anything. You are a professional. And he's just a boy with a stick."

My throat thickened with those words because Vince Tanev was *far* from a boy.

And as if he'd heard the words and was intent on proving me wrong, he answered his door shirtless, in nothing but a thin pair of dark green pajama pants that rested so low on his hips, I could see the band of his briefs beneath them.

"Well, good morning, sunshine," he greeted, holding the door open farther as if I was supposed to come inside. The motion set his biceps on display, his massive palm flat on the door and propping it wide.

His hair that had been carefully styled at the gala was a chaotic mess now, the brown and gold strands of it sticking up this way and that. He looked like he'd either just woken up, or just rolled around in the sheets with a passionate lover.

Maybe both.

His hazel eyes danced as they stared back at me, that scar lining his eyebrow somehow more pronounced when he wore nothing to distract from it.

I had to clamp my jaw shut to keep it from hanging open. The muscles of his abdomen and ribs stretched like art under the light coming from inside his condo. It cast half of him in a warm glow, and the other half in dark shadows from all the lines and cuts, his body carved in the way only an athlete's can be.

Clearing my throat, I held my chin high and checked the time on my watch. "I apologize, your general manager told me seven AM sharp. I can wait downstairs while you get ready."

"I believe he told you seven because that's about thirty minutes after I usually wake up," Vince said. "And this is supposed to be a month of my life, right? It doesn't start when I get dressed. And good thing, since I like to be naked most of the time."

Heat scorched my neck, but I held a blank expression and blinked at him. "Can you please not make this difficult?"

"Me?" He pressed a hand to his bare chest, and my eyes followed the movement before I flicked them back up to meet his gaze. "I'm an angel. It was *you* who insulted me the first night we met."

"I imagine your ego is inflated enough to handle the blow."

Vince smirked, his eyes trailing down the length of me. And just like that night at the gala, he took his time, not even a little shame finding him as he let his gaze linger on every inch of my skin. His Adam's apple bobbed before he pushed the door open even farther, his eyes snapping up to meet mine.

"Come inside, Maven."

It wasn't a request, but a command — one I felt like a bolt of lightning cast down from Zeus himself. I wet my lips, resisting the urge to argue since I'd have to work with the asshole for the foreseeable future.

With a contained sigh, I slid past him, hugging the opposite edge of the door frame so I wouldn't brush up against his half-naked body. He seemed to notice, too, because he wore that damn smirk again when the door was shut and I was inside his condo.

I, however, wasn't smiling at all, not when I took what I could see of the expansive penthouse.

The architectural design was sleek and masculine, dark metals mixing with rich natural woods to create a space that felt as cozy as it did dangerous. I'd walked directly into the living area, which was decorated with expensive modern furniture and eclectic art that was tasteful and sparse.

The windows were the art I was most drawn to, though, reaching from the floor all the way to the ceiling and showcasing a bright orange glow slowly rising beyond the lights of downtown Tampa. The city was stirring to life, the darkness being overtaken by the warm sun that would bring another hot, humid October day.

It was silent, save for the soft sound of a beat-heavy R&B song that started with a deep voice singing melodically in English, but then slid into French and Arabic as the song progressed. The music set a distinct vibe as my eyes trailed the space, from the decorative fireplace that I was sure was never used for heat, to the spotless, sleek kitchen.

But my eyes didn't linger much on the carefully decorated space. Instead, they snagged on the messiest corner in the entire condo.

It was the area designed to be used as a dining area, but instead, it was an explosion of pottery.

It was also the most warm and inviting space inside the otherwise cool and clean room.

An unfinished wood table was covered with clay, metal tools I didn't know the name of, and half-finished bowls, vases, mugs, and more. Next to it sat a potter's wheel, the pedal and edges of it covered in the same specks of clay that decorated the table. There was also an electric kiln, along with shelves and shelves of everything from supplies just waiting to be made into something to fully finished pieces of art.

"Go ahead," Vince said, shaking me from my trance. "Take your best shot."

I turned in a daze and realized my lips had curled into a soft smile from taking in the pottery corner. It slipped when I found Vince leaning a hip against the edge of his kitchen island, his eyes curious where they watched me as he sipped something hot from the mug in his hand.

A mug I had no doubt he had molded himself.

It was oddly shaped, but beautifully colored and glazed, and he'd made it. He'd created it from raw materials with hands that were usually wrapped around a stick, or punching an opponent in the nose.

Without thinking, without *asking*, I pulled out my camera. I took only enough time to adjust a couple settings for the low light before I snapped a photo of him.

He chuckled. "Okay, not the kind of shot I was referring to, but I guess it's better than the alternative."

"Sorry," I said, looking down at the camera in my hands.

Why did I suddenly feel shy, as if I'd seen him fully naked or indisposed?

Maybe it was because that little corner of creation felt like the most vulnerable part of him, and I'd walked right into it without warning.

"It's fine," he said. "I imagine that's something I'll need to get used to for this..." He waved his hand in the air. "Whole ordeal. Pictures and videos when I least expect them."

I offered a smile. "I should have warned you. I just..." I paused, rolling my lips together before I pointed at the mug in his hand. "You made that, didn't you?"

He didn't even look down. "I did."

"It's beautiful."

I said the words before I thought better of them, and he cocked a brow in surprise.

That. *That* was why I much preferred to be thought of as a bitch than anything else. Because in one moment, with just a touch of softness showing, I'd exposed my neck. And now, Vince was looking at me like his prey rather than his opponent.

I slung my camera around my neck, sniffing and tearing my gaze from his as I looked around. "Anyway, I guess just... go about your usual routine. I'll ask questions when I have them, and take a lot of pictures and videos. When I know your schedule better, I'd like to steal you for some interviews, and maybe some fluff content for the podcast. If there's ever anything you're doing that you don't want on camera, make sure to tell me beforehand."

"So I can request things to be off the record?" he asked, and I didn't miss the salacious smile that accompanied that comment.

I ignored him, carefully placing my bag on the edge of his couch before I pulled out what I needed — pens, notebook, laptop, phone.

"What time do you expect we'll head out?"

Vince set his mug on the island before sliding his hands into his pockets. That motion perfectly framed an area of him I was very much trying not to look at, a feat that was increasingly hard considering the thin material of the pants he wore. Add that to the fact that he had massive thighs straining against the fabric, and an ass so rock solid he didn't even have to turn around for me to notice, and it was a miracle I kept my eyes on his.

"Practice is at ten, so we'll walk over at about half-past eight."

"Great," I said, swallowing and picking up my notebook to write down a few notes about his condo. "Just pretend like I'm not here."

"Easier said than done when you look like that."

I blinked, turning to find him wearing that cocky grin again, his eyes trailing the length of me in that slow, carefree way they loved to do so much.

"This is a professional relationship, Mr. Tanev," I said with what I hoped was more resolve than I felt.

"I'll be on my best behavior," he said, crossing the space between us in just a few smooth, slow strides.

He walked until he was less than a foot from me before he stopped, close enough that I could feel his body heat like the uncomfortably warm sensation of standing too close to a fire.

When I didn't back down, Vince smiled at me, his eyes bouncing between mine.

Then, he pressed a hand to the bare skin over his heart. "Promise."

Chapter 6

Break the Internet

Maven

"Is your head spinning yet?"

I chuffed out a laugh, writing notes frantically in my phone as I followed the Tampa Ospreys' Executive Director around. We had finished our tour of the arena, landing back in the rink after she took me through the locker rooms, training areas, the team gym, the kitchen and cafeteria, and the executive suite. It had taken nearly the entire hour of practice, but the team was still out on the ice, and I finished the note I was writing on my phone before switching it to video mode so I could get some content.

"Yes," I admitted to Mrs. Lopez. "But in the best way."

She smiled, but her hand shot out to stop me before I could make my way up to the bench where the players sat during the games so I could get an unobstructed shot of the guys on the ice.

"Be careful," she warned. "Behind this glass, you're safe." She knocked on the glass as if to illustrate her point.

"But out there, you've got to be aware. Trust me when I say you don't want a puck to the jaw."

I thought about all the gruesome stories Livia had told me from working with hockey players over the years, and I grimaced.

"Fair point. Maybe I'll stay back here for now."

Mrs. Lopez nodded her agreement before checking her watch. "Okay. I need to get everything ready for the team to fly this evening. I'll see you then."

She left before I could ask what she meant, and then my phone was buzzing hard in my hand. I answered the call from Reya, only to be greeted by high-pitched squeals.

"THE ACCOUNT ALREADY HIT ONE-HUNDRED-THOUSAND FOLLOWERS!"

I held the phone away from my ear, blinking, but a smile spread on my lips despite my eardrums nearly being blown to bits.

"And ESPN just shared your post!" Camilla added. "So that number is about to shoot up."

"A Morning With Vince Cool," Reya sang. "I mean, I don't know what I expected, but it wasn't a shirtless Vince Tanev in nothing but his PJ bottoms as our first official post." She let out a low whistle. "Those *thighs*. Too bad we didn't get the view from the back."

Camilla giggled. "I think we broke the Internet."

I barely got out a *thank you* before Camilla was rambling off a bunch of logistics, including the surprise that I would be traveling with the team *tonight,* and that they'd secured me a small condo rental in the same building as Vince, just a few floors down, for when we got back.

"Tonight?" I squeaked, glancing out on the ice where the guys were still practicing. "I... I wasn't prepared for that. I need to pack. And why do I need to live in his building? My house is only twenty-five minutes away."

"It's an all-access, twenty-four-seven affair," Reya reminded me. "Trust us. This will be easier on everyone. And you'll be fully immersed. Gah. I'm actually *jealous* of you."

"Same," Camilla said on a sigh.

"I don't even have anyone lined up to house sit or anything. My plants," I whimpered.

Reya and Camilla cooed an *aww* before Reya said, "We will handle it. I have a copy of your house key from the photoshoot we did there when we announced you as the newest Babe."

"Let us take care of everything else. *You* just focus on Vince Tanev, and give these hungry new followers what they're asking for," Camilla added.

They were making kissing noises and shooing me off the phone before I could argue, and when the call ended, I tapped the Instagram icon on my phone, and my eyes nearly bulged out of my skull.

They were right. One-hundred-and-eight-thousand followers and counting.

I'd posted that picture of Vince holding his handmade mug, that little smirk on his face while he stood there shirtless and bathed in morning light. A quick glance at the comment section showed me that I wasn't the only woman in the world who drooled at the sight of him like that. It was impossible not to with how his abdomen rippled with muscles and lines, with how the waistband of those pajama bottoms hugged him in the most perfect way.

He was so hot it wasn't fair, and now, the hockey world was panting and begging for more.

When I saw that ESPN had reposted the picture and tagged our account with credit, encouraging everyone to follow us, I almost squealed.

Excitement buzzed through me like an electric current.

This really *was* the opportunity of a lifetime.

So what, hockey wasn't exactly what I pictured myself being known for. This was a way to get noticed, to break out as a Babe and establish myself in the eyes of our city and beyond.

Once I had their attention, I could focus on what I really wanted them to see.

Our community and the people who serve it.

My chest was still light and airy when I switched to the story mode and took a video of the guys on the ice, zooming in slowly on Vince as he ran a drill with his team. He was so calm and confident, carefree as he glided across the ice, his shoulders squared and hands gripping his stick like an expert. He wore a white practice jersey, and even under all the pads shielding his body, he moved with ease in the way only a pro can.

I held the phone steady in my hand as I framed him on the screen.

And as if I'd planned it, he shucked the puck right into the net with my camera rolling, ripping his helmet off in a victorious battle cry like it had been a game instead of practice.

His hair was drenched, and he shook it out as he shot off some smartass remarks to his teammates. They met him with a mixture of groans and insults, but a few of them clapped him on the back as they skated by.

Then, his eyes found me.

I had about fifteen seconds left in the story clip as he skated toward me, his face coming into view more and more. And with his mouth slightly parted and a grin curling on his lips, he pointed at my phone with his glove.

And the motherfucker winked.

It was so hot I nearly dropped the phone, but managed to hold my hands stable until the clip ran out.

Vince tore his attention from me just as quickly as he'd given it, slipping his helmet back on and fastening the chin strap just in time to line up for what coach had planned next. I watched the clip play back, and the intensity was even more powerful the second time around.

I debated what text to write to accompany the clip, but everything I thought of just didn't match the energy.

He was the story.

Just him.

So, I put nothing more than a winky-face emoji with its tongue out at the lower left-hand corner of the screen, and I tapped the button that sent the story live into the social media atmosphere.

I'd just tucked my phone away and pulled out my camera for a few shots when Coach McCabe blew his whistle, and the team gathered around where he stood for a quick chat before they were all skating off the ice and toward the tunnel I was standing in.

I pressed myself against the wall, trying to be invisible, but I didn't miss the chance to capture them all on video as they hopped the boards and took off their helmets, making their way back toward the locker room.

Each of them eyed me either curiously or like I was already annoying them as they passed. A few of them goofed off for the camera, smacking their ass as they passed or making faces so close to the lens that they fogged it up.

Vince held back, making himself the last player off the ice, and he paused right in front of where I stood, ignoring the camera and focusing on me, instead.

"Having fun, Maven King?"

"That's one word for it," I said. I debated recording the exchange, but tucked my phone away, instead. "Nice shot out there."

"I did it just for you."

"Mm-hmm."

"I did," he insisted. "I just imagined you jumping up and down when I scored, chanting my name. It was great motivation."

"I'm sure you *would* love to hear me chant your name, but I'm not one of your fan girls."

He tilted his head, smirking like he had a comeback to that, but he kept it locked behind those curled lips of his. Then, his eyes flicked down, and his scarred eyebrow arched high.

"Let me grab you one of my jerseys from the team shop," he said, staring a bit longer before his gaze found mine again. "Looks like you're a little *cold*."

He was already hobbling toward the locker room on his skates when I glanced down, immediately mortified to find my nipples so hard they were distinctly visible through my top.

I had dressed for a hot Florida day, not an ice rink.

Idiot.

"I'm not wearing your jersey," I shot at him, folding my arms over my chest.

He turned, walking backward through the tunnel on his skates. "Wanna bet?"

"Only if you want to lose."

Vince shrugged, smiling like he'd already won. "I'll take my chances."

And then he turned and disappeared down the tunnel, just in time for Coach McCabe to stop right in front of me and block my view.

"Sorry I didn't get a chance to introduce myself before," he said, extending a hand.

I was still shaken up from the exchange with Vince, which was supremely annoying, and I blinked out of the daze with a smile as I took Coach's hand in my own.

"It's perfectly okay. You're a busy man. I just want to thank you for agreeing to all this."

"Well, it wasn't my choice, if I'm being perfectly honest," he said, withdrawing his hand.

"Oh." My cheeks heated.

"I want you to feel welcome," he said. "And I am happy to give you the all-access my general manager promised. However," he amended, holding up one stern finger. "The last thing we need on this team is a distraction."

"I understand," I said before he could continue. "I'll be like a fly on the wall, sir."

Coach gave me a quick once over, then smiled and shook his head. "I don't think that's possible for you, Miss King."

Heat blasted my neck once more. It wasn't like he was checking me out, more like he was just a man appreciating the beauty of a woman.

Also, a coach realizing what a distraction I could be to his team.

"I'm sorry I didn't dress appropriately."

"You can dress however you feel comfortable," he said quickly. "I'm pretty sure you could wear a burlap sack and still stop traffic. All I'm asking is that if the guys start yucking it up for you, if Vince or anyone else starts to lose focus because they're wanting to be a part of all this." He waved his hand. "Just... help me keep them on track. Okay? We have a real shot at a winning season this year, and I don't want that to go up in flames."

"Neither do we," I promised him.

I spoke for us as the Tampa Bay Babes, the organization. But in my head, I was also making that statement for me. The last thing I wanted was the attention of a rich, cocky athlete.

I'd been there, done that – still had the scar to prove it.

Plus, this was my first real test from Reya and Camilla. I wasn't about to mess it up.

He nodded, and then blew out a breath, checking the time on his watch. "Flight is at four. We'll take you to the airport in one of our cars. Be back here at two-thirty sharp."

He paused then, and heat washed over my neck as his eyes found mine. He was sexy as hell, a dark line of scruff on his jaw and his suit all tailored to perfection. I half-wondered if maybe it should be *him* we were covering – especially considering he was one of the youngest coaches in the league.

"And I'd suggest you pack something a little warmer," he added with a wry grin as he turned toward the locker room. "Boston is cold as hell."

Chapter 7

An Asshole Rocket

Vince

"Ohhh shit, there he is!" Jaxson said when I boarded the team plane, and he started a slow clap that the rest of the team joined in on as they cheered and made catcalls.

I arched a brow, storing my backpack in the space over my seat. All our equipment and luggage was taken care of by the staff, so that backpack was all I had until we landed in Boston.

When the applause died down, Jaxson wrapped his arm around my neck like he was going to take me down in a wrestling move, but he just ruffled my hair instead.

"Our little pigeon has the whole world losing their minds."

"And their panties," Carter added with a grin.

"Want me to rub you down with oil next time, Tanny Boy?" Jaxson asked when he released me. He rubbed my pecs to illustrate before I smacked his hands away with a smile of my own.

"Wow, I've never heard jealousy ring out quite so loud before," I said, taking my seat before I stretched my legs out confidently. I'd dressed in my newest custom suit from Stefano Ricci, and I unclasped the buttons of my jacket as I kicked back. Will was in the seat by the window across from where I sat, and Jaxson took the seat next to him.

"What's next? Posing on the beach in a banana hammock?"

"Nah, Brittzy," I said, flicking my sunglasses down over my eyes. "My cock wouldn't fit in one of those. Now *you* on the other hand..."

He kicked me before I could finish the joke, but we were all laughing. Well, all of us except Daddy P, who looked out the window with his headphones on.

The team plane was expansive, large enough to fit close to two-hundred passengers if it was designed like a normal commercial plane. But it wasn't. Instead, huge leather seats donned the space — two facing forward and two facing backward — in little pods of four on either side of the aisle. The coaches and staff usually sat at the front of the plane, while the rest of us filled the middle and back, and before we even took off, we were waited on by the flight attendant staff — the same ones who flew with us each and every away game.

"Seriously, man, is it weird?" Carter asked when he took a seat across the aisle from me. "I heard she's moving into your building and everything."

That was news to me — enticing news, if I was being honest — but I pretended I already knew as I took a water from the flight attendant and thanked her.

"It hasn't even been a full day," I reminded him. "But so far, it feels like normal. She told me to just pretend she isn't here."

Will snorted at that, which told me he was wearing those headphones more for show than anything else.

"I agree with Daddy P," Jaxson said. "Fat chance in hell you can ignore a woman that fine."

"I'll never forget that yellow dress," Carter added with a far-off look.

"That *ass.*" Jaxson whistled through his teeth as the both of them shook their head in mutual agreement that those two words were enough to convey a whole story. "She's an absolute rocket."

I didn't know why my jaw tightened a bit as they joked about Maven and how attractive she was, because they were right. It was true. She was the kind of woman who belonged in magazine spreads, the kind who made you forget how to speak. I'd also tossed around these same remarks and worse with the guys about dozens of women before.

Why did it make my hands roll into fists when they talked about Maven the same way?

"That's enough," I clipped.

Their smiles fell along with mine.

"She's essentially a part of the team now," I said. "She's going to be uncomfortable enough as it is in a new environment with a bunch of smelly brutes like you two. Show her some respect, or I'll make you show it."

Jaxson and Carter bit back smiles, glancing behind me and then at each other before Jaxson put his hands up in surrender.

"Sure thing, Pidge," Jaxson said. "We won't rag on your girl."

"Don't hit on her, either," I threatened, chest puffing a little when he called Maven my girl. She was nowhere near that, but I liked the thought of establishing that claim even when I didn't have the right to.

Suddenly, someone cleared their throat over my head, and I glanced up and back to find Maven standing there with her arms folded over her chest and an amused look on her face.

I didn't have to glance back at the guys to know she'd been there for a while, especially when I could hear their laughs fizzling out of their chests. I ignored them altogether, standing and extending a hand for Maven's bag.

"Window seat's yours, doll," I said, smoothing my knuckles over her slim shoulder as I removed her bag. She kept her arms crossed until the last second like she didn't want my help, finally releasing the strap so I could tuck her bag in the bin overhead.

"I'm not your doll," she bit back. "And I want the aisle."

I clucked my tongue. "No can do, peach. I've got long legs I need to stretch out."

"More like he's afraid of flying and being too close to the window makes him shit his pants," Carter chimed in.

I didn't even look at him as my fist jutted out and slugged his arm. He laughed on a yelp, rubbing the spot while Maven watched the exchange and I watched her.

"Vince Tanev, scared of flying?" She tilted her head a bit. "That's something I didn't expect."

"Oh, I'm full of surprises."

"I'm sure," she said with a slight roll of her eyes.

I took the opportunity then to appraise her outfit change. I missed that tiny scrap of white fabric she'd been wearing as a top earlier, especially since I'd had the sinfully delicious view of her hard nipples earlier that morning. My cock twitched a little at the memory of those peaks, of how goosebumps had trailed over her arms when I'd let my eyes rake over her and discovered that fun little surprise like a toy in a cereal box.

Now, she had on light-colored jeans and a black long-sleeve shirt. Her hair was held back by a bright blue bandana tied in a knot at the front, and silver hoops hung from her ears. And even though she was showing less skin now than she did this morning, she was somehow even more alluring.

It should have been illegal for that woman with an ass like hers to wear jeans that tight.

I didn't hurry my perusal of her, and when I finally dragged my eyes back up to meet hers, she gave me a look that said *well, are you going to move or...?*

I stepped a bit to the side, just marginally, like I didn't have the space to move much farther. My smile climbed on my lips in a dare as Maven assessed the tiny sliver of space between me and the seat that I'd left her to slip through.

Her jaw tightened as she took the challenge, and at first, I thought she was going to ram through me and bulldoze her way into the row. But at the last moment, her pace changed, and she held her chin high as she turned toward the seats, her hands bracing on the back of them to steady her while she squeezed by me.

That little turn meant her ass was practically in my lap as she did.

"Excuse me," she purred, smirking back at me as she slowly dragged that perfect, round, apple-shaped ass across my groin. She did so achingly slow, and my nostrils flared at the contact, hand clamping on the seat behind me to keep from reaching out and grabbing her to keep her against me longer.

When she slid by, she watched me out of the corner of her eye before she carefully took the window seat and crossed her legs.

I finally exhaled, glancing at Carter and Jaxson who were watching me with shit-eating grins now. Even Will arched a brow at me before turning to look out the window again.

I cracked my neck, unfastening the button on my suit jacket before I slid into the seat next to her.

"And don't call me peach, either," she said.

"What should I call you, then," I asked. "Girl of my dreams? Siren of the seas?"

"How about Maven, since that's her name," Daddy P cut in, blinking slowly at me like I was a teenage boy who had climbed too high on his nerves. To be fair, I was *acting* a bit like one, but I couldn't help it.

I liked to push Maven's buttons.

I wondered what would happen if I pushed all the right ones.

Maven tongued her cheek at me with that little input from our goaltender, and then she turned to him, extending her hand. "Thank you. I don't think we've officially met. I'm Maven King."

"Will Perry," he said gruffly with a firm, short shake.

"We call him Daddy P, though," Jaxson cut in.

Maven's brows tugged inward. "Why?"

"Well, because he's a daddy — like *actually* a dad. He has the cutest kid you'll ever meet."

"But also because he's iron-fisted and hands out punishment like a dad," Carter explained. "And he treats the puck like a boy trying to take his daughter on a date and his daughter is the net. No access granted."

Maven's cheeks tinged a bit pink at that, and she smiled at Will. "Daddy P. I like that."

"We all have nicknames," Carter said. "It's kind of annoying, honestly, but inescapable, nonetheless."

"What do you mean?" Maven asked.

"Well, it just sort of happens in hockey. Sometimes it's a play on your last name, or sometimes you do one stupid thing and it becomes your identifier for years. Sometimes it's a name earned from performance, like Daddy P is part for his last name, Perry, but also part P for Pickles."

"Pickles?" Maven's nose scrunched up.

"Yeah. Because he's cool as a cucumber on the ice," Jaxson said.

Maven laughed, and the sound was so airy and light that I wanted to bottle it up. She seemed to be relaxing the more the guys talked to her, and the bite she loved to nip me with was slowly receding, her teeth no longer bared.

"So, he's Daddy P," she said, pointing at Will before her finger moved to Jaxson. "And you are?"

"Brittzy," he said. "My last name is Brittain. And then Carter here is Fabio."

"Because of the flow," Carter said, sliding his hand back through his medium-length brown hair before that same hand ran over his scruff. That made Will snort again and pin him with a glare.

No one had better hair than Daddy P.

"Because his last name is Fabri," Jaxson interjected. "And because his game with the ladies is absolute shit, so calling him Fabio is ironic."

That earned Jaxson a wet willy from across the aisle.

"And what about you?" Maven asked, finally turning to look at me. When she did, her honey golden eyes danced a little. "What's your nickname?"

"Mr. King."

She frowned. "Why?"

"Because when we get married, I already know you're too independent to take my last name, so I guess I'll have to take yours."

An incredulous laugh burst from her lips, and she shook her head, folding her arms over her chest again. "You think you're so cute, don't you?"

"Like a puppy."

"More like a dog," she said just as quickly.

"He's Vince Cool to the outside world, but with us, he's Tanny Boy," Carter said. "Because on our first night out he got wasted on car bombs at O'Briens and kept requesting 'Danny Boy' even though the band was playing Southern Rock, not Irish music."

"Nah, he's just Pidge to me," Jaxson said, crossing one ankle over the opposite knee and bringing his hands back behind his head. "Always will be."

Maven hadn't taken her eyes off me.

I wasn't sure I ever *could* take my eyes off her.

"Pidge?" She finally asked.

"Pigeon," I answered. "Just another word for rookie."

"Ah," she mused. "I like that one. Pigeon. Can I use it, too?"

"You can call me whatever you want to. Just make sure you like the name you pick." I leaned in a little closer, lowering my voice. "I have a feeling you'll be saying it a lot. Maybe in different decibels, too. Might want to try screaming it loud and high-pitched, just to make sure it feels right."

Maven's cheeks reddened again, just a light pink flowing over those warm brown cheeks peppered with freckles. I smirked at the sight of that blush, but it wasn't there long before Maven clamped her mouth shut and shook her head.

"You aren't going to make this easy, are you?" she asked.

I leaned even closer. "Be honest. You would hate it if I did."

She didn't answer, but she didn't have to.

The smile that played at the corner of her dusty-rose lips told me I was right.

Chapter 8

Precious Little Rituals

Maven

Present Me never been so thankful to Past Me than I was the afternoon of the Boston game when I rolled out my yoga mat.

Past me had wondered if it would be necessary to pack, if the staff would be annoyed that I brought it, if I'd even have time to use it. But *present* me was sighing with relief at the small bit of normalcy as I stepped onto it.

I knew it would be impossible to meditate this morning, to find any way to clear my mind, and I had been right. Everything kicked into gear quickly, and I had barely woken up before I was on the bus with the team headed to the rink for their morning skate.

So now that I had a little time alone in the afternoon, I succumbed to all my thoughts, letting them race through me as I began my practice in child's pose. I needed to be grounded. I needed stillness.

The last week had been such a chaotic blur, I didn't know where to start to even try to piece it all together. It was beyond me how one little gala with my best friend had turned into my entire life being uprooted. It was an exciting opportunity, but it was also draining – and I was completely out of my routine, out of my comfort zone, and more than anything, out of my usual energy level.

I was so tired, I could sleep for a year and still need more.

I decided a yin practice was what I needed, so I transitioned into a butterfly pose and settled in.

The plane ride with the team had been wild – and *fun*. Will Perry, or *Daddy P* as they called him, seemed the only one who was quiet and focused. The rest of the players let loose, singing loudly, talking, laughing, and playing cards.

I'd been a quiet observer for most of it, taking photos and videos and scratching notes down in my notepad in-between texts to Livia. She was the only person I knew I could talk to who would actually understand, given that she worked with these brutes on the daily.

I watched them with a smile on my face, marveling at how much they seemed like a family. It was like a plane full of twenty brothers, and the coaches and staff were like their cool uncles rather than their dads. At least, all of them except McCabe, who seemed to be the only one able to wrangle the boys with as little as a whistle and a stern glare.

When the guys were playing a card game in our little pod, Vince dealt me in, and though he didn't pry, he made me a part of the conversation.

I hated how much I loved that.

I'd had my mind made up about him, and when he slung his stupid pickup lines or cocky jokes my way, it was easy to keep him in that box. He was a playboy, a cocky athlete who was used to the limelight, and even more used to always getting his way. I had no interest in him other than what he would do for my career.

I just needed him to stay there, in that box I'd placed him in, because when he asked about me, when he stood up for me to the other players when he didn't realize I was behind him?

Things like that made the lid on the box pop open, and I didn't like the thought of him getting out of where I'd placed him in my mind.

Throughout the day, I'd posted pictures and videos to my stories on the One Month with Vince Cool account, showing everything from the guys dressed in their travel day suits on the tarmac to them wrestling each other to the ground in the hallway of the hotel on the way to their rooms. All day long, the followers had ticked up, and any time I posted anything, it took only seconds to have thousands of likes and comments. I was also receiving direct messages with requests for what they wanted to see.

Please show us what they do after the game when they win!

OMG, please post what bar they'll be at so I can show up and make Vince my husband.

Can you tell us what music he loves to listen to?

Can you show us pictures of him as a kid?

What does he like to do when he's not playing hockey?

Is he DTF? If so, how do I get in on that?

How do I become his wife?

Tell Vince I said he's a pussy.

That last one was from Jaxson Brittain, which made me laugh.

By the time my head hit the pillow last night, the account had half-a-million followers.

In one day.

That made my chest tighten with a performance anxiety I wasn't sure I'd ever felt before. It also made me shake off my thoughts and focus on my mat. I needed to let go of all the noise. Otherwise, I'd drown in it.

I flowed through a gentle thirty-minute practice before I had to take a quick shower and get over to Vince's room. I'd filmed a little of him at the morning skate, which was just as relaxed and fun as the plane ride had been, but then the team had retired back to the hotel to get ready for the game.

I didn't realize that, for most of them, part of that process was taking a long nap.

So I'd retreated to my room for a little much-needed silence, and I felt a bit refreshed as I got dressed and ready for my first NHL game.

Before heading over to Vince's room, I checked my reflection in the mirror. My outfit was much more appropriate than what I'd worn the day before. I chose a chic pair of cream slacks and a white blouse, pairing a royal blue blazer with it to match the team's colors *and* to keep myself warm. My curls were bouncy and voluminous, but without the frizz I usually had in Florida. I absentmindedly wondered if women in the Northeast ever had to deal with humidity or if their hair always looked flawless. I'd also decided to wear my favorite pair of nude heels, giving myself a little height. I just prayed my feet wouldn't be in too much pain by the end of the night.

My makeup was soft and neutral, the way I applied it when I wanted it to look like I wasn't even wearing any at all. I used just enough concealer and foundation to smooth my skin but still let my freckles pop through, and I enhanced my brows with a little gel before running mascara over my lashes. A nude gloss finished the look, calling attention to one of my favorite assets. I loved my lips, my teeth, my smile as a whole.

When I added a delicate pair of gold ear climbers and a dainty chain necklace that hung perfectly in the V of my blouse, I called it done, and then I was out the door and on my way to Vince's room.

Which was, conveniently, right next door.

I pulled a deep inhale through my nose, forcing a smile before I rapped my knuckles on the wood. I was about to knock again when the door flew open.

Vince was once again shirtless, and this time, he was in nothing but a pair of navy blue briefs.

It happened so fast — him slinging the door open, running a hand back through his messy hair as he yawned and held it open wide for me to come in. He was just a tired man waking up from a nap in his underwear, nothing out of the ordinary for him.

But for me, it was like seeing one of the seven wonders of the world.

Even if I *was* used to his ridiculous abdomen and chest — which I wasn't, by the way — I was now face to face with his monster thighs, too. They strained against the fabric of his underwear, though not as much as another part of him, which was framed perfectly by the white stitching in the front of those blue briefs.

He was also *very much* at attention.

Vince didn't seem to notice. He just held the door open wider, and then once I had my hand on it, turned to walk farther into his suite. And when he did, I gaped for another reason altogether.

Vince Tanev had an ass of stone.

It was the largest I'd ever seen on any man in my life, but it was also cut, the muscles lean and a dip in the side of each cheek showcasing as he walked. I'd had a sneaky suspicion when I'd seen them all dressed in their suits earlier, but now, I had that suspicion verified.

Hockey players had the best asses in the entire world.

There was just no debating it.

"Coffee?" he asked me as he walked into the kitchen area of his suite, already pouring a cup for himself. He turned and leaned against the counter, and once again, my eyes flicked to where his erection was.

He followed my gaze.

And then the bastard smirked, shrugging.

"Sorry about that," he said, reaching down to adjust himself. I had to tear my eyes away and look up at the ceiling, because seeing his gargantuan hand wrapped around his massive cock as he casually grabbed himself was too much for any woman to withstand — even one who knew he was a playboy.

"Good dream during that nap, I take it?" I said, hoping that came out as a joke more than a question I actually wanted the answer to.

"A very good dream," he said, sipping the black coffee in his mug. "You were in it."

That made me suck my teeth, and when I leveled him with a glare, he chuckled.

"I'm going to start getting myself ready," he said. "And... I know it's kind of been fun and games up until this point, but it's game day, and my pre-game ritual means a lot to me. So..."

"I'll stay out of your way," I promised. "Just ignore me."

His eyes flickered a little bit where they ran over me. "You're entirely oblivious to what a fox you are, aren't you?"

My neck warmed at his words, but I didn't let myself smile or blush beneath them. Instead, I pulled out my phone and snapped a picture of him.

"Keep making comments like that, and I'll post this picture of you in your underwear."

"Go ahead," he dared on another shrug, pushing off the counter and heading toward the bedroom part of the suite. "Maybe a Boston Bunny will see it and find me after the game."

"Pig," I called after him, and his deep laugh was the last thing I heard before he was running the shower.

True to my word, I tried to be invisible as Vince ran through his pre-game routine. The only question I asked was what he did before I got there, to which he told me he had a big pre-game meal – which apparently was the same for him every game, a huge heaping pile of some sort of pasta – and a long nap with the air conditioning turned down to sixty degrees. I'd wondered why I had been freezing when I first walked in, and now I had my answer.

That little tidbit of knowledge along with what I observed him do had me smiling to myself.

Vince Cool was superstitious.

He didn't shave on game days, and he also brushed his teeth not once but twice – once after he finished his coffee and another time after he had his pre-game snack, which was a piece of wheat toast slathered in peanut butter and topped with bananas.

He got dressed in a very particularly order, and he packed his bag to take to the stadium in a very particular way, too. When we were getting close to ready to leave, he dropped to the ground and did four pushups. *Only* four. Then, he surprised me further by calling his little sister.

Her bright blue eyes filled the screen, and she looked so much like Vince I wondered if they were twins. But a quick Google search told me she was a year-and-a-half younger than him.

"Hey, big bro," she sang, her smile wide, teeth like the ones you saw on orthodontist billboards. "You ready to kick ass?"

"Almost."

She sighed on a laugh. "You know, I might be getting too old for this."

"You're not allowed to. Ever. You know the rules."

"Yeah, yeah, pre-game ritual," she said with a grin. She perked up when she saw me standing behind her brother. "Oh! You're Maven King!"

Vince held the phone at a better angle for her to see me. "I am," I said with an awkward wave. "Hello."

"Hi! I'm Grace, Vinny's sister. Nice to meet you. I'm so excited for this piece you're doing on my brother." She paused, her nose wrinkling. "I could do with you showing him with more clothes on, though."

I laughed, and Vince pointed the phone back at himself. "Come on, sis. Gotta give the people what they want."

"Isn't what they want supposed to be you scoring goals?"

"Yes," he said. "*And* making them cream their panties."

"Ew!" she screamed at the same time I said, "Gross!"

Vince smiled victoriously. "Alright, we need to get downstairs for the bus. Let's go."

"Fine," she sang again, and then she propped her phone up so she could stand in the middle of the room. I didn't know where she was, but it looked like a college dorm, and she swung a leg out like she was testing the space around her.

I pulled out my phone and recorded Vince from behind, arching a brow at him and then the screen.

Then, Grace started singing.

Well, it wasn't really *singing* as much as it was half-cheering, half-squawking like a bird. She did the most ridiculous dance, her hair flying about as she chirped something about *forty one, best under the sun, forty one, let's have some fun, Vinny, Vinny, you're so cool, you're so cool you rule the school* and then she ended it all with a back tuck into a split.

Vince held up his fist when she finished. "Perfect ten."

"I know," she said, climbing to her feet. "Go get 'em, big bro."

"Later, sis."

The call ended as abruptly as it had begun, and I turned off my own video, momentarily stunned.

"Um..." I laughed. "What was that?"

Vince shrugged, and I noticed he'd slipped out of his usual goofy demeanor into one more serious. The transition had been slow, starting from the moment I'd walked in the door and getting more severe as the hours ticked on.

He was mentally preparing himself for the game, that much was easy to see.

"Just a little tradition," he said.

I couldn't help but laugh again. "What – your little sister doing a bizarre dance and backflip?"

"Yes," he said, snapping his eyes to mine. "Is there an issue?"

I swallowed under his gaze, which was harder than it ever had been when it was on me. "No," I said. "I just wasn't aware you needed someone to squawk like a bird to feel game ready."

He narrowed his gaze, standing from where he had been on the couch. It always took my breath away, how tall and broad he was. "It was something she did to cheer me up before a game in high school when I was on a shit streak. I got a hat trick that game, and so now it's routine."

"But... you've lost games since then," I pointed out. "So it can't always work."

"You don't get it."

He was gathering the last of his things to head out the door when I cut him off. "So explain it to me."

He sighed, looking up at the ceiling. The movement exposed that long column of his throat, and I traced his Adam's apple with a bolt of electricity firing off between my thighs.

How *is this man's throat so damn hot?*

"I can't. It's just... I don't know. Something I have to do."

He walked toward his bedroom then, which confused me, since we needed to head downstairs. I followed him, and when he turned *on* his closet light instead of flicking it off like a normal person would do before they left, I laughed.

"Don't tell me this is part of it, too?"

He didn't answer, but the muscle in his jaw ticced.

I shook my head on another quiet laugh, jotting it all down in my notes. "What's next? Going to hop on one foot, rubbing your belly and patting your head at the same time?"

At that, Vince gritted his teeth, the muscle of his jaw flexing under his skin. "Can you stop being such a bitch?"

My jaw fell open at that.

"*What* did you just—"

"A bitch. That's what I called you. Because that's what you're acting like." He stepped into my space, sucking all the air out of the room when he did. "Maybe this isn't important to you. Maybe all you can focus on is getting your little photos and videos and likes and shares. But just like that's your career, this is mine, okay? It's my whole fucking life." He stepped even closer. "It's important to me. And if you can't respect that, then we can't work together."

We were chest to chest now, and his was heaving almost as hard as mine.

"You're such a bastard," I said, lifting my chin to let him know I wasn't backing down. "So, what? I'm a *bitch* because I didn't smile and tell you how adorable you are when you do idiotic, superstitious stunts before a game?"

He puffed his chest even more, and that scarred eyebrow dipped low and menacing.

I couldn't explain it, the electricity buzzing through me then. He was angry. He was staring at me like he wanted to wring my neck.

And something inside me was giddy about it.

"Fine," I said after a moment, dragging the word out. I knew I sounded like the bitch he'd accused me of being even as the words came out of my mouth, full of sarcasm and not genuine in the least, but I couldn't help it. I wanted to test him, to see just how far I could push. "I'm *sorry*. How dare I not understand why it's *so important* to turn on your closet light before a game? I promise to be more respectful of your precious little rituals." I smiled sweetly. "Okay, *Tanny Boy*?"

His hand shot out so fast I couldn't register it.

One minute, I was smiling up at him with my little jest.

The next, he had my chin gripped tight between his thumb and forefinger, his knuckle guiding my chin up even farther so he could properly look down at me. He was just above me, his lips maybe only an inch from mine, so close I could smell the mint on his breath when he spoke.

"If only you had something better to do with this smart mouth of yours."

He spat the words like a curse, like he wanted to throw me to the ground and leave me there. Instead, he held my chin in place, dark hazel eyes flicking between mine before they fell to my lips and stared hard and long.

Shock zipped through me from where his bruising grip held my chin, but it was quickly washed away by the stronger, more prevalent sensation I couldn't quite name. It was hot and charged, reckless and consuming.

I should have been appalled. Intimidated. Scared, even.

Instead, I was aroused.

I didn't have a single ounce of fear in me that he would hurt me. I wasn't afraid of how hard he gripped me, or how he was so close I could feel his breath on my lips.

All I could focus on was his hazel eyes and how they darkened the longer he stared at my mouth.

He blinked, three times in rapid succession, like he was waking up from a sleepwalking dream. His expression softened, along with this grip.

Vince released me, tilting his chin a bit higher before he turned and took all the heat with him.

He grabbed his bag without another look in my direction, tossing it over his shoulder and barreling out of the suite with the door clicking shut behind him.

And I just stood there, blinking, sucking in a breath that burned as my hands floated up to trace where his had been.

What the actual fuck was *that*?

Chapter 9

Extra Credit

Maven

Am I crazy?

Those were the words on repeat in my mind as I loaded up onto the bus with the team. They grew even louder when we arrived at the stadium, the guys much more subdued now than they were on the plane ride or even during the morning skate. Now, they were all quiet and focused like Daddy P had been, whether they were taping their sticks or watching film or stretching in the corner of the locker room.

Meanwhile, I was pretending to focus while my brain turned over what had happened in Vince's room.

I should report that, I thought. But that notion only lasted for a split second before the more pressing one took its place.

That shouldn't have turned me on.

I knew it was true, and yet, my body was still tense in the most exhilarating way from the exchange. I could close my eyes on a blink and see the whole scene play out again — him standing over me, his hand gripping my chin tightly, his eyes hard on mine before they fell to my mouth.

I shivered, and then my skin crawled like a cold front had just blown in. I looked across the room at where Vince was taping his stick.

His hands were at work, but his eyes were on me.

He watched me for a long pause before he tore his gaze away, his jaw tight, and continued working on his stick.

That was the last time he looked at me the entire game.

It wasn't my first time watching an NHL game, but it *was* my first time watching one live. And, to be honest, it was my first time where I actually paid attention. Hockey was big in Tampa. As a life-long resident, it was impossible to escape the big playoff parties hosted all around the city. I'd gone with friends or even watched with my dad a time or two, but the games were mostly background noise while I talked to my friends or scrolled on my phone.

Tonight, I was standing behind the glass at the mouth of the tunnel, right next to where the players lined the bench. I had chills lining my arms and my phone clamped in shaky hands.

The rush of adrenaline I felt was like riding a roller-coaster without a seatbelt.

From the moment the puck dropped, I was in a trance, taking photos and videos while also frantically writing out notes in my phone — and questions. *So* many questions I wanted to ask Vince later, like how they were able to change lines so seamlessly, how they were able to skate so hard for minutes at a time, how they were able to catch their breath before being put back on the ice. Also, what were those salts they smelled? And *why* did they do it? Why was tripping a penalty, but being shoved hard into the boards was seemingly fine?

The energy from the crowd only amped up my buzz more, and this was an *away* game. I couldn't imagine what it would be like at home, and I couldn't wait to find out.

At the end of the first period, no one had scored, but it wasn't because the teams weren't playing well. It was the opposite, actually, Boston and Tampa duking it out like they'd sooner get nut tapped than let the other one score.

In the locker room, Coach McCabe gave a few words of encouragement, telling the guys to keep doing what they were doing but to fight harder.

"You want this," he reminded them. "But so do they. Wanting it isn't enough. You've got to *need* it. You've got to need that win so badly you will fight like it's win or die."

Coach let me sit at the edge of the bench the next period after I'd begged him for a glass-free video. I had a helmet strapped to my head, just in case.

As the puck was dropped, I thought about what Coach had said to me yesterday, about how they had a real shot this season. I knew Vince Tanev was a big part of why he believed that, and when Vince scored a goal within the first minute of the second period, I understood why.

He was a beast.

Or, as I heard a couple of guys on the bench call him, *a beaut.*

That one goal seemed like a match that lit his fuse, and he went off like a bomb after that. He had an assist to the center in his line, bringing them up by two, and then when Boston caught up and the game was tied in the third period with just four minutes left to play, he scored again, rendering the arena completely silent while he and the team celebrated.

It was after that goal that he finally looked at me.

His eyes sparkled behind the shield of his helmet, and he skated over so fluidly to where I sat, it was like he'd been born on those blades. I took my phone out and focused the video camera on him, and a little smirk climbed on his lips.

"Sick celly, Pigeon," a player yelled from the bench beside me, and Vince lifted his head in a little nod of acknowledgement before hopping over the boards.

But he didn't sit on the bench.

Instead, he sat right there on the ledge, right in front of me, all padded up and sweaty and hot as hell as he leaned forward, elbows resting on his knees. I had the camera trained on him, but he wasn't looking at the lens.

He was looking directly at me.

Vince didn't say a word, just sat there, smirking, his eyes zeroed in on mine with some sort of challenge lying behind them. Slowly, I dropped the camera, meeting his gaze with my own instead of watching him through the screen.

His smile climbed higher.

"Alright, Tanev," Coach McCabe said from where he stood against the glass. "There's still a game going on. Ass on the bench."

Vince kept his eyes on me as he stood, and then he winked, wetting his lips a little as he strode to the end of the bench to take a seat.

My heart was hammering in my chest when the puck was dropped, and my phone buzzed so hard in my hand I jumped. When I checked the text, it was from Livia.

Livia: Ohhhh, girl. You are in trouble.
Me: What? What happened?
Livia: They just showed that whole exchange between you and Vince on TV, that's what happened.

I swallowed.

Me: I don't know what you're talking about.
Livia: Sure. Let's go with that.
Livia: But be honest... you need to change your underwear, don't you?
Me: You're disgusting.
Livia: And YOU are lying to yourself.
Me: This is an assignment, Liv. Nothing more.
Livia: Uh-huh. Looks to me like you might have an extra credit opportunity. ;)
Me: Goodbye.

I couldn't help the little laugh that left me when I saw the string of emojis my best friend responded with, but I exited the conversation and pulled up my video camera just in time to catch the last ten seconds of play. Our team celebrated on the ice while the home team skated off silently, and only a handful of fans cheered in the crowd while the rest were hanging their heads on the exit.

After a quick celebratory skate around the rink where all the guys hammed it up, I followed them back to the locker room — the very, *very* smelly locker room — halfway listening to their celebrations while I posted Vince's goal and the final score.

Just because I was curious, I refreshed the app after thirty seconds.

And the post already had more than ten-thousand likes and hundreds of comments.

I shook my head. It was just... *ludicrous,* the amount of people who were invested in him, in his life, in his body. I absentmindedly wondered what kind of pressure that would put on a person as I tucked my phone into my purse.

Once it was put away, I kneaded my temples with my fingers. So much screen time was giving me a headache, along with the insanity of the past week and wearing a helmet not made for me. And we still had to pack and fly home.

I understood the appeal of flying after the game, of being able to go to sleep in your own bed back in your own city, especially since we had a home game in a couple days. But I hoped it wouldn't be too loud on the flight. All I wanted was to catch some Zs.

"Aw, come on, it can't be *that* bad."

I opened my eyes to find Vince standing over me. His hair was soaking wet, sticking to his forehead and neck just like his t-shirt was sticking to his chest. I assumed he wore that under his pads, because it was completely drenched. He also wore a pair of equally wet shorts and still had his shin pads on.

"Oh, are you talking to me again?"

"For now."

I smiled, my skin still buzzing from our earlier exchange. But that menacing gaze of his was gone, and he was the Vince Tanev I knew again. Playful. Charming. Annoyingly so.

"Congratulations on the win," I offered.

"Thank you. Still think my pre-game rituals are stupid?"

"I never said they were stupid," I defended. "But... does this mean we have to fight before every game now? Because we did, and you won, so..."

He scrubbed a hand over his jaw with a devilish grin.

"Sounds like fun to me," he said, his eyes following the line of my necklace where it dipped under my blouse. "But only if we get to kiss and make up afterward."

He waggled his brows as I flattened my lips.

And then he was tackled from behind by Carter before I got the chance to tell him that was *never* going to happen.

Chapter 10

Good Morning to Me

Vince

I woke up bright and early Sunday morning in Tampa with a raging hard-on.

I had so much testosterone flowing through me after winning an away game against one of the best teams in our division, I felt like I could pick a car up over my head and throw it a hundred yards. Add in the fact that I'd now spent forty-eight hours with Maven King invading every inch of my life, and it didn't surprise me to wake up with morning wood.

My eyes closed on a groan as I palmed myself, and the first thing I thought of was her rubbing her ass against me on the plane in those tight-as-sin jeans. I kicked my sheets off, not even a little ashamed as I gave in and pumped myself to the memory. I saw her in that yellow dress from the gala, pictured her daring eyes and that sweet mouth of hers that loved to sass back when I challenged her.

When I thought of how those honey eyes had widened when I took her by the chin, when I forced her to look at me while I stared at her mouth, I came.

It was a memory I'd store away for life, how her delicate neck had been exposed for me, her pulse thrumming under the surface and begging to be kissed, to be licked, to be bitten. I could replay the way her eyes dilated for years, how all that gold had been swallowed up, her chest rising and falling in a hypnotizing rhythm as she stared up at me and waited for a command.

She liked it, when I took control of her like that, when I shut her up.

Whether she'd ever admit it or not was another story entirely.

After I cleaned up, I ran a hot shower, and my thoughts of Maven turned less sexual and more guilty. Not that I felt guilty for fucking my hand at the thought of her, because I didn't, but rather that I felt bad for snapping at her before the game, for being the asshole she already thought I was.

If we were going to work together for a month, I needed to make things right.

With a towel around my waist, I padded into my bedroom and grabbed my phone off the nightstand, thumbing out a text to her.

Me: Breakfast?
Maven: Where?
Me: My place.
Maven: You... cook?
Me: Told you I'm full of surprises.
Maven: You better not serve me burnt toast. See you in twenty.

Right on time, she knocked on my door just as I finished mixing up my mom's famous waffle mix. She was a fucking vision in my doorway, wearing a flowy bohemian dress that cinched her waist and framed her slight breasts in two triangle slips of fabric. The skirt draped down to her ankles, but two slits on each side revealed her toned legs beneath. She offered a tentative, almost nervous smile when I answered, her face void of makeup, and only a simple pair of earrings donning her lobes. Her black hair was pulled up into a poof on top of her head, the edges of it styled in swirling designs that framed her forehead and temples.

"Damn," I said, and I thought I'd said it to myself, but when the corner of Maven's lips curled softly, I knew I hadn't. So, I owned it. "Good morning to me."

"Shut up," she said, softly pressing her hand against my chest as she pushed past me and into my condo. I shut the door behind her before making my way into the kitchen, and Maven slid into one of my barstools like she'd been there a hundred times, setting her purse on the island.

"I hope you're hungry."

"And I hope you're not trying to poison me," she said, eyeing the goop I was mixing up. I sprayed the waffle maker before dumping the mix in and closing the lid.

"Now why would I do that? You're working wonders for my brand right now."

"Well, you *did* look like you were two seconds from killing me last night."

My throat tightened at that, and once I had flipped the waffle-maker, I leaned a hip against the counter and crossed my arms, turning to face her.

"I'm sorry, Maven."

She seemed surprised by the genuine apology.

"It's fine," she tried, waving me off. "I—"

"It's not fine. I was a jerk, and you didn't deserve that. I'm sorry."

She swallowed. "Oh. Well... thank you."

"I just... I am a creature of habit and routine, especially when it comes to game days. I can get a little crazy, I guess."

"I'm sorry, too," she said. "For making fun of the process. I was curious at first, but then, I admit I found it a bit bizarre." She chuckled at that. "And then I saw how worked up you were getting and I..."

"You wanted to push my buttons."

She bit the inside of her lip like she was ashamed. Then, her smile leveled out, eyes searching mine, and I wondered if she was remembering what I'd done after she mouthed off to me.

I wondered what she'd do if I did it again, right now, without all that anger simmering between us. What would her eyes look like if I wrapped my hand around her throat and squeezed *just* a little bit...

"It's okay," I told her. "I like to push yours, too."

I turned back to tend to her waffle before I got the satisfaction of seeing the look on her face. Once it was on a plate, I dressed it with the sweet cream cheese I'd mixed up, along with the blueberry compote and fresh blueberries and strawberries on top. It looked like a culinary sensation by the time I slid the plate in front of her, and Maven's eyes lit up.

She eyed me curiously before taking out her phone and snapping a picture of the waffle. She snapped one of me, too, standing at the island with my palms on the counter, smiling at the camera. I had no problem cheesing it up for the public – especially since I wanted my name at the top of everyone's mind when it came to selecting Rookie of the Year.

Once she had her pictures, she tucked her phone away and forked off the corner of the waffle.

"Make sure you get the berries," I coached, which made her smile.

Then, she took her first bite, moaning with her eyes closed as I tried not to stare at where her tongue darted out to lick the compote from her lips.

"*Hngg,*" she said around the mouthful, swallowing before her eyes popped open and locked on mine. "Holy shit, this is good."

"Always so surprised," I chastised, but I smiled in victory when I turned away to make my own waffle.

Maven was almost done with hers by the time I sat down next to her with my own, and she rubbed her belly as if it was a beer gut, sinking back in her chair.

"Call me impressed."

"I thought I was only supposed to call you Maven."

She stuck her tongue out at me before leaning her chin on her palm, watching as I took my first bite. "So, I take it you and your sister are pretty close. Especially if she loves you enough to do that whole pre-game dance thing every single game."

"She's one of my best friends," I answered honestly, stacking a few berries on my fork. "We were only a year apart in school, so we grew up together with the same friends and the same problems."

"You ever date any of her friends?"

"Define *date*."

Maven snorted. "Pig. Okay, did she ever date any of yours?"

"Never."

"Never?"

I shook my head. "My friends didn't want to die, so they stayed away from my little sister."

"Oh, that's rich. You can mess around with her friends, but yours are forbidden, huh?"

"Grace is too good for any of my friends."

Maven smiled a bit at that.

"I take it you're the oldest of your siblings," I observed. "You've got the first-born attitude, too."

"Only-born," she amended, and her face softened a bit. "I was a miracle baby."

I frowned, swallowing another bite before I asked, "How so?"

"My parents weren't sure they wanted to have kids when they first got married. They were in AmeriCorps together, which meant they didn't really have roots set in place. They were so focused on helping other people, they didn't really think about themselves. But one day, Mom decided she wanted a baby, and Dad has always done whatever Mom wants." She smiled, making designs with her fork on the leftover compote on her plate. "That's when they found out Mom had cervical cancer."

My heart bottomed out in my chest. I wasn't expecting such a vulnerable admission, not from the woman who had been hard as steel around me.

"They caught it early, thankfully, but the doctors still weren't sure she'd ever have kids." Maven looked at me then. "She had two miscarriages before she had me, and not too long after I was born, the cancer came back, and she had to have her uterus removed."

I balked. I didn't have a single word to say to that.

"So, it's just me," she said, smiling on a little bounce of her shoulders. "Their miracle baby."

"You three are close." I said it as a statement, not as a question. "You post a lot of photos with them."

"I do. Creeper."

I smirked. "Hey, you left an impression on me at the gala. Not my fault your bestie dropped your full name, and I couldn't resist the urge to look you up."

"Damn it, Livia..."

"It surprised me," I admitted. "What I found when I did."

She propped her chin on her palm again. "Why? What did you expect?"

"Not a barefoot hippy working in her garden."

Maven sighed. "I'm not sure I classify as a true hippy," she said. "Not with how conflicted I am. Part of me feels like throwing caution to the wind and living my life in a tent. The other half of me wants a career and money and a nice, clean place to lay my head at night."

"Why does it have to be one or the other?"

"It doesn't, I guess." She considered. "It's just odd. I feel like the loudest inner parts of me are at war. I enjoy my job, especially the thought of using it for good. But then I think about what my job *is*, social media, and I just... laugh at myself. Because it's ridiculous."

"It's not," I told her. "It's essentially you being a modern-day journalist. And trust me, the fact that you want to use all those followers you have for any kind of good sets you apart from the norm."

She offered me a soft smile, and then another longing breath left her chest. "I miss my plant babies, and my bed. I miss my *life*, honestly."

"I'm sure it's hard, walking away from your routine for all of this." I waved my hand in the air.

"I mean, I'm not sure I have as much of a routine as *you* do," she teased. "But, yes. It's... different."

"In a bad way?"

"Just... different. I'm not used to such a lavish lifestyle." She gestured to my condo. "This place costs more money than me or my family have ever seen in our lives. I flew on a private plane to and from Boston in twenty-four hours' time. I stayed in a plush hotel suite with a balcony overlooking the city and a bathtub big enough to fit five people in it."

"It is a lot," I admitted.

"I'm sure you're used to it."

"I've kind of grown up in it," I admitted, and for some reason, I felt a little ashamed. "But I guess you already knew that, judging by your comments the first night we met."

Maven's eyes flicked between mine, almost like she was sorry. But then, she snuffed a laugh out of her nose. "Please don't act like you were offended. Or like you don't enjoy the women who fall all over you or the guys who would lick your skate if you let them."

"I've always wanted to be the best," I said, taking our plates to the sink. "And not *all* the women fall all over me," I added pointedly, glancing at her as I rinsed the dishes.

She rolled her eyes, popping out of her barstool to stand. "So, Vince Cool. What do you do with a day off?"

"I'll show you," I said. "But first... what do *you* want to do?"

"Me?"

I nodded. "You said you're missing your normal life. What would Maven King be doing on a Sunday morning if she wasn't babysitting a pro hockey player?"

At that, she folded her arms with her brow slowly arching. "You really want to know?"

"I do."

She watched me for a long moment before shaking her head. "Alright," she said, grabbing her purse off the island. "Let's go, Tanny Boy. Wear something casual that you don't mind sweating in. Oh," she added with a wry grin. "And bring your credit card."

"Am I taking you shopping?"

"Something like that."

Chapter 11

For My Eyes Only

Maven

"I can't believe you did all this for us, Vince," Mr. Pruitt said, smiling his signature gap-toothed smile. Mr. Pruitt was a white man, sixty-two, with long gray hair and more unbelievable road trip stories than a circus troupe. "You know you didn't need to."

"Yeah, we're happy just to hang out. We didn't think we'd see you much once the season started," Lonnie added, clapping Vince on the back. Where Mr. Pruitt was pale, Lonnie was bronzed like he lived at the beach. And to be honest, on some occasions, he did. He was also very proud of his full head of brown hair and matching long beard.

And while I usually would be hugging them and asking how they'd been, I was currently standing there on the edge of the conversation, completely shocked.

When Vince had asked me what I would usually be doing on a Sunday morning, I'd thought I'd be throwing him for a loop when I told him. Because every Sunday morning, I either made egg sandwiches myself, or grabbed some from McDonald's, along with some orange juice, and came downtown to the park where a handful of Tampa's displaced population tended to congregate.

It was something I started doing when I was in college, and the tradition continued once I made so many friends. While it killed me to see their situation stay the same for so long, it also filled me with joy to spend time with them, to hear their stories and show them kindness that I knew they weren't showed often. When I had a little extra to give, they were usually the first people I gave it to. Sometimes I took them to get their hair cut. Sometimes I put them up in a hotel when a cold front swept through, which wasn't often in Tampa, thank goodness. And sometimes, *most* times, I just came out to chat with them, to remind them that regardless of how some might treat them, they were still worthy of love and respect.

This morning, with Vince's credit card in hand, I'd decided to spoil them not only with a hot breakfast from McDonald's, but with Publix subs to save for later, *and* brand-new packages of socks and underwear, too. And the entire time, Vince had been quiet, wearing a smug little smile that I thought meant he was just amused and confused about what was happening.

But when we pulled up to the park and walked over, all of its residents greeted Vince before they did me.

And I'd been standing there confused ever since, watching as they interacted the way family would.

"Well, to be fair, you probably won't see quite as much of me," Vince admitted, scrubbing a hand over the back of his neck. "But this one dragged me out this morning. And I'm glad she did."

"Ah, Maven is an angel on Earth," Nonna said. I didn't know if that was her real name or just what she had everyone call her, but she was one of the only women who stayed at the park with all these rascals. She had olive skin, and an accent I couldn't quite place, along with a smile that felt like a warm hug any time she geared it toward you. The guys here respected her like she was their grandmother even though she couldn't be more than sixty years old, so maybe that was why they called her Nonna. "You picked a good girl to date, son."

"Oh, she's not my girl," Vince said, his eyes twinkling a little bit when they met mine. "Not yet, anyway."

Lonnie and Mr. Pruitt exchanged glances on a snicker at that, but I was still too shocked to even roll my eyes. Here was this man who lived in a multi-million-dollar condo not even five blocks from this park, who wore designer suits and drove a car that cost more than my parents' *home* — and somehow, everyone here knew him.

How?

I watched them all chatter for a bit as Vince handed out the underwear and socks before digging out breakfast from the multiple paper bags. Everyone chowed down and laughed beneath the large oak trees covered in Spanish moss that shaded the park. I joined in, but still couldn't hide my *what the fuck* face, apparently, because after a while, Vince nudged my arm.

"What's wrong, Maven? You look a little perplexed there."

I glared at him. "Are you going to tell me what's going on or just sit there all cocksure?"

"I like the sound of that second option," he said, biting into a McGriddle even though we'd already eaten a massive waffle. He was so lean, I found it hard to believe he ate as much as I'd seen him eat in the past couple of days. Then again, when you skate nonstop for hours at a time, I guess you need to pack it on so you have the energy to do so.

"How do you know everyone here?"

"Oh, we met Vince during rookie camp," Lonnie answered for me. "He was walking back to his place after practice one day and we called him over, started chatting."

"Yep. I told him how I set up outside of every home game with my bamboo roses for sale," Mr. Pruitt said.

"And I told him how I play my bucket drums," Lonnie added. "Before you knew it, Vince was inviting us up to his place."

My jaw nearly hit the grass. "To... his place?"

"Oh, that was such a lovely day," Nonna said all dreamy-eyed. "He let us all take showers, made us a hot meal, and even let us sleep in the air conditioning for a while. We made a big camp there in his living room."

I blinked, sure I wasn't hearing this right.

When I looked at Vince, he was chewing, silent, staring down at his sneakers with his cheeks a bit pink.

"I tried to convince him to give us a key, but..." Nonna said wistfully, a rascally grin on her face.

"Now, Nonna — if I would have done that, I would have woken up with you in my bed by now," Vince said.

"And it would have been the best morning of your life," she combatted.

He winked at her, and she pinched off a piece of her hashbrown and tossed it at him.

"Since then, we been friends, haven't we, Vince?" Mr. Pruitt declared with a grin. "He comes by and says hello when he can, and Lonnie beats the drums extra loud when we win here at home."

"I even painted his number on the side," Lonnie said proudly. "Forty-one, baby."

Vince looked at me then, lifting a brow.

He knew without me saying it.

He'd surprised me yet again.

"Excuse me?"

We all turned to look toward where the soft voice had come from, finding a woman with a young boy tucked into her side. She smiled shyly.

"I'm sorry to interrupt, but my son is your biggest fan. He'd really love to take a picture with you, if that would be okay."

Vince wiped the crumbs from his hands and stood from where we'd been sitting on a blanket. "Of course. What's your name, little man?"

"I'm The Machine."

Vince's eyes shot up, and the boy's mom let out a little laugh.

"His name is Matty."

"But my teammates call me The Machine because I'm the best goalie, and no one ever scores on me."

Vince bent down to Matty's level. "Ever?"

Matty seemed a little unsure, looking at his mom, but then he smiled and shook his head. "Never."

"Think you could come give Perry some lessons?"

Matty laughed at that, and suddenly he was shy, his cheeks a flaming red as he tucked behind his mom a little bit.

Vince took the photo with Matty alone before the mom handed her phone to Lonnie so she could get in, too. I took a video from behind them, scanning the whole park to show the clothes and food Vince had brought out.

But I didn't post it, not yet, mostly for fear of fans swarming the park, but also a little because I didn't want to.

It was a dangerous admission, because it was quite literally my job — to show Vince's life to the world. But in this moment, my heart was beating a little odd, my mind swimming with the contradiction of the man before me. Last night he was pinning me with an angry glare, his hand holding my jaw like he didn't know if he wanted to kiss me or throw me to the ground.

And this morning, he was spending part of his day off with people most of the world turned their back on.

Therefore, the world could wait.

Right now, in this moment, Vince Tanev was for my eyes only.

Chapter 12

Free of Expectations

Maven

The amount of times I yawned throughout the day was impressive, but even as tired as I was, it was fascinating following Vince around on a day off.

It surprised me that we went straight from the park to the stadium, where he changed and headed to the team's private gym on the top floor. There were only a few other players in there, and they goofed off a bit before each settling in to their various workouts. They weren't lifting weights, though. It seemed to be all cardio, a couple of them jogging on the treadmills while Vince spent almost an hour on the bike.

When he was done, he spent a lot of time in what he told me was recovery. One of the trainers did an intense cupping session with him before a long massage, and he finished it all off with a twenty-minute sauna session. I had followed him in long enough to take a photo before quickly exiting, because being in a literal hot box with shirtless Vince was a sure-fire way to test my professionalism.

Afterward, he ate *another* meal prepared by the team's chef before we headed back to his condo. His housekeeper had come while we were gone, and the place was now spotless.

He spent a long time meditating, which surprised me, and then he journaled, which about put me on the floor with shock. When I thought about having *one* day off, I imagined him bingeing Netflix, or going out with the guys. And he admitted that sometimes, he did just that. But most of the time, he had a routine he stuck to, especially during the season.

While he was journaling, I stepped onto his beautiful balcony to call Reya and Camilla. They were losing their *minds* over the content. Between the game and all the footage from his day off, our followers were feral. And so were my bosses.

"All of this is gold," Reya told me. "And don't worry about your garden, your plants, or your house. We've hired someone to take care of all of it for the month."

That brought me as much relief as it did anxiety, because caring for my home and my garden was something *I* wanted to do — not have someone else doing.

Still, I would be lying if I said I wasn't having fun, that this assignment wasn't exciting. I decided to take my dad's advice and *live in the present*. What were the odds I'd ever do anything like this again?

Answer: slim to none.

With the end of that phone call, I committed to throwing myself completely into the experience and getting the most out of it. And when I quietly stepped back inside, Vince glanced up at me from where he was journaling with a crooked grin.

I ignored the way my heart skipped a beat when he did.

Throughout most of the day, he was silent, and I just took photos and videos and observed from the outside. I'd told him to pretend like I wasn't there, and after the park, he'd been incredibly proficient in adhering to my request. I almost missed it — his playboy attitude, cocky lines, and quick banter. But there was something magical about watching him from the outside, being a little fly on the wall during a professional hockey player's day off.

I wasn't sure what I'd expected, exactly, but it likely involved women and drugs and spending money like it would never run out. I *definitely* hadn't expected him to be so focused on the season, to work on his body and his mind, to stick to a routine that would help him recover from the games this past week while also gearing up for the ones to come.

There was a reason he was one of the best rookies in the league. Maybe luck and talent had something to do with it, but this? His dedication to what he did? That played a part, too.

I thought I'd be ignored until I excused myself from his apartment, but when the afternoon bled into evening, and the sun began to sink over the city skyline, Vince grabbed two local IPAs out of his fridge. He cracked the top on one of them before arching a brow at me to ask if I wanted the second one.

And *usually*, I was not a beer girl.

But I thought *what the hell — part of the experience, right?* and nodded.

"Is it Netflix time?" I asked him as I took the first sip.

He smiled the way the Cheshire cat would, rounding the kitchen island and walking past me and across the room.

"Not quite," he said.

And he placed his beer on the end table by his pottery wheel.

"Wait," I said excitedly, hopping off my barstool and all but skipping over to him. "Am I going to get backstage access to the making of a Vince Tanev ceramic masterpiece?"

"I can't tell if you're being sincere or sarcastic."

"A bit of both." I grabbed one of the spare rolling stools in the area and took a seat, wheeling up to where he was. "So what are you doing? What are you making? Tell me everything."

I couldn't explain it, but Vince was the most relaxed I'd seen him all day when he stepped into that little corner of his home. It was like watching someone kick their shoes off after a long, hard day.

"This guy is going into the kiln because it's finally dry enough," he said, picking up a wide, shallow bowl. It was sage green and looked like one you might use for pasta or a salad. "And I'm going to fuck around with some designs on these guys," he said, motioning to a set of tiny glasses.

"What are those, anyway?"

"I had Japanese teacups in mind when I made them," he said. "Mainly for sencha. But we'll see how they turn out."

"They look okay to me."

"Now," he said. "But I could screw them up in the design process or in the kiln. Especially since we live in Florida." He shook his head. "The moisture here fucks everything up."

I felt like a little kid in Santa's workshop, an excited smile spreading on my lips as I leaned forward and took it all in.

"And then," he said, reaching for a plastic container on one of the shelves behind his wheel. He set it on the table and popped the lid, revealing multiple sealed bags of clay of all different colors. "I'll start something new."

"What do you do with all of them?" I asked. "When you finish?"

He shrugged. "Depends. I keep some, give some away as gifts, throw some right into the garbage where they belong."

"Use some to make ten grand for charity."

"Someone's gotta make the rich assholes of the world feel good about themselves," he said pointedly, and we shared a knowing smile.

I continued peppering Vince with questions as he got started, and he had the patience of a saint as he walked me through everything he was doing, step by step. I had just as many questions about this as I did about hockey, except this was more exciting to me because it was something I had personal interest in.

I loved tending to my garden with my hands, loved cleaning up the earth with my hands, too. The thought of creating something with them, of taking something from the earth to make something beautiful and useful... it was enticing.

"How did you get into this, anyway?" I asked after he had placed a few pieces into the kiln. He grabbed a bag of clay next, adding pieces of it to a scale until he had the right weight of what he wanted to work with.

"I don't really know, actually," he confessed, covering his workspace with a large piece of plywood. He plopped the clay onto it before taking a seat, readjusting the stool and table until they were at the perfect height. Then, he dug his hands into the clay and began to knead it. "I kind of stumbled upon it."

"How does one *stumble upon* pottery?"

"I was a freshman at Michigan, my first year playing hockey at that level. And I knew it would be tougher than when I was in high school, but I didn't realize how much of a toll just being a college athlete would have on me. It's not just hockey," he said, molding the clay with long, smooth presses of his fingertips. "And it's not high-school-level classes. It's grueling practices, high-pressure games, *and* getting a degree, a career. I mean, of course we all want to go pro, and most of us know we'll play in the circuit in *some way*, at least for a while." He shrugged. "But what if you get a career-ending injury? What if you only play a few years and then get let go altogether? We can't all play pro forever. There are too many players with the same dreams."

"I never thought of that," I admitted softly, mulling on all he'd said. I'd always assumed college athletes had a free pass, that they were the lucky ones who didn't have to try as hard as the rest of us.

I felt a little guilt at that assumption now.

"Anyway, I was stressed, to put it lightly," he continued, and I marveled at how his hands spread and shaped the clay, how gracefully his fingertips and palms worked in sync to wedge it.

I'd never stared so much at someone's hands, and I found myself appreciating the makeup of his, the large knuckles and smooth, bronze skin that stretched over them.

"When I wasn't in class or studying, I was at the rink, either practicing or playing in games. We partied, of course, but that was stressful sometimes, too, because one night of partying too hard could mean a shit game performance the next day.

I needed something for me," he said after a pause. "Something that wasn't goal-oriented, that didn't have any pressure tied to it. One night when I couldn't sleep, I was scrolling on my phone, and this time-lapse video of a vase being made came up. I must have watched it a dozen times." He smiled as if he were back in the memory. "And then, I signed up for a class."

"And you loved it so much, you made yourself a home studio?"

"Not until I got my signing bonus," he said. "This shit's expensive. But, yeah. I knew I'd need it now, in the NHL, even more than I did in college."

He seemed to be satisfied with whatever he'd done to the clay to prep it, and he balled it up in his hands before rolling over to his wheel.

"When I'm in here, in this space," he said, looking around at the shelves of clay, at the finished and half-finished and completely *un*finished projects. "I'm... free. Free of expectations, free of the pressure I put on myself in every other aspect of my life. If I fuck up," he said, wetting the wheel a bit before firing it to life. The clay spun centered and beautiful for just a moment before he pushed too hard on it and it warped, nearly flying off before he cut the power on the wheel. Then, he quickly reshaped the clay and put it back in place again, as if it'd never happened. "I just start over."

My chest tightened as a smile found my lips. "That's kind of beautiful."

"That's not what you said the first night we met," he teased.

"Yeah, well, I thought I had you pegged."

He arched a brow. "Is this you admitting that you were wrong?"

"I didn't say that," I said quickly. A flash of James struck me so hard I held my next breath for a moment.

He had been just as charming as Vince, just as surprising. He'd made me laugh, made me hot with desire, made me feel safe.

And then he'd broken my fucking heart.

"But..." I added, almost regretful in my admission. "You're definitely testing my beliefs."

"How so?"

He settled in at the wheel then, and I lost myself watching him mold the wet clay with his fingertips.

"I dated a guy like you once."

That made him pause, and the clay warped before he cursed and started over again.

"Rich, I mean," I clarified. "An athlete. Someone cocksure and popular with the whole world in his hands. And let's just say he and his entire family showed me that I don't belong in their world."

Vince was quiet for a moment, focusing on the clay. I thought I saw the muscle in his jaw tense. "What did he do?"

I sighed. "Well, we were in love. Like... *stupid* in love. And he made me feel like it didn't matter that my family was poor and always had been, or that his had more money than God. He lit up when I shared stories about my past with him. He loved introducing me to things I'd never experienced, like fine dining or spending a day on a boat bigger than every house I've ever lived in put together. And when he met my parents? He charmed them. He had that power, the ability to make any and everyone fall in love with him."

For a long pause, I just watched Vince shape the clay, watched him work to get the perfect thickness on all sides.

"He gave me a promise ring." My voice cracked a bit with that. "It was... stupidly expensive for a promise ring.

And gorgeous. And it meant something to me. I was living inside the fairytale where Cinderella gets the prince." I chuffed out a laugh. "Until I went to his brother's wedding.

I was... completely out of place," I said, the memory making my skin burn with a mixture of embarrassment and rage. "Wearing a dress I'd found on the rack at Goodwill while everyone else had on ballgowns and tuxes. From *that* season, of course, because wearing anything from a line released the year before would have been atrocious. I hadn't graduated from college yet, didn't have a job where I could afford even the modest clothes I have now. I was living on loans and scholarships.

James assured me it was fine, but he broke up with me not even a week later. And his parents then called me to explain *why*," I said, laughing again. "As if I couldn't already piece it together." I straightened my back, mimicking his mother's voice that was so prim and proper. "*You're a sweet girl, Maven, but this just isn't the world for you. You have to understand that James has a very promising life ahead of him. He needs someone who understands that, and what their role in his life will entail.*"

Vince was quiet, but his nostrils flared, his hands working a little too aggressively. The clay folded in on itself and he had to start over again.

"And I know it's not fair," I said before Vince could speak. "But I listened to his stories about his family, and I watched them with their friends. I heard everyone at that wedding talk about how charitable they were, how much they gave to this organization or that one. Meanwhile, they had no *idea* what it was like to be someone like my parents, to sacrifice time and money and truly *give* to others." I shook my head. "It's hard not to have a sour taste in my mouth when I was so close to both sides. Add in the fact that James was able to so easily lie to me, to be with me for *years* and give me a fucking ring and then just... change his mind, all because..."

I couldn't finish that sentence, but the words I didn't say hung in the space between us.

Because I was poor. Because I wasn't good enough. Because I didn't fit in.

Vince finally looked at me, his eyes flicking between mine like he wanted to say something as his hands paused over the wheel.

"What?" I asked.

He opened his mouth, then shut it again. Then, swallowed and asked, "What's his last name?"

"Why?"

"Just think I should know his last name before I wipe him from the face of the planet."

I blinked at him, and then I laughed, tilting my head back and letting it bark out of my chest. "Shut up."

Vince smirked in victory, like his only goal was to lighten my mood and make me laugh about a situation that had so permanently marked me.

He went back to molding the clay, and with his eyes on his hands, he said, "All jokes aside, he's an idiot. And I'm sorry his family made you feel that way."

"It's fine."

"You should meet mine," he added, and I was thankful he wasn't looking at me when my eyes bulged out of my skull. "I think we could change your mind."

I offered a pathetic smile, but didn't respond. I didn't want to tell him I was pretty sure that was impossible. Part of my job was researching who Vince Tanev was, and I knew he came from a family maybe even more affluent than the one that had dismissed me. His parents had a mansion in East Grand Rapids, a cabin in the Rockies, a beach house here in Tampa, *and* a yacht on Lake Michigan that they were known for hosting private parties on. They both came from wealthy parents who had wealthy parents, too.

Maybe they weren't exactly like the Long Island and Hamptons crew James was a part of, but they were one in the same.

"What about you," I asked, eager to change the subject. "You ever have anyone break your heart?"

He blew out a breath. "Oh, boy. Did I just walk into an interrogation?"

"You don't have to answer, if you don't want to."

Vince smirked, shaking his head a bit as he worked the clay. "I guess you can't really have your heart broken if you've never dated anyone seriously."

I snorted internally.

I was not the least bit surprised.

"It's not because I don't want to," he said, glancing at me like he knew the assumptions I was making about him. "I just haven't found the right person yet."

"Interesting, because from the many photos I've seen posted of you online, you seem to find multiple *right ones* pretty frequently."

"To warm my bed," he clipped, his eyes finding mine. I shrank a bit under his gaze. "That's different."

"Meaning you couldn't take those women home to Mom?"

His eyebrows jumped up a bit, as if to say, "*Your words, not mine... but yes.*"

I held in my unsurprised laugh. That alone told me his mom was just like the one who had told me I didn't belong with her son, that I didn't measure up. Moms like that, who had money and an athletic son with prospects, had high expectations for who their daughter-in-law would be.

Glancing down at my unpolished nails, I swallowed past the knot in my throat when I said, "It's good to have standards."

"I guess," he said. "I just want someone who challenges me, who fires me up and makes me want more. Someone who makes my life better." He swallowed then. "Not someone who just wants me because of what I do, of who I am, of what they think they can get from me."

That response surprised me a little. It seemed the theme of the day. "I'm sorry you have to deal with people like that."

The corner of his mouth crooked up. "Careful. You said that almost like you care about me."

We both fell silent after that.

My head was spinning from the one-eighty from the day before. I'd gone from having him seething in my face with my chin clutched in his hand to being front row and center to the softest parts of him.

I didn't know what to think anymore.

And I damn sure didn't have a box to put him in.

But one thing I *did* have was the climbing numbers on our social media channels to remind me that this was all a job. There was only one reason why a man like him and a woman like me were in the same place — because it was an assignment. For both of us.

I could think about my subject all I wanted, and I'd even give myself the pleasure of appreciating how unfairly good looking the man was. But that was where it ended.

There wasn't a time that existed where the two of us mixed past this one we'd found ourselves in by happenstance.

The night crawled on, and Vince put on that music I'd heard the first morning I'd walked into his condo. It was a cross between French and Arabic, and it set a vibe unlike any other, especially paired with the views of him creating.

I had expected it to be beautiful, watching Vince mold that clay into a vase.

I had *not* expected it to be erotic.

But there was no better word for it. Watching this beast of an athlete work with something so fragile and delicate with his massive, calloused hands was sexy as hell. The clay covered his fingers and knuckles and palms, and he moved each muscle in his hand with perfect precision to turn a lump of terra-cotta clay into something sensational.

I pulled out my camera, taking a long video of him when he was halfway through. I started zooming out, catching a smirking Vince as he glanced at me and shook his head before focusing on his work again. Then, I carefully walked closer, zooming in the camera to focus on his hands.

On *only* his hands.

And to add a little cinematic touch, I slowed parts of it down in post, editing the video so that for ten seconds of it, the viewer saw Vince Tanev's hands and fingertips dancing around that wet clay and shaping it in super slow motion.

Watching it playback before I posted it made my throat dry, like it was almost too hot to post, like I was about to push a sex tape into the world instead of an innocent video of a man molding pottery.

I wrote out a long caption, one that detailed a little bit of the story Vince had told me about how pottery came into his life, and I highlighted one quote in bold.

This is the one thing in my life that isn't goal-oriented, the one place where I can be free.

By the time I woke up the next morning, the video had gone viral.

With over eight-*million* views.

Chapter 13

What's With the Fish?

Vince

The long drag of the buzzer sounding was music to my ears.

The home crowd in Tampa went wild, blue and white towels being waved overhead in a battle cry as I was tackled from all angles by my teammates. We celebrated the goal, one Carter had assisted me in, with a cheeky dance to the roar of the stadium. It was a mixture of applause and laughter, and even the referees smiled while shaking their heads and giving us the look that said we'd better wrap it up and get ready for the next play to start.

We were up three to zero with less than eight minutes left to play.

One of the wingers for the opposing team knocked me hard in the shoulder as I passed him, and I turned with the hit, smiling as I skated up next to him.

"Oh, are you the tough guy?" I chirped. Then I pointed my stick at him and called out to Jaxson. "Watch out, this one's the tough guy."

"Fuck off, Pigeon," he spat.

"This pigeon is shitting all over your goalie," I reminded him. "Like he's a bench seat in Central Park."

He shoved me hard, which just made me laugh as I skated backward toward the bench. I took off my glove and wiggled my fingers at him in a wave that made him grit his teeth.

"Alright, Tanev. That's enough," Coach warned when I was close enough to hear him. But I saw his grin. "Save the fights for when we need them."

I jumped the boards and took a seat on the bench, graciously accepting water from one of our trainers as I tried to catch my breath. The puck was dropped, and my focus zeroed in on my teammates.

But I felt Maven where she stood in the tunnel like a current of electricity buzzing through my veins.

The last week with her had tilted my world on its axis. And where she'd been like a thorn in my side that first game in Boston, she'd been more like a soothing balm today, quietly observing me while I got ready to play.

We'd spent my entire day off together on Sunday, and then she'd followed me all yesterday, too, during practice and film and everything in-between. The frost she'd iced me out with in the beginning was thawing now, and she talked to me, laughed with me, and let me peel back a little layer to see more of who the girl was beneath it.

She was a walking contradiction, Maven King — simultaneously a fascinating, generous, free-spirited hippy, and also a closed-off, teeth-bared in warning brat. It was so far from what I was used to when it came to women, I couldn't help but be enamored by it, by her.

And whether I chose it or not, she was now a part of my routine.

The corner of my mouth twitched up when I recalled her standing in my doorway when it was time to head to the stadium earlier. She'd leaned a hip against the frame, the white pencil skirt she wore hugging her slight curves, and the midnight blue top she wore with it cinching her slim waist. Her hair framed her face in a curly halo, and her glossy lips had spread into a smile as she watched me grab my bag and head for the door.

She didn't move once I reached it.

"I'm afraid I can't let you pass," she'd said, tilting her head a bit. "Not until we fight."

It was a tease, a reference to the game before, and I'd folded my arms over my chest and sized her up. "What do you want to fight about?"

"Dealer's choice."

"Hm..." I'd said, tapping my chin in thought. "I need to figure out a way to piss you off."

"Shouldn't be too hard for you."

I'd smirked at that, and then, I'd dropped my bag to the floor and dug my fingertips into her sides, tickling her mercilessly.

I smiled wider remembering the squealing peals of laughter that she'd let loose, how she had tears coming out of her eyes as she tried to break free from me. In her attempt, her body had been completely pressed into mine, and I'd felt the weight of her slight frame in my arms, had inhaled her scent — lemon and vanilla, like a refreshing dessert I was more than curious to taste.

She was breathless by the time I'd finally relented, and as soon as she had her breath back, she'd socked me right in the gut.

I'd doubled over with an *oof,* but had laughed all the same.

"You're such a prick," she'd yelled. "I couldn't breathe!"

"Is it time to kiss and make up now?"

She'd sucked her teeth at that, turning on her heels that matched her blouse before strutting down the hall like a model.

And I'd spent the last few hours trying to stay focused on the game, and not on how it had felt to have my hands on her.

I blinked back to the present just in time to hop the boards and skate out onto the ice with my line. We played hard, not letting up even when the score told us we could. We wanted this team and the rest in our conference to hear our message loud and clear.

Tampa is the team to beat, and we won't make it easy to do so.

Sweat dripped into my eyes as the last buzzer sounded, and the crowd cheered so loud the stadium shook with the sound of it. Then, a flurry of stuffed animal fishes of all kinds rained down on us.

We had to watch where we were skating to dodge the toys as we took our victory laps, but none of us minded. It was tradition, one that had been around for decades. The fish were a sacrifice to the Osprey, our mascot. When the tradition started, they had thrown *actual* fish. Of course, that had been a smelly, disgusting, and rather inhumane practice that quickly turned into what it was now. A rainbow of color filled the ice just like a hat trick did, and at the end of it all, every toy would be donated to local shelters and families in need.

We took our time on our victory lap, and not a single fan moved from their seats as we went back into the locker room. Minutes later, the three stars of the team were announced.

I was one of them.

I skated a lap with the lights flashing and the crowd chanting my name, and I searched for a kid to give my puck to. When I spotted a familiar face by the glass at center ice, I grinned.

The Machine.

I skated over to him, and he jumped up and down more excitedly when he realized I'd spotted him. He tugged on his mom's jersey, and she only laughed and thanked me with a sweet smile and tilt of her head.

Instead of tossing the puck up over the glass like I usually did, I nodded toward security and motioned for them to find a way to get him on the ice. When they did, I pulled him up onto my shoulders, handing him the puck and letting him celebrate like the victory was his as we skated another lap with the other stars.

When the celebrations were done, I bent to let him down and rejoin his family, and I turned to find Maven watching me from the bench. I cocked a brow, silently asking what she thought.

She smiled, something light and soft about her for just a moment. But then, she scrunched her face up and waved her flat palm side to side, as if to say, *Meh, it was alright.*

I scrubbed a hand over my smile at that.

Back in the locker room, the celebrations continued, my teammates stripping their clothes off and chugging beer as the DJ played our win song loudly through the speakers.

"Great job out there," Coach McCabe said when we were all gathered. "It was a rough first period, but you found your groove in the second, and if we keep playing like that, we'll have the trophy in our hands by the end of the season."

We roared our agreement.

"Have fun tonight, but be smart," he warned. His expression was severe for only a moment before he grinned, and we all cheered and whistled as he shook his head and left us be.

He knew as well as we did that tonight was going to be lit as fuck.

"Let's fucking party!" Jaxson belted out once Coach had ducked out of the room, and the team responded by beating on the lockers and dancing as if we'd already won the championship.

I joined in, grabbing my jersey at opposite ends and threading it between my legs as I thrust my hips in a ridiculous dance. I whipped it overhead like a helicopter next before sending it flying into the team laundry basket.

It soared right by Maven's head on the way, and she caught the whole thing on camera.

I hopped down from where I'd been on a bench, slowly making my way toward her. Where I was a sweaty, smelly mess, she was just as pristine as she had been standing in my doorway hours ago. I noted the freckles on her cheeks the closer I got, loving that I could see them even through her makeup.

"Well, did I give you enough content tonight?"

"Indeed, you did," she answered on a smile. "I just have one question."

"Shoot."

"What's with the fish?"

"Sacrificing to the Osprey!" Carter answered for me, slinging his arm around Maven. She grimaced a bit at how sweaty he was, but didn't pull away. "It's tradition after a win."

"You know what else is tradition," Jaxson said, waggling his brows as he sidled up next to me. "Boomer's."

"And Boomer Bunnies," Carter added with his own salacious grin.

"Shut up, Fabio. We all know bunnies don't come for your rookie ass," one of our defensemen chided. Dimitri Volkov. He was Russian, an older vet, his accent thick and his tolerance for bullshit somewhere around Daddy P's. I loved him, though, because he was essentially like having a second goalie. The man was a weapon, one I was glad to have on my team.

Carter flicked him off.

"Boomer Bunnies?" Maven asked carefully.

"Boomer's is the bar we go to after a win," Brittzy explained. "And let's just say, there are some very attractive women in the area who are well aware of that fact."

"They're also aware of how fat your pockets are," Daddy P grumbled from the bench. "You're a fool if you mistake it for anything else."

"Some of them are nice," Carter defended.

"Just because one of them let you poke her in the butt doesn't mean she's Miss America, Fabio."

The words shot out of Jaxson like a barrel, and we all burst into a fit of laughter as Carter shamefully took his arm from around Maven. He sulked for a moment before punching Jaxson in the arm.

"Um... she let you... *what*?" Maven asked.

Carter's face flamed a furious red.

"Carter here was a virgin the first night we all went out," Jaxson explained, all too happy to fill in the blanks. "And a couple teammates took some bunnies home, a few of them excited to... *play*." He grinned.

"One of them told Carter he could *put it anywhere,*" I said. Maven's eyes doubled in size when her gaze snapped to mine, and I loved it. I loved seeing her squirm, watching her reaction to that little tidbit.

It made me wonder what she was thinking, if she was disgusted by the thought, or maybe, just *maybe*, a little turned on.

"And you... you chose..." Maven slowly turned to Carter again, who threw his hands up like he'd had no other choice.

"I just figured I wouldn't get that offer as much in my lifetime!"

My stomach hurt from laughing so hard with the rest of the crew in that corner of the locker room, and even Maven cracked a smile, shaking her head.

"Please, don't post that," Carter said, sobering up.

"Your virgin escapades aren't exactly the content we're going for, Fabio," Maven shot back just as quick.

"Hey, I'm not a virgin anymore."

"Does it count if it's just the ass?" Maven asked.

That made us all laugh harder.

Maven felt like one of us already.

"Alright, twat lickers," one of our veterans called. Shane Lomberg, a left-winger who was also the first of us to fight when necessary. "Shower your smelly asses, and let's get this party started."

Maven shook her head, writing something in her phone before she tucked it away on a sigh. "Alright, well, you guys have fun."

"You guys?" Carter asked, frowning.

"Ohhh, no. You're coming, too," Jaxson said, pointing at her.

"Me?" She laughed a little, like it was a joke, before her eyes scanned each of us. She swallowed when she looked at me, fidgeting with her hair as she shook her head again. "No, no, this is your night. I'd cramp your style."

My chest tightened at that because I knew she wanted it to land lightly, but I also knew she actually thought that.

She didn't think she belonged.

My jaw was a little tighter then, thinking about her douchebag ex-boyfriend and his family. He'd hurt her so bad she had a permanent belief about the people she perceived as "rich" and how they were as human beings.

Which meant she was looking around this locker room thinking there was no chance in hell she'd feel comfortable going out with us for a night.

"Come on," I said, calling her attention back to me. I waited until her eyes met mine. "Twenty-four-seven access, right?"

I threw out the work line because it was an easy one to get away with, one I knew would make her reconsider simply because she cared about doing the job right.

It was also an easy way to cover the truth, which was that I wanted her to come.

And I didn't want her going home without me.

"Yeah!" Carter agreed. "You've gotta come."

"I'll buy your drinks all night," Jaxson chimed in.

"Don't listen to these guys," Will said, standing. "If you want to go home, go home. This motley crew will have you out until dawn if you let them."

"Leave us alone, Grandpa," Jaxson said, waving him off. He stood between Daddy P and Maven then to hammer his point home. "Don't make us beg, Maven."

"But we will," I said. "If you want."

The guys and I shared a look before I dropped to my knees, clasping my hands together with big puppy dog eyes.

"Oh, *please*, Maven! Please come celebrate with us!"

Jaxson and Carter dropped, too, and we chimed it over and over, like kids begging their mom for an ice cream cone.

Maven laughed, shaking her head before she held up her hands and said, “Alright, alright, *alright.*” We quieted at that last one. “I’ll come.”

Her eyes found mine when she said those last two words.

And I couldn’t help but lick my bottom lip, hoping for the chance to make that statement true.

Chapter 14

I Am the Mayhem

Maven

The crowd was so thick outside of Boomer's, I had a panic attack when the black car dropped us off.

I'd ridden with Vince, Jaxson, and Carter, and while all their eyes lit up with excitement at the multitude of people clamoring to party with them after their win, I'd shriveled into the corner of the car. I was cursing Livia under my breath for not agreeing to come out with us. She had clients early in the morning, so I understood, but I hated that I didn't have her here.

It wasn't that I had an issue with crowds. Hell, I'd been in one of thousands of people at the stadium without issue. But a sea of people clamoring to get a glimpse of who's in this car, a sea of people who would be staring at *me* when I exited this thing?

My brow was sweating just thinking of it.

I was used to being *behind* the camera, and Vince must have picked up on that fact, because he frowned when he looked at me over his shoulder and saw what was no doubt my very hesitant expression.

"Hey," he said. "Look at me."

Screams ripped out when our car came to a stop, and security fought to keep people back, like the guys were rockstars instead of athletes. I supposed it was one and the same in this city.

A warm palm sliding over my knee called my attention away from the chaos, and I found Vince, his eyes set on mine as his hand squeezed.

His massive, talented hand, one that could score goals and mold art from clay. He smoothed his thumb over the skin just below the hemline of my skirt, and I swallowed, not daring to look down at where he touched me.

"You're with us," he reminded me. "And we've got you. Okay? We have a VIP area in there that's completely roped off. You only have to be in the crowd for a few minutes while we make our way in."

I nodded, a little embarrassed by my anxiety. "I'm sorry, I just..."

"Your phone."

"What?"

"Pull out your phone. Pretend like you're recording, or actually record it, we don't care," he added, and the guys nodded behind him.

"The seas will part for you, Maven. Everyone knows you."

Those words from Carter made me blink.

Everyone knows you.

I hadn't considered that, hadn't thought about the fact that my social media accounts were the most watched in the city right now. I didn't know if that made me feel better or worse.

With a final nod, I pulled a deep inhale through my nose to prepare me, and Jaxson opened the door for us to climb out.

The crowd cheered when we did, but it wasn't the nonstop, high-pitched screams you'd hear for a rock band. It was loud and deep, a sea of grown men hollering their approval and respect for the team. Of course, there *were* some women in there, too. Plenty of them. But they didn't crowd us when we got out like I thought they would.

Vince grabbed my hand, anyway.

I tried not to focus on that, on how small my hand was in his as he led us through the small opening they'd made for us to make our way into the bar. I tried not to let it impact my breathing, how confidently he held me, how proudly. He pulled me through that crowd like I belonged to him.

My free hand held my phone, and I clicked the button on the side to start the video as I followed Vince in.

"Maven! We love you!"

I followed the source of the chant, smiling a little when a group of three college-aged girls waved excitedly at me.

"Told you," Vince whispered in my ear, tugging me close enough to do so. I felt his breath warm on the shell of my ear, and a shiver spread over my skin.

"Are you two dating?!"

"What's it like, Maven?"

"Vince, let's do pottery together!"

"Vince, let's fuck," someone else cheered louder, and that made everyone laugh.

Except me.

Vince took all of it like a champ, winking at the girl who'd offered herself up before we ducked inside the bar.

It was even louder once inside, but the bouncers didn't stop us for an ID check or anything else before ushering us to the back corner, and up a small set of stairs to the VIP area.

I felt like I could finally breathe once we were behind the ropes, and Vince dropped my hand, high-fiving one of his teammates with it a moment later while I tried to gather my bearings.

Boomer's was more of a club than a bar, as the guys had made it sound. Strobe lights and lasers flashed in the foggy darkness, go-go dancers shaking their asses on the bar while patrons slipped dollar bills into their garters. A DJ was front and center, and he pointed back to the team's VIP area before spinning right into their win song, which made the crowd roar and jump and dance wildly as the team celebrated from our little corner.

I couldn't believe they were still letting people in. The place was already packed, and all I could think of was what the hell would happen should a fire break out.

Warm, long fingertips wrapped around my hip, nearly encompassing the whole of me as Vince pulled me into him from behind.

"Drink?" he asked in my ear.

My eyes fluttered shut, but I forced them open again, turning more to break contact than anything else.

"Please," I said over the music.

Vince nodded toward one of the tables in the back of our secluded area, each piled high with bottles. He poured ice into a tumbler and topped it with mostly Grey Goose, and a small splash of pineapple juice before handing it to me.

I downed the whole thing.

I was still grimacing when Vince took my glass and refilled it on a laugh. "You can hang out back here if you want to be out of the mayhem." He nodded toward some cushioned booths in the back. One was empty. The other had two hockey players with a girl in each of their laps.

"What about you?" I asked.

A slow, lazy grin spread on his beautiful mouth. "I am the mayhem."

I didn't have Vince long before he was being pulled away by his teammates, and I took his offer, curling into the smallest form of myself I could on a booth in the back. I watched from afar as the team partied in a way I hadn't witnessed since college. They took shot after shot, dancing and horsing around as they raged into the night. Smoke swirled from vapes and cigars alike, mixing with the lights to create a heavy, neon fog.

But even as I tried to make myself invisible, the guys wouldn't let me.

Carter came back to grab me at one point, pulling me to the front to meet his brother who was in town for the game. I'd no sooner sat back down before Jaxson was sitting beside me. He'd brought two girls and a couple other teammates with him, and he made me part of the conversation, making sure I felt comfortable.

And I did.

I felt like I belonged there with them, like no one was judging me for being the lowly reporter, even though they *knew* I was in a different class than they were.

At one point, I noticed Vince saying something to one of his teammates. The next moment, that teammate was walking over to introduce himself to me, to sit and talk and make sure I wasn't left alone.

I wondered if he'd done that all night, if he was the reason I hadn't had a spare moment to feel out of place.

It made my chest hurt in a way I wasn't familiar with, to think he cared about me, that he wanted to make sure I had a good time.

But it also put all my defenses up.

I hated that. I hated that even when someone was doing something nice for me, I had this devil in the back of my mind telling me it was all a farce. I couldn't trust Vince, or anyone who I felt was bred from a different cloth.

James had done that to me.

I wondered if that damage could ever be *un*done.

But then I remembered what my therapist had said — that trauma response was good for us. It kept us safe. It kept us from repeating a mistake, and thus the pain that came with it. It showed us red flags when we used to ignore them or make excuses for them.

I was glad I had my guard up. It was a sure-fire way not to get hurt again.

The night went on.

Every now and then, one of the guys from the team would invite women from the crowd behind the ropes. They danced with some of them, pulling their barely covered asses into their laps as they swayed to the beat. Others, they tugged into a corner to make out with, wasting no time.

I took photos and videos from my corner when the moment felt right, mostly when Vince was goofing around and smiling that megawatt smile of his. But as the night dragged on, I felt less and less inclined to stay — especially when the heavy bass of the music seemed to thrum like a heartbeat between the players and the girls who were desperate for their attention.

"Dance with me."

I was in a daze when the request came, and I glanced up, finding Vince smiling a drunken smile down at me. His hair fell into his view a moment before he ran a hand back through it, styling the messy waves with just that motion. His pouty lips were curled slightly at the corners, his eyes glazed and dangerously inviting.

He held out a hand for mine.

"Oh... I'm okay," I said.

He cocked a brow. "You've been sitting there all night. Come on," he said, wiggling his fingers. "Dance with me."

There was a dare in his eyes, and if I gave in to the way my heart raced at the way he watched me, I would have slid my hand into his and let him lead me onto the floor.

But where this was a night out celebrating for him, it was a job for me.

Things were going better than I'd ever imagined. Reya and Camilla were ready to hand me anything I wanted if I continued to pull this off. And nothing mattered more to me than remaining professional – which dancing with the devil disguised as Vince Tanev would make very difficult to do.

"I'm really okay," I said again, offering a small smile.

Vince looked a little disappointed as he dropped his hand, but it lasted only a moment before he shrugged. He refreshed his drink and sucked half of it down with his eyes still on me.

"Suit yourself," he said.

He disappeared back into the crowd just as easily as he'd popped out of it, and I watched him go, checking the time on my watch as I blew out a breath.

It was almost three in the morning.

I looked around at the crowd, which despite the hour, only seemed to be thickening. I slid my purse onto my shoulder and decided I would make my way back to the condo to get some much-needed sleep.

But when I looked for Vince to tell him I was heading out, I found him just in time to watch him pluck two women from the crowd dancing outside the ropes.

He pulled them in, security fastening the barrier back in place as soon as they were at his side. One of the girls was tan and tall and lean, with platinum blonde hair and a perfect heart-shaped ass. The other was tall, too, but was a creamy pale, shaped like an hourglass, with short brown hair and a mouth like Angelina Jolie.

The women encircled Vince once they were behind the ropes, sandwiching him between them, and all three of them began to move to the beat of the music thumping through the club. The women draped their arms over him like he was theirs — not even a hint of hesitation, or a single thought that he wouldn't want them to.

My heart stopped in my chest, and then kicked back hard, racing faster and faster as I watched them.

I watched the blonde trail her nail up Vince's arm, over his neck, until she dragged it along his chin and guided his mouth toward hers. She didn't kiss him, just held him there, where he had no choice but to look at her as she stared back at him and moved her body against him.

Her body that he moved his hands to hold, to feel as she rolled to the music.

The brunette danced to the other side of him, straddling his leg with her thighs as she tugged at the collar of his shirt for his attention. When the blonde kept it, the brunette licked his neck before biting down.

Even from across the room, I saw Vince hiss, saw a smile curl on his lips as he turned to face her, and she grinned at the victory.

I was rooted in place.

Like a masochist, I watched it all unfold with my stomach bottoming out.

A front-row show to Boomer Bunnies in action.

And when both women started kissing on his neck, Vince looked up at the sky on a curse.

Then, he looked directly at me.

His eyes were dark and mischievous, locked on mine as the girls battled with each other for who could make him unravel the quickest. But he wasn't smiling anymore, and he wasn't giving either of them what they wanted.

He was too busy staring at me.

I sucked in a stiff breath, blinking repeatedly before I finally tore my gaze away and adjusted my purse on my shoulder. I muttered unheard *excuse me's* as I pushed through the team and the lucky girls who'd been selected to join them. I pushed farther, out of the ropes and through the crowd until I burst out into the humid night air. It was so hard to breathe, I gasped, trying and failing to fill my lungs.

I didn't see the car we'd come in, didn't even give myself time to think of calling one. I just started walking in the direction of the skyscraper holding me prison for the month I was doing this job, squeezing my eyes shut hard to try to clear what I'd just seen before I opened them again and put one foot in front of the other.

I hadn't made it twenty steps before I was spun in a circle, Vince sliding his hand into the crook of my elbow and pulling me to a stop.

"You're leaving?"

I blinked at him, eyes catching where he had lipstick smeared on his neck.

A harsh laugh burst from my chest.

"I'm surprised you noticed," I snapped, and then I ripped away from him and started off in the direction I'd been walking before he stopped me.

"Let me get you a car."

"I can walk, it's not far."

"You're in heels. And it's three o'clock in the morning."

"I'm fine."

Vince jogged around to stand in front of me, blocking my path. "What's going on? Why are you mad?"

"I'm not."

"So you breathe like an angry dragon and storm around town because you're having a grand time?"

I scoffed, skirting past him. "Go back inside, Vince. I'm sure your *fans* are missing you."

He didn't follow for the next several steps, but then he jogged to catch up to me, blocking my path once more. I noted that he had been texting something on his phone, but he slipped it into his pocket when he caught up to me.

Probably telling his little groupies to meet him back at his place.

"Maven," he said. "Talk to me. Tell me what's wrong."

His eyes were lazy and glazed. He looked so sleepy and sexy and confident, and he watched me like he already knew the answer.

I glowered. "Oh, I don't know. I guess I just wanted you to surprise me again, and found myself dreadfully disappointed."

That beautiful, scarred brow lifted into his hairline. "How so?"

"You're just like every other rich, professional athlete that the rules don't apply to," I said, shaking my head. "And it's just so unoriginal."

Vince frowned at that, almost laughing like he was confused. "The *rules*?"

But then the laughter faded, and something like recognition washed over him, smoothing out every feature of that beautiful, stupid face.

"You're jealous."

My eyebrows shot up into my hairline, indignation swirling with something akin to being stripped naked and put on display for the world to dissect. I swallowed all of it down, guard firmly in place.

"Wow." I pushed past him, shaking my head, but he rounded me before I could take two more steps.

"You are, aren't you?"

"Get a grip, *Tanny Boy*," I shot at him, lifting my chin and standing even higher on my heels. "You couldn't make me jealous if you tried."

"Is that right?"

"It is."

"Huh," he mused, and before I could decide what to do next, he grabbed me by the hips, backing me into the brick wall of the building I'd been storming past.

I hit it with enough force to make me gasp, and Vince smiled down at me, blocking me in, surrounding me like a predator about to devour his first meal in days.

"So you don't want me to take you up to my condo right now?" he asked, his voice low and seductive in the space between us.

He pressed into me harder when I didn't answer, eliciting another gasp I wished I could keep inside. His thick thigh slid between mine, spreading me for him so much my skirt raked up six inches.

"You don't want me to touch you the way I was touching them?"

He didn't have to clarify who *them* was as his hand wrapped around my throat, my pulse thumping against his palm. He lifted my chin even more, forcing me to look at him.

"You don't want me to haul this sweet ass over my shoulder and carry you inside," he asked, running the tip of his nose along the bridge of mine. I tasted his breath when he finished his question. "To pin you against my window, hike this skirt up over your hips, and fuck you for the whole city to watch?"

My chest heaved against his, and he drove that thigh a little higher, taking my skirt with it as my eyelids fluttered shut.

His grip on my hips tightened, just a fraction, just enough to break me.

And I kissed him.

All it took was me pressing up onto my toes a centimeter more to press my lips to his, and I sucked in a breath when he groaned at the contact, his hand moving from my throat to the back of my neck and holding me to him for a long, ravenous kiss. His lips were so big, so firm as they demanded mine. I opened for him, moaning and squeezing my legs together when he dipped his tongue inside to taste me.

But as quickly as the kiss had come, he pulled it away, along with the rest of him.

My body convulsed at the loss of heat, at how the humid air suddenly felt cool when it washed over my exposed thighs from where my skirt had ridden up.

And Vince Tanev, that cocky motherfucker, wiped the corner of his mouth with his thumb while a wicked smile spread on his lips.

"Sorry, pet," he said, tucking his hands in his pockets. "You'll have to admit you want it before I give it to you."

I gaped at him.

And then, I growled out a scream, righting my skirt and shoving him so hard in the chest that he stumbled backward.

"I am not your *pet*," I seethed.

He barked out a laugh that made me shove him again. "*God*, you are such a bastard. I hate you!"

"Sure you do."

His hand shot up in the air, waving at a black car as it pulled up to the curb. It was the same one from the beginning of the night, and the driver dipped his head at Vince in acknowledgement as he put the car in park.

"What is this?"

"Your ride," he said, pulling the back door open. He all but tossed me inside before shutting it again. The window was rolled down, and he braced his hands on the edge of it, leaning down so he could see me. "Goodnight, Maven. See you in the morning."

Vince winked, standing and thumping on the roof of the car before he backed up a few steps. He wore a cocky smile like I'd just handed him the winning lottery numbers, and I'd never felt more betrayed by my body than I did in that moment — my chest heaving, head dizzy from our kiss, panties wet under my skirt.

The car sped off before I could tell him to go fuck himself.

Chapter 15

Sexual Awakening

Vince

Two days after the win in Tampa, we flew to Pittsburgh for a Friday night game.

It was back-to-back away games — Pittsburgh on Friday and Baltimore on Saturday. We flew out Thursday evening to get settled, and with a home win under our belt and a three-game winning streak flying with us, we were confident.

I held onto that confidence, onto the fact that we knew what we were doing, and we had the chance to really have the league's attention if we won these away games, too. That would be five games in a row.

Tampa hadn't won five games in a row since 2015.

Nothing motivated me like the potential to make headlines, other than the chance to silence sports analysts and their assumptions about me and my team. I could do both with these wins, and I kept that in the forefront of my mind.

After the morning skate on Friday, I went back to my hotel room to do my usual pre-game routine. But something felt off.

I couldn't place it, but I *knew* without overthinking it that I needed to shake things up.

"I'm going somewhere."

Maven peeked up at me from where she was working on her phone on the couch in my suite. She wore olive sweatpants and an oversized black t-shirt that swallowed her small frame. Her bare feet were tucked beneath her, no makeup on her face and her hair natural. I didn't have to guess that she also didn't have a bra on under that shirt, which killed me as much as it made me count my lucky stars.

It stole my breath a moment, seeing her like that — comfortable, relaxed, like she was just wasting away an afternoon in her own home.

I'd been buzzed the night after our home game, but I still remembered everything. I remembered following her out of that bar, remembered the exact moment I realized she wasn't mad at me.

She was jealous.

I didn't need her to confirm it, because when I'd backed her into that wall, her body had betrayed whatever lie she was trying to tell me and herself.

She'd kissed me.

It had taken everything in me not to take her right then and there. The way she melted into me when I kissed her back, how she trembled when my hands framed her face and my leg slid between her thighs. I loved pushing that skirt up to her hips, loved pushing that girl to the edge even more.

Neither of us had said a word about it since.

I knew why *I* hadn't. I told her all I needed to that night — that if she wanted me, she was going to have to admit it. She was going to have to use her big girl words and say it out loud.

But she hadn't broached the subject either, either because she was still pissed at me, or she was trying to convince herself it didn't happen.

Regardless, it didn't bother me.

I was a patient man.

Or so I told myself.

"Okay?" she said carefully when I didn't elaborate.

"You don't need to come," I said. "It's nothing that needs to be covered."

That made her eyes narrow in suspicion, and she set her phone aside before sitting up a little straighter. "Where are you going?"

I shrugged. "Just somewhere to clear my head."

She watched me a moment longer before hopping up from the couch. "I just need to change real quick."

"You really don't have to come," I said. "If you want a break."

"Twenty-four-seven, remember?" she reminded me, and then she slipped out of my room and over to hers to change.

I smirked in victory. Reverse psychology worked a little too well on this woman. She was nothing if not stubborn, but sometimes, that worked to my advantage.

Though we hadn't spoken about what happened between us, I felt a charge of electricity anytime she was near. When we sat next to each other on the plane, her laughing and playing cards with Carter while I pretended to listen to a podcast, I saw the hair on her arm stand on end when she brushed against me, felt how she drew her breaths a little shallower.

The guys had taken my coaching from that night at Boomer's and done everything to make sure Maven felt comfortable with us — whether we were in the public's eye or alone in the arena. I didn't know why Maven had felt vulnerable enough to open up to me about what happened with her ex, but I knew one thing.

I didn't want to be lumped into the same category as him, and I wanted my team to prove to Maven that we weren't all the same.

When we were in the back of the black car I'd arranged for us, she watched the city pass out the window, taking in the cool, gray day painting the city.

I watched her.

She frowned when we pulled into the parking lot of the old, beaten-down rink – first at the scenery, then at me, and then again at the building as we both got out of the car. I tapped the trunk twice with my fist until the driver popped it, and then with my duffle bag slung over my shoulder, I led the way.

"What is this?" Maven asked.

"You'll see."

It was quiet when we walked into the rink, save for the sounds that always came with it – skates gliding, pucks being hit, sticks scraping the ice. I smiled at the familiarity of it, of how it took me back to a simpler time when Mom and Dad put me in pads as a kid and told me to just have fun.

Bobby Green stood in the box, his hands on his hips while he watched the kids skate around on the ice. He had a whistle between his teeth, and he shook his head at something before he glanced over at where Maven and I had just walked in.

The whistle fell from his mouth, and a grin split his face. "Well, I'll be damned. Vince Tanev."

That made half the rink stop skating, and one by one, the kids lit up with recognition.

"Nice to see you, *Coach*," I said, shaking his hand. His players had stopped skating, and were standing at various places in the rink watching us and whispering to each other.

"I thought you were joking, you know."

"Well, here's proof that I was serious."

Bobby and I had played at Michigan together. But where I went to the show, he came back to his hometown to coach at the rink where he'd learned how to play. He wanted to give back to the community that gave so much to him, and to give more kids with lesser financial means the opportunity to play.

Hockey wasn't exactly cheap, and I respected him more than I could say for giving up his own dream to help the kids in his community chase theirs.

I was far too selfish, too driven to be the best for me to ever do the same.

When we'd graduated, on our last night out, I told Bobby I'd come see him when I was in the city. He'd laughed me off, saying I'd be too busy fighting off girls to remember him.

Seeing his smile right now was worth more than any night I'd ever had with a puck bunny.

Without a word, he clapped me on the shoulder, his eyes speaking volumes. "How long do we have you for?"

"Maybe an hour."

His eyes flicked behind me to Maven then, and he arched a brow at me before extending a hand for her. "Excuse my former teammate for being a rude sonofabitch," he said. "I'm Bobby."

"Maven," she said, smiling as she shook his hand.

I realized then that only half the kids on the rink were staring at me, because the other half were very firmly staring at *her*. They had to be somewhere in the twelve to fourteen range, so I couldn't blame them.

Maven was a sexual awakening if I ever did see one.

"Ah, you're the one giving us all access to *Tampa's Hotshot Rookie!*" he said, giving me a fake one-two punch with the words. He shook his head once he was upright again. "I think they should have *you* in front of the camera, if you ask me."

Maven smiled. "I'm nowhere near as interesting as this one," she said, pointing to me.

"And he's nowhere near as jaw dropping."

Bobby always had a way with the ladies, which was exactly why he was already married at twenty-three.

"Alright, easy there, Bobbers," I said.

"What, you two dating?"

"No," Maven answered quickly.

Bobby grinned, looking at me like he saw something I didn't. "Then I guess I'm free to remark on her beauty all day if I want to, Vinny."

"And I'm free to tell your wife about it?"

He pointed at me. "You win. Alright!" He blew his whistle, calling his team over. "Well, boys. We have approximately sixty minutes with Vince Tanev." He grinned at me when they all buzzed with excitement at the confirmation of it really being me. When he turned back to them, he asked one simple question. "Where should we start?"

He was met with silence.

And then, every player talking over each other trying to be the one to answer first.

Once I had on skates and pads, I took to the ice, running drills with the team and offering pointers where I had them. When I'd look over at Maven, Bobby was always yakking it up beside her. The guy couldn't help himself.

I spent about forty-five minutes on the ice, and the last fifteen taking pictures and signing autographs. Then, with one last hug from my former teammate and friend, Maven and I were back in the car and on our way to the hotel.

I already felt more refreshed, energized by the excitement of the kids at the rink.

"Bobby had some fun stories to tell," Maven said as we rode across town.

"About all the records I broke at Michigan?"

"More about how many girls you left heartbroken in your wake."

My smile flattened.

Damn it, Bobby.

Maven snuffed a laugh through her nose. "Don't worry. I told him it was nothing I didn't already know."

I realized then she was preparing a post on her phone, a video of me skating drills with the kids pulled up. I covered it with my hand.

"Don't."

She frowned. "What?"

"Don't post it."

Her jaw went slack, confusion drawing her brows together. "But..."

"Some things aren't for public consumption."

I held my hand over her phone while she watched me, only pulling it away when I was sure I'd made it clear. She kept her eyes on me even after I removed my hand.

And there was something in her gaze, something that was becoming my new favorite drug.

Proof that I'd proven her wrong about me.

Not with any help from my former teammate, it appeared.

I looked out the window for the rest of the ride, and when we got back to the hotel, the rest of my pre-game routine was waiting for me. I didn't have the nap, but I did have the pasta, and the pushups, the call to my sister and the closet light.

Maven and I didn't fight, but then again, we hadn't really talked at *all* since that night outside the bar.

So maybe it counted.

When we won in overtime against the Pittsburgh Venom, I decided that it did.

Chapter 16

Hot Streak

Maven

The Ospreys managed to squeak out a narrow two-to-one win against the Baltimore Railers, sealing them their fifth win in a row. This game hadn't been as pretty as the last few, and Vince said as much to the reporter interviewing him on the bench after the game.

"As you and the team prepare to head back to Tampa, what's your focus going to be?" the reporter asked. She was beautiful, professional, with a tailored skirt suit and makeup applied to perfection. She had champagne blonde hair and skin as pale as moonlight. I didn't miss the way she batted her eyelashes at Vince and leaned in a little closer than necessary during the interview.

"I'm going to continue to play like we're already in the playoffs," he said. "Like every game counts. I'm disappointed that I didn't score tonight, but I'm proud of my team for showing up and getting the job done. I can do better," he added with a nod. "And I *will* do better."

I recorded the interview on Instagram Live from behind the cameraman who was with the reporter. The comments rolled in faster than I could read them.

Tampa loves you, Vince!

Take your shirt off, Vince!

It's a jersey, not a shirt, idiot.

You did great tonight, Vince!

You played like shit, rookie. What are we paying you for?

My kid can skate better than you, Tanev.

Perry won this game tonight — not you.

I didn't know how he put up with it, the constant chatter from his fans. Most of them loved him, but some of them were just... *mean*. It was appalling to me how much they felt like they had claim over him, over the team.

My inbox was so out of control these days that I only checked a handful a day, randomly picking ones to respond to with a heart-eye emoji. I saw everything from letters of devotion to Vince or the team to rants about stats and insults that felt personal — and they weren't even about me. I couldn't imagine what Vince dealt with on his own social media. Then again, I imagined he probably didn't care — not when he was so confident he was the best.

When the reporter thanked him and the interview was over, I followed him back to the locker room. For a moment, he was quiet, his head hanging, a deep line between his brows. I wondered if he really was beating himself up for his performance. Sure, he didn't score, but he played well. They won.

I could tell from his expression that that wasn't enough for him.

But when we made it to the locker room where celebrations were already in full swing, he took one deep breath, plastered on a smile, and slipped right back into the Vince Cool persona.

"We're getting tanked tonight," Carter said, jumping on Vince's back. "Five-game hot streak, boys!"

"Maybe Maven here is our lucky charm," Jaxson added, and before I could protest, he had me thrown over his shoulder like a sack of potatoes. "We'll have to kidnap you when your month is over."

"Put me down," I said on a laugh, beating my fists on his back. It was like hard stone.

"Only if you agree to go out with us tonight."

"Put her down."

Those last three words came from Vince, and it was the deepest I'd ever heard him speak. Slowly, Jaxson did as he asked, and then the locker room was quiet for a moment — all eyes on the exchange.

"Easy, Pidge. I was just messing around," Jaxson said, and he looked almost scared before a grin split his face, and he eyed Vince like he knew all his deepest secrets.

Vince didn't respond. He just glanced at me, back at Jaxson, and then sat down on one of the benches to begin the arduous process of stripping out of his pads.

I waited in the hallway outside the locker room, uploading some of the content I'd filmed while the boys took quick showers and got ready to load the bus. We were spending the night in the city, flying out first thing in the morning, and while the guys were ready for a night out on the town, I, for one, was missing what little semblance of a routine I had back in Tampa.

My whole life had been thrown off-kilter, and the more I slipped into this new lifestyle, the less I knew what day it was or what was going on. I did yoga when I could, called my parents, and saw Livia when she was at the stadium, but other than that, my life revolved around Vince Tanev.

"You okay?"

I startled at the voice, but recognized it immediately. Slipping my phone into my purse, I pushed off the wall to stand, trying for my best smile.

Vince was freshly showered, his hair damp and messy, eyes wide and alert like he was ready to tear up the town. He wore gray joggers and a royal blue Ospreys long-sleeve shirt, one that hugged the lean muscles of his chest and arms and tapered at his waist.

We hadn't talked much since we left Tampa, but I could still feel the brand of his lips on mine. When he was close like he was now, I felt it burn even hotter.

"Yeah. We heading out?"

Vince eyed me like he didn't believe me. "I'm not getting on the bus."

"Oh?"

"Are you tired?"

I laughed as a yawn stretched my mouth open right as he asked. "Full of energy."

He smirked a little, but it fell quickly. "I got a car. Want to come with me?"

"Where?"

"Anywhere."

"You don't want to go out with the guys?"

Our conversation was broken when a few of his teammates passed, and he high-fived one of them, nodding to the others. They had already cracked open a few beers.

"Not tonight," he answered when they were gone.

"Why?"

He shrugged.

"And you don't want to go to bed?"

"I can't," he said. "Not after a game. It takes a while for the adrenaline to wane."

I chewed the inside of my lip, debating. It would be easy to just go back to the hotel and get some much-needed rest. But something about the way Vince watched me, about how he seemed to not want to be alone... it had me reconsidering.

"I'm still mad at you, you know." I breathed the words low enough so only he could hear.

The corner of his mouth ticked up, but he didn't say anything.

He just grabbed my hand in his, leading me through the hallway and out to where a car waited for us.

Chapter 17

That Face

Maven

The Inner Harbor in Baltimore reminded me of Tampa's Riverwalk, the lights of the city serving as a backdrop and reflecting off the water. Except I would have been sweating in Tampa, even though it was early November.

In Baltimore, I was shivering.

Vince and I walked quietly side by side, and I thought that was what he'd brought me here for. When the car had dropped us off and he'd just started strolling, I assumed that was it. He just wanted a walk to clear his head.

I was wishing I'd worn more comfortable shoes — and a heavier coat.

But we didn't walk more than a hundred yards before he turned us toward a dock, and he shook hands with a man halfway down it before climbing aboard a boat.

Although, calling it a *boat* felt silly.

It was more like a small yacht.

I shook my head in disbelief at the pristine luxury of it — the crisp white hull gleaming under the moonlight, the plush leather seating area surrounding a hot tub, the tables covered in a spread of hors d'oeuvres. Vince watched my expression as the captain introduced himself to me, along with the crew, and then Vince and I were handed glasses of champagne and given a tour. We ended it at the front of the ship, Vince taking a seat on one of the couches while I sat in a chair across from him. The teak was gorgeous, the deck furniture more expensive than all my belongings combined.

"How on Earth did you manage to get a yacht chartered at almost midnight?" I asked when we were alone, the crew working to get us off the dock and out into the harbor.

"Gary is a friend of Bobby's," he explained on a shrug, referring to our captain. I remembered Bobby well enough — especially the stories he shared about Vince in college. If I'd had any doubt that Tampa's shiny new toy hid his playboy activities behind his well-curated façade, it was obliterated with Bobby's recounting of their days at Michigan.

James had been like that.

He had a shiny reputation on campus, and even more so when it came to the media that followed his college career as he worked toward being invited to play in the PGA Tour when he graduated. He was one of the few amateurs who received an invite to play at the Masters, and he'd made the cut, which had everyone in a tizzy about him and his future.

To everyone who thought they knew him, he was an All-American boy next door. But I'd seen him not-so-covertly check out another woman's ass as he put his arm around me. I'd watched him wink and flirt with girls on campus as he signed autographs, only to quickly kiss me and tell me it was all for show. I'd seen him play in charity tournaments, only to make fun of the poor and complain about taxes with his buddies at the country club.

So many red flags, and yet I'd ignored them all — because I thought I was the exception to the rule. I thought I was the girl who broke the mold. I thought he was telling the truth when he said he was loyal to me, that we had forever in our hands.

I shivered, the past as icy cold as the air sweeping through my hair.

"Don't you think this is an activity a little more well-suited for Tampa?" I asked, wrapping the blanket one of the stews had given me tightly around my shoulders. "It's freezing."

"We have the hot tub," Vince said in way of a solution.

"Right. And no swimwear."

"Who needs swimwear?"

I snorted a laugh, but Vince downed the last of his champagne with his eyes locked on mine. Then, he stood.

He shrugged off his jacket first, kicking his shoes off at the same time. Next, he reached one hand back over his head, gripping his long-sleeve shirt by the neck and tearing it off in one smooth pull.

The city lights cast him in a soft glow — his lean abs and arms, his chest, the unmistakable cut of muscles that made a V, the apex of which was still hidden by his joggers. The corner of his mouth lifted when I didn't look away, and he pulled his joggers down next, kicking them off his ankles before removing his socks.

In nothing but a pair of black briefs, Vince stood on the deck of that yacht like he owned it. His thick thighs stretched the fabric, and it didn't seem to bother him that it was freezing. I could see the outline of him, thick and proud, his cock so big it looked like he'd stuffed his pants.

When he slid his thumbs beneath the waistband, I looked up at the sky just in time to hear him shed that last bit of clothing. I thought I also heard him chuckle before there was the distinct sound of a body wading into water.

When I was mostly sure it was safe to look again, I brought my eyes back to the hot tub — where Vince was reclining, his arms draped over the edges, hazel eyes watching me.

"You joining me?" he asked, the steam wafting around him.

"Keep dreaming."

He shrugged. "Suit yourself. This water is perfect." He almost purred the words, sinking down more into the hot tub with a groan. His eyes fluttered shut. "And we have the boat for three hours."

I clenched my teeth as a particularly brisk wind whipped through my hair then. Even Mother Nature was playing dirty.

"But I guess you have your blanket," he said, his eyes still closed. "That should keep you warm enough."

His smile grew an inch.

"You're so sure of yourself, aren't you?" I scoffed.

"I'm sure you'll have more fun in here with me than out there in that wind."

"I'll take my chances."

He smiled even wider, and I was thankful there wasn't a light in that hot tub because from this angle, I was pretty sure I'd be able to see everything.

When we made it out of the harbor, the wind picked up even more, and I curled in on myself, teeth chattering. Even with the third glass of champagne I eagerly downed, hoping it would bring a little warmth, there was no use.

I was a Popsicle.

"Fine," I gritted out, standing and reluctantly shrugging off my blanket. "T-turn around and c-close your eyes."

"I like it when you're bossy," Vince said, and I flicked him off before he did what I asked.

Quickly, I undressed, leaving my thong and bra on. I figured I could change and get home without them under my clothes later, but it seemed pressing to *not* get into that hot tub naked with Vince Tanev.

The water stung at first when I stepped in, prickling my skin until I was fully submerged. When I was, I let out a long sigh of relief. The water was perfectly warm.

"Aren't you glad you didn't let your stubbornness win?" Vince asked, turning to look at me. I didn't miss how his eyes immediately went to my tits, and he almost looked disappointed to find them covered.

I splashed him.

For a while we sat in a comfortable silence, relaxing in the bubbling water. I didn't realize I let out another long sigh until I opened my eyes and found Vince looking at me.

"You needed this."

I was tempted to argue with him, but the water had me feeling more relaxed than I had in weeks. "Maybe I did."

"Something wrong?"

"No," I said on another sigh. "Just... a lot going on, I guess."

"You need to unwind."

I laughed. "Right, with all my free time."

That made Vince frown, and I waved him off.

"I'm fine. I do yoga when I can, which helps, and this is all temporary. I'll be back to my normal routine before I know it."

I thought that made him frown even more, but he smiled so quickly on the edge of it that I couldn't be sure.

"Turn around," he said, moving slowly toward me. He was like a snake in the water, gliding through it, head just above the waterline, his muscular shoulders making a small wake.

"What are you doing?" I asked, backing away.

His hand caught my wrist under water, and he tugged me forward before spinning me to face the opposite way.

"You are a terrible listener," he said in my ear.

Chills swept over me, and in the next breath, his massive hands were wrapped around my shoulders, thumbs kneading into the tense muscles.

I moaned so loudly my face flamed with embarrassment.

Vince paused only a second before continuing his delicious assault, and I had no choice but to melt into him. The water, his hands — it all felt so fucking *good.*

The silence was no longer comfortable.

It was heavy, weighted with something that made me want to run for my life. So I cleared my throat and reached for the first thing I could think of to break it.

"That was really sweet," I said, biting back another groan that I wanted so desperately to release when he rubbed my sore rhomboids. All my focus was on *not* focusing on how Vince Tanev was naked behind me with his hands on my body. "What you did with the kids at that rink yesterday..."

"Just paying a visit to an old friend."

My stomach soured a bit. "Yeah. Bobby seems to know you really well."

He nodded. "We were close at Michigan. He's a beast of a defenseman, just as good, if not better, than Brittzy."

"Why didn't he go pro?"

"He could have. He had teams who wanted him. He probably would have started in the AHL, though," he said.

"But even if they would have told him he could have come straight to the NHL, I don't think he would have. Bobby has always wanted to coach, to be at that rink that helped him so much. Not everyone has parents who can afford to drop the kind of cash hockey requires."

I let that sit for a moment, wincing as he dug his thumbs into my neck. I let my head fall back when he moved to my shoulders again.

"You've been off on this trip."

It was a statement, not so much a question, and Vince didn't answer for a long moment.

"I need to play better."

I barked out a laugh. "Why, so you can win all three stars of the game instead of just one?"

"I didn't score in either of these games," he said.

"You had an assist."

"It's not the same."

I pulled away, turning so I could face him. I immediately missed the feel of his hands on me — which was a problem in and of itself — but I wanted to look at him when I said, "You don't have to carry the weight of the team on your shoulders."

"No," he agreed, his eyes glued to mine. "But I can play better."

"You're a perfectionist."

"I just hold myself to a high standard."

"That must be exhausting."

He smiled, looking up at the sky before he looked at me again. "It's the opposite, actually. I feel energized when I'm performing well, when I'm scoring goals and training hard. I feel my best when I'm performing on and *off* the ice."

"What are you afraid of?"

The question seemed to catch him off guard, and Vince watched me for a long pause before he answered.

"Being worthless."

I wasn't expecting such an honest answer. In fact, I guess I'd been expecting a joke, because the vulnerability with which he said those words struck me like a bat against the head.

I frowned, and the longer I watched him, the more Vince shifted under my gaze. Eventually, he cleared his throat and motioned for me to turn around again, swirling his pointer finger in the air. When I did, he went back to massaging my shoulders.

I groaned. "God. This feels so good."

"Still mad at me?"

I felt under the water for his side, and then pinched it hard enough to make him squirm away.

"Ow," he said, pointedly.

"You deserved it."

"Why? What'd I do?"

I didn't humor him with a response, which made him let out a soft laugh.

"You really are tense," he said, finding a particularly stubborn knot under my shoulder blade and digging into it. I hissed, but didn't pull away, knowing I'd feel better once it was worked out.

"Yeah, well, let's just say, I'm not used to your hours yet."

"Tell me about your life. What did a normal day look like before you got this assignment?"

I sighed. "Well, I usually start my morning on my mat."

"Yoga?"

I nodded. "And then coffee, of course."

"Of course."

"From there, it depends. On the weekends, I'm probably tending my garden, or spending time at the beach, or hitting a new brunch spot with Liv. Sundays start at the park, as you know. If it's a weekday, I'm either in the office or out on the town, depending on what my job is that day."

"Is this your dream job?"

I laughed. "I don't know if I *have* a dream job."

"Sure, you do. What would you do if money were no object, if your bills were paid and all you had to do was fill your time?"

A long moment passed before I found the words to answer.

"I don't know."

It was the most painful admission, one I was surprised I made. It dredged up the embarrassment I'd felt when I admitted that to James when we were together, how he'd judged me for it even before I realized that's what he was doing.

People like him, like Vince, didn't understand what it was like to not be born knowing exactly what you wanted to do with your entire life.

"My parents, they've always known their path," I said. "They were in AmeriCorps together, shaping communities for the better. They dedicated an entire decade of their life after college before they got out and started making a life of their own. Now, Mom works with a women's shelter, and Dad builds houses in communities where owning a home seems more like a pipe dream than a reality within reach. They brought me up with those same values, and I want to give back. I want to make Tampa, and the *world,* better."

"But?"

I hated that he knew there was a but, and I was glad to be facing away from him, to not have those hazel eyes peering into mine when I answered.

"But I don't necessarily love it the way they do. Don't get me wrong," I said hurriedly. "I enjoy giving back, I do. I love feeling connected to people, and making them feel valuable, worthwhile — reminding them they're not alone. It's just... I don't know. I guess I just wish I had the same passion for it. I wish it fueled me the way it fuels my parents." I paused. "You should have seen their faces when I told them I didn't want to go into the Peace Corps. I think a small part of them died that day."

"Does anything fuel you that way?" Vince asked.

I let out a long exhale, my heart squeezing. It felt so foolish to say the answer to that out loud. Because when I thought of what made me feel passionate, it was creating content — editing videos, getting the perfect photograph, creating presets that, in turn, create an entire vibe. I loved writing captions. I loved making something that went viral, that reached millions of people worldwide.

Right now, it was Vince Tanev and the Tampa Ospreys and hockey.

But maybe one day, it could be more.

Instead of saying any of that, I just shrugged.

Vince's grip on me softened. "You don't have to have it all figured out right now, you know?"

I nodded, but refrained from pointing out that *he* had it all figured out, and he was younger than me.

"What you *do* need," he continued, moving to massage my neck again. "Is to relax."

"Says the perfectionist."

But my joke was cut short because Vince moved his hands from my neck into my hair, massaging the base of my skull.

I moaned, melting.

If his hands on my shoulders weren't already enough to unravel me, feeling those massive fingers cradle my skull and massage my scalp was enough to make me spontaneously combust.

I couldn't help but lean into the touch.

And in the process, my ass brushed against him, our skin connecting underwater and sparking an impossible fire.

Time stopped, Vince pausing only a moment before his hands were working again. I thought I heard him swallow, thought I heard his next breath come a bit more labored.

I didn't pull away.

My heart thumped loud in my ears as we stayed like that, connected both with his hands in my hair and his thigh just barely brushing the bare skin of my ass. And when his hands moved down, fingertips gliding over my shoulders before disappearing under the water, I felt him grow hard behind me, his erection pressing into the small of my back.

And still, I didn't pull away.

Those fingertips danced down the span of my arms, gliding back up before they were on my back. He touched me so softly it was almost like he wasn't touching me at all, and yet I couldn't let out the breath lodged in my throat.

He nuzzled the space behind my ear with the tip of his nose as his hands slid down lower, fingertips drawing a circle around the dimples at the small of my back. They found my hips next, pulling me flush against him, letting me feel what I did to him.

His breath was in my ear, louder now, more unsteady. He didn't say a word as his fingers skated over the slim band of my thong, and then one hand pressed against my stomach as the other traveled farther up. Just the tip of one finger slipped beneath the band of my bra, and his cock twitched against my back.

"Fuck," he whispered.

The sound was so raw, an admission and a prayer all at once, and it rumbled through me. My nipples peaked, thighs clenching together at the jolt of electricity I felt from that one little word.

His hand slid up just a fraction of an inch more, pushing my bra out of the way. I wondered if he could feel how hard my heart was pounding, if I was trembling as much as I felt like I was.

I held my breath, angling my chin toward him until I could taste his exhales. The tip of his nose ran along the back of my jaw, and just as he gently, *barely* cupped my breast, his tongue snaked out and licked my earlobe.

"More champagne?"

I tore away from Vince as the stewardess's voice pierced the heavy night air. I was on the other end of the hot tub by the time her smiling face rounded the corner, and she offered a glass to Vince, who declined, before I took one and downed it.

"Unfortunately, we had to turn around to head back into the harbor. There is some weather coming in that we weren't expecting. But you have a little more time to enjoy the hot tub, if you wish."

As soon as she left, I climbed out of the whirlpool, not bothering to ask Vince to turn away. I just grabbed one of the towels rolled up on a chair and covered myself with it before swiping my clothes off the deck and retreating inside.

In the bathroom, I composed myself as much as I could, which was to say not much. I stared at my reflection in the mirror, at my hair, wild from having Vince's hands in it, and my eyes, rimmed with my mascara.

I was so wet I didn't know how I was going to go commando without soaking through my slacks.

Red flags. Red flags *everywhere* and yet still, I burned for that man just like every other simpering puck bunny.

I was as angry at myself as I was turned on.

I still hadn't completely caught my breath when I reemerged on the deck, and we were already pulling into the harbor. Vince was dressed, too, his hands in his pockets as he watched me.

I had plans to stay on the opposite end of the deck from where he was, but he crossed it, sidling up next to where I was leaning over the railing and watching the city glide by.

"I like what you posted tonight," he said, as if he didn't just have his hard cock pressed against my back, as if he hadn't just tasted my skin and palmed me under my bra. "The video, it was cool."

I'd put together a mashup of the two away games, matching the explosive hits of him pummeling an opponent into the glass or stealing a pass with the beat of the music.

"Glad you like it," I said, still a bit breathless.

"You should post a picture of us."

That got my attention.

"Um..."

"Here," he said, and before I could react, he had my phone in his hand. He held it out to me to unlock, which I did in a daze, and then he had Instagram pulled up, the screen reflecting us in selfie mode.

It was dark on the boat, but the lights from the city showed just enough of us to make up a grainy, golden image.

Vince threw his arm around me, pulling me into him. He was so massive, his arm hooked around me completely, shoulder over one of mine while his hand hooked the other.

"Don't look so scared," he whispered against my neck, watching our reflection on the screen.

I reached up, hooking my hands on his arm that was around me. His chin was on the crown of my head, his smirk sexy as hell, eyes like that of a leopard who just spotted his prey.

His extended arm captured all of it — me pulled into him, his arm holding me close, my hands curled into the sleeve of his jacket. The flash went off, and before I could even see the picture, Vince pulled away.

"What are you doing?" I asked, watching him walk across the deck, thumbing away on the keyboard.

"Posting it."

"No one wants to see me. This is about you, remember?"

He didn't reply as I followed him.

"What are you writing?"

He didn't answer me, and he got a lucky break because the stews were getting us ready to dock and disembark. He slid my phone into the pocket of his jacket and didn't give it to me until we were back in the car.

It was so late by the time we made it to the hotel, but the rooms were quiet enough that I assumed the rest of the team was still out on the town. There was no way they were asleep yet, not with nothing to do in the morning other than fly home.

"Goodnight," I said to Vince when we made it to our rooms. I was already tapping my key card and opening my door when he just leaned against the frame of his, watching me.

I paused, arching a brow.

"You'll be in my bed soon."

My mouth parted at his words, and I blinked before letting out an incredulous laugh. Then, I let my door shut without going inside it, crossing to where Vince was, instead.

I folded my arms, lifting my chin high. "Never going to happen, *Pigeon*."

He pushed to stand, invading my space so quickly I backed up and hit the wall in-between our doors. Vince stared down at me, a lazy smile on his lips.

"I can't wait to make you eat your words."

He pressed into me, just a little, just enough to make my breath catch. He reached up and trailed the back of his knuckles up the line of my jaw, tugging on my earlobe as if to remind me that his teeth had done the same tonight.

Then, he grinned wider, stepping away completely and unlocking his door.

"I love that face, by the way," he said, glancing at where I was still frozen in place. "The one you make when you realize you've met your match."

ʘ ʘ ʘ

I didn't think to check my phone when I made it inside. I was buzzing from his touch, mind and body on fire from the night's events and how I felt about them. I was also *exhausted*, so much so that I barely washed my face before I fell into bed and let sleep take me under.

The next morning, I woke to a flurry of texts.

Reya: Camilla and I are freaking out over last night's post. In the best way. Call me when you're up!

Camilla: I smell an assignment extension… way to

break the Internet! And every Tampa girl's heart. ;)

Livia: Told you you were in trouble. Can you tell me I was right over a glass of red soon? I need details.

I clicked out of my best friend's text with my heart hammering in my ears, pulling up Instagram next. I clicked on my profile picture, quickly tapping through the stories I'd posted of last night's game until I came to the picture of me and Vince.

The image was so striking, I covered my mouth with one hand, staring at it in disbelief.

My eyes were a bit squinted from the flash, which just made me look sated, the smile on my lips subtle and soft. My normally curly hair was styled in soft waves and blowing in the wind, fresh from the blowout I'd had done earlier in the afternoon. Strands of it stuck to my lips, my hands clutching Vince's arm tightly, fingertips curled into the fabric of his jacket. And even though I knew that I'd just been tired, I looked like I'd just been freshly fucked.

And there was Vince behind me, wrapping me up like he owned me, his eyes low and sexy and commanding all of the camera's attention.

His lips were pressed against my hair.

My chest tightened. *How* had I not noticed that?

But I didn't focus on it long before I was gaping at the text overlaid on the screen.

night out celebrating with my girl

I clicked out of it, blinking, only to be hit with it in my feed.

The photo had already been picked up by ESPN, and they'd reposted it.

Sonofa*bitch.*

Chapter 18

All the Right Webs

Maven

I pulled my hood over my head in the back of the plane the next morning, ignoring Vince, along with the rest of the team, as my phone continued to blow up. Reya and Camilla wanted me to call as soon as I landed. So did Livia.

When we touched down in Tampa, I bolted, getting my own ride downtown so I could make my calls in peace. But before I had the chance to call my best friend, my phone buzzed in my hands with my parents' faces lighting up the screen.

It was a photo from Christmas two years ago, all of us in pajamas and huddled together for a selfie by the tree. Dad had taken it, his long arm stretched out and his smile wide. Mom was curled into his side, and I was there in front of them, a blend of the two humans who made me.

I always felt that I favored my mom — the same gold eyes, same slight frame, same warm smile. But my dad was evident in all my features, too. Our eyes were the same shape, we shared the freckles smattering our cheeks, and

I knew I got my attitude solely from him. Dad's skin was a pale white, though it turned red with emotion, alcohol, or even ten minutes in the sun. Mom's skin was a deep brown, like the soil of Mother Earth. And I was a blend of the two.

Normally, I would have been answering their call with a smile, excited to hear how they were and to tell them about my life, too.

But today, I answered with anxiety bubbling in my gut.

"Hello," I said just as I slid into the back of a cab. I quickly told the driver which building to take me to before my dad's voice rumbled through the phone.

"Are you dating this hockey player?"

I chuckled, letting my head fall back against the seat as I stared out the window. "Well, good morning to you, too, Daddy. Yes, I'm doing well, thank you for asking. What was it like in Pittsburgh and Baltimore? Well, the weather was—"

"I don't care about the weather," he said, and even though his voice was deep in its severity, I still smiled. My father loved to act like a protective Rottweiler when it came to me, but in reality, he was just a teddy bear. "I care about this young man with a reputation who seems to have become very comfortable with my daughter."

"What your father is trying to say," my mom interjected, her voice sweet like maple syrup. I could picture her gently placing a hand on my father's arm, could see the deep inhale that touch would force him to take. "Is that we wanted to check in on you and make sure you're doing okay."

"And that you're keeping your head on straight and remembering that this is a job," Dad added.

Mom sucked her teeth, and I tried not to bristle with defense as I slid in my earbuds so I could talk hands-free. "I'm not dating him, Daddy. It was a publicity stunt. Just giving the people something to talk about."

My throat tightened a bit at that, because it had been an *unplanned* stunt that I did not actively participate in. I was trying not to blow a gasket. My bosses were clearly fine with that photo and the implications behind it, but it didn't stop me from feeling like a fool.

An unprofessional, simpering fool.

That's how everyone else would see me. I was no longer the woman behind the camera, the one on assignment with my job at the forefront of my mind. I was no longer a content creator, a reporter, a force to be reckoned with, taking the sports world by storm.

Now, I was a joke.

The fact that my parents were calling me was proof of that.

"Some stunt," my father said on a harrumph. "Don't let your guard down, Maven. I know he's a handsome young man, but keep your wits about you. He has a reputation, and no matter what he says to you, he's probably only got one thing on his mind."

"Dad," I chastised.

"We just worry," Mom said softly, and those words hung in the silence between the three of us like a loaded gun.

My parents had been there for me when everything blew up with James. They quite literally had to peel me off the floor and convince me that life was still worth living, that I needed to walk across the stage at graduation, that life would go on without James Baldridge.

And maybe they had a right to be worried.

Because had that stewardess not interrupted us on the boat, I might have let all sense leave me.

My skin burned from the memory, as if Vince were still naked in the water behind me, his knuckles dragging over my skin. I heard his words in my ear, felt my skin prickle with chills just like they had last night.

My stomach fluttered, but I pinched the bridge of my nose and tried to snuff him out with the motion.

"You don't need to worry," I promised my parents. "Trust me — I am in no hurry to have my heart smashed again." My next swallow was dry and painful. "Besides, like I said, it was just a stunt. Vince and I are nothing but professional."

I'd never lied to my parents, and was surprised my voice didn't shake more with that one. Because being half-naked in a hot tub with Vince rubbing my shoulders did not feel professional.

I was caught between being ashamed and angry, with a little dash of *why do I feel like I would go back and do it again* thrown in, too.

"You tell him to keep his hands to himself, or he'll have me to answer to," Dad said. I could picture his bright blue eyes hardening into the cerulean they did when he was angry, could picture him wagging his finger at me like he does the crew on work sites.

I chuckled, despite feeling like a senseless little girl. "I will do that."

My phone buzzed in my lap, and when I glanced at the screen, I was already telling my parents I needed to end the call. I figured it was Reya, or Livia.

But it was a number I didn't recognize.

I assumed it was likely someone from the team then, so with a promise to get lunch soon, I ended the call with my parents and switched over.

"Hello?"

"Maven King."

My entire body froze as the familiar voice crooned in my ear.

"How's it feel to be the hottest thing on the Internet?"

He chuckled on the end of that stupid fucking question, but I was too busy reminding myself to breathe, to blink, to not pass out in the back of a cab.

"Hello? Did I lose you?"

I snorted a laugh at that, my senses coming back to me in a whoosh. "Yes, actually. Years ago. Why are you calling me, James?"

I glanced down at my phone again, pissed that he clearly had a new number. I'd blocked his old one, making sure something like this could never happen. Then again, he was on the PGA Tour now. He probably had some fancy new phone on some fancy private plan that the normal population didn't have access to. I didn't even know if that was a thing, but I *did* know that he tied for *tenth place* at a tournament earlier this year and still made three-hundred grand. In *one weekend.*

I hated myself for knowing that, for the night I drank a bottle of wine and went down a Google rabbit hole with my ex as the target.

"Hey, easy now," he said, his voice as deep and smooth as I remembered. I could still picture his smile, could imagine him holding up his hands like he came in peace right before he wrecked my whole world. "I was just thinking of you. It's been a long time."

"You were just thinking of me," I repeated, deadpan. "Meaning, you saw the photo Vince posted of us last night."

He barked out a laugh at that. "Transparent as an ice cube, aren't I?" He let his laugh die off, a moment of silence before he added, "So... is it true, then? Are you two together?"

"That is none of your business."

"No," he agreed. "I just didn't peg you for someone who would throw away a great opportunity for the chance to jump in bed with a rookie."

My jaw nearly hit the floor of the cab.

"Ex*cuse* me?"

"I'm just telling you to be careful."

"Be careful," I repeated. I actually could not believe the audacity of this man.

"Look, I understand how guys like him tick. I also know you've worked your ass off to get where you are."

"Don't act like you know anything about me anymore," I spat.

"I just don't want you to jeopardize your career because he's spinning all the right webs and saying all the right things."

"Oh, the way you did?"

The words popped out of me so quick, I didn't have time to think about whether I actually wanted to say them or not. What I should have done was hang up. But instead, I was starting a fight like I wanted it, like I still cared about him and what happened between us.

It felt like showing my hand.

It felt like losing.

And it made me grit my teeth so hard I nearly chipped one in the process.

"I loved you," James said, his voice just above a whisper. "You know that."

"No, I don't," I clipped, fuming. "Thanks for your concern, but it's no longer needed. You were the one who exited my life, James, so at least have the decency to stay gone."

I hung up before he could respond, immediately blocking his number just in case he tried to call back. Then, I threw my phone in my purse and let out a frustrated growl that turned into a high-pitched scream.

My driver eyed me in the rearview mirror, and I muttered an apology just as he pulled up to the skyscraper I was calling home for the month. I tipped him graciously before kicking the door open and lugging my bag out of the trunk, dragging it behind me like it was a weapon, and I was going into a street fight.

I stewed the entire way up the elevator, flinging my bag into the foyer once I'd made it to the condo. I nearly cried at the sight of the place — all the furniture and art and appliances that weren't mine. Everything was modern and expensive and cold, nothing like my bungalow that was just a twenty-minute walk from the beach, and tears pricked my eyes before anger washed them away again.

I roared, kicking off my shoes and pacing as I dragged my hands over my hair. I was so fucking *pissed* — at my parents, at James, at Vince, at *myself*. One night. One stupid photo and everything was blown to shit.

And I *knew* in that moment what I should have done.

I should have gone for a walk. I should have gone to the beach. I should have rolled out my yoga mat and found poses to ground myself. I should have meditated. I should have called Livia.

I should have done a million other things.

But what I *actually* did was pick up my phone and open Instagram.

Because I didn't want to calm down.

I wanted to rage.

I wanted *payback*.

And I didn't stop to think about the repercussions until it was too late.

Chapter 19

Such a Little Brat

Vince

Coach McCabe looked ready to blow a gasket.

He reminded me a little of my father in that moment, the way my dad would hold in his anger until he could go to the gym or get out on the boat. He never wanted us kids to see it or be on the receiving end of it. I loved and admired him for that, how he could bottle it up and find the proper release.

Coach, on the other hand, was ready to unleash — and I was his target.

"Look, it's not a huge deal," Dick said, my general manager much calmer than the red-faced man standing against his office window. Coach could barely look at me without seething. "It pulled in some good publicity for you and for the team, and it was a kind thing to do. But—"

"But it's against your fucking contract," Coach filled in for him, nose flaring. "What the *hell* were you thinking, Tanev?"

I swallowed, knowing that wasn't a question he wanted me to answer. I was expected to sit there and take my lashing like a good boy, and I was content to do just that.

But anger simmered in *me*, too.

Because I told Maven not to fucking post about that day.

Our away games had gone just how we wanted them to. We were on a five-win streak and back in our city to try to make it six. Yesterday was a hungover flight home for most of the guys, and we spent the rest of the day recovering. I hadn't seen Maven, other than where she was already sleeping when I boarded the plane. She was in the back, hoodie on, pillow against the window, and headphones covering her ears.

When we got back to Tampa, she muttered something about seeing me later before she disappeared. I had no idea where she'd gone, and I hated to admit how much I missed having her around — especially since I wanted her to talk to me about what happened the night before.

She was so goddamn stubborn, it infuriated me as much as it made me want her more.

This morning, when I'd shown up to practice, I'd no sooner laced my skates up before Coach was pointing at the elevator. Wordlessly, I followed him, and when he hit the button for the executive floor and handed me his phone with his jaw clenched, I knew I was in trouble.

Maven had posted a video of me at the rink in Pittsburgh with Bobby and his kids.

I only watched a few seconds of it before I handed the phone back, knowing my ass was grass.

"Oh, come now, McCabe," Dick said, leaning back in his chair with that jovial grin of his. "The boy is fine."

"He could have gotten himself hurt. *Before a game.*"

"But he didn't."

The way Dick said those words told me he wanted Coach to back off, and the way Coach fumed told me that was the last thing he planned to do.

"I'm sorry," I said to both of them, and I meant it. "I needed to clear my head, and I knew my buddy from Michigan was coaching at that rink. I promise, I didn't do anything that would have put me at risk."

"Being on the ice *period* put you at risk," Coach argued. "You weren't even wearing a mask. What if you got a puck to the jaw? What if one of those kids wanted to prove he was big and bad and shoved you into the boards? What if you pulled a fucking hamstring? *Anything* could have happened. And then what? You would have been out of the game. And what would you have told your teammates?"

"Alright, he said he was sorry," Dick said, holding out his hands.

Coach let out a hot exhale through his nose, running his hands through his hair and turning away from me. I'd never seen him so pissed, but I knew without him saying so that he was less mad and more scared.

He didn't want to have to figure out how to win a game without me on the ice.

Dick pointed at me next. "Let this be a one-time thing, okay? It was a nice gesture, and I'm sure those boys will remember that day for the rest of their lives. But Coach is right. We can't afford to lose you, son."

I nodded. "Understood."

Coach didn't talk to me the rest of practice. He hammered my ass, though, and made sure I was sweating and sore as hell by the time he called it for the day.

And where *he* ignored *me*, *I* ignored Maven.

She was there, just like she had been the last two weeks, recording from the sidelines. When we were dismissed, I didn't wait for her as I shoved through the doors that led from the stadium into downtown. I walked with my headphones on, duffle bag slung over one shoulder, ignoring everyone who walked past me and recognized who I was. A few of them snapped photos, others just pointed and smiled and called out my name. The best of them left me alone altogether.

I'd no sooner made it home and started my shower before I heard a knock at my door.

Maven didn't look scared when I swung it open, staring down at her with my jaw set. In fact, she folded her arms and lifted her chin in defiance.

"Bad day?"

"What the hell is wrong with you?"

"Me?" She balked, catching the door before it could shut when I let go of it. I headed back toward my bedroom, to where I had the shower going. "What is wrong with *you*?!"

"You posted that video when I told you, I *told* you not to." I spun to face her in the hallway, the sound of the shower serving as white noise behind our screams. "But you did it anyway. Because you're Maven King and you just do whatever you want."

She scoffed. "In case you forgot, you agreed to this."

"Oh, my bad. I thought when I specifically asked you not to post something, you'd listen. Didn't you tell me that in the beginning? That if I wanted anything off the record, all I had to do was say so?"

I didn't know why I took that exact moment to take her in, to really look at her. Her eyes were as tired as mine, and yet still, she was glowing — her skin fresh and smooth, her hair curly and held off her face by a colorful bandana tied at the crown of her head. She wore her classic silver hoop earrings, a white t-shirt that fit her perfectly, and a pair of light-washed jeans that fit even better.

Even when I was pissed at her, I wanted her.

"This is a good thing," she said after a moment — but it felt like she was trying to defend herself more than convince me. "Every news outlet in the city has picked up the story, along with some of the national stations. You're welcome for the great publicity."

"Did it ever occur to you that I wasn't supposed to be there?"

She blinked.

"Yeah. It's against my contract. I'm not supposed to play any kind of sport or do anything that can put me or my body in danger during the season. I can't so much as swing a golf club without risking my job."

The color drained from her then, and I knew I had her.

"Coach McCabe filleted my ass today."

"Okay, well..." She stammered, then stood tall again. "Well, you let the kids take pictures, which I'm *sure* they posted. So what's the difference?"

"The difference is that in those photos, I wasn't skating on the fucking rink, Maven!" I scrubbed a hand over my jaw. "Sorry, I didn't mean to yell. But there *is* a difference between me just hanging out with some kids playing hockey, as opposed to playing along with them. And Coach is *pissed*."

Maven had the decency to shrink a bit at that, but then she squared her shoulders. "Yeah, well, I guess we're even then."

"How the hell do you figure that?"

"The picture? You kissing my hair? *My girl*?"

A smile curled on my lips, that anger I had before ebbing a bit. "What, not ready to admit that yet? Because let's face it. It's true."

She shoved me, *hard*. Her hands found my chest and pressed until my back hit the wall. I let her think she had that power, that she could move my six-foot-one brick of a body with her slight one.

"This is my career," she seethed.

"And this is mine," I argued. "So, you're right. I guess we *are* even."

"It's not the same. *You* got a slap on the wrist and some damn good PR. Do you realize how unprofessional that photo looked for me?"

"Are your bosses mad?"

Her mouth was still open, ready to fire her next argument, but it snapped close at my question.

I laughed, shaking my head, and then I pushed off the wall.

"You," I said, moving slowly, step by step toward her as she matched my pace walking backward the other way. When her back hit the wall, I enveloped her, reveling in the little gasp she elicited when my hand found her throat. "Are such a little brat."

I waited for her to slap me.

But she just swallowed, the movement vibrating under my palm, her eyes locked on mine.

"You're so used to getting everything you want." I tilted my head. "Well, *almost* everything."

"What's that supposed to mean?"

I dragged the tip of my nose along the bridge of hers, smiling. "You want me."

Her next breath shuddered out of her, her eyelids fluttering.

"You are seriously deranged."

The words were a breathless lie, the warmth from them sweet like vanilla on my nose. I squeezed her throat a little tighter, her eyes dilating as my free hand slid over her hip. I trailed it up, the back of my knuckles slowly skating over her waist, her ribs, along the swell of her breast. I brushed against where her nipple was pulled tight before flattening my hand and pressing it against her chest.

"Your heart is about to pound out of your chest," I said, voice low and taunting. I swore I felt her heart stutter under my palm. "Why do you fight it?"

She swallowed, her eyes flicking to my lips.

Then, she pushed me back with whatever semblance of control she was still holding fast to, peeling my hands off her and storming down the hall.

"There's nothing to fight," she said over her shoulder.

I stood there in the hallway until she ripped my front door open.

"I'm not your girl, Vince Tanev." She turned to pin me with her gaze, more determination than ever before etched into her features. "Allow me to prove that to you."

Chapter 20

Backfire

Maven

"This is hotter than the Skinemax movies my Aunt Rosie used to watch," Livia said, fanning herself as she leaned back in her chair. "I mean, usually I'm more into being the domineering one," she added, tilting her head side to side. "But to each their own."

"It's not hot. It's maddening," I told her, taking an angry sip from my cocktail. We had escaped the chaos of our Tuesday for a long overdue bestie lunch at a spot near the stadium. Vince was in a film meeting with the team for at least another hour, which meant there was nothing to post about.

"You are a shit liar."

"He posted a photo of us," I barked at her. "And called me *his girl.*"

"Oh, no!" Livia gasped, sitting up straighter and pressing her hand to her chest like she was appalled. "What a jerk, liking you so much he wants to claim you. And to be hot and rich, too? With a nice cock? God, I don't know how you're surviving."

She sat back with a roll of her eyes as I flicked her off, looking around to make sure none of the other diners were shocked by my best friend's casual use of the word cock.

"Don't act like you wouldn't be just as upset."

"Yeah, well, that's different. I don't date hockey players."

"Because you're too busy making them writhe in pain on your table?"

"Exactly," she said, pointing at me before she sipped her martini. "*And* because they're never the right candidates for what I like in the bedroom."

I smirked at that. "Kinky bitch."

"You're just mad I'm not *your* dom."

"A girl can dream."

Livia smiled, shaking her head. "Stop trying to flatter me and get back to the point at hand. Why, exactly, are you so upset? You think he's hot, right?"

"Well, I'm human, so yes."

"And he's cool, he's fun, you like to be around him."

"I guess, but—"

"So *what* is the problem?"

"He's a hockey player!" I said, exasperated, my hands jutting toward her. "Just like you said. He's a *player*. Period. I've literally seen him sandwiched between two women in a crowd of people. If I wasn't there, he would have taken them both home."

"But you *were* there," Livia said.

And that was it.

That was her whole argument.

I had been there, and so Vince had left those girls dancing by themselves in the bar — all to chase after me.

I sighed, shaking my head as I sat back and drained my cocktail. I didn't care that it was lunch and I had more work to do. I ordered another one. My heart was thumping in my ears, a panic attack rising.

"Are Reya and Camilla mad?"

"No," I said on a laugh. "They're tickled pink. But that doesn't make it any less professional. I mean, let's be honest, Livia — how many people are going to think I only got this gig because Vince Tanev wants to fuck me now? How many people are going to say that I was lucky, that I got plucked from the crowd of females desperate for his attention?" I paused, my voice softer when I added, "You should see the comments already. They're awful."

"Who gives a fuck what anyone on the Internet thinks or says?"

"It's my *career*," I said. "I just... I don't want this to be what I'm remembered for. And besides, even if I did entertain whatever it is he's offering. Which I'm not," I added pointedly. "He's a playboy, Liv. He can have whoever and do whatever he wants. What do I honestly expect?"

Livia's eyes softened in understanding. "This is about James."

I blinked, that panic that had been simmering under the surface boiling over now.

"No," I said, but the admission was so weak not even I believed it.

"Oh, babe." Livia leaned forward, wrapping her hand around my wrist on the table with a gentle squeeze. "Vince is not James."

"He's not that much different."

That made Livia quiet, like she wanted to argue but wasn't sure she had a leg to stand on. Because just like Vince, James had been an athlete. Just like Vince, James had been charming, and magnetic, and easy to fall for. And just like Vince, James was rich, from an affluent family, with certain expectations of who he should be with.

"He called me."

"Who?"

I flattened my lips when I looked at her, but it was actual surprise on her face when she damn near choked on her cocktail.

"*James*? How? Didn't you block his number?"

"He got a new one," I said flatly. "Don't worry — I blocked it, too. But not before he rattled me and gave me his unwarranted advice."

"He *what* now?"

I sat up straighter, using my straw wrapper to make a mustache like the one James sported now. Then, in my best impression, I said, "*Look, I understand how guys like him tick. I also know you've worked your ass off to get where you are.*"

"No he did *not*—"

"*I just don't want you to jeopardize your career because he's spinning all the right webs and saying all the right things.*"

Just like mine had, Livia's jaw hit the table, and she slow blinked twice before letting out a menacing laugh. She dabbed the corners of her mouth with her napkin before tossing it on the table. "Alright. That's it. I hope that prick is enjoying breathing today, because he won't be soon."

She acted like she was about to stand and go find James, like she was my knight in shining armor. I tried to laugh, but it fell flat, and Livia frowned before reaching across the table to squeeze my arm again.

"I'm sorry," she said.

I didn't let myself overthink it before I was blowing a breath through my lips, shaking the whole thing off. "Whatever. It doesn't matter. But in a way, it was a good reminder of what I already knew to be true."

Livia's lips pulled to the side, but she didn't argue.

"And I'm going to show Vince that, despite him ignoring me every time I've told him, this is a professional relationship."

"Oh, yeah?"

I nodded, smiling wickedly as I sat back and sipped my martini. "I have a date. Tonight."

"A date?" Livia almost laughed. "With who?"

I waved her off. "I don't know. Some guy from the apps. I swiped right a few times and got a match."

"Let me get this straight. Your plan is to go on a date with another man, presumably let him pick you up at the condo where you're currently staying, and for that to somehow make Vince Tanev realize you're off limits?"

"Yes."

"You think," she said, slower now, like I wasn't understanding. "He'll see you leave with this guy and take the hint, that he'll leave you alone and think to himself, 'Well, I guess that's that. Maven is clearly taken and not at all interested in me?'"

"Exactly."

This time, she did laugh, shaking her head as she plucked the olive out of her martini and popped it into her mouth. "Oh, honey," she said. "This is going to backfire right in that pretty face of yours."

Chapter 21

This Fucking Dress

Vince

"Man, I'm *starving*," Carter said, rubbing his stomach like an old man waiting for Thanksgiving dinner. "I feel like I could eat a whole cow."

"Maybe if you did, you'd be able to hit the puck better," Jaxson said, pinching Carter's biceps with his fingertips. "That wimpy shot you made in our scrimmage today is going to reverberate in my nightmares."

"Fuck off. It was bar down."

"It would have actually had to go in the net to be bar down," Will grumped. "Not doinked off like a missed field goal."

"It went in and you know it, Daddy P. You just don't want to admit this rookie scored on you."

"That's because you didn't, Fabio. And you never will."

Carter and Will were still horsing around when we pushed through the front door of the restaurant. We were immediately greeted by five employees at the hostess stand, all of them eager to welcome us and see us to our table. There were more eyes on Will than the rest of us, mostly because Daddy P didn't make public appearances often. He was usually home with his kid, where he loved to be. I was glad we'd managed to pull him out for an evening, even if just for dinner.

But that wasn't my sole focus of the evening.

"You good?" Jaxson asked me, pulling behind a bit to walk at my side.

"Peachy."

"That's convincing," he said on a laugh, and then he narrowed his eyes when he saw me searching the place as we were walked through the restaurant to a back room. "Who are you looking for?"

I didn't answer him, but when I spotted Maven and her date at a table by the window, I stopped dead in my tracks.

She was so gorgeous it hurt.

Her onyx hair was blown out in a soft, wavy style that reminded me of the night we spent together in Baltimore, her warm brown skin glowing in the candlelight. The gloss on her lips was almost as enticing as the heels strapped to her delicate ankles, and even from a distance, I could see the slit in her velvet blue dress, could trace the lines of her legs that it revealed beneath the table.

I wasn't sure how long I stood and stared before Jaxson's laugh cut through the haze.

"You sly dog," he said, shaking his head as he clapped me on the shoulder. "She know you're here?"

"Not yet."

He laughed again. "I'll write a good eulogy for your funeral."

He left me then, following the rest of the guys to our table as I stayed rooted in place. A few tables of diners began to recognize me, the chatter getting louder, and Maven must have picked up on it. Because she was in the middle of a beautiful, sing-song laugh that floated through the restaurant and right to my ears when she paused, turning toward the noise.

Her mouth went slack at the sight of me.

For a moment, I just stood there and stared at her, my heart hammering in my chest. A cocky smile slid on my lips easily, without me prompting it, like it was my natural state of being. Then, I slid my hands into my pockets and winked at her before turning and heading in the direction of our table.

I didn't say a word when I sat down, letting the rest of the guys carry the conversation. Jaxson was watching me with a curious look over his menu, though — especially as my gaze stayed fixed on Maven across the restaurant. She was doing her best to ignore me, but when her eyes would flick to mine, I would always smile.

And she would always glare.

It was a good thing looks couldn't *actually* kill, because I was pretty sure my life would be over.

Showing up here was a bold move. I knew as much when I decided to make it. Maven had politely told me after practice that she wouldn't be around this evening, and when I asked her why, she hid a shy tinge of her cheeks with her hair when she said, "I have a date."

Four words.

Four words was all it took to make my blood boil and my brain cease to have any common sense or rationality.

I'd pretended to be cool about it, shrugging and telling her to have fun. But as soon as I'd shut the door to my place, I'd called Livia.

"Tell me where he's taking her," I'd said when she answered.

She'd laughed, and I was almost certain she wasn't going to tell me. But then, after a long pause, she'd asked, "You really like her, don't you?"

I hadn't been able to respond.

"You've got a long road ahead of you to earn her trust," she'd warned me, and when I didn't back down, she'd given me the name of the restaurant.

Something about that fueled me even more. Livia was her best friend, and if she'd willingly told me the location of Maven's date, that said loud and clear everything I needed to hear. If Maven really hated me, if she really didn't want me, Livia would have told me to leave her alone, to kick rocks, to back the hell off.

Instead, she'd handed me an invitation.

I wasn't going to waste it.

After we placed our order, I excused myself from the table. But instead of going to the restroom like I'd said I was, I strolled right over to Maven's table.

Her eyes nearly bulged out of her skull as I approached, and she smiled at her date while trying to subtly shake her head at me.

Do not *come over here*, those eyes said.

But I was on a mission, and I wasn't backing down now.

When I didn't relent, she gritted her teeth, scratching the back of her neck with one fingernail and avoiding eye contact until she had no choice.

Because I was right there, standing at her table with a smile of my own.

"Holy shit," her date said, beaming up at me. "You're Vince Tanev!"

His chair made a horrible sound scraping against the floor as he stood in a hurry, taking my hand in his and shaking a little too aggressively.

"It's amazing to meet you, man. You've really put Tampa back on the map." He looked at Maven, hooking his thumb toward me. "Did you do this? Is this a surprise for me? Because if so, you just won the award for best first date."

"She *did*, in fact," I said, smiling at Maven as she set her jaw and folded her arms over her stomach. I turned back to her date. "But I didn't realize this was your *first* date. Wow. Maven made it sound like you two had really hit it off."

Maven rolled her eyes.

"You must really be a catch..."

"Damon," he said.

"Damon," I repeated. Then, I unfastened the button on my sports coat and pointed to the empty chair at the table behind him. "Mind if I sit for a bit?"

"Please!" he said at the same time Maven muttered, "Yes, we mind."

Damon looked at her with a strange expression before laughing and pulling up the chair for me.

Before I could do anything else, a couple guys interrupted and asked for a photo and autograph. I scribbled one out quickly, smiling for the picture, and then I sat right between Maven and her date.

"Maven," I said, finally greeting her properly. I let my eyes rake over her, fully appreciating the blue velvet dress up close. "You look beautiful."

She blinked at me, her jaw clenched.

"So, *Damon*. What is it you do?" I asked, declining the waitress when she offered me something to drink.

"I'm in real estate."

"Fascinating," I mocked, leaning my chin on the heel of my hand. "Isn't that fascinating, Maven?"

She smiled, dabbing at the corners of her lips with her napkin daintily before she folded it beside her plate. "It is. If you'll excuse me," she said, and then she got up from the table as calmly as she could.

I didn't have to look at her over my shoulder to know she expected me to follow.

I entertained her date for a moment longer, mostly listening to him tell me what a huge fan he was of the team, and how he had been for years — *even when we sucked*. He took full advantage of Maven being away from the table, sheepishly asking me if he could have my autograph and a photo before she returned. I told him we should wait, that she'd want to be in the picture.

Because fat chance in *hell* was I giving this guy anything when he was here with my girl.

Then, I told him I needed to get back to my table, but I'd stop by later.

And I followed the trail Maven had made toward the bathrooms.

It smelled of smoke, like she'd burned the entire way.

There were two bathrooms, each gender neutral with one stall inside. One was empty, and one was locked. I knocked only twice, softly, before the door was ripped open and a hand jutted out, grabbing me by the collar and yanking me inside.

"Wow, really? Here, Maven?" I teased when she slammed the door shut again, locking it and pressing her back to the metal. "It's kind of kinky, but hey, who am I to deny your fantasies..."

I took two steps toward her, and then she poked me hard in the ribs.

It would have hurt, had I been a man of smaller means. As it was, I laughed, which made her wind up like she was going to sock me in the jaw. I caught her fist, holding it in my hand as I backed her into the sink.

"*What* are you doing here?!" she seethed, shaking free of my hold. She kept a hand on my chest, forcing a foot between us.

"I thought it was quite obvious."

"You," she said, poking me in the chest with one long nail. "Are such a prick. I am on a *date*, Vince. Go to your table and leave us alone."

"Is this you trying to *prove it*, as you so eloquently stated yesterday?"

"It's not me *trying* to do anything. I am dating. Other people — not you."

I inhaled a stiff breath, the muscle in my jaw locking at that statement. I stared back at her, my fire-breathing girl, but then my eyes were traveling down again.

"I'm sorry," I said. "Could you repeat that? Because I'm having a hard time focusing with you in this fucking dress."

Maven flushed, but then let out an, "Ugh!" She pressed into my space, the universe answering my prayers as she did. "You're exhausting."

"Oh, so *that's* it. It all makes sense now."

She frowned, confused.

"You're tired," I said. "That's why you can't open your eyes and see the truth."

"What truth?"

"That I want you," I said, and I pressed right back, my hands finding her hips and pinning her to the bathroom sink. Even then, I pushed in farther, my nose centimeters from hers. "I want you so badly, Maven. I *like* you, goddamnit."

She swallowed, attempting to wriggle free, but I held her tighter.

"No," I said, shaking my head as my forehead fell to hers. "Don't. Don't make a joke. Don't deny it. You want me, too."

She turned her face, my lips falling against her temple as she swallowed again and looked away from me.

"Admit it," I pleaded.

A long pause settled between us, the air charged, waiting for one tiny spark that would engulf us both in flames.

"You're a playboy, Vince," she breathed, just a whisper, but the words struck me as if she'd yelled them. I pulled back, and her eyes found mine. "You only want me because I haven't let you have me."

I shook my head, brows folding together. "You... you don't honestly believe that." I laughed, sure it was a joke. When she didn't prod me further, that smile fell, my throat tight. "Tell me you don't see me that way."

But she didn't.

She didn't answer at all.

Her eyes flickered down to her shoes, and she kept her gaze there as I slowly backed away, releasing her.

This was the persona, the one I played into with everyone else. But with her? I'd let her in. I'd shown her parts of me the rest of the world had never seen before. I was nothing but honest with her, right from the start.

I let her see me.

And yet all she saw was a player.

I nodded. Again and again, laughing a little as I scrubbed a hand over my mouth.

And then I left.

The bathroom, the restaurant, and her.

Chapter 22

No One But Me

Maven

I bailed on my date before he had the chance to order dessert.

My emotions were so tangled up I could barely hold down what I *had* eaten, let alone consume anything more. So, with a polite kiss on the cheek and a hug, I parted ways with Damon and headed home.

Home.

That made me laugh.

The fully furnished condo I was staying in with giant windows, a sweeping city landscape, and a bed far too big for only me could hardly be considered home. It was my clothes in the provided dresser, and my toiletries in the bathroom, and my usual food in the fridge. But it wasn't my small bungalow near the beach. It wasn't my garden or my macramé wall art or my compost ready to be put to good use.

Still, it did bring me a small comfort, and I sighed when I kicked my heels off once I was inside.

I poured a glass of wine, which I wasn't entirely sure I wouldn't regret in the morning. We had a game the next day, and that meant I'd be up early reporting on all of it. My head was already pounding from the night's events.

But not as much as my heart.

What was even happening?

I sank into one of the leather armchairs in my living room, crossing my legs and attempting to relax. But I didn't sit there for more than sixty seconds before my thoughts started whirring, and I couldn't make sense of a single one of them.

I wanted to feel victorious, to bask in the glow of having succeeded in what I'd had planned for the evening.

But the look on Vince's face, the way he'd tongued his cheek and nodded like I'd disappointed him...

It left me feeling sick.

Before I knew it, I was up and out of the room, out of my new home, taking the elevator up a few floors and walking barefoot down the hall to Vince's door.

I knocked hard three times, knocking again when he didn't immediately answer. I didn't even know what I was doing. I didn't know what I would say. Did I still want to fight? Did I want to apologize?

Did I want to *fuck*?

I knocked again.

When he didn't answer, and it was suspiciously quiet inside, my heart leapt into my throat. I immediately wondered if he'd gone out, found someone, and gone home with her.

Then, I immediately chastised myself for caring, because the whole point of tonight was to cement how *not his* I was, and yet...

"He's at the gym."

I jumped at the unexpected voice, a little scream slipping from my lips. When I turned and found Jaxson at the opposite end of the hall, I sighed.

"Jesus, you scared me. You live here, too?"

"Nah, just dropped something off at Carter's," he explained. Then, he repeated his earlier sentiment. "Vince went to the gym, the team one at the arena. Third floor."

I nodded, swallowing. "Is he okay?"

"Why wouldn't he be?"

Jaxson arched a brow, giving me a pointed look like he wanted me to confess something. When I didn't, he saluted me before disappearing inside the elevator.

I still didn't know what I was doing as I went back to my place, threw on a pair of sneakers, and headed for the lobby. Those Nikes looked ridiculous with the dress I was wearing and my full face of makeup, hair blown out and styled, but I didn't care.

I also wasn't thinking straight, as evident by the fact that I was on my way to the arena in the middle of the night to find the guy I had worked so hard to get off my ass in the first place.

The walk was quick, the arena just a couple blocks from the condominium. It was dark and quiet at the arena when I arrived, and I was surprised when the key card they'd given me allowed me access in at all. It was almost eerie, walking through there with just a few lights on. There was someone cleaning the floors, and they nodded at me as I passed, but didn't bother to ask who I was or why I was there. I guess they assumed that if I had a key to get in, it was fine.

My hands shook as I took the elevator up to the third floor, which was where the executive suite was. I wandered around a bit aimlessly before I finally made my way to the team gym, and when I did, I stopped, watching Vince through the window.

He was the only one in there. Hell, we had to be two of only a handful of people here at this hour. There were no concerts tonight, no events at all, and it was damn near midnight.

For a moment, I let myself watch him, taking in the gleaming muscles of his back as he pedaled on the bike. His powerful thighs worked as hard as they did on the ice, his arms flexing where they held the handlebars. He was an absolute machine — steadfast and focused.

He was dripping in sweat, watching himself in the mirror like he hated the person he saw.

Then, those eyes flicked to me.

I swallowed, using my key card and again surprised that it granted me access to join him. He didn't slow his pace, though. Just kept his eyes on the mirror and pedaled even faster.

He wasn't wearing headphones, and the gym was completely quiet, save for the sound of his labored breaths and the whir of the bike.

"I didn't know the team gym was open twenty-four seven," I said in way of greeting, folding my arms and looking around at all the equipment. I remembered spending his first day off here, watching him go through his routine with the rest of the guys before working on recovery.

Vince ignored me.

"I'm surprised to find you here, especially the night before a game," I continued. "Figured you'd be resting."

His watch made a buzzing noise, and he slowed his pace, sitting upright and hitting a button on the side of it. Then, he grabbed the white towel hanging over the bars and mopped the sweat off his face.

He still didn't say a word.

I moved closer. "Look, about earlier..." I paused, because I didn't know exactly what I wanted to say. "I... I'm sorry, okay? If I..." I laughed a little before finishing that sentence with *hurt your feelings*, because I was certain Vince Tanev didn't have the capability of having his feelings hurt.

He slowed all the way to a stop, hopping off the bike and draping the white towel around his neck. He grabbed a wipe next, cleaning the bike seat.

Then, he strode right past me on the way toward the exit.

A voice in the back of my mind told me I should apologize. No, it urged me to *grovel*, to admit I was wrong and immature for playing whatever stupid game I had been playing at the restaurant. I shouldn't have said what I'd said.

But I did, because I had to. I *needed* to. It was the only way to protect myself.

Everything was such a mess inside me, two opposing forces battling for dominance. On the one hand, I wanted to give in, to throw myself at this man's feet. On the other, I wanted to fight.

It was that urge that won out.

"Wow," I said, turning to face him and watch him go. "Cool. So this is how it's going to be now? I turn you down, so you give me the silent treatment?"

He paused then, and I noted how his fingers rolled into fists at his sides, those back muscles still rippling in the low light of the gym. Only one light was on overhead, and it bathed him in menacing shadows, highlighting the cuts in his body even more.

It was psychotic, how much I loved that I'd made him stop with those words, how much I got off on knowing I had the power to make his fists clench.

"I said I'm sorry," I repeated.

He cracked his neck.

"Well, that's *real* mature, Vince," I said, tonguing my cheek on a laugh when he didn't respond. "I'm so glad we're both adults. I'm so glad—"

My next words were sucked out of the room, along with all the oxygen in it, because Vince spun on his heel and charged toward me. My heart lodged in my throat, eyes wide as I took in the snarl on his lips, the furrow of his brows.

He was a man on the edge, and I'd just shoved him over.

But I wasn't scared.

I stood there, not moving, waiting for him to wash over me like a barrel wave that would take me down to a world I'd never known. My chest heaved with my next breath, and in four long strides, he invaded every inch of my space.

Every inch of *me*.

He sucked in a harsh breath through his nose as his hand reached out for me, snatching my chin just like he had that day in Boston. His eyes flared when I didn't pull away, when I leaned into the touch, pushing until I was sure his fingers would bruise me.

I held his stare, both of us breathing hard and shallow as he squeezed my jaw and tilted my head even higher.

It was just the permission he was looking for.

"I've had enough of that fucking mouth of yours," he husked.

And then he kissed me.

We both inhaled a fiery breath the moment his lips crashed down onto mine, and he held me there like he was afraid I'd pull away. But I didn't. I *couldn't.*

I pressed up onto my toes, threading my hands into his hair and twisting the strands between my fingertips – tugging, pulling, demanding more.

Vince released his grip on my jaw, reaching down to palm my ass, instead. He lifted me, pulling me into his massive arms as my legs wrapped eagerly around his waist.

We were on the move then, his mouth still devouring mine until my back slammed against the wall.

No, not the wall.

The mirror.

"This fucking mouth," he breathed, biting my lip until I winced. As soon as he released it, I was kissing him again, asking for another lashing. "This fucking *dress,"* he said, his hands fisting in the velvet fabric at my hips. He nudged my chin with his nose at the same time, giving me no choice but to let my head fall back as his lips descended on my neck.

His hands gripped my hips while he wedged himself between my thighs, and he ran his tongue up my neck and along my jaw before sucking my earlobe between his teeth.

"You have me so fucked up, Maven. Every waking hour, every waking *minute* of my life is wrecked by thoughts of you."

I whimpered as his hand slid under the hem of my dress with those words, and he teased the line of my lace panties, running one fingertip along the edges that hugged my inner thighs. I spread wider, wanting him to cross that fabric boundary.

"You are so deep-seated in my mind, in my *being*. I will never be rid of you."

That made my heart stop, my anxiety trying to snake its way in. I pressed my hand to his chest, making him look at me, ashamed of the weakness in my voice even before I spoke.

"Even once you've had me?"

His eyes danced under those bent brows of his — one scarred, one perfect — and he dropped his forehead to mine on a long sigh.

"Especially then," he breathed against my lips.

For a moment, I thought he was second-guessing, thought he might pull away and put my feet back on the ground, help me right my dress, and tell me we shouldn't.

So, before he could, I grabbed him by the back of his neck and pulled him into me again.

"Then I guess we're both fucked," I said, and I licked his lip until he opened his mouth and let me in.

He kissed me on another deep inhale, smothering the curse and any resolve I had left to fight the chemistry between us. Even if it was just once, even if this was all we had — I wanted it.

It was all-consuming, that kiss — his hands completely destroying my blowout, his mouth completely destroying my lipstick.

Him, completely destroying *me*.

He wrapped me up in his arms, holding me to him as my back left the mirror. He held all of my weight then, and he kissed me every step of the way until dropping me carefully onto a weight bench. I didn't have a chance in hell of catching my breath when he released the kiss, and as soon as he did, he yanked my hips until my ass was hanging over the edge of the bench, my body in a tilted, awkward angle.

My hands flew up to grip the first thing they could find — a cold barbell — and then Vince smacked the outside of my thigh.

"Lift," he commanded.

I pressed weight into my heels on the floor, just enough for my ass to rise off the bench. Vince shoved my dress up to my rib cage, wetting his lips at the sight of my thong before he hooked his thumbs in the band of it.

"Let me see you," he said, slowly peeling the fabric down over my thighs. As soon as it was past my ass, I sat down again, and I had no choice but to lift my legs and let him peel it the rest of the way off.

When my panties were tossed somewhere behind him, I tried to put my legs back down, but he clamped his hands over them and held them up — ankles wrapped together in one of his hands, legs fused together, my bare pussy framed by the swells of my ass propped on the edge of the bench.

"Fuck *me*, this is a beautiful sight." He quirked his scarred brow at my sneakers next, laughing a little as he popped one off and then the other.

"Don't judge," I breathed.

"Pet, the only thing I'm judging right now is how fucking soaked you are," he said, kissing the inside of my ankle once he had my socks discarded. "Stubborn girl. How long have you been this wet for me?"

I ripped out of his hold, pressing my toes into his chest. "Don't call me pet."

"You like it."

I tilted my chin in defiance, but couldn't fucking deny it — so I kept my mouth shut.

Vince smirked in victory, and then he grabbed one of my ankles in each hand and slowly, *painfully* slowly, opened me.

His eyes drank me in as he spread my legs, and he stared at where I knew I was glistening for him before he dropped to his knees in front of me. He placed one of my feet on the bench, the other on the floor, and then he hooked my hips and tugged me even closer, my hands holding the bar now working overtime to keep from falling on top of him.

He seemed to notice because he nodded at that bar with a wicked grin. "Hold tight," he said, and then he descended.

It was a slow, teasing torture — his lips kissing up my thigh that was propped on the bench. He flicked his tongue over my clit just once before he was kissing down the other thigh, and I squirmed, gripping the bar so hard I wondered if I'd callous.

Vince Tanev was on his fucking knees for me.

There was no thought more erotic than that one.

Just when I thought I'd combust from him kissing and licking and nipping at all the skin *around* where I really wanted him, he wrapped his arms up and under my thighs, holding the weight of me before burying his face.

His tongue covered me, hot and wet and with the perfect pressure to make me tremble beneath the touch.

"Oh, *fuck*," I cried, trying to sit my ass back on the bench so I could spread wider for him. But he kept me up, kept me shaking and holding on for dear life as he worked. My heart was pounding, the reality of the moment stealing my breath. Somewhere in the back of my mind I knew it was a bad idea, that I wasn't being professional, that this would all blow up in my face.

I couldn't find it in me to stop. I *never* wanted him to stop.

"Jesus, Maven," he breathed against me, swirling his tongue over my clit before sucking it between his teeth. I bucked my hips, and he did it again, and again, finding the rhythm to drive me toward an orgasm. "So fucking sweet. So fucking *you*."

"God." In a feat of strength, I held onto the bar with one hand, and the other jutted out for his hair, guiding him where I wanted him.

And then all contact was lost.

My ass dropped to the bench, and Vince grabbed my hand, guiding it back to the bar.

"I said *hold tight*," he reminded me, and then he kissed me hard, his mouth wet with my pleasure before he crawled down my body again. And he moved even slower this time, taking the opportunity to forcefully tug at the top of my dress until my modest breasts spilled over the top of it.

He licked his lips, my taste there, like he was savoring every sip of me as he palmed my swells and rolled his thumbs over my nipples.

"I knew you had pretty tits even before I felt you that night in the hot tub," he said, shaking his head in awe as he took in the sight of me. And what a sight it had to be — my dress shoved up over my hips, pussy wet and spread open, breasts spilling out, hair mussed, lipstick smudged. "But *fuck*, my imagination was so far off. These," he said, squeezing me before he leaned down to circle one of my nipples with his tongue. "Are *perfect*."

"Vince," I breathed.

"Mm? Is there something you need, *pet*?"

I glared at him, but before I could press my toes into his chest and kick him away, he snatched my ankle, spreading me wide.

"You need only say it," he teased, a challenge in his eyes as he held me like that.

I was tempted to kick out of his grasp, but instead, I leaned up a bit, enough to stare down at him when I said, "Eat. Me."

He grinned. "With pleasure."

He didn't delay this time. He enveloped me — wrapping my thighs in his arms again, balancing me in the air as my grip tightened on the bar. His mouth was ravenous, his tongue that of an expert, sliding up and down and *in* me. He used the tip of it to flick my clit in a quick, merciless motion, holding me to him when I tried to back out.

"*Ohhhh fuuucckkk,*" I cried, my legs trembling so hard it hurt. It was like having a full body spasm, but I pushed and stretched and opened, reaching, holding tight.

And then I let go.

It struck me only then that we were in a public place, when my cries rang out in that gym and echoed off the walls. I hoped the people who *were* still in the building weren't on the third floor, and I *really* hoped there weren't cameras in this gym.

Those thoughts lingered only a second, though, because the orgasm was so powerful, it eradicated everything else from my brain. I was lost in that moment, that climax, the waves after waves of pleasure that rolled through me and made my toes curl — all courtesy of Tampa's hotshot rookie.

When I was spent, I let out a short burst of a breath, collapsing onto the bench. My hands were red and raw when I released them from the bar, my legs still quivering.

Vince smiled against my pussy, kissing it lightly before crawling up to kiss my mouth.

"Cameras," I breathed.

"I already took care of it."

I blinked. "How?"

He nodded toward the top right-hand corner of the room. To my horror, there *was* a camera, but his t-shirt was thrown over it, blocking the lens.

"I didn't want to get reamed by coach for working out the night before a game," he explained.

"Audio?"

"None," he promised. He captured my mouth again with a long, slow kiss. "No one gets my girl like this. No one but me."

Those words unraveled me, sending any paranoia I had skittering away. I tried not to overanalyze, not to latch onto the way his lips curved when he said *my girl*. I knew as well as he did that this was just one night. It was giving in to the fire between us that refused not to burn. It was fighting and fucking because that's what we were meant to do, from the moment we met.

All thoughts were wiped clean when he grabbed my wrists and pulled me to stand, his eyes skating over every inch of my skin.

"You should see yourself right now," he said, biting his lip.

And then, like a lightbulb went off, a little smile curled on his lips, his eyes wide.

He tugged me away from the bench, stealing another kiss, and then he grabbed my hips and spun me around.

Until I was looking at myself, at *us*, in the mirror.

Chapter 23

Look at You

Vince

This is it.

That was all I could think as I stood behind Maven in that gym, the light from above painting her in a masterpiece of shadows, me holding her hips and watching her eyes widen at the sight of herself, at what I'd done to her.

This was it for me.

This was the peak of my life — this view, this girl, this fucking dress.

"Look at you," I said, leaning down so those words could caress the skin at the back of her neck. I grabbed her wrists, holding them up to spread her wingspan, and then I trailed my fingertips along her arms.

One of my hands dove down, palming her breast where it swelled over her dress. My other hand rose up, gliding along her collarbone before I wrapped it gently around her throat.

Her lips parted, head falling back a bit as if to offer me better access. So I grabbed her jaw next, tilting her even farther back, until her head was against my chest and those pretty doe eyes were looking up at me.

My bottom hand slid lower, over her velvet dress, down to where she was dripping from between her legs.

"You're going to watch while I fuck you for the first time," I said, kissing her hair.

"You say that like there will be a second."

She quipped it so fast it shocked me, and for a moment I just stared down at her. Then, I blinked on a laugh that ripped from my throat.

"Baby, *believe me* when I say there will be a second," I said, rubbing my palm over her clit. She shook in my arms as I did, and then I lifted my hand just a little, enough to slap her pussy with enough bite to make her moan. "And a third, and a fourth, and so on, and so forth until this pussy molds to my exact shape, it's so sure it belongs only to me."

Maven moaned, and then I grabbed her arms and pinned them behind her back, her dainty wrists caught in my grip. I held her there with one hand as the other struggled with my shorts, edging them down one side at a time until they were at my ankles along with my briefs.

And that's when it hit me.

"Fuck," I cursed, forehead falling forward to rest against her hair. "I don't have a condom."

Maven stilled, a long stretch of time and disappointment passing between us.

"I have an IUD," she said, quietly, as if she wasn't quite sure what those words meant in this context. "Are you... um... do you have any..."

"I was just tested at camp," I told her. "And I haven't fucked anyone since."

That seemed to surprise her.

I didn't want to ask the same of her, but my mom had given me too many talks about safe sex for me not to. "Maven," I said, her eyes fluttering shut at the sound of her name as my hand slid between her legs to cup her. "Tell me you're tested, too. *Please*, tell me I can fill this needy cunt the way I want to."

"Yes."

The word might as well have been a prison sentence and a freedom flag all at once. I slid one finger inside her from where I was cupping between her legs from behind, and she mewled, bucking into the touch.

I withdrew just as quickly.

With one hand at the crook of her hip, that velvet fabric of her dress resting on my wrist, I placed myself at her entrance, gliding my cock up and down her wet seam until I was coated.

I wedged myself inside just half an inch, both of us hissing at the feel of it.

Then, I hooked my hands around her elbows, holding her arms back and her chest puffed until she had no choice but to look at me in the mirror.

"Watch," I commanded.

And I slid it home.

The room shrank as I did, the air suffocating, neither of us able to breathe until I was all the way in. Everything snapped back at once then, and Maven shook in my grasp, her knees buckling, eyes fluttering shut.

"Come on, baby," I coached, kissing her hair. "Watch as I fuck you."

She peeled her lids open, her eyes connecting with mine in the mirror. She was so wet from my mouth, from her climax, that she stretched open for me with just that flex of my hips. I slowly pulled out, watching her as I did, and then pressed back in again, finding more depth.

It was me who closed my eyes this time.

My head lolled back, and I bit my bottom lip on a curse before I looked in the mirror again.

Maven just smirked, hinging at the waist, allowing me better access to drive it in.

My first strokes were slow, calculated, like I was pushing reps in the gym. Withdrawing for four breaths, pressing in for one, holding for two, and then repeating again. And the whole time I was torn between watching Maven's ecstasy in the mirror, or where her ass rippled every time my hips slammed into her.

I wanted to savor it, every second, committing the whole thing to memory. I wanted it tattooed on me.

I wanted her in my fucking bloodstream.

Slowly, I picked up my pace, kissing her neck and shoulder and jaw as I held her arms behind her. My mouth was on her neck when I glanced in the mirror and saw her eyes closed, her lips open in a moan, her tits bouncing wildly where they were shoved up and over the top of her dress.

"Eyes on me, baby," I said, nipping at her neck.

She seemed drugged as she forced her head up, her gaze toward me, and when those heavy golden eyes locked on mine, I pumped faster, harder, never breaking our stare.

I released one of her arms, my free hand scooping up under her thigh and lifting one leg. I held her steady, stretched her open, and sucked on her earlobe before saying, "Again. Play with that pussy until you come again."

She whimpered like she wasn't sure she could, but then her hand dove down, nudging her dress out of the way so she had access to her clit. She circled it slow at first with just a couple fingers, and I slowed my pace to match hers. But when those two fingers turned into her whole hand, when she was bucking and trembling and circling her palm quickly over that sensitive part of her, I railed her, letting out a long, slow curse as I came.

I groaned with the first release, and Maven was right on my heels, crying out as she found her second orgasm. She was melting into me, and I took her weight even as my body convulsed and shook with her. It was so fucking good, so fucking *us* — hot and angry and unpredictable.

"Yes, baby," I moaned, filling her again and again. I could feel my cum dripping out of her already. "Just like that."

She cried out, bouncing against me, riding out the last of her climax until we were a trembling, filthy mess. Sweat slicked our skin, and our breaths were still haggard and harsh as I carefully set her foot back down on the ground, releasing her arm, both of us wincing from how we'd been tangled up now that the rush had passed.

"Jesus. Fucking. Christ," she panted between breaths, and she turned to face me, leaning her back against the mirror.

She smiled.

I smiled.

And then she laughed, shaking her head as she started to right herself.

"I told you."

"Told me what?" she asked, attitude present as ever as she tucked her tits back into her dress.

"That I'd have you in my bed soon."

She looked around with an arched brow. "I didn't realize you slept in the weight room."

I bit my lip before letting a growl out, laughing a little as I pinned her. "Smart ass," I said, and then I kissed her smile.

"Vince, wait," she said, pressing a hand to my chest. She looked at that hand, then up at me. "This... this can't happen again. I know we have this... this *thing* between us, and that was... *so* hot. But it was just once. Just to scratch an itch."

"Scratch an itch," I repeated.

She nodded, brows tugging inward.

"What happened to what you asked me?"

"I don't know what you mean."

"You asked if I'd feel the same, even after having you," I said. "Why would you ask that if this was just to *scratch an itch*?"

She swallowed, her eyes flicking between mine before she stared at where her hand still pressed into my chest and held me at a distance.

"It was a one-time thing," she murmured again.

"Uh-huh."

"I mean it."

I wanted to ask her why again. *Why* was this a one-time thing? *Why* "couldn't we," as she had put it? What was she hiding?

What was she so damn afraid of?

But I knew, even then, with her looking me dead in the eyes and saying that this was it — she was a damn liar.

This wasn't it.

Not even close.

So, I humored her, stepping back and giving her space.

Because if there was anything I loved more than fucking Maven King, it was proving her wrong.

"Fine," I said.

Then, I crossed the room, bending to retrieve her panties. I walked back to her just as she was sliding her dress down over her hips.

"Put these on," I said.

"I was going to—"

"No," I said, cutting her off. Her finger was pointed toward the bathroom, and I pulled that fingertip to my lips and kissed it before draping her panties over the knuckle. "You're not allowed to clean up yet."

"Not *allowed*—"

"Put these on, and walk home with my cum dripping out of you. I want you to feel a reminder of what just happened with every fucking step."

Her lips parted, eyes wide.

I didn't say another word.

I waited, ready for her to fight me, for her to say I was disgusting and I didn't own her, that I couldn't tell her what to do.

Satisfaction buzzed deep in my being when she didn't do any of that. Instead, she slid the thong on, showing me more than her words that this was far from over.

Once her dress was in place again, I pressed her against the mirror, running the pad of my thumb over her bottom lip.

"I promise... the next time I touch you?" I hooked my thumb over her bottom teeth, swiping her tongue and prying her mouth open. "You'll be begging me to."

I sealed that promise with a bruising kiss, and then I released her, turning my back and pulling on my briefs and shorts. I grabbed a wipe and ran it over the bench, too, because I wasn't a monster.

That made Maven laugh.

"Where are you going?" she asked when I was heading for the door.

I turned, walking backward as I shrugged and offered one last smile. "Gotta take care of that tape."

I nodded toward the camera in the corner that was still covered by my shirt, and Maven's little mouth popped open, eyes bulging.

"I thought you said there was no audio!"

"You're not the only one who's a good liar."

The laugh that rumbled out of my chest was almost as satisfying as the dumbstruck look on her face.

"Vince! Do *not* keep that tape."

I held up two fingers. "Scout's honor."

"I mean it. You better destroy it."

I just laughed again as I kicked the door open and made my way toward security.

We both knew there was no chance in *hell* I'd be doing that.

Chapter 24

Roller Coaster

Maven

The next week passed in a dizzying blur.

I'd been in a daze the morning after my night with Vince, waking up with a cacophony of questions and thoughts screaming at me all at the same time.

What the fuck happened last night?

Oh my God... what the fuck happened *last night?*

That was a mistake.

That was the hottest experience of my life.

It can never happen again.

I can't wait *for that to happen again.*

I need to talk to Livia about it.

I shouldn't tell anyone it happened.

It was just for fun.

It was more than just a little fun.

At some point I let out a scream, stalking to the shower to scrub off the night and the memory and all the questions that paraded on the heels of it.

So what, we'd had sex. So *what*, it had been the best sex of my life by far.

I was a professional, and he was my client, for all intents and purposes. He was *also* a professional, and it would all be fine. We'd made an agreement that it was one time and one time only.

I only half-believed that as I made my way to his condo, feeling like I was doing the walk of shame even though I was showered and refreshed, and no one knew Vince had had my ass hanging off a weight bench while he ate my pussy last night.

I wondered if he'd smirk at me all knowingly when he saw me, if he'd tease me about the noises I'd made, or how embarrassingly wet I'd been for him.

But when Vince opened his door, he just offered me a polite *good morning* before letting me inside, and his pregame rituals got underway. We went to the morning skate, he retired for his nap, we had fettuccini alfredo together, I posted a video mashup of him doing his pushups and turning on his closet light and calling his sister for their traditional dance.

And all the while, he didn't say a word about the night before.

Sadly, we lost the game at home that night, ending the hot streak we'd been on. Vince had scored, but a nasty fight had broken out between the teams that seemed to tip the momentum into the hands of our New York opponents. They scored twice, back to back, leaving our fans going home as disappointed as the team was.

After that, the week just sort of... happened.

The *One Month with Vince Tanev* account had grown into a feeding frenzy. As soon as I posted a story, it was screenshotted or recorded and shared on other accounts, everyone thirsty for more content. My messages were so insane, there was no prayer of keeping up, and I couldn't post a photo or video without it having thousands of likes in mere seconds.

When the account broke one-million followers, Reya and Camilla gave me a generous bonus.

And an extension.

One Month with Vince Tanev was now just *Rookie Season with Vince Tanev*. The Ospreys' GM was so thrilled with how tickets were selling and all the coverage, that he wanted me there at least through the holiday season, and my bosses agreed.

It was business as usual.

I spent my days and nights with the team, almost feeling like I had always been a part of it. And though I worried it would, Vince's demeanor didn't change. He made his snarky little remarks and smiled in victory when he managed to make my skin heat. He tested out a few new pet names – *darling, sunshine, sweetheart* – all of which were shot down by a smack or glare from me.

Things weren't weird, and he also didn't push me, didn't press for another night together.

Which was exactly what I had asked him for.

So *why* was I perturbed by it?

I felt like a toy that had been wound up tightly and then bound in rubber bands. I was ready to go, all this pent-up energy crackling beneath my skin, but I was stuck, unable to release any of it.

I masturbated more in that week than I had in the last year, even going so far as to buy a toy.

Each and every time, I thought of Vince, which only pissed me off.

After that picture he posted of us, the Internet had been buzzing with rumors. Camilla and Reya loved it, but they didn't read the comments that streamed in under every post, or the messages that plugged my inbox.

You're too ugly for Vince.

What does he even see in you?

You only got this job because he wants to have sex with you.

How big is his cock, Maven?

When he's done with you, send him to me.

Whore.

Slut.

Puck bunny.

No one wants to see you. This is about hockey, not some romance fantasy.

I tried to ignore them, and when Vince was asked about us in interviews — which wasn't often, but enough to make me grind my teeth each time — he would always laugh and politely defer. He spoke highly of me, saying I was a professional and I was good at my job, that the team loved having me around, but that there was nothing romantic between us or me and anyone else on the roster.

The first time he said it, that there was nothing between us, I'd felt queasy.

Even though it was what I wanted him to say.

... Right?

I was a damn mess.

Livia told me as much the night before I traveled with the team to Atlanta, me sprawled on her couch while she steamed one of her dresses.

"You're a damn mess."

I sighed.

"You like him. And he clearly likes you. Stop being a dumdum."

"He's fun, sure," I conceded. "We have a good time together. But I don't *like* him. And he doesn't like me. He just wants to get me naked."

She leveled me with a look, hanging one hand on her hip. "Bitch."

I held up my hand to stop her. "I can't like him, Livia."

That made her pause, her brows folding together.

"I *can't*," I said again, throat thick. "I get hives just thinking about it."

My best friend watched me for a long moment before she put her steamer down and sat beside me on her couch. "Can you walk me through why you feel this way?"

My eyes welled, and I laughed at myself, thumbing a tear away before it had the chance to fall. "I can try."

Livia was quiet, patient, waiting for me to try to find the words to explain it. I kept coming up empty. How did you explain how someone left such a permanent mark on you?

I loved James. For nearly two years, he was my everything. I saw a future with him. We were building that future together. I believed him when he told me I was enough, that we were going to go the distance. I believed him when he said we were going to get married, that I'd bear his last name and, one day, his children. I'd built up a whole future in my head, one that felt so solid and sure.

And then he discarded me like an old golf club.

All it took was one event for him to feel ashamed of me, to go from viewing our differences as something beautiful to something insurmountable. He was the first person to make me second-guess my gut instinct, the first person I trusted who proved I was wrong for doing so.

When I was with Vince, when he opened up to me, when he asked me about what made me... *me*... it was terrifying.

Because I wanted to trust him. I wanted to spend my time with him. I wanted him to look at me, to touch me, to say I was his girl — even though I screamed at him when he actually did that.

But I knew, deep down in my gut, that we were from two different worlds.

And I knew even if I *wanted* to trust him, I shouldn't.

After a long pause, I tried to explain it to my best friend. "I guess the best way I know how to put it is that it's like if you were at a theme park, right? And you've heard terror stories about the roller coaster — how scary it is, how high it goes, all the loops. But you've also heard it's *amazing*. And you're an optimist, you're a believer in good things happening to good people. So, you decide you're going to take a chance, you're going to ride the roller coaster.

"Your stomach is in knots as you wait in line, and when they strap you in, they look you right in the eyes and say, *you're safe*.

"So, you throw your hands up, you laugh and feel the pure joy and excitement of riding that first slow incline up. You keep your hands there, and you revel in the joy of the first drop, the notion that you really *are* safe."

I swallowed.

"Only for the seatbelt to break, and for you to fly out at the first loop, being tossed to the ground like a rag doll."

I laughed a little through my nose, shaking my head.

"You end up maimed, physically and mentally, forever changed. And it doesn't matter if it was a fluke accident, if the odds of it happening again are slim to none. Your body, your brain — they won't let you take that chance. Any time you even *think* about it, you tremble. When you get close to it, you panic. You don't even realize it, but you're in survival mode, your instincts doing everything they can to protect you." I looked Livia right in the eyes then. "You aren't getting on another roller coaster again. You just... *can't*."

She rolled her lips together, nodding. "That was some powerful shit."

"Maybe I should be an actress."

"Nah, you're too nasally."

I laughed through the threat of tears, sniffing.

"Okay," she conceded after a moment, her brows furrowed in thought. "What if you played within the safety net? What if it didn't have to be serious? Maybe you don't ride the roller coaster, but you still go to the theme park. You know — hang out on the spinning teacups, get your thrills on the water rides, eat too much cotton candy, stay late for the fireworks."

I laughed. "Okay, I know this is my analogy, but you lost me."

"Let him rock your world," she said, leaning in and patting my leg. "Get your kicks, girl. You deserve them. And you need them, if I'm being honest. I can smell your sex-deprived desperation from here."

I smacked her as we both laughed.

"That is a dangerous game to play," I told her. "The *friends with benefits* route."

"Could be fun, though."

I chewed on her suggestion for a moment, but not long enough to actually consider it before I was waving her off. "Look, Vince and I are fine. We scratched the itch and got it out of our system. And now things are back to normal."

"Normal," she repeated, arching a brow. "Which is what, exactly, when it comes to you two? Because I'm pretty sure he's been undressing you with those sexy eyes of his since that first night at the gala."

"Maybe, but he's seen the goods now. He'll lose interest. He's got a hundred girls throwing themselves into his lap every day. And we're professionals."

Livia pursed her lips. "Uh-huh."

"I need to get going, long day tomorrow." I popped off her couch. "Thank you for celebrating with me."

"Hey, Reya and Camilla extending your assignment through the Christmas holiday is a pretty big deal." She stood, too, grabbing my hand. "*You* are a big deal, my friend. Don't forget that."

I squeezed where she held me. "Thank you. I... I think I could actually see myself doing this for real, Liv. I love it. I'm *good* at it. Maybe this is just the start."

"You can do anything you want to do. I've always told you that."

"Best friend obligations."

She pinched me. "It's the truth. I just can't wait to see what you do next."

That made two of us.

Chapter 25

If I Didn't Know Better

Maven

We were losing.

The crowd in Atlanta was vicious, their chants callous and loud as we fell behind by another point. It was four-to-one, our guys making a poor showing, and every single member of the team was wearing their emotions on their sleeves.

I stood behind the bench, phone in my pocket with absolutely no desire to film what was happening now. Coach McCabe stood beside me, arms folded over his chest, brows bent and lips in a firm line. He was pissed, but underneath it, I could see the worry winning out.

This wasn't his team, and he knew it.

I heard him mutter something under his breath as the guys battled for the puck by where Will was defending our net. Carter managed to dig it free, and then he was skating down the ice, and Vince was flying out ahead of him, his focus on getting in position to score.

"Yes! Go, go, go!"

I didn't realize the words had come from *me* until Coach glanced over at me with a smirk before his attention was back on the puck. I chewed my thumbnail as Coach called out instruction, trying to make a play happen. The puck went back and forth, around the back of the net, down to the middle of the ice before they were back in the offensive zone.

I held my breath the entire time, visualizing the puck going into the net.

"Come on, come on," I chanted quietly.

The guys kept the puck moving, Carter making an attempt that was batted away by one of the opposing defensemen. Vince swooped in, and I saw with the rest of the crowd that he had a wide-open shot.

Before he could take it, an Atlanta player skated up quickly and pummeled him right in the face with a high stick.

The sickening *crack* of contact echoed through the rink, and Vince went down to the ice, curled into a fetal position and writhing in pain.

My heart stopped in my chest, ears ringing, everything happening in slow motion as Coach tried to keep the guys from clearing the bench. The Ospreys players who were already on the ice were taking off gloves and helmets, everyone ready to fight as Carter helped Vince stand.

Fists flew. Whistles blew repeatedly. The crowd roared, encouraging the fights.

But all I could do was stare at Vince.

He was bleeding, the skin between his nose and cheek bone split wide open. The sight of it made me woozy, and I planted a hand on the glass behind me to hold me steady.

"Vince!" I cried out, embarrassingly, but he didn't seem fazed at all. He wiped his glove over his cheek, brow arching a bit when he saw the blood smeared, like he was impressed at the hit.

The referees broke up the various fights on the ice as Carter helped Vince skate back to the bench. He hopped the boards, and his eyes caught mine as the trainers immediately tugged him back toward the locker room.

I must have been wearing my concern like a neon vest, because he pulled to a stop right in front of me. He smirked, his face already swelling, the blood leaking down into his teeth.

"Hey, I'm good," he said, pulling off a glove. He tapped my chin with his knuckles. "I'm good."

I thought I nodded, thought the next breath came maybe a little bit easier. Then he was being toted back to the locker room, and I allowed myself one full inhale and exhale before following.

Vince

Maven was like a fretting mama bird, the way her brows pinched together as she held ice to my cheek after the game. I'd been cleared by the medical staff, no stitches needed — but it was too late. By that time, we'd already lost the game, not even scoring during the power play my injury provided us.

The loss stung worse than the cut that was currently numb, thanks to all the ice I'd had on it.

But as much as I was pissed over the game, I didn't mind the current view — Maven in her sweatpants and a hoodie four-times too big for her, her hair wrapped in silk, eyes wide and concerned as she took in where my face was swollen and bruising.

"If I didn't know better, I'd say you might be worried about me, Maven King."

She flinched like I'd screamed, like she'd been lost in her own world. Then, she sighed, finally taking the ice off my face. She looked down at where she held the bag in her hands, trying to force a smile.

"More like concerned for the stick you broke."

I smiled, too — mostly at the fact that it was so difficult for her to even joke like she wasn't upset. I liked that thought, that she worried about me being okay.

It had been hell, pretending like everything was normal between us since the night in the gym. Behind hockey, there was nothing I thought more of than the moans I elicited from her on that bench, of her breasts spilling over that dress, of spreading her ass when I took her against that mirror.

My cock twitched at the memory, and I cleared my throat, sitting up a bit on the couch. We were in my suite, the lights low, television quietly filling the background with sports highlights — including the nasty high-sticking that split my skin tonight.

I'd made it this far without pushing her, letting her think what happened between us really was a one-night thing.

But my patience was wearing thin waiting for her to admit it was more.

"This might be the most I've ever seen something akin to distress on your face," I said.

Maven let out a long sigh, tossing the ice on the coffee table beside her. She was on the ground next to the couch, balancing on her knees, and even sore as hell from the game and with a splitting headache from the hit, I still had a hard time not imagining what it would be like to stand

and tower over her in that position, to stretch her throat and take both our minds off the game.

"How do you do it?" she asked, shaking her head. "I just *watch* you out there, and I'm groaning in pain. I mean, tonight, you got a stick to the face," she said, gesturing to my injury. "But even on a regular night, you're skating nonstop, getting thrown into the glass and the boards and onto the ice, taking elbows to the ribs..." Her eyes found mine. "It's insane."

"I told you," I said with a shrug. "I'm the mayhem."

She rolled her eyes on a smile, but it fell flat when her eyes skated over my cut. "Does it hurt?"

"A little," I confessed. "But not too bad. This is pretty minor."

"*Minor*?!"

"Nowhere near getting a couple teeth shattered," I said, tapping my veneers with my pointer finger. "I'm sure Livia could tell you all about that."

She grimaced, waving her hand. "I've heard enough of her gruesome stories to last a lifetime." Maven watched me a moment before hesitantly reaching out, her cool fingertip gliding over the scar on my eyebrow. "And this?"

"Ah," I said, mirroring her touch once she'd pulled back. I missed that touch as soon as it was gone, longing to reach out and snag her hand and hold it in my own. "I wish I had an epic hockey story to back this one up, but sadly, it happened off the ice."

"Fall off the monkey bars?"

"Took a steel-toe boot to the face, actually."

Maven's jaw dropped. "*What*?!"

"Senior year of high school. Picked a fight with a guy who was three years older and about a hundred pounds heavier than me. All muscle."

"Let me guess — over a girl?"

"You see right through me."

She chuckled, shaking her head. "Why am I not surprised? Did he steal your date to prom or something?"

"He got drunk and decided to use one of our cheerleaders as a punching bag because she was his girlfriend at the time."

The color drained from Maven's face.

I shrugged. "I didn't care if I was younger or smaller than he was. And I got a scar, but he got the lesson of a lifetime."

"Did he press charges?"

"Against a high-schooler who kicked his ass?" I scoffed. "He was too embarrassed. Limped off like the coward he was and left my friend alone, which was all I wanted."

I thought I saw a new level of respect in her eyes as she watched me like I was a brain bender puzzle she couldn't quite figure out.

"What?" I asked when she didn't say anything.

"It's hard for me to picture."

"Me beating someone's ass? Come on, Mave, give me some credit. You see me do it nightly on the ice."

I thought I saw her cheeks redden at the shortening of her name. I made a mental note to do it again.

"I just mean... I can't picture you in that scenario. I pegged you for a more... *posh* school environment."

"Believe me when I say, prep schools have more drama than public ones. When everyone has money, and everyone thinks money is power... it can feel like living in a fantasy world, one where the rules don't apply."

She huffed out a laugh at that, her eyes on the floor like she was thinking about her own past instead of mine now. I saw the ghosts dancing in her eyes.

"I will say, I think wearing my scar is easier than bearing the hidden ones you have to live with."

She stilled, her next breath paused in her chest for a moment before she looked at me.

I wanted to ask her more about her ex, about the fucking bastard responsible for all the barbed-wire-lined walls she stood so shakingly behind. He'd hurt her. That much she'd admitted. But it was deeper than what she'd let on, little remnants of him sticking to her like shrapnel from an explosion.

Suddenly, her phone vibrated, the screen lighting up and breaking through the darkness in the room.

She swiped it off the table, sighing a bit before she glided her thumb over the screen and fired off a message.

"What's up?"

"Reya is asking for an update." She looked at me like she was ashamed of what she was going to say next. "Everyone wants to know you're okay."

I maneuvered myself to sit up straighter on the couch. "Well, let's give the people what they want."

"Really?"

I shrugged like it was no big deal, giving her a wink.

She cared about her job, about what people thought of her. Maybe if I showed her I cared about it, too, I could break out of the box she'd put me in in her mind. I thought about what Livia said when I'd called her, before she'd told me where Maven was on her date.

You've got a long road ahead of you to earn her trust.

Maven watched me for a moment before tapping on her screen until she had Instagram pulled up. She snapped a picture of me holding up two thumbs, and when she showed it to me, we both laughed at my swollen, bruised face, and the gnarly cut covered by bandages.

Once the photo was posted, Maven hopped up from the floor, wincing a bit from the position she'd been in for so long. My stomach immediately sank, knowing she was about to leave. It was the first night I'd spent with her without her teeth being bared, the first time I felt her peeking over those walls — even if just a little.

"We better get some sleep," she said. "Do you need anything before I go?"

Stay.

The word reverberated in my mind, in my chest, but I snuffed it out like a candle flame.

"I mean, I could use a massage," I said. "Or maybe a kiss — that would make it all better, right?"

"Vince," she warned.

"Maven," I echoed.

She looked so cozy in that moment, so relaxed, and yet I watched in slow-motion as she snapped every single guard back into place, a little line between her brows showing before she turned away.

"Make sure to keep icing," she said, grabbing her bag off the table by the door.

"Careful. You're doing that thing where it seems like you might care about me again."

She turned, hanging a hand on her hip. "Don't flatter yourself."

There she is, I thought. *My feisty girl.*

I couldn't resist the chance to play with her.

"Oh, by the way, I forgot to ask... how was your walk home from the gym last week?"

Maven's face slackened as my grin grew.

"I know it was a bit... *hot* that night. Humid. Things can get a little... sticky."

Her mouth popped open for just a moment before she scoffed and turned on her heel.

"You're unbelievable."

"Did it rain?" I called behind her, arms resting on the back of the couch as I watched her go. "I heard things were a little *wet*."

"Good*bye*."

I laughed long after she slammed the door.

Chapter 26

One Stubborn Girl

Vince

The rookie party was a highly anticipated event for the Tampa Bay Ospreys.

At a point in the season where things were relatively calm – meaning we had at least a few days between games and our record wasn't too shitty – the veterans would essentially kidnap the rookies on the team for a night of debauchery in their honor.

Coach McCabe was noticeably absent for the affair, and thankfully so, because I was currently in my underwear on stage at a strip club with a bucket of water being poured over my head.

I threw my hands up when I was drenched by the strippers, shaking my hair like a wet dog to the roar of my teammates. We were the only ones in the club other than the women who worked there, and they were good sports, playing into our chaos and making it a memorable night for everyone.

I, personally, was amazed at how they were so steady, walking in their eight-inch heels across a soaking wet stage like slipping and falling wasn't even a risk on their radar. And when they grabbed the poles behind us and swung themselves up and into a plethora of contortions, the team erupted again, nearly blowing the ceiling off the joint.

I used the distraction as an excuse to hop down from the stage, thanking the girl who handed me a towel and my clothes with a wink. It was poor Carter's turn next, and he was throwing back another shot to prepare for his torture.

"If only my mom could see me now," I said when I flopped into a table booth next to Jaxson.

"Ew, bro, you're soaked." He tried to shove me away, but I shook my hair again, flinging droplets of water at him before I tugged my jeans on over my wet briefs. I left the shirt off, graciously accepting the beer delivered by the cocktail waitress as Jaxson used my towel to wipe his arms.

"Was your party this wild?" I asked him, glancing around the bar at the absolute animals I called teammates. Everyone was blasted, and Carter was being dragged on stage, the DJ cueing up a new song with our teammates throwing dollar bills at him while he stripped. I laughed when his shirt got caught on his head and he nearly fell off the stage.

"We had a private beach house for mine," he said, shaking his head on a smile as he tilted his beer to his lips. "I remember approximately two percent of that night, but one thing I'll never forget is waking up with clown makeup and four girls in my bed."

I chuckled, then turned to the stage just in time to cat-call Carter as he attempted some half-ass spin on the pole that made him fall flat on his butt.

“Real nice what you assholes pulled with the dinner, by the way,” I said. All the veterans had taken us out to eat at the nicest steakhouse in town before heading to the club and told us it was on them, only to hand us the bill at the end.

“Hey, just be thankful they didn’t hold you down in the locker room and shave your hair and beard off,” Jaxson said. “You never realize what an ugly sonofabitch you are until you have a naked head and face.”

Carter threw his hands up in the air like he would at a game, telling us he needed us to get louder. And as the cheer grew in volume, he moonwalked across the stage, did a spin on one sneaker, and landed in a jazz split that made me spit out my beer.

We all roared our approval, and then Carter was thrown down into a folding chair on stage, and four of the club’s dancers descended on him.

I smirked, shaking my head.

And then, just like they had all night, my eyes scanned the crowd until I found Maven.

When she’d been dragged along for the shenanigans, I was sure she’d either bow out early or sit silent for the entire night with her brown cheeks flushed. Instead, she’d fit in like she was part of the team, even throwing dollar bills at me when I was on stage.

I had no idea how she was going to find any safe-for-Instagram content from tonight. The only time I’d seen her actually recording anything was at the dinner.

She was currently sitting with Will, the two of them laughing and watching Carter try not to pop a boner with three half-naked women in his lap. But as if she could sense me watching her, she smoothed her hair back over her shoulder and glanced over it.

Our eyes connected, my heart jolting, and she offered me a small smile that I responded to with a wink. She flushed a little when she looked down at where her fingertips daintily held the stem of a martini glass, and then Will was saying something to her, and she turned her attention back to him.

Jaxson pinned me with a shit-eating grin when I turned back toward him.

"What?"

"Don't *what* me, you lovesick bastard."

I took a swig from my beer.

Jaxson angled himself toward me, elbow on the table. "Is that silence admission or denial?"

"I don't know what the hell you're talking about, so neither."

He snorted. "Sure. Okay, so, you're telling me there's nothing going on between you and Maven?"

It took all the effort I had to keep my eyes on the stage. "What do you think?"

"I think she showed up at your door about ten days ago when you were throwing your pity party the night before the New York game, I told her you were at the gym, and that both of you seemed *very* tired the next day."

"It was a long week."

Jaxson poked me in the chest when I wouldn't look at him. "Bullshit."

I clenched my jaw, fighting back the urge to tell him anything. Maven had made it more than clear that she didn't want anyone to know.

It had been killing me, the last week and a half of being around her after knowing what it was like to be *inside* her. I was exhausted at the end of every day, and not from practice, but from the effort it took to keep my hands off her, to respect her wishes, to be as close to normal as I could after knowing what her pussy tasted like.

Every time I pumped myself in the shower, I heard her moans, saw her body arched in the mirror, felt her cunt swallowing me whole. I was convinced I'd never have an orgasm again in my life where I didn't think back to that night.

And every time our skin brushed by accident, I felt it — the electricity that charged that entire night. I knew she felt it, too.

But she was still fighting it.

And that hurt worse than the cut healing on my cheek.

I took an aggressive swig of my beer, blowing out a breath through my nose like a bull.

I still believed what I'd said to her that night — that there was no way in hell that was a one-time thing.

But Maven was one stubborn girl, and my patience was being tested.

"Alright," Jaxson said when I didn't indulge him. "So, if there's nothing going on between you two, then I guess you won't mind if I shoot my shot?"

Ice pricked my veins.

I turned toward him, slowly, my eyes menacing when I met his goading grin.

"What?" He feigned innocence, already sliding out of the booth. "I'm just being a good friend. Had to check and make sure you were cool with it, that there wasn't anything there, and I guess there's not, so..."

"Brittzy," I warned, shooting daggers at him when he stood and smoothed a hand over the seam of his button down.

He ignored me, staring at where Maven was with Will. She tossed her head back on a laugh, and he blew out a low whistle.

"She's such a fucking smoke show, man." He sucked his teeth then, socking me in the arm. "Wish me luck."

My hand involuntarily crushed the beer can I was holding, what was left of the IPA squeezing out onto the table. I thought I heard Jaxson laugh, but he didn't stop. He strode right over to her table and sat down, making it so Maven had no choice but to scoot closer to Will.

And there she was, sandwiched between two of my teammates.

Jaxson threw his arm over the back of the booth, and consequently over *her*. He leaned in, too fucking close, his lips by her ear as he said something that made her smile and roll her eyes.

But she didn't pull away.

She didn't excuse herself, didn't push him out of the booth, didn't so much as glance in my direction. She leaned into him, into whatever he was saying to her, playing with her hair and laughing like those laughs weren't supposed to be reserved for me.

I nearly broke a tooth watching it, and then Carter was flopping down next to me with a goofy grin. He slid me a shot, holding out a lime to go with it.

"You look like you need this."

I didn't answer him.

But I threw it back, letting it sting almost as much as watching Maven.

As the liquor burned my chest, I allowed myself one last glance at her.

Then, I cracked my neck and felt a new resolve settle into my bloodstream just like the alcohol had.

Maven was mine. She knew it as much as I did. But she was hell bent on pretending otherwise.

Fine.

Two could play that game.

Chapter 27

Told You So

Maven

Somewhere around midnight, the rookie party wrapped up and the strip club opened its doors to other patrons.

I didn't notice at first. One second, Carter was on stage being hazed while I got to know Will Perry more. The next, I was sandwiched between him and Jaxson Brittain as the crowd thickened around us, and it went from easy to hear the two of them to damn near impossible.

The strippers took the stage, customers crowding the front row just as much as they packed the VIP tables in the back. Go-go dancers jumped up on the bar, and the lights flashed to the beat the DJ was spinning. People talked and laughed and whistled and yelled, all of them fighting to be louder than the music — which was a feat.

Even with his mouth right by my ear, I had to make Jaxson repeat himself at least twice when he tried to keep our conversation going. He'd been telling me ridiculous stories for the past hour, mostly about the shenanigans he and Vince got into during the preseason.

At about half-past midnight, I excused myself to the restroom, laughing at my reflection when a yawn stretched my mouth wide. I was ready to call it a night.

I searched the packed club for Vince. I didn't know why, really, but I felt like I should tell him I was heading out. It wasn't like I'd post any of the content that would be captured after this point, anyway, and the team was getting a little too rowdy for my tastes.

I smiled a little as I recalled how carefree he'd seemed all night. I sat next to him at the rookie dinner, our knees brushing under the table, my heart pounding in my chest every time I glanced at where his massive hands held his cocktail. I couldn't look at those hands without remembering what they did to me, and that was a very bad image to conjure up in a fancy restaurant — especially when I was wearing a dress with only a thong on underneath it.

When we'd arrived at the club in a collection of limousines, I'd thoroughly enjoyed watching him get dragged on stage to be hazed.

I loved that he was laughing, that he was having fun.

I also loved that every time I looked at him across that club, he was looking at me, too.

I internally scolded myself as my neck heated with that thought.

His cut was healing already, the bandages removed, but the bruising, tender flesh reminded me of our night together in Atlanta. It had felt a little too intimate, him opening up to me the way he had. I was thankful Reya had texted me and interrupted us before I could lose myself too much.

It was easy to do with Vince, which was a very big problem.

The crowd had a heartbeat now, and I weaved my way through it, hunting for Vince to say goodnight. I knew he was far from turning in. It was *his* rookie party, after all.

I thought of what he told me about pottery that first week I was on assignment, how it helped him release stress, helped him re-center. I also noted that he hadn't been able to carve out enough time to sit at that wheel since, and I knew it had to be wearing on him.

I was glad he was cutting loose tonight. He needed it.

I asked a few teammates if they'd seen him, feeling a bit helpless when none of them could point me in his direction. I was pulling out my phone to just text him that I was heading out when I finally spotted him.

My heart split in two when I did.

It wasn't fair, the way my breath caught at the sight of him in a VIP booth with a woman straddling his lap. It wasn't fair how my chest squeezed the life out of my lungs when I catalogued the scene: his hands on her ass, her hips grinding against him, his panty-melting smirk, her hands running the length of his chest as she rode him to the beat.

They were both fully clothed, but it didn't matter. I felt like I'd just walked in on him with his cock in her mouth.

She was stunning — deep brown skin, a long, midnight braid falling down her slender back. She moved on him so seductively it was like the music lived within her, and Vince let his eyes crawl over her body as she did.

He didn't look like himself.

I registered it even as bile rose in my throat. Something was off. He seemed pissed, almost... *distant*, not engaged, numb.

When his eyes slowly swept up to mine, they stuck, his jaw hardening.

Like he wanted me to see.

My nostrils flared, but I turned on my heel before my eyes could water, pushing through the crowd toward the door. I gasped on the first sip of clean oxygen on the outside, and then I climbed into one of the limousines, promising the driver none of the other players were ready to leave yet, and to please just take me back and then he could return.

Blessedly, he listened, and he didn't ask a single question as I stewed in his back seat.

I shook my head over and over, laughing and then scoffing and then growling in frustration. I shouldn't have cared. I shouldn't have felt sick at the sight of him with someone else. This was what I wanted.

One time, and one time only.

Back to professionals.

And that meant I had no fucking right to be upset that he had another girl in his lap.

But it killed me. The betrayal swam in my gut like a virus the whole ride back downtown.

Once the anger subsided a little, disappointment scurried in to take its place. I shouldn't have been surprised. This was exactly what I pegged him for. It didn't matter that he'd fucked me against a mirror ten days ago, or that he'd watched me like he saw right through me when we were alone in the hotel in Atlanta. It didn't matter that he'd opened up to me, that he'd let me see a little more of the man behind the show.

He had already moved on, his mission accomplished. He'd seen me naked, gotten his dick wet, and now I was just another conquest he could put behind him.

I'd told him as much that night in the restaurant, when he'd cornered me in the bathroom and told me he wanted me. I'd looked him right in the eyes and *told him* I saw him for what he was.

But even then, there was a small part of me that wondered if he was different, if I was judging him too harshly, if he'd prove me wrong in the end.

I knew now not to hold my breath.

When the limousine pulled up in front of the skyscraper I called home now, I climbed out and all but ran up to my condo. When I kicked off my heels, I looked around at the space — at the couch that wasn't mine, the chairs that weren't mine, the windows and the artwork and the stupid fucking fireplace that made no sense because we lived in Florida.

I was so homesick, I let the first tear fall free.

Swiping it away as soon as it fell, I grabbed my bag out of the closet and began packing. One night in my own house wouldn't impact my job, and tonight, I wanted *my* bed.

"Shake it off, Maven," I coached myself as I packed. "It's fine. You are fine. Everything is *fine*."

I almost believed it.

Until I strapped my bag over one shoulder and heaved my door open, only to find Vince standing in the middle of the hallway.

I halted, my bag swinging and nearly taking me forward with it before it slung back in place. Vince was stone where he stood, like a tortured god captured in statue form. It was like he was coming to get me and then had stopped himself, but then didn't know where to go or what to do next, so he just stayed, waiting.

But for what?

We stood like that a long time before he started moving toward me, his pace slow, eyes never leaving mine until he was standing in front of me at my door. His gaze flicked to my bag then, and he swallowed, finding me once more.

"Where are you going?"

The spell was broken then, and I remembered the woman writhing in his lap. I chuffed a laugh out of my nose. "Home," I said, then I let the door shut behind me, locking it and stalking down the hall.

Vince was on my heels.

"What's wrong?"

"Nothing."

"Liar."

I growled, turning to shove him hard in the chest. "If you know, then why are you asking, you pompous prick?"

"Because I want to hear you say it."

"Say *what*? That I'm disgusted by your public display of lust?"

"You're not disgusted," he challenged. "You're mad. You're jealous."

I scoffed. "I am *not*—"

"You are. I know because I felt the same way when I saw you cuddled up in a booth with Brittzy."

I blinked at that, letting it sink in.

Then, I laughed.

"You've got to be fucking joking me. So, what, you just found the first girl who'd let you grope her and took her to the VIP booth, hoping I'd see?"

His jaw locked, but he didn't answer.

"Wow." I laughed again, shaking my head and pushing the button for the elevator. "Real nice, Tanev."

"God*damnit*, woman." He snatched my bag so fast I couldn't register it, and then his hands were on me, sweeping up to cradle my face as he backed me into the nearest wall. I gasped when we slammed into it, heart racing at the mixture of anger and passion ignited in his golden-green eyes.

"I don't want to do this," he choked, Adam's apple bobbing hard with the admission. "I don't want to play these fucking games with you. I don't want to be in pain when I see you with one of my teammates because I don't have the assurance that you're mine, and I don't want to try to make you jealous with some random fucking girl I don't even know. This isn't who I am, but it's who you make me because I'm fucking *crazy* for you."

My insides melted to mush at those words, at the sight of this confident, powerful man so raw and exposed.

All for me.

It was sick what that did to me, how my thighs clenched together and my pulse picked up a notch.

The last bit of my good sense hanging on was screaming as loud as it could for me to remember what I'd just been feeling in the car ride home, to remind myself who I was playing with here. But the screams were like the buzz of a fly — annoying, and then something I could ignore altogether because my heart was humming so much louder.

Vince read right through me, something shifting in him, too.

I didn't mean to do it, but I didn't have a choice.

It was a green light.

His forehead met mine on a sigh, one hand sliding to palm my throat, while the other ran the length of my body and hooked my hip.

"I thought I could be patient," he said, his breath warm on my lips. "I thought I could wait it out, wait *you* out, but I can't."

He pulled back, but held me close to him as his fingers splayed over my neck. He lifted that hand until his thumb could run the length of my bottom lip, and I just stood there and let him touch me, trying not to black out from the rush of adrenaline surging through me.

The elevator dinged, the doors opening, my last chance to escape.

I let them close.

Vince's eyes smoldered when I didn't smart mouth him, when I didn't shove him away, when I didn't bolt for that elevator. His breath was as shallow as mine, and I focused on that hollow point in his throat as he unhooked my hip.

In the next breath, that hand was up and under my dress, cupping me as I gasped and let my head fall back against the wall.

"Look at me," he husked.

It took all my effort to do what he said, to look into his eyes as he rubbed his palm up and then down, slowly firing me to life like only he could. I wanted to fight it, and I didn't even know why. I wanted to clamp my knees together and walk away and tell him to go fuck himself.

But my body was a traitor, and I felt myself spread for him — thighs opening, beckoning for more.

The corner of his mouth twitched, the small smile of victory.

"There's my girl," he said, toying with the seam of my panties. My eyelids fluttered, but I kept my focus on him, on where his eyes were dancing more and more as I let him in. "There's my fucking girl."

When he teased me with just the tip of one finger brushing through my wetness, I sighed, his name rolling off my tongue without permission.

"Vince."

"What is it, pet? What do you want to say?"

I rolled my lips together, fighting against the full body tremor that racked through me when he palmed me again, harder this time, rubbing me with the friction needed to start the fire I wasn't sure ever stopped burning from the first night he touched me.

I whimpered, melting into him, and he took my weight greedily.

"Say it," he whispered in my ear, his fingers toying with me under my dress, tuning me like an instrument only he could play.

"Please."

The word leaked out of me like air from a dying balloon, and the smile on Vince's lips curled up even more.

"Please *what*."

"Touch me," I moaned, wrapping my arms around his neck as I mounted him. "*Take* me."

He captured that plea with a passionate, demanding kiss, one that stole my breath and what was left of my resolve all at once. His tongue met mine, his hands holding my ass as I writhed against him, desperate for that friction he'd given me with his hand.

The rubber band snapped.

I was off the wall before I could register it, Vince still kissing me hard as he swiped my bag from the floor and carried both it and me down the hall.

"I told you so," he grumbled against my lips.

"Excuse me?"

He bit my lip, sucking it between his teeth on a grin. "That the next time I touched you, you'd be begging me to."

I didn't have time to scoff or pin him with a remark of my own before he set me on my feet in front of my door, digging through my bag until he found the ring of keys I'd thrown in there.

"Unlock that door," he said, dangling them between us before he dropped them into my hand. "And then get on your fucking knees."

Chapter 28

Say Please

Maven

She was such a good fucking girl.

As soon as the door was unlocked, Maven shoved through it, pulling me in with her. I slung her bag into the corner of the foyer, following where she led me into her living room.

Then, she released my hand, and dropped to her knees just like I'd asked.

It was my first time in her place, one that looked so much like mine, and then again, nothing like it. Hers was smaller, bland, filled with furniture and artwork that was no reflection of who she was. I made a mental note to ask her to take me home — to her *real* home — as soon as possible.

But for tonight, I had more pressing matters to attend to.

"For the record," she said, her ass balanced on her heels, knees against the hardwood floor. "Me *talking* to your teammate is not the same as you having a girl grinding on your lap."

I smirked, widening my stance as I folded my arms and stared down at where she knelt. "If you want to demand something, Maven, just say it."

Her eyes flicked between mine. "You're not mine to command."

"No?" I asked, tilting my head. Then, I walked slowly to where she was, tilting her chin with my knuckles so she looked up at me. "Don't let another man touch you unless you have my permission. I don't care if you're just friends."

Her eyelids fluttered a bit, and I arched a brow, waiting.

"Don't touch another woman," she said carefully, quietly.

"What was that?"

"Don't *touch* another woman," she said, louder, eyes on mine. "And don't let another woman touch you."

My smile climbed, her steely command making my cock twitch. I leaned down, taking her chin in my hand and kissing those sweet words left hanging on her lips. When I released her, I stood tall again.

"As you wish. Now, pull your dress up to your hips."

I saw it, the moment her breathing intensified, the moment the rules were laid out and it was time to play again. Her lids fluttered as she slowly folded her fingertips into the fabric at her waist, scrunching it up little by little until it popped over her ass and settled there, ruched at her hips.

"Spread your legs."

Her nostrils flared as she did.

"Wider."

Again, she obeyed, feet together under her ass and knees spread wide. I could see the brown fabric of her thong, how it blended with her skin.

"Pull those perfect tits out of that dress."

With her eyes still on me, she slid the thin strap off one of her shoulders, and then the next, peeling the fabric down until her breasts tumbled out. She didn't have a bra on underneath, and my cock hardened to stone at the sight of her.

The city spread out in the window behind her, lights reflecting off the water of the Hillsborough River. And she was a piece of art against that backdrop.

I swallowed, making quick work of my shoes before my hands moved to unbuckle my belt. Maven's gaze fell to watch me, until I had it and the button on my dress slacks unfastened. I tugged the zipper down next, and then shrugged my pants off, followed by my sports coat and button-up shirt.

I left the shirt on, open, exposing my chest and stomach with the sleeves shoved up to my elbows. My briefs were a fucking tent, cock aching to be free, but I stayed clothed as I walked over to her again.

"Are you wet?" I asked her, smoothing my thumb over her jawline.

"Yes," she breathed.

"Show me."

She slid one hand between her legs, eyelids fluttering a bit as she swiped her finger under her thong. When she pulled it out again and showed me her glistening fingertips, I bit my lip at the sight.

"We can do better than that," I said, and then I pulled my briefs off, kicking them to the side. I palmed myself, wrapping my fist around my cock and smoothing it with two slow pumps. Maven practically salivated when I did, her thigh muscles activating like she wanted to clench her legs together.

I used my feet to spread her knees even wider, and then held them there just in case — so she had no choice but to stay splayed.

"Open that pretty mouth for me, pet."

"Say please."

My eyebrows shot into my hairline at how quickly she combatted my request, and with a short laugh barreling out of my chest, I held my cock at the seam of her lips.

"Please," I said with a smirk.

Her eyes glittered with amusement as she opened her mouth, tongue skating out to flick my tip.

I hissed at that first touch, shaking my head as her eyes smiled up at me. But she held her mouth open, and I slicked the crown of me with her tongue before dipping my cock inside her mouth just an inch.

"Fuck," I groaned, every nerve in me firing to life at the feel of her wet heat. I withdrew, running my head over her bottom lip before I pressed inside again, this time a bit deeper.

Maven tilted her head down a bit, angling her jaw so she could take me in without gagging. It was the most torturous, beautiful sight — her knees spread wide, nipples peaked, mouth open and ready to be fucked.

My hands found her hair, and I carefully held her to me, working myself out and then deeper inside. Each time she made room for another centimeter of me, I groaned my approval, flexing my hips and watching my cock disappear between her lips.

"Eyes on me, baby," I said, and when she looked up at me with teary vision, I cursed. "Yes, baby. Just like that. Watch me while I fuck your mouth."

She moaned around me, which made me see stars, and I held onto the back of her head and picked up my pace. I slid in over and and over, deeper and deeper, until she had all of me inside her.

And she didn't choke, didn't gag, didn't tap on my thighs and ask for a break.

She kept her eyes glued to mine, holding her mouth open wide, tongue gliding along the underside of my shaft. When she took me so deep I felt the tip of her tongue on my balls, I shivered, holding her there for a long moment before I pulled out completely.

A strand of saliva connected us, from her lips to my glistening cock, and Maven panted, looking up at me like she was ready for more.

"You wicked thing," I said, smoothing my thumb over her wet bottom lip. "You're far too good at that."

"Apparently not," she said, still breathing hard. "I don't have your cum down my throat."

I bit back a groan, holding out my hands to help her stand. When she carefully made her way up, I framed her face, kissing her long and deep.

"That's because I want to come in this cunt again," I said, palming her roughly under her dress. I smiled against her lips when I felt how drenched her thong was, and I rubbed it against her before sliding it to the side with one fingertip. "I knew we could do better," I said, slicking that finger inside her and curling it deep. "You're fucking *soaked*, Maven."

"Vince," she pleaded, and I nipped at her bottom lip before I withdrew my finger from her pussy and smacked the side of her ass.

"Strip for me," I said against her mouth. "I want to see my girl."

I backed up then, grinning at her as I took a seat on the couch. I spread my legs wide, wrapping my hand around my wet cock and waiting.

For a moment, she stood there slack-jawed, but then she breathed a laugh and shook her head before sliding her thumbs into the band of her thong. She slid it down her thighs and knees, letting it rest at her ankles before she grabbed the hem of her dress and lifted it overhead.

Her hair fell over her shoulders when the dress was discarded, the long, thick, jet-black strands falling to cover her breasts. But as if she knew I'd ask, she pulled that hair into one hand and draped it behind her, letting me take her in.

And my God, was she a sight to behold.

I let my eyes wash over her, taking in the lines of her collarbone, the swells of her breasts, the brown pebbled peaks of her nipples. My eyes continued down the lean line of her abdomen to her lush hips, to her thighs and the way those two parts of her met in an apex and framed her pussy.

I shook my head, pumping myself. "Come here."

I thought she looked a little shy then, her eyes falling to where she stepped out of her thong that still rested around her feet. She played with her hair as she walked to me, pulling it all over one shoulder until she stood at my knees.

I reached out a hand for her, helping her to straddle me, and then I swept her hair back again so I could view her up close.

"You are sensational," I whispered, letting my hands rove over her. Chills erupted everywhere my fingertips touched, and I smiled as they did, loving that I had that effect on her.

Her hands slid up and over my chest, my shoulders, until her wrists caught the fabric of my shirt. I released my hands only long enough for her to wrangle me out of the fabric before I had her in my grasp again.

My hands wrapped nearly all the way around her waist as I lifted her up, lining myself up below her. We both inhaled a hot breath when my crown slid between her lips, and she rolled her pelvis against it, coating me, feeling me thick and hard at her entrance.

Her hands found my shoulders, and then I pulled her down, inch by blissful inch, until she was sitting on my cock and shivering at the fullness.

"*God*, Vince," she said, nails digging into my shoulders as she lifted and slid back down. "You feel so good."

"This is all I've thought about since that night at the gym," I told her, groaning as I filled her once more. "You and this magnificent mouth and this perfect pussy."

She moaned, and then her lips were on me, and she took control. Her movements were slow and savoring, her hips sinking all the way down before she'd lift them again and repeat the motion. Soon, every bit of her was moving with the pace, her back arching, body rolling, head flung back in ecstasy.

"You look so pretty riding my cock," I praised her, palming her breasts and rolling her nipples between my thumbs and fingertips. She cried out when I did, body erupting in chills again. "So fucking pretty."

She spread herself even wider at those words, and her movement became erratic, her hips not able to grind as fast as she needed me. I took control then, leaning up to wrap one arm around her while the other hand slid into her hair. I held her to me for a bruising kiss, and then started to pump my hips underneath her, meeting her thrust for thrust.

"Fuck," she cursed, trembling, clawing. "*Fuck*, Vince, I—"

Her words melted into a symphony of moans, and I helped her ride out her orgasm, eating up every cry she let out with eager kisses. I wanted to capture them all, to keep them forever.

I earned those fucking moans. They were more priceless than any goal I'd ever scored.

When she was satiated, she melted into me, falling completely lax. Her breaths were hard and shallow, her forehead against mine.

"Need a break?" I asked, slowly withdrawing before I flexed deep inside her again.

"Please. I've got more stamina than you and your whole team, Tanev."

I barked out a laugh, flipping her into the couch cushions. She landed with a puff of the down feathers, her hair splaying out under her as she smiled up at me with tired, sated eyes.

"Let's test that theory," I said, and then I stood on my knees, hiking one of her legs up onto my shoulder and then the other.

I kissed the inside of each of her ankles, positioning myself at her entrance again before my hands found the arm of the couch above her head. I nearly bent her in half when I did, her knees lining up on either side of her jaw. Her legs stayed fixed on my shoulders, and I grinned in appreciation as I just barely pressed inside her.

"I didn't know you were so flexible," I mused, hips thrusting until I entered her another inch.

"You didn't know I don't have a gag reflex, either," she clipped. "Tonight is full of surprises."

I smiled wider, leaning down to capture her mouth in a passionate kiss as I flexed all the way inside. She sucked in a breath when I did, and I held myself there, deep enough to leave a permanent mark as her legs shook around me.

Then, slowly, I found my pace.

My lips claimed hers, cock driving in and out as her ankles balanced on my shoulders. Her fists held tight to the cushion underneath her, grounding her, until I was fucking her so hard she had no choice but to hold onto me. Her arms wrapped around my neck, nails digging into my back as I hissed and drove deeper.

"Grab your ankles," I groaned when I was close, and when she did, I moaned her name and filled her, pumping out my release as a searing numbness took over me. Maven's pussy was the kind that hugged you until every drop was spilled, and I rode out that feeling of ecstasy with my toes curling until I was empty.

Slowly, I pulled out of her, but not before I made sure to pump myself completely dry one last time, squeezing out another drop of cum and leaving it there between her legs.

She went to release her ankles, but I snapped my fingers to stop her.

"Spread your legs," I said.

Her shyness was back, her cheeks flaming, but she did as I said, slowly spreading her legs until she was on that couch in a straddle, the V of her legs pointed up to the sky.

"Squeeze your pussy, baby," I said, taking in her sweat-slicked body. "I want to see my cum dripping out of you."

She whimpered, and I loved that sound — because it affirmed that she wanted that dirty talk as much as I needed to give it. With her hands wrapped around her ankles, I watched as her walls clenched and opened, again and again until my seed streamed out of her pussy and down the crease of her ass.

"Fucking hell, Maven," I said, hovering over her again. I reached down and slid my finger inside her, pushing my cum back in. Then, I kept my eyes on hers and added a second finger, curling it deep.

She bucked against the touch, and this time, when I withdrew my fingers, I slicked them in my cum and lubed her ass with my release.

Her eyes widened a bit, but she didn't stop me. With my heart racing and my cock already growing hard again, I slid my finger inside her ass, slow and steady, careful not to stretch her too quickly.

Maven's legs shook so violently I thought she'd fall off the couch, her eyes rolling shut. "Oh, my *God*."

I worked her slowly, fucking her ass with my middle finger and watching her pussy clench like it wanted to be filled, too.

"I want to fuck this ass," I husked.

"Now?"

"Right now."

A little mewl escaped her when I pulled my finger completely out, and she leaned up onto her elbows to watch as I wrapped my fist around my cock and lifted her hips until I could press myself against that forbidden entrance.

"Touch yourself, baby," I said, guiding her hand to her clit. She started circling slowly, her eyes still rapt where they watched as I slicked the head of my cock with the mixture of her release and mine. I made sure she and I were both slick before I pressed, opening her just half an inch.

"Oh," she cried, circling faster.

I paused there, letting her play with herself and adjust to the feeling. I had no idea if it was her first time, but I knew anal needed to be taken slowly, carefully. I wanted her to love it as much as I did.

When she flexed her hips, giving me the sign she was ready, I pressed in more, taking my time, both of us breathing hard where we watched me disappear inside her. It was centimeter by centimeter, a slow stretching that had us both crossing our eyes in ecstasy.

"This feels fucking incredible," I told her, sliding out and back in just a little. She tightened around me, and I groaned. "So fucking tight."

"Yes," she breathed, closing her eyes and falling back against the couch cushions. Her other hand shot down to join the first, one circling her clit as the other slid inside her pussy.

"Goddamn, Maven," I praised, pulling out and sliding back in. I was more than halfway now. "You're going to make me cum again."

"*Yes.*"

It was the only word she had, and it echoed as she fucked her pussy with two fingers, circling her clit with the opposite hand as I filled her ass. She was stuffed as I held her legs open, driving in and out, sweat slicking my forehead. I felt another orgasm building, and the sensation nearly knocked me on my ass. I hadn't come twice in one night since I was a fucking horny teenager, and that had been just me and my hand.

This was Maven King destroying me for all other women.

When she started writhing, bucking her hips and crying out, I picked up my pace, matching hers, and I was finally all the way in her. Driving, stretching, feeling her hugging every inch of me.

"Oh, fuck, fuck, *fuckkk*," she dragged out, pinning her lip between her teeth. I felt the moment she came again, her walls tightening around me and driving me to tumble over the edge with her.

I had to fight to keep upright, to let her work the rest of her release while I spilled inside that tight ass. The sight of her falling apart at the same time made my climax feel even more powerful than the first, and when she was done, I carefully pulled out, pulsing out the last of my release on her stomach. My cock jumped even after I'd released my hold on it, cum dripping out and landing on her lean muscles.

And as if I couldn't be any more turned on, Maven dragged her finger through the line I'd left, and then sucked that finger dry.

"Good *God*," I said, finally collapsing. I savored the giggle Maven let out when I fell on top of her, our bodies slick and heaving.

After a moment, I pressed up onto my elbows, tenderly sweeping her hair out of her face. "Was that your first time?"

I didn't have to clarify. Maven smiled shyly, nodding.

"Fuck." I kissed her then, framing her face and holding her to me. "Thank you."

"For letting you fuck my ass?" she asked on a laugh.

"For trusting me to," I said, and I pushed up so she could look into my eyes, so she could see that I cherished the fact that I got to touch her, taste her, fuck her. "Did you like it?"

She drew a line down my chest. "It was really hot," she confessed, her skin heating against mine with the admission. "It felt... *different*. The orgasm. Like... deeper, somehow. I can't believe I came like that."

"I think I'm keen to make you come again," I said, kissing along her collarbone before sucking one of her nipples between my teeth. "I have yet to taste you tonight."

"We both need to clean up first," she said on a laugh.

I paused at that, noting where we stuck together with a smile. "Fair point."

Then, I stood, hauling her up into my arms as she laughed and wrapped her arms around my neck to hold on.

I carried her to the shower, dropping her only long enough for her to put a cap around her hair. When we were both inside, the hot water streaming down our backs, we were silent, each of us washing the other and stealing kisses in-between.

I lathered her body with soap, washing every inch, careful when I slid a cloth between her thighs and gently cleaned her there, too.

But when we were rinsed, I didn't turn off the water, didn't let her reach for one of the towels we'd laid out.

Instead, I knelt in front of her, hiking one thigh onto my shoulder and leaning her against the wall for my first taste of the night.

Chapter 29

Dirty Little Secret

Maven

My entire body was sore.

It wasn't the kind of sore after an intense hot yoga flow, either. It was bone deep, the kind I could only imagine a person might feel after running their first marathon. In my case, it had been a sex marathon — one I did not train properly for. But I didn't regret it. That soreness was delicious, the kind that reminded me in little flashes of everything that had happened.

My hands ached from gripping onto Vince the night before, my toes from how they'd curled, my thighs from how they'd quivered, my neck from how it'd held my head up while I watched him fuck me. My core burned from the cardio, my pussy from being filled, and — a new sensation — my ass from being taken for the first time.

And while I wanted to stretch out all my sore muscles, I couldn't, because I was covered by thick thighs and hair-dusted arms, Vince's warmth surrounding me and holding me to him.

I tried to wriggle free, laughing when I didn't so much as make the behemoth of a man budge. But he did stir at my attempt, and he wrapped me up tighter, kissing the back of my neck.

"Trying to escape already?"

His words rumbled through me, and I bit back a smile, snuggling into his arms. It had been so long since I'd been held like that.

Of course, that reminder made my eyes bulge open wide.

Because the last man who had held me like that had also broken me completely.

I swallowed down my panic, drawing circles on Vince's arm. "I need to stretch."

"Mm, I can help with that," he said, his voice low and seductive as he pressed his hard-on against my ass. I'd no sooner let out a laugh before I was pinned in the sheets, his hips between my thighs, my wrists overhead and held against the pillows.

"No, I mean seriously, I am sore as hell," I said against his lips. "I need to stretch."

"I'll stretch you out," he promised. "After breakfast."

And then he was kissing down my body, his scruff tickling the entire way.

I wiggled away from the touch, breaking out of his grasp just in time to catch his face in my hands before he could land between my legs.

"I don't think I could come right now even if you stayed there all morning," I said.

He kissed the inside of my thigh. "Not with that attitude."

"You already got me *three times* last night."

"We call that a hat trick. But I still think we can do better. Let's go for four."

I laughed when he tried to descend again. "Sir, am I going to have to kick you out of this bed?"

"I'd like to see you try," he said, but he conceded, balancing back on his knees as he took in the sight of me spread out in the sheets below him. The morning light was coming in through the sheer curtains covering my windows. "Alright. What's sore, how can I help?"

"Everything," I said.

He frowned, gently kneading my thighs with his massive hands. I groaned at the sensation. "I'm sorry."

"Don't," I said on another laugh. "It was the best night fucking of my life."

"Do you mean it was the best fucking night of your life?"

"That, too."

He chuckled, hands moving to massage the insides of my thighs as I winced. "How are you... internally?"

I peeked an eye open, smirking at him as he continued his massage. "Is that your way of asking if my asshole is okay?"

He grinned.

"I'm fine," I said, resting in the pillows again. I pointed to my calf to tell him where to touch me next.

"Still think it was hot?"

My neck burned. "Yes."

"Want to do it again?"

"Right now? Absolutely not." I opened my eyes to meet his. "But, yes."

His chest swelled with his next breath, like he was restraining himself, like he owned me and just remembered how proud he was of that fact. I felt like a trophy, like a million-dollar car in his garage that he couldn't wait to drive down Bayshore Boulevard.

For a while, Vince worked my sore muscles as we listened to the morning sounds of the city waking up outside the windows. Eventually he rolled me onto my stomach, massaging my legs and ass and moving up to my lower back.

The more the silence stretched between us, the more my brain raced.

Last night had been hot. It had been... life-altering. That was the kind of sex a woman dreamed about, knowing deep down it would likely never actually happen. Maybe in the movies. Maybe in books. But never, *ever* in real life.

Still, I could close my eyes and see the girl grinding on Vince's lap, the ones that sandwiched him between them in the bar after that first home win I'd witnessed. He was drowning in pussy. Right now, mine had his attention, but I knew this thing between us was a fleeting one, a snapshot in time.

Part of me wanted to run.

It was the loudest part of me, if I was being honest – the one that knew I'd end up hurt at the end of all of this. Vince lived a different life than I did. He was surrounded by riches – literally – and the attention of the entire world. Everyone wanted a piece of him.

I was just the one who had his focus at the moment.

My heart picked up its pace at another thought – my job. I'd just landed this extension, proving to Reya and Camilla that I was serious about elevating our brand to the next level. I wanted my own segment. I wanted to showcase community heroes, to use our followers and my reputation in Tampa for good when this was all over.

I didn't want anyone, least of all my bosses, to think I was losing control of the situation.

Control.

The word struck me like a lightning bolt.

That was what I needed in this moment.

I knew it all would end, eventually. We would crash and burn, just like every passionate romance does.

But maybe I could avoid being hurt if I was the one driving the car.

"So," I said when he moved to my upper back.

"So?"

"Should we talk about this?"

"About me massaging you and trying not to have a boner?"

I chuckled. "No, I mean... this. Us." I swallowed, rolling until Vince climbed off of me. I sat up in bed, folding my legs beneath me as he crooked a sleepy smile.

"What about us?"

"Well," I said, reaching up to fidget with the silk wrap around my hair. "Obviously, we have chemistry. We enjoy each other's company."

He cocked a brow.

"I think... we should keep seeing each other." I swallowed, lifting my eyes to his. "Friends, with perks."

I tried to read his expression then, because it changed — just slightly. He still wore a little smile, but it didn't feel quite as genuine.

"I just mean, we have fun, we... we can keep it that way. No expectations, no promises for more. Just... sex."

"Just sex," he echoed.

Again, I couldn't read him.

But he almost looked... relieved.

It made sense. Maybe he was already thinking this, listening to me fumble for words while in his head he's like, "*Well, yeah, duh.*"

"I still want what we talked about last night, though," I clarified. "If we're going to do this, I don't want you to have sex with anyone else. And I won't either."

"Damn fucking straight, you won't."

I arched a brow a little at his tone. "I just want us to be safe."

Vince scratched the back of his neck, opening his mouth like he was going to say something, but I kept talking.

"I also think this is the best for both of us, professionally. I'm finally making a name for myself, Vince. I… I *really* enjoy what I do. And I don't want to spoil this opportunity. I don't want to be the punchline of a joke everyone in Tampa loves to tell."

His brows folded together at that. "And you think being seen with me would make you the butt of a joke?"

I laughed. "I mean, honestly? Yes." I reached for him when I said the word. "You should see the comments that are already rolling in after that photo you posted of us. Everyone knows you could never actually be serious about someone like me. They're calling me names, saying I only got this job because you wanted in my pants, telling me to let them know when you're done with me so they can have their turn." I shook my head. "When this is all over, I'll go back to work, back to my life that never crossed paths with yours. And you'll go back to being Vince Cool, with your whole career ahead of you, and the whole world at your fingertips."

I ignored the way my stomach somersaulted as I tried to play off the nonchalance of that assessment. Because I knew that also meant he'd move on to fucking someone else into oblivion, and to waking up next to them with bed hair and a sleepy smile I wished was only for me.

Vince watched me for a long moment before he blinked and pulled his hand away from mine. He stood, giving me a beautiful morning view of his backside before he ran a hand roughly through his hair.

For a small, microscopic moment, I let myself envision an alternate universe. I imagined him turning around and shaking his head, his jaw tight as he said, "*Fuck no.*" I imagined him wanting me for more than just sex, wondered what it would be like to be claimed by him, to be on his arm after every game, to watch him from the box where all the wives and girlfriends sat. The *WAGs*. Could I be one of them? Would he ever want me to be?

But I only let myself daydream for a moment before I exhaled the thought away.

I'd literally let the guy fuck my ass last night. *That* was the kind of sexual power he had.

I would be a fool to think he'd ever spend it only on me.

After what felt like forever, Vince turned to look at me, hanging his hands on his hips. He watched me for a long time, his eyes flicking between mine under furrowed brows.

"If that's what you want," he finally said.

My heart cracked.

I didn't know what I expected. I was in control of the situation, just like I'd wanted to be. I was setting the ground rules, the terms.

But he didn't even fight me on it, and I felt so silly for thinking that he might.

"It is," I lied.

He nodded. "I can be your dirty little secret, Maven."

I thought I saw a bit of sadness with those words, but a wicked smile spread on his face before I could fully catalog it. And there he was, right back to playful Vince, knowing he could have his fun with me and was completely off the hook for anything past that.

It was what every guy wanted, especially a world-renowned professional athlete like him.

The theme park without the roller coaster.

I tried to channel my best friend's words, her idea that this could be fun. I wanted Vince, even if this was the only way I could have him. Because I knew if we didn't draw lines in the sand now, I'd read too much into every look, every touch, every sweet word he whispered against my skin.

Vince Tanev was far too easy to fall in love with.

And I knew I wouldn't survive it if I did.

Now, I had him wrangled back into a box. It wasn't the same one I'd shoved him into after that first night we met, but it was a box nonetheless, one with solid walls and a lid I could shut and tape up when the time came.

But my heart squeezed painfully in my chest, because even being in control, I had a feeling I was already too far gone to come out of this unscathed.

"Now," he said, climbing back into bed with me. He grabbed his phone off the nightstand and looked at the screen before tossing it back face-down. "I have forty-five minutes before I have to be at practice."

He kissed me, long and slow, his lips massaging mine as he settled between my legs. My core fired up at the feeling of him pressed against me, at his tongue dancing with mine.

"How about you sit this pretty pussy on my face," he mused, reaching down to slip a hand between my legs. "And show off that lack of gag reflex you teased me with last night."

"Is this your proposal to sixty-nine, Vince Tanev?"

He slid a fingertip inside me, and I bit my lip, rolling into the touch.

"Oh wait," he said, withdrawing. "I forgot. You're too sore. Maybe we should—"

Before he could finish that sentence, I kissed him silent, rolling until I was on top of him and crawling up to straddle that sexy scruff around his smile.

Chapter 30

Witchcraft

Maven

Fall slipped away like a summer vacation after that.

In so many ways, nothing had changed. Vince still had practices and games and travel. I was still there with him every step of the way. We still volleyed back and forth with each other around the team, nothing out of the ordinary, him trying his best to push my buttons only for me to turn around and do the same to him. I grew closer with the other players and the coach. I spent what spare time I could wiggle into my schedule catching up with Livia over cocktails or a greasy pizza at her place.

But in every other way, my life was unrecognizable.

Whenever we weren't traveling or at the arena for practice or a game, Vince was inside me.

He took me every morning, every night, and every afternoon we could make it work. Any time we were alone, his hands were in my hair, his lips fastened to mine, his thighs spreading mine open until he could find the contact he so desperately searched for.

I knew that man's hands and mouth and body more intimately than I knew my own now. I knew how his fingers pressed into the skin at my hips when I straddled him, knew the exact sighs and moans he would set free the moment he was inside, knew the gentle sweep of his tongue when we were warming up, and the passionate frenzy it became when foreplay turned to fucking.

And I was content.

No, I was *floating,* high on life and on the elixir Vince pumped into me with every single touch. I didn't think about the rules we'd set or the fact that it all would end after that first morning together in my bed because I didn't have *time* to think.

We were wrapped up in each other in every possible way, and I was living in the present moment as if the future didn't exist.

November bled into December, the holidays kicking up in a whole new way in Tampa. We were always a bit cheeky in our Christmas celebrations, anyway — lawns boasting Santa Claus in his swim trunks on the beach, palm trees glittering with lights, our weather staying firmly in the eighties while the rest of the country battled its first falls of snow.

But this year, the city hummed with an exciting energy, because for the first time in over a decade, the Ospreys had a winning record.

We were 14-11-1, and every home game was packed to the hilt now. The city was lit up in blue and white, too — buildings painting their bricks with *Ospreys Nation* or *Fly Birds Fly*. Our players were healthy and hungry and out to prove a point, and every eye in the city was on the prospect of making playoffs.

Every eye in the *nation* seemed to be on Vince Cool.

Our accounts had swelled to a combined three-million followers in just two months, sparking the demand for me to have not one, but *two* social media associates to manage the comments and messages while I focused on content creation. Reya and Camilla also worked with our marketing team to launch an entire store of branded merchandise, everything from t-shirts and stickers to beach chairs and umbrellas.

And in the midst of all the chaos, Reya had pulled me to the side and told me to start drafting my concepts for what would come after the season.

"You've earned the spotlight," she'd told me. *"What you do with it next is up to you."*

Full control. I had full control of my content, my subject focus, my future career, and — most excitedly — my sex life. I was flying so high I was dizzy off the lack of oxygen. And, strangely enough, this new chaos somehow felt... comfortable.

I found a home within the mayhem.

One afternoon before a five home-game stretch, Coach gave all the players the day off to rest and recharge. I snuck away long enough to have brunch with Livia, who was just as busy as I had been lately with the team dentistry and her other South Tampa clients, before finding a text from Vince.

Vince: I have a surprise for you.
Me: Sounds dirty.
Vince: Oh, you have no idea. Wear something you don't mind getting stained.

My interest piqued, I stopped by my bungalow long enough to change into a t-shirt and overalls before I made my way back downtown and up to Vince's floor. When he opened the door, he took in my appearance with a shit-eating grin.

"How did you know the perfect way to dress?"

I laughed, looking down at the overalls that had remnants of projects past etched into the jean fabric. There were paint splatters from working on houses with Dad, grass stains from gardening with Mom, and a host of other organic matter that had collected over the years.

"Lucky guess? What are we doing?"

"Hang on, I'm still appreciating the view," he said, reaching out for my hand. He held it over my head and gave me a spin before letting out a low whistle. "How the hell you manage to make overalls sexy is a puzzle I'll never solve."

"Witchcraft," I said as he pulled me into his arms, one hand hugging me tight to him while the other slid up to frame my face.

"Mm." He kissed me long and slow before adding, "Then I'm gladly under your spell."

It was moments like this, so small and quick I'd miss them if I blinked, that I felt it. My heart would stutter and expand, brain going haywire trying to stop myself from reading more into things than I should.

"Close your eyes," Vince said, and when I did, he circled me until his hands were on my shoulders and guiding me inside.

I held out my hands, walking slowly so I didn't slam into anything. My face was split in a smile, wondering what the hell he had in store as he kissed behind my neck and muttered about how he couldn't wait to peel my overalls off me later. I didn't have any context for where we were by the time he pulled me to a stop, but something smelled earthy, and sunlight warmed my face.

"Okay," he said, releasing my shoulders. "Open."

I blinked my eyes open, pupils dilating a bit as the sun streamed in through the window.

And then, I gasped.

I'd never been in this room before, but judging by the equipment that was shoved out of the way, I assumed it was a sort of multipurpose area for Vince before. A treadmill was pushed against the back wall, along with recovery equipment like bands and rollers, and there were some trophies displayed in a floor-to-ceiling case.

The rest of the area had been cleared, and the entire floor was littered with gardening tools, soil, seedlings, and plants.

It was too much to take in at once, my eyes shifting from one corner of the room to the next in a frenzy before I closed my eyes tight and took a deep breath. When I opened them again, I started over, beginning at one inch and letting my gaze float to the next.

There was a brand-new wooden plant shelf, its pine surfaces empty and begging to be filled. Next to it was a working table and two low stools. The table had gloves and trimmers and other tools, all brand new.

The floor was a jungle of color — marble queen pothos, African violet flowers, pearls and jade pothos, a rubber plant, an arrowhead plant, a Christmas cactus, a split-leaf thaumatophyllum, neon pothos. I shook my head as I identified more and more, everything from tiny tugela cliff-calanchoe succulents to a large and healthy monstera.

My hand floated up to my mouth, covering it as my eyes welled without me willing them to. I turned to find

Vince watching me with his hands in his pockets, his brows furrowed, a slight tilt in the corner of his mouth.

"Do you like it?"

"What *is* it?" I breathed.

He ran a hand back through his hair. "I know you've been missing your plants. I thought maybe you could make a home for some new ones here."

I blinked, turning back to survey the room with my heart thundering in my chest. "Did you build that shelf?"

He nodded, his smile shy.

"And these," I said, bending to carefully retrieve one of the empty pots. There was an assortment of them in the corner, from five-inch to twenty-four inch, if I was guessing. They all had the perfect drainage holes drilled into the bottom. The one I had was creamy white, with painted black bohemian designs swirling around it. "Did you make these?"

My eyes floated back to him, and he shrugged. "I thought it could be a blending of the things we love – your plants, my pottery."

I tried to swallow, but my throat was thick, blocked with a wad of sandpaper. "You did this for me?"

His eyes searched mine, worry etched into his brows as he moved close enough to slide his thumb along my jaw. "Oh God, I didn't freak you out, did I? I just thought–"

"I love it," I said, interrupting him. And as soon as I carefully set the pot back down, I threw myself into his arms, inhaling his masculine scent and how it mixed with the earth in that room. "I *love* it."

He sighed, as if he were relieved, burying his nose in my neck.

Every part of my brain wanted to overanalyze in that moment. He'd bought a whole fucking indoor garden for me.

But he'd also immediately worried that it would freak me out, that I would read too much into it.

So I did my best not to, squeezing him tight and shoving anything that resembled feelings into the pit of my stomach where I hoped they'd stay.

When he released me, he rubbed the back of his neck. "I hope you know I'm completely clueless when it comes to what to do next. I don't even know if I got the right supplies."

I looked around with a smile so big it hurt my cheeks, excitement thrumming in my veins. "You got plenty. Let's get to work."

Vince put on a playlist before letting me take charge, directing him how to help me. I started with assigning each plant to its new pot, making sure we had them all in the right sizes and with the right drainages. Then, I showed him how to repot them, arching a brow when I asked if he realized what a mess this was going to make on his beautiful wood floors. But he didn't care. He promised me the cleanup would be worth it.

After that, we fell into a comfortable rhythm, repotting each plant and clipping any dead leaves off before we situated them on the shelf. I smiled wider each time a new one was placed, feeling a fuzzy warmth spreading in my chest at the notion that we were displaying a little piece of each of us.

"Why do you listen to French music?" I asked as I worked on the monstera and he carefully packed soil into one of the pots with pothos.

"It's soothing," he said.

"Do you have any idea what they're saying?"

"Not a damn clue."

I laughed, listening to the song currently playing. It was slow and romantic somehow, even though I couldn't comprehend it. "It is quite lovely."

"I feel about music the way I feel about pottery, I think," he said. "I don't have to fully understand it to know that it's beautiful." He paused, frowning at his own words, and then his gaze sifted to me. "Funny. I kind of feel that way about you, too."

I fought back a smile, grabbing a bit of soil and rolling it into a clump before I tossed it at him. "Flattery will get you nowhere, sir."

"You sure about that?" he asked, and he dropped the plant he was working on, crawling across the floor to me, instead.

"Hey, do not interrupt me. This monstera needs—*hey!*"

I laughed as he tugged me by one leg from the stool, and I tumbled into his lap, inhaling a breath as he caught me with a kiss. We were both dirty, soil under our fingernails as our kisses went from lazy and sweet to urgent and intentional.

The afternoon slipped into evening, the sun moving slowly across that room as Vince undressed me and laid me down right there on the dirt-covered floor. It felt like fucking in a forest, the French music adding a magical element that would burn that memory into my mind forever.

ʚ ʚ ʚ

Later that night, while Vince was sound asleep, I pulled up an article on my phone in bed next to him.

I must have wanted to torture myself.

I must have wanted to remind myself who I was, and who Vince was, and how the rules we'd outlined were the ones I needed to remember to play by.

I must have been determined to cast a dark cloud over the most beautiful day, to rain on that sunny afternoon before anything had the chance to bloom.

Because I googled *wives of NHL players*, and doom-scrolled.

Models. Actresses. Sports broadcasters. Pop stars. Hotel heiresses.

My stomach tied itself up into an impossible knot the more I read, and when a tear pricked my eye, I sniffed, batting it away and closing out of the app. I laid there, staring up at the ceiling with the phone on my pounding chest.

Then, I blew out a breath, opened my phone and started a new note.

Bullet after bullet, I listed out goals and to-dos: create name for new account, build six months of content with local community outreach programs and heroes, link website with resources for people who want to get involved, invest in new camera equipment and upgraded phone, take a girls' trip with Livia, spend a long weekend with Mom and Dad, remodel my patio, try a new hairstyle, get a new dress, get a tattoo, get a cat?

I sighed when it was twenty-bullets long, staring at the list with my heart in my throat.

I titled it *Life After Vince Tanev.*

Then, I quietly slid my phone onto the nightstand and curled up behind the nation's hottest rookie hockey player, wrapping my arms around him and letting myself admit in that dark silence what I'd never admit out loud.

Chapter 31

A Real Fucking Problem

Vince

We were up by three when I dropped my gloves and picked a fight with a guy much larger than me.

One of the goals tonight was mine, along with an assist, which must have pissed Austin Marchand off, because the Atlanta defenseman checked me hard against the boards. When he did, he sneered through his face mask and said, "Cute show tonight, Tanev. That girl of yours must have a golden pussy, huh? Make sure you pass her on to me when you're done."

I ground my teeth, elbowing his ribs before I started wailing on him. He threw me to the ice, where we tussled for a minute before I jumped up. When he was standing, too, he grinned a bloody smile like he'd won.

So, I dropped my gloves, and we duked it out to the roar of twenty-thousand Osprey fans.

I was still fuming when the refs peeled us off each other and made me skate to the penalty box. Normally, I'd be revving up the crowd after a fight like that, but I was still pissed. I wanted to punch that fucker's teeth through his lips so he'd learn to never talk about Maven like that again. Having to deny allegations anytime a reporter asked if there was anything between us was hard enough as it was, but having another player — shit, having *anyone* — talk about her like all she was was a piece of ass?

That wasn't going to fucking fly.

Marchand's teammates goaded me when I was in the box, along with a few Atlanta fans beating on the glass behind my head, but I ignored them all. My eyes skirted to Coach, who arched a brow at me that said he'd be wanting an explanation later. He wasn't pissed, though, because we were winning — and now, we had even more momentum, our crowd fired up and chanting. A few stuffed animal fish toys flew onto the ice prematurely, a sign that they were confident we had the win.

My eyes found Maven next.

I sucked in a breath at her smile, the one that beamed across her entire face. Her eyes were shining and bright behind where she held her phone, and I could tell she was zooming it in on me. She shook her head as she did, and when I winked, she laughed, typing something on the screen before posting the video, I assumed.

I watched her for a moment more before I closed my eyes, and set my gaze back to the game.

Before her, it had never been an issue for me to focus on hockey. It didn't matter what kind of pussy I was getting before or after the games — when I was on the ice, that was all that mattered.

But with her in the tunnel, it was impossible not to notice.

I felt her eyes on me, felt her smile like it was my own. I could predict the exact shape of it, how it would spread slowly, like she was fighting it before she let it take over her completely. I could close my eyes and see hers, could feel her pulse under my palm just like the stick I held right now.

She was engrained in me.

Which was a real fucking problem, considering what she wanted.

An unfamiliar numbness fell over me like fog as we did our victory lap around the rink at the end of the game. We were on fire. *I* was on fire.

And yet I felt like a man standing on a hilltop watching a tornado touchdown, knowing it would be blazing a path of destruction straight toward me, but unable to move my feet.

Maven was laughing in the locker room when I made it back after the star ceremony, and her eyes caught mine from across the room. She smiled, her gaze mischievous and stirring my body to life.

I could fuck that girl twenty times a day and still not ever get enough.

"So... Boomer's?" she asked me when I walked over to where she and Carter were.

I hoped my smile was more convincing than it felt. "Of course. I just want to run upstairs and bike for a bit. Legs are tight."

She nodded, smirking a little bit as she reached up and thumbed my brow. I still had a little bit of dried blood on it from the fight.

"What did he say to get you so worked up?"

I shrugged. "Nothing. I just felt like fighting."

She gave me a look that said she knew better, but dropped it. "I'm going to go change. Text me when you're wrapping up?"

With a nod from me, she swept out of the locker room, and I watched her go with a boulder sitting on my chest.

When I turned toward my locker to start changing, I found Will Perry staring at me.

He didn't say a word, but when I went upstairs to the team gym, he followed. Silently, he climbed onto the bike next to mine, and it was just the sound of the equipment whirring for a while before he finally spoke.

"When are you going to tell her?"

Sweat dripped into my eyes, my ribs burning. "Don't."

He shook his head, sitting up and slowing his stride. He watched me in the mirror, but I stayed bent, pedaling faster. The longer I felt his eyes on me, the harder I worked, until I was out of breath and cursing, sitting up to mirror his stance. I swiped my towel off the handlebars and covered my face with it, slinging it over my shoulder before my hands wrapped around the bars once more. I stared at my knuckles where they were turning white, all while he stared at me.

"You love her."

I closed my eyes on a long exhale.

"You don't have to admit it," he continued. "I know it when I see it."

My brows bent together then, and I turned to look at him, stunned to see a bit of vulnerability on that normally grumpy face of his. He didn't have to tell me for me to know the ghosts in his eyes were the ones of his late wife.

I sighed, sitting up again and folding my arms over my chest. "I'm going insane."

"It's terrifying, isn't it?"

I laughed through my nose, but didn't say anything more.

"Have you two been..."

"Fucking like porn stars every waking minute of the day? Yes."

He smirked, wiping a hand over his mouth. "Not what I was going to say, but good to know." He fell quiet for a moment before adding, "So, what's wrong?"

I didn't even try to say *nothing*, because the fact that he could read me well enough to follow me up here told me I didn't stand a chance of convincing him of that.

"I don't know," I admitted. "We're having a great time. She's... *God,* she's fucking phenomenal. Funny. Smart. Stubborn as hell. That woman knocks me on my ass daily."

"She's a good one."

I nodded.

"So... again, what's the issue?"

I swallowed. "The issue is that I think you might be right." I looked at him then. "I think I love her."

Saying the words out loud felt like stabbing my own chest with a dull, rusty knife. I felt the air leak out of me along with them, and I stared down at my shoes on the bike pedals.

"When are you going to tell her?"

"Never."

He sucked his teeth. "Don't be an idiot."

"She doesn't want that," I said. "She doesn't want... *me.*" That made the knife twist deeper. "We're just having fun, friends with benefits, no expectations."

"Good God, *why*?" Will wrinkled his nose. "Don't tell me that was your idea."

"Hell no," I said quickly. "I don't know, it just kind of... happened. The first time we hooked up, she said it was a one-time-only thing. We didn't even last two weeks before we hooked up again, and then she put these... I don't know, these *rules* in place."

Will was silent for so long that I turned to look at him, and found him slow blinking at me like I was stupid.

"What?"

"I'm just trying to figure out if you really are an idiot."

"She doesn't want anything more. She told me as much. She said she just wanted us to enjoy the time while we have it and then..."

I didn't want to finish that sentence.

"And you didn't fight her on it?"

"Of course not," I said quickly.

"Dumbass."

I leveled him with a glare. "What was I supposed to do? Tell her I didn't care what she wanted, that I don't respect her boundaries, and I want to be the one calling the shots?" I continued before he had the chance to answer. "She had her heart obliterated by a rich asshole athlete, and she lumps me into the same category." I ground my teeth. "I saw it in her eyes when she told me she just wanted this little arrangement."

"Who?"

"I don't know, some pussy golfer."

Will wrinkled his nose. "I bet I could beat him."

"Your swing is weak, Daddy P," I said, tilting my head to the side. "*Me*, on the other hand."

He snorted. "So this guy fucked her up?"

My hands tightened into fists. "She thinks if we let it go too far, I'd break her heart just like he did."

"Would you?"

I was silent at that, because the truth was that I didn't know.

I couldn't make her promises, not when I was only in my first season in the league with no fucking clue what came next. If my career took off, what would that look like for us? Would she follow me if I got traded to another team, another city?

Could I expect her to?

And even if they did extend my contract and I got to stay in Tampa, it wasn't like she'd have this twenty-four-seven-access pass forever. The only reason I had so much time with her now was because her job called for it.

Would I be enough for her, if she only had me in-between practices and games? Would she put up with me traveling all the time?

Would she trust me?

And even if she did... would it ever be fair, to ask that of her, of anyone?

"I've never thought about any of this," I admitted, shaking my head. "I assumed I'd never have to, at least not for a while. Hockey and partying and girls, that I can handle. But Maven..." I swallowed. "Fuck, I didn't see her coming."

A little laugh puffed out of William at that. "We never do."

I tried to smile, but it fell short. And for a while, we sat there in silence, both of us in our own worlds.

"Look, I won't lie to you. If she's been hurt before, the road ahead of you will be bumpy at best, and a pothole-ridden shit show at worst," he said. "But... if you're serious about her, maybe you just need to give her time to see that, to see that you're different, and that history doesn't have to repeat itself."

I nodded, hating how my chest lit up with hope at his suggestion. I thought of earlier that week in my condo, when I watched Maven smile and hum along to the music while she tended to the plants I'd bought her. She'd had her hair pulled back, a blue-jean bandana tied around the crown of her head, her lips nude and begging to be kissed.

The domestic nature of it had slammed into me so hard I could barely breathe until I laid her down and flexed inside her. I had to be connected, to feel that she was mine, even if just for that moment.

And that's what it was — a moment.

I didn't want to press her for more. I couldn't.

She'd made the rules, and I was following them, because if I didn't, I'd lose her even sooner than I already had to.

I cracked my neck. "Thanks, man," I said, hopping off the bike. "But I think if this is all I can have with her, I'm just going to soak up every minute of it and not overanalyze the situation."

"Sure," he said, hopping off his bike, too. "Because you don't seem like you're worried at all."

He leveled me with one last look before he left the gym.

Once I'd showered, I headed back to the condo, promising the guys I'd see them out at the bar when I knew it was a lie. I didn't want to have to explain myself.

But all I wanted that night was Maven.

I texted her and asked her to come up, and as soon as I opened the door, I pulled her into me, kissing along her neck and collarbone as I worked to undress her.

She didn't fight me, didn't insist we go or ask if the guys were waiting on me. She opened like a flower more and more with each sigh, and then we were in my bed, and I lost myself in the present moment with everything that she was.

When we were spent, I watched her from the bed as she washed her face in my bathroom. She had a toothbrush in there, too – and her shampoo was in my shower.

She frowned a little when she caught my gaze in the mirror, turning and looking over her shoulder covered with one of my t-shirts.

"You okay?" she asked with a curious grin.

I swallowed down the truth, shoving Will's words out of my head before they could echo any louder.

"Never better," I lied. "Now bring that sweet ass back to bed."

When she did, I peeled my t-shirt off her body and slid inside her until I felt whole again.

Chapter 32

Making a Mess

Maven

The night before we had to travel to Ottawa, I showed up at Vince's door in nothing but his jersey.

Christmas was just around the corner, and I wanted to give him a gift. Of course, giving him an *actual* gift would cross over our friends with benefits boundary and head right into relationship territory. So I wrapped myself up in the package he'd been dying to see me in, finding a creative way to have the best of both worlds.

I was barefoot, looking up and down the hall and praying no one would come out of their condos and see me. They might assume I had on shorts underneath, but I didn't — nor was I wearing a bra or panties. I swallowed down the nerves I still got every time I anticipated being touched by Vince, smirking at the peephole until the moment the door swung open.

As soon as it did, a sturdy hand wrapped around my wrist and pulled me inside, and then I was pressed against the door when it closed behind us, and Vince was everywhere.

His hands pinned my hips to the wood, one thigh sliding between mine as he kissed me with a low, deep growl rumbling out of his throat. He slid his hands up to palm my breasts through the jersey next, and I moaned into his mouth, threading my arms around his neck.

"Woman," he said when he pulled back, his eyes taking in the full sight of me. "You're wearing my jersey."

"I am."

He shook his head, fisting his hands in the fabric as his eyes grew hungrier. "This makes me fucking feral, Mave."

"I thought it might be good luck," I said, heating under his stare. "Letting you win a bet the night before we go to Canada."

He wet his lips. "I *did* bet that I'd have you in this one day, didn't I? Past Me was a genius."

"Maybe it can be a new tradition," I said, linking my arms around his neck again. "Me wearing your jersey to the games."

His nostrils flared, one hand sliding up to cradle the back of my neck and bring me into him. "Careful. People might think you're mine."

My lips parted when he hovered his just an inch away, my heart thundering in my ears.

"They'll just think it's part of the gig," I assured him, even as it made my chest squeeze painfully around my lungs. "Don't worry. Your bunnies will only take it as motivation to try harder."

I didn't know why the joke fell so flat, why it didn't land with the sassy bite I intended. It sounded almost... sad, petty, and I shook my head and smiled quickly to cover it.

That's when I noticed Vince was speckled with clay, and that now, the jersey I wore was, too.

"Shit," he said, following my gaze and looking down at his hands. "I'm sorry, I ruined it."

"Or did you make it better?" I asked, thumbing over one of the places where his fingerprints were etched in a rust orange clay against the white jersey fabric. I smiled up at him next. "Are you making something?"

He shrugged, nodding to where he'd left a heap of clay wet and ready to be molded on the wheel. "Not yet. Just... fucking around."

"Stress relief before the big game?"

He swallowed. "Something like that."

I knew there was a lot riding on this trip. The Ottawa Otters were currently first in our division, and everyone assumed we were flying up to get our asses handed to us. They'd beat us in a shutout when they came to Tampa earlier in the season, and the Ospreys wanted a redemption game.

That had to be a lot of pressure on Vince.

So I grabbed his hand in mine and tugged him toward the wheel. "Teach me."

"Teach you?"

I nodded, pushing gently on his chest until he sat on the stool by the wheel. Then, I carefully sat in his lap, rolling the sleeves of my new jersey up several times until they stayed above my elbows.

"I don't know how I'm supposed to focus on pottery when you're in my lap."

"Did I mention I'm not wearing a bra?" I asked, sneaking a peek at him over my shoulder.

He groaned, wrapping his hands around my hips and grinding into me.

I swatted his hands away. "If you want to touch me, you have to teach me."

His head hit the top of mine on an exasperated sigh, and I smiled, flicking on the button that made the wheel start to spin. Of course, I had no idea what I was doing, and apparently you needed to have your hands ready because the clay began to wobble and spray over both of us and the table and the surrounding area, too.

Vince thumbed it off quickly, laughing and digging his fingers into my side to tickle me.

But then, he trailed his hands up and over my shoulders, palms floating down every inch of my arms until they covered the backs of my hands. He threaded his fingers over mine, moved us closer to the wheel, and started it again — this time, bringing my palms to the clay.

He didn't actually *explain* anything, just used his hands to guide me. He'd dip our fingertips in the bowl of water at the station before showing me how and where to press against the clay to shape it. We molded it into a fat, shallow shape before he showed me how to lengthen it, to make it deeper and more narrow.

As always, his French music served as the soundtrack, and the longer we worked, the more I understood.

It was peaceful.

We didn't make anything of perfection or beauty. Quite the opposite, actually. We'd mold for a while, only to destroy and start again. But there was something magical in that process alone, that we could build and then change our minds, shape and then wipe clean, start over at any point.

Just like the first time I'd watched him in this space, I found myself mesmerized by his hands. They were wet and covered in clay, just like mine, and the way they cupped and pressed against the terra-cotta was so erotic it made me wet without him even touching me.

When he felt like I had the hang of it, Vince removed his hands from behind mine, letting me try out shaping on my own.

But that left his hands with nothing to do.

And so, they began to roam.

He rested them on my knees, marking my bare skin with the cool, wet clay before he dragged it up, up, up, toward the hem of the jersey that just barely covered my thighs. I sighed when his fingertips slid under the fabric, my head falling back against his chest, eyes closing.

"You're making a mess," he mused in my ear before kissing behind it, and I peered my eyes open long enough to see where the clay had begun to warp and spray again.

I flicked the machine off, twisting in his arms to straddle him.

"So are you," I said.

"Of your panties?"

"I'm not wearing any."

He cursed. "So there's nothing underneath this," he said, rubbing his hands on the fabric of my jersey. He used it like a towel, absolutely destroying it in the process of wiping his hands clean.

I hoped that meant he had other plans for them.

"I mean... there's *something,*" I teased, nipping at his bottom lip. "Maybe you should explore."

When his hands were as clean as he could get them, he did just that.

It was a shock of cold lightning, one hand jutting between my thighs as the other reached up and under to palm my breast. I balanced haphazardly in his lap, trying to maneuver to give him more room as he teased my slick entrance with one thick fingertip.

He groaned when he felt me, flicking my nipple and sliding just a fraction of that finger inside me at the same time. Then, he withdrew both hands and smacked the side of my ass.

"Up."

I jumped off him, and as soon as I was out of the way, he made quick work of his shorts and tore his t-shirt over head. His briefs went next, and then it was just him – tan and toned and gloriously naked.

Vince tugged me back into his lap and caught me in a rough kiss, our teeth clashing when he did. He held me steady with one hand as the other reached down and placed the tip of his cock against my opening, and he pulled my hips down at the same time he flexed hard, filling me with brute precision that made me gasp and see stars.

"Oh, *fuck*, Maven," he groaned when he filled me, withdrawing only to press all the way in again. I felt his pelvis curl under me, felt how he flexed his ass and dug himself as deep as possible, until I was sitting all the way down. "I love the way you feel. Every single time." He shook his head like he was in disbelief. "I'll never get enough of this, of you."

We were both needy, kissing and clawing and fucking each other hard. It was like we only had minutes before the clock struck midnight, before the spell was broken and we were without each other again.

I tangled my hands in his hair, matting it with clay as I rolled my body and bucked my hips. He filled me, again and again, his brows etched together as if he were in pain, as if he needed to bury himself inside me to feel anything at all.

Every now and then, he'd look down at where his team's name was on my chest, his hands curling over the stitching on the back that spelled out *Tanev*, and I swore I felt him fuck me harder then, deeper, with more intensity than I'd ever felt before.

My climax built furiously fast, and I tossed my head back, moaning and bouncing in his lap. Deftly, I felt his hand wrap around my throat, and he squeezed with just enough pressure to make my vision go dark and heighten all my other senses.

"Open your mouth," he said, and when I did, he slicked his fingers inside.

I could still taste a bit of the earthy clay mixed with his salty skin, and I swirled my tongue around those fingers like it was his cock. He groaned like that's what he was imagining, too, but then he pulled out and trailed his slick digits down and under my jersey.

They slid between my cheeks, toying with the hole he wasn't currently filling as my eyelids fluttered.

"Yes," I breathed.

Vince smirked against my neck, answering my plea with one smooth plummet of his middle finger deep inside me.

I gasped, shaking, clinging to him as he set my orgasm on fire. He filled me in every way — his mouth on mine, his cock buried inside me, his finger stroking the inside of my asshole with the same perfect rhythm. The combination made me combust, and a numb fire licked at my nerve endings before spreading and consuming my entire being.

I moaned his name as I came, and with a groan, he followed. I felt him spill inside me, and it only made me come harder, made the orgasm echo like that was the key to unlocking a series of aftershocks.

It was unbridled and messy and so fucking *hot*.

When we finished, Vince carefully removed his finger, but kept me there in his lap, his cock softening a bit inside me. We were sweating, my forehead pressed to his as he wrapped me up in his arms.

As our breaths evened, he moved my hair from my face, holding at the back of my neck like he was afraid I'd pull away. I could hear his heart racing, felt his head shake marginally as his brows pinched together even more.

"What?" I asked.

But he just shook his head again.

We stayed like that a few minutes, holding tight to each other without a single word, and then he began moving again.

Pump. His hips flexing into me. *Pump*. His mouth claiming mine. *Pump*. His hands sliding under the fabric of the jersey before sliding it up and over my head.

He dropped it to the floor, hands exploring my newly revealed skin that had been covered the first round. He roamed every inch of my navel, my rib cage, my breasts, and back down to my hips.

And he grew harder inside me, his release mixing with mine and providing the lubrication to keep going.

Everything was more sensitive this time, our bodies already sated as we pushed them to give us more. My eyes locked on his, and Vince held me there, grabbing the back of my neck and making me watch him as he flexed deeper.

It was too much.

I wanted to close my eyes, to look away, to disconnect. Because the way he looked at me, the way he slowed his pace so much that he was just barely moving inside me, the way he held me so tight like he thought I might disappear...

It was intimate.

It was heavier, more weighted than any time he'd touched me before.

"Vince," I warned.

He only held me tighter, and when I closed my eyes, he smacked my ass.

"Look at me."

When I did, he shook his head, rolling his lips together as he started to fuck me faster.

"What have you done to me?"

He whispered the words so low I thought I might have misheard them, and then he was kissing me so hard it hurt.

Vince was so deep, so needy, and the power that sent rushing through me sharpened into an electric fire. I reached between us, circling my clit, and my second orgasm shot through me so quick it didn't seem possible. It was more intense, my clit already sensitive, my walls swollen. I cried out every last wave of it, and then Vince came, too, and he held me down on his lap, his cock twitching inside me, cum leaking out and down the insides of my thighs.

I'd never felt anything like that before, not in all my life.

As soon as we stopped moving, tears pricked my eyes.

I panicked, not wanting Vince to see, so I climbed off his lap and muttered something about cleaning up before I padded down the hall to his shower. My face warped when I made it to the bathroom, and I pressed a hand over where my heart squeezed under my rib cage, like that could soothe it.

It was too much.

That first time was fucking.

But that second time...

It felt a whole lot like making love.

I closed my eyes, shaking my head and swiping the tears from my cheeks before they could stain. This was what had gotten me in trouble with James – all the times he made it feel so real, made *me* feel so safe and wanted. It made it impossible not to trust him, to believe him when he said we had a future together.

And in that moment, I realized that was what had fucked me up the most.

It was one thing to hear a man spurt his lies and know they're lies, to smile at them in amusement that they thought they could pull one over on you. But the power is still in your hands then, and you can detach. You can enjoy the moment knowing it will end. You can let go before you've even started to hold on.

It was when they were convincing like this, when they made you second-guess if you were wrong about men. Could this one be different? Could he care?

Could he be the one?

Sucking in a shuttering breath, I dug my heels into my eyes and internally groaned in frustration.

I was being a fool.

Wiping my nose with the back of my wrist, I hastily turned the shower faucet on and climbed in, scrubbing my skin like I could eradicate my feelings from the outside in.

It wasn't long before Vince joined me, and he wrapped me up in his arms, pulling my back to his chest as I fought not to feel anything, not to let my body and mind and heart float away in a balloon of hope.

Chapter 33

Tell Me What You Need

Vince

The plane ride home from Canada was a circus.

We'd managed to squeak out a win in overtime against Ottawa, who were the number one team in our division. And it didn't matter that, really, we didn't play our best, or that we got lucky on a shot that tipped off their own player's skate and got us the W.

We partied like we'd just won the Cup.

It was a Saturday, and it had been an afternoon game, so it was just past nine when we touched down in Tampa. The night was young, it was the weekend, we had a late practice the next day, and we'd just won the game every sportscaster in the nation was sure we'd lose.

The energy was untouchable.

Jaxson shotgunned another beer as the front half of the plane debarked, smashing the can on his head when he was done. He shook his head with his tongue hanging out like a dog, and then started barking at Maven, which made her throw her head back in a laugh in such a carefree way it made my chest tight.

"You guys are insane!" she yelled in-between peals of laughter just as Carter started twerking on the seat in front of her.

"Come on, Maven. Match our energy," he goaded her.

She snorted and waved him off. "I don't think that's possible."

"The night is young, *we* are young, and Tampa is waiting to celebrate us," Jaxson said, grabbing Maven by the hands and pulling her up reluctantly from her chair. "You're part of this team now. Time to show it."

"And exactly how do you propose I do that?"

Will smirked as he grabbed her shoulders from behind and gave them a little squeeze. "Show us your celly dance."

"My *what*?"

The guys who were still on the plane cheered, clapping and whistling before Carter started a chant.

Cel-ly dance, cel-ly dance.

Our pilot played right into our hands, cranking the music on the stereo system. It was a club mix of "Ferrari," and our cheers grew louder as Maven's mouth popped open in an amused smile.

"You brutes are dreaming," she said on a laugh. Her eyes found mine then, and I made a fake pouty face, clucking my tongue.

"Aw, I think she's embarrassed, guys," I said, crossing the plane until I was behind her. I rubbed her shoulders, brushing my thumb along the slope of her neck and loving that I made chills break out when I did. "It's okay, Maven. We know you can't dance for shit."

The guys laughed and made a deep *ooohhhh* sound, watching as Maven narrowed her eyes and looked over her shoulder at me.

"Is that what you think?"

I shrugged, egging her on. "Prove me wrong."

The team started chanting her name, and she arched a brow, breaking out of my hold with a determined nod.

Using the hand Carter had outstretched to help her, she climbed up onto one of the large leather seats, and then she started pumping her fists to make the team roar even louder.

When she had their attention, she cast me one last *watch this* look, and she broke it down.

She was goofy at first, waving her hands in the air and bobbing her head. Then, her shoulders shimmied, and she pointed at one of our wingers before doing his signature celebration dance – brushing off her shoulders with her brows pinched together before she pretended to shoot a basket. She held her hands up in the little flick and we all went wild.

One by one, she pointed at each teammate and mimicked them, whether by doing their dance or, like in Daddy P's case, crossing her arms and scowling hard while imitating his crouched goalie position.

My stomach was in stitches, and just when I thought she couldn't shock us all any more than she had, she pointed right at me with a wink.

Then, she bent in half, her hands finding the leather of the seat. She kicked one foot up behind her to balance on the head rest, and then the other, until she was inverted and stacking her hips over her shoulders.

The plane quieted a bit with confused murmurs, the music growing in a crescendo toward the beat drop. When it did, Maven knocked us all on our asses.

Because she started shaking *hers*.

She twerked upside down, her ass bouncing side to side, up and down, and then in a circle as she threw it to the beat. The team went absolutely ape shit, but when Carter wound up like he was going to smack her ass, I caught his wrist before he could, pinning him with a glare.

"Do you want to die tonight?" I asked him.

He just laughed, holding his hands up in surrender while he and Jaxson exchanged looks.

Trying to play it off before they could read too much into it, I picked Maven up and hauled her over my shoulder, dancing us down the aisle and off the plane with her little fists beating on my back, and the team following behind us with hoots and hollers.

I didn't drop her until we were on the tarmac, and she came up breathless, laughing and smacking my chest.

"You interrupted my celly!"

"That's because it was about to get me thrown off my team and possibly in jail, too."

She grinned, leaning forward with a little shimmy of her shoulders. "What's wrong, Vince Cool? Don't like other guys looking at my ass?"

She waggled her brows as I leaned in and tilted her chin up with my knuckles. "I'm going to spank that ass later."

"Promises, promises."

Maven was so light, so playful in that moment that I couldn't help but mirror her smile.

I wanted to kiss her.

Right then, right there, without a fucking care in the world who saw us. I wanted to kiss her until she melted into me the way she always did, until she begged me to take her home.

"SURPRISE!"

I didn't realize how close my lips were to Maven's until the sound broke through the haze, and we both jumped away from each other, snapping our heads in the direction it came from.

When I saw my family standing there with wide-open arms, my jaw dropped.

"Mom? Dad? *Grace*?" I shook my head in disbelief as they crowded me in a group hug. "What the hell are you doing here?"

"We knew you wouldn't be able to come home for Christmas with your schedule," Mom said.

"So, Mom insisted we bring Christmas to you," my little sister finished, rolling her eyes. "Precious Prince Vince, always the favorite child."

Mom narrowed her eyes, but we all laughed at the joke, the same one Grace had made for years. My dad clapped me on the shoulder, beaming, his chest puffed. "You look good, son. Damn good. And what a game!"

I was still in shock that they were there, shaking my head as my heart swelled. If I wasn't surrounded by my teammates, I probably would have cried. It'd been so long since I'd seen them, my first season in the NHL sweeping me up and making it impossible to get back up to Michigan for a visit. It had been hard at first without them, but then I'd been so focused on the schedule, and most recently, on Maven. I hadn't stopped long enough to remember how homesick I was.

Now that they were here, it was like a sigh of relief, a deep breath I didn't know I had been needing so desperately to take.

My mom and dad were dressed to impress, just like always, Mom in a pencil skirt and elegant blouse, and Dad in slacks and a sports coat. Grace was in a simple sundress, which I knew she had probably been so desperate to wear that she put it on even before they left the freezing cold weather in Michigan. My sister was born to be a beach bum, and I knew it was just a matter of time before she'd leave our home state behind and find refuge in a state that didn't have a winter. Where I was at home on the ice, she was at home in the sun.

I saw my own features staring back at me when I looked at them — the eyes I got from my mom, the smile I got from my dad, the way my sister's nose was the same blend of our parents as mine was.

"Okay, you are so rude," Grace said, flicking me in the arm before she brushed past me. She swept her long blonde hair over her shoulder and walked right up to Maven. "Hi! It's so nice to finally meet you! Especially after the embarrassing amount of times you've seen me dance."

Maven seemed as surprised as me, her eyes flicking to mine before she extended her hand for Grace's. "Trust me, you're better than I could ever be."

Grace didn't shake Maven's hand. Instead, she grabbed her in a crushing hug.

"Don't let her lie to you," Carter said, popping up out of nowhere and grabbing my shoulders from behind as he joined us. "Maven just rocked that whole damn plane."

"Oh my, I bet that was quite the show," Mom said, smiling at Maven next. "I'm Lorraine. This is my husband, Derrick."

"You," Dad said, pointing at Maven before crushing her in an even more powerful hug than Grace had. "Are one talented lady. I downloaded Instagram because of you."

Grace groaned like she was embarrassed.

"The videos you post?" Mom shook her head, smiling. "Just... incredible! Do you do all that editing yourself? The way the clips match up to the music?"

"It's called a Reel, Mom," Grace said.

"Well, whatever you call it, this one has turned our son into a superstar," Dad beamed.

Maven smiled nervously. "Oh, he did that all on his own."

Her eyes flitted to mine then, and my chest swelled in a completely new way.

"We've got cars coming," Jaxson said, running over to join us. He smiled and introduced himself to my family, and I didn't miss how he nearly swallowed his tongue when he met my sister.

I cocked a brow at him when he stared at her a little too long, and then glowered when his face turned like I'd caught him doing something he wasn't supposed to.

I hoped that look told him not to get any ideas, because I loved Jax, but I'd kill him if he tried something with my sister.

"I think we're going out without Vince Cool tonight," Carter said, nodding toward Jaxson. "Let's give him space to enjoy the family reunion."

"I'll hit you guys up later," I promised, but the way they smirked at Maven, then my family, and then me — I knew they wouldn't hold their breath waiting for that call.

Once they were gone, I turned back to my family.

"It was nice to meet you," Maven said. "I'm just going to—"

"Come with us."

I cut her off with the request, and she furrowed her brows, trying to communicate something to me with that look alone that I couldn't decipher.

Or, maybe I could, but I chose to ignore it.

"Yes, *please* do not leave me alone with these three," Grace said, linking her arm through Maven's. "I'll be the forgotten child in the corner. At least with you there, I'll have someone to talk to while they fuss over their precious baby boy."

"Grace," Mom warned on a smile. And then, Dad took Mom's hand in his and started walking, Grace following and toting Maven right along.

She looked over her shoulder at me, and I shrugged, smiling.

It looked like there was a change of plans.

ଓ ଓ ଓ

We went to dinner at a chic rooftop restaurant on the Riverwalk, which was at Grace's request. At Mom's, we ended up back at my condo, she and my sister fussing over all my pottery, and even more over the garden room Maven had brought to life. Dad and I talked with the ESPN highlights on in the background until he whipped up some of his famous cocktails and we all ended up outside on the balcony enjoying the balmy Florida night.

We talked and laughed and shared stories of the past, most of which made me groan and hide my face because my family was all too eager to try to embarrass me in front of Maven. They seemed especially keen to tell her about the time I wore my underwear on my head for two weeks because we were on a win streak at Michigan, and I was convinced that was why.

Through it all, Maven fit in like she was already part of the family.

My mom all but interrogated her at dinner, but not in the way she would if she were sizing someone up. It was more like she was so genuinely curious about Maven and everything that she was that she just couldn't stop asking.

She lit up with every answer, fascinated by Maven's upbringing and career.

Grace was just as bad, squealing when she found out Maven loved yoga and begging her to take her to a studio for a class while they were in town. She also told Maven repeatedly how jealous she was that Maven's place was so close to the beach.

And while Dad was quieter with his interest, he loved how quick-witted Maven was, how she volleyed back and forth with me *and* with him. She made him bust a gut more than once throughout the night, and when Maven told him what her plans were once this assignment wrapped up, Dad's eyes shone like she was his own daughter, and he had a right to be proud.

He pegged me with a curious look, too — one I couldn't bear for long before I looked down at my cocktail and took a long pull.

It was surreal — having them there in my new home, having Maven there with us. And as much as I pretended to be annoyed with all the questions my family asked her, the truth was I loved it — because I got to know more about her, too. And every new little story she told, every piece of herself she revealed? It made me feel like a greedy kid in a candy store.

I wanted more of her.

I wanted *all* of her.

It was almost three in the morning by the time Grace dragged my yawning parents toward the door. They were staying at a hotel on the Riverwalk just a few blocks away.

"Thank you for changing your plans for us tonight, son," Dad said, clapping my back in a tight hug. "Hope we didn't cramp your style."

"Please, he's got no style to begin with," Grace said, but she hugged me like she'd missed me, and I knew she had.

"It was a great surprise," I told them earnestly. "Hopefully I can show you around a little before you have to go."

"We know you're busy," Mom said, yawning again as I tucked her into my side. "We're just happy to steal you away for whatever you can manage." Her eyes lit up on a smile as she pulled away from me and framed Maven's arms with her hands. "And *you*, young lady. You are just... sensational. It was so lovely spending the evening with you."

Maven flushed. "You, as well, Mrs. Tanev."

"I want to meet these amazing parents of yours. Let's all have a little get together, yes?" Mom looked back at me with the question.

I glanced at Maven, who had the strangest look on her face then — like she was sick or sad or both.

"We'll see, Mom," I said, guiding them all toward the door.

Everyone hugged again, and I noticed my dad speaking to Maven in a low voice while Grace and Mom asked me about the International Mall in town. I tried to make out what he was saying but had no luck, and when he patted Maven's arm with a grin, she smiled, but that same sad look was etched into her expression.

My stomach tied up in knots at the sight.

The goodbye dragged on for twenty minutes before they were gone, and as soon as the door shut, silence fell over me and Maven like a cold, wet blanket.

I stood there with my hand on the knob for a moment before swallowing and turning to face her. She looked as if she were in a daze, her eyes unfocused where they stared at the floor between us.

"Sorry about that," I said, rubbing the back of my neck with a smile. "They can be a lot."

"They're lovely," she whispered.

And then her eyes welled with tears.

I'd never seen her like that, never watched as her face warped and all the walls she held so firmly around her crumbled into dust. It tore through my chest like a gunshot, seeing her sad, seeing her in pain.

"Mave," I said, crossing the room to where she stood. I wrapped her up in my arms, which made her go stiff before she softened and gripped onto me, burying her head in my chest. I held her tight for a long time, feeling the air around us growing heavier, colder.

"What's wrong?"

She shook her head, over and over, sniffing before she pulled away from me. "I'm going to go. It's late."

I blinked as she swiped the tears from her face and grabbed her purse. "What? You're leaving?"

"You have practice tomorrow. You should get some rest."

Her voice sounded detached, dead.

"I can think of a more fun way to energize," I said, hoping the joke would make her laugh, that we could slip back into the place we'd been on the tarmac when she was teasing me and I was trying not to kiss her in public.

Instead, her face warped, and she turned away from me so I wouldn't see as more tears broke through.

"Hey," I said, slipping my fingertips in the crook of her elbow. She wouldn't look at me until I tilted her chin and gave her no choice. "Talk to me."

She shook her head, over and over, swiping furiously at the tears that kept coming. She was the strongest, most stubborn woman I knew — and she was crying.

It fucking wrecked me.

I lifted my hands to take the place of hers, thumbing away each tear, and that made her sob before shoving me away. "Stop," she pleaded, the word croaking out like it pained her.

"Tell me how to help."

"Stop looking at me like that, stop touching me, stop..." She buried her face in her hands.

I didn't dare reach for her again.

After a long moment, she let her hands fall to her thighs, her eyes pitiful when they found mine. "We can't do stuff like this, Vince," she whispered, licking the tears from her lips. "Because when we do, I... I feel like..."

My heart stopped in my chest before firing back to life with a thunderous kick. "You feel like what, Maven?" I asked, nostrils flaring as I took a step toward her. "Like I love you?"

Her eyes snapped to mine, wide and terrified.

"Like I am compelled by you, by everything that you are, by how you have annihilated whatever version of my life existed before you?"

"Don't," she whispered, but I couldn't stop now.

I closed the last of the distance between us, grabbing her hand and forcing it to my chest. "Do you feel me holding on tighter every time you're in my arms? Do you feel time slipping away too fast when we're together?" My jaw tightened with restraint against the emotion strangling my throat. "Do you feel my heart fucking *breaking* at the thought of losing you? Is that what you feel, Maven?"

Her chin wobbled, two silent tears streaking down her cheeks.

"Look at me," I begged, and when she did, I swore the world stopped spinning, waiting for us to give it the cue that we were ready again. "Tell me what you feel."

Her eyelids fluttered, cheeks glistening under the soft light, but her gaze didn't waver.

"Like I want to believe you," she admitted softly.

Hope flittered through my ribcage.

"And like I'd end up broken if I actually did."

Her words slammed into me, knocking my breath from my chest like a hard check against the boards.

This wasn't her talking. I knew it like I knew every play in the Osprey's playbook. This was the remnants of the one who came before me, the one who scarred her, who made her feel like she couldn't trust another man.

Like she couldn't trust herself.

I opened my mouth, but closed it again, shaking my head. I didn't say anything.

What else *could* I say?

"I have to go." Her voice trembled with the words, more tears searing her cheeks as she tore her gaze from mine. She brushed past me and ripped the door open, sliding through it and tugging it shut behind her before I could so much as blink.

She left.

And I had no choice but to let her.

Chapter 34

Break Shit

Maven

Four days before Christmas, the Ospreys had their last home game before the holiday. It was going to be *my* last game with full access, my last assignment before everything wrapped up. Reya and Camilla were ready for me to tackle what came next, and the Osprey's GM didn't want any distractions for the team as they headed into the second half of the season and, hopefully, toward playoffs.

This was it. We'd had our fun, and now, it was time for life to go back to normal.

I should have been with Vince, but instead, I was curled up in the fetal position on my couch with my head in my best friend's lap.

It had been all I could do to show up for the morning skate, to post a few clips of content and then duck out before I broke down in front of the entire team. When Coach McCabe had asked if I was okay, I'd nearly lost it.

The worst part was that Vince looked just as miserable as I did.

And that was my fault.

I hadn't just left his condo after that night we spent with his family. I'd left the building, too. I'd packed my belongings and moved back home.

And I'd barely seen Vince since then.

The only content I posted was of him at the rink, where I felt like I could take some photos and videos and then quickly get away.

And any time I *did* see him, I lost the ability to breathe.

I was so sick, my stomach in dreadful knots, lungs operating at low capacity as if I had a box of bricks on my chest. From the outside in, it all seemed so simple – Vince had caught feelings, and I knew I had, too. All I had to do was tell him that I felt the same and we could be together.

But I couldn't do it.

It was like trying to convince myself to jump out of an airplane when I had a gut feeling my parachute wouldn't work. It was like someone else telling me it's fine to take a step, but I'm blindfolded, and when I hover my foot, I'm just certain there's a cliff there, and that I'll tumble off it and to my death.

I was frozen in place, fright-stricken, trying to survive by just staying still.

"I hate seeing you this way," Livia said softly, but I jerked as if she'd screamed. We'd been silent for so long, her playing with my hair while I cried quietly.

"I know."

"You love him, too."

I squeezed my eyes shut, and how more tears found their way out, I'd never know. I couldn't believe how much I'd cried. It had to be a Guinness World Record by now. My eyes were so swollen I was surprised I could even see at all.

"You do," Livia repeated, smoothing a hand over my hair. "Babe, why are you torturing yourself?"

"You know why."

She sighed. "Okay, yes, I do, but..." She paused like she was gathering her thoughts. "If there was ever a time to move forward, or a person to move forward *with* – is this not it?"

"Livia, James broke me," I said, pushing up so I could look her in the eyes. I hated how my voice trembled. "But Vince? He... he could kill me."

"Or he could bring you back to life."

I rolled my lips together, tasting the salty tears there.

"You're scared of being hurt again," she said, my face warping as she did. "And that's okay, that's normal," she assured me, covering my hand with hers. "And truthfully, I cannot promise you that it won't happen. No one can, not even Vince. That's what's so fucked up about relationships, about love. We give ourselves, we trust, and then we get hurt. We wonder why we ever did that, we hate everyone for a while, until... we don't. Until we meet someone, and we laugh again, and we *feel* again, and we start to wonder if we can fall in love again. So we do." She laughed a little. "And then, they fuck us over or we fuck them over and we're right back to square one."

"So you *do* get it."

She squeezed my hand. "I do. But listen, you want to know the difference between the people who end up alone and the ones who end up with the love of their life?" She leaned in on a smile. "The former never open themselves up to love again because they're too afraid of the pain that might come with it. And the latter understand that love is worth it, and that they're strong enough to survive whatever comes before they find it."

I nodded, eyes bubbling over again. "You do realize how stupid that sounds coming from someone who has told me dozens of times that love is a construct, right?"

"Yeah, well, I'm not you," she said, quickly waving me off. "I get my kicks in different ways. But baby girl, *you* are in love. And if I was ever in your shoes, I'd want you to smack me and shake me until I saw it and listened to you, too."

"You haven't smacked me yet."

"I'm close."

I chuckled, leaning my head on her shoulder and thinking about the night I spent with Vince and his family. They were so lovely, so different from James's that it had knocked me for a loop. With James, he made me feel like we were invincible, but his family only made me feel like a bug that needed to be squashed. Vince's family only spent a few hours with me — one night — and somehow, they made me feel like I'd been in the family for years, like I belonged there with them.

The words his dad had said to me before they left made more tears pool in my eyes as I recalled them.

"I wondered when my boy would give his heart to someone. I'm glad he waited for you."

Squeezing my eyes shut, the tears were released, my bottom lip quivering.

"I want to, you know," I whispered. "Trust him. Jump in. Try. I just... I feel frozen. I feel... scared. I'm *so* fucking scared, Livia. I can't sleep, I can't eat, and the sickest part of me keeps saying it's better to feel this now than later, that losing him today will be easier than a year down the line."

"Probably true. But what if you didn't have to lose him at all?" She nudged her shoulder up until I lifted my head and looked at her. "What if he stayed? What if you made it?"

I covered my heart where it fluttered at the thought. "I felt this way once before, you know. I thought I was getting married, I thought we would be together forever." I shook my head. "I think that part of me is broken now. I don't know how to access it."

Livia frowned, and we were both quiet for a long moment before her eyes widened and she lit up. "Oh, my God. I'm a genius."

She jumped up from the couch before I could ask what the hell she meant, and then she ran back to my bedroom. I heard her rummaging through something, and then a curse before a loud thump rang out.

"Liv?" I called, dragging my ass off the couch to go get her. But she swept through the living room before I had the chance, a familiar box tucked under her arm as she grabbed my wrist and tugged me toward the sliding glass door that led to my back yard.

"Come on."

"Livia, what are you doing with that?" My chest was even tighter now in the presence of the box.

"I'm not doing anything," she said, plopping it on my outdoor table. She tore the lid open. "*You* are."

"Wha—"

"Here," she said before I could ask anything, taking out the first item she found and shoving it into my hand.

I froze the moment it touched my skin.

It was a golf ball, neon orange, from one of my first dates with James. We'd gone putt-putting, him showing off and me letting him because I liked that he wanted to show off for me. At the end of the night, he'd drawn a black heart on the ball he'd won with, and I'd kept it in my purse for longer than I'd ever admit.

"Okay..." I said, staring at it.

"Throw it." Livia said, pointing across my yard toward where my compost bin was. "Or stomp on it or light it on fire or get a sledgehammer and destroy it."

"A sledgehammer?"

"Listen to me," she said, grabbing my shoulders in her hands. "You've cried over this fucker. You've gone to therapy. You've picked yourself up and you've started building a career and you've moved on. But you can't let go of him, of what he did to you, until he's no longer taking up any space. Not in your head, your heart, or this stupid box you keep shoved in the top corner of your closet." She pulled out a picture frame of me and James next, pressing it into my chest. "It's time to break shit, bitch."

As soon as the words left her mouth, she pulled out her phone and thumbed through it until Limp Bizkit was playing that exact song she'd just referenced, and she gave me a nod of encouragement, bopping her head to the beat.

"Livia, this is—"

"BREAK SHIT, BITCH."

I let out a long sigh, because I did not see how this was going to fix anything at all. But I took the frame from her anyway, and when I looked down at it, I paused.

It was a photo of me and James at the beach, my head on his shoulder, his arms wrapped around me, both of us smiling. That was the night he'd asked me my ring size. We'd spent the weekend with friends, and it was one of those perfect kind of weekends when the weather is gorgeous, and the days are long and lazy, and the nights are hot and wild. It felt like a turning point in my life. The man I loved had asked for my ring size, and we were joking about how many kids we wanted.

For so long, I looked at that photo and felt my stomach ache with how happy I'd been in that moment, with how scared I was I'd never be that happy again.

But looking at it now, I only thought one thing.

He's not Vince.

It felt wrong, to see me in another man's arms. I thought about the picture Vince took of us on the boat, and I compared my smile in that one with the one I stared at now.

I didn't even recognize her anymore, the girl on the beach.

But I knew the girl on the boat.

I shivered.

The longer I stared at the photograph in my hands, the more upset I became. I didn't want his arms around me, because they weren't Vince's. It was... *gross.* It was disturbed. It was not okay. It was *wrong* in every possible way.

And that made me laugh.

It was a short laugh at first, one that bubbled out of my chest. But then I was cackling, shaking my head as tears from *laughing* filled my eyes this time.

"Oh, God," Livia said, blinking as she stepped away from me with her hands raised. The song played out, the lyrics calling to me while my best friend stared at me like a psycho. "Did I officially push you over the insanity line?"

"No," I managed through another fit of laughter, wiping tears from my eyes. "I... I think you just saved me."

I ran a hand over the photograph, shaking my head. How did I ever think *that* was joy? How did I ever see *him* as forever?

What James and I had was love, yes — it was important in its own way. He did make me smile, and I did feel safe with him until the very moment I didn't.

But God, comparing him to Vince, comparing how I felt with James with how I feel now?

It was laughable.

Literally.

Vince pushed me. He challenged me and made me want to be spontaneous, to be free, to be *more*. I felt alive with him — not just when we were tangled in the sheets, but any time we were together. He was quick to tease me, and I loved that he did. He never shut me out. He'd been open from the first moment I'd walked through his door with my camera in tow.

I wanted to walk a hundred riverwalks with him. I wanted to be at every game. I wanted to watch him create at his pottery wheel and watch him destroy on the ice. I wanted to laugh and dance and *play,* and know that no matter where we went or what we did, he would be there, protecting me, taking care of me, *loving* me.

I tossed the golf ball up in my hand, taking one last look, and then, I heaved it with all my might just as Fred Durst screamed *motherfucker*.

I didn't even watch where it went, because in the next breath, I threw the frame down on the concrete and watched it splinter, the glass shattering with the most satisfying sound.

"Fuck YES!" Livia said, and then she handed me the next victim — a ticket stub from when we went to the zoo.

I tore it in half.

"AGAIN!" She cheered, wiggling her hips with a fist pump before another memento was tossed my way. It was a snow globe with a beach inside it. He'd bought it for me as a birthday gift.

I didn't even like snow globes.

I smashed it with so much joy I laughed like a mad woman.

"FINISH HIM!" Livia bellowed in a deep voice trying to mimic the old Mortal Kombat video game, and then I had another frame in my hand only long enough to heave it up and throw it to the ground.

Piece after piece, object after object, picture after picture, we destroyed every item in that box while "Break Stuff" played on repeat. Love notes, photographs, Christmas ornaments, books, jewelry, old dried flowers – none of it was safe. And each time I touched something new, I felt what little of James I was holding onto tear away more and more, until the last shred of him was eradicated with the satisfying breaking of a necklace, the beads on it flying everywhere and skittering across the concrete.

When we were done, I was panting, smiling, and Livia high-fived me like a proud mother.

"Good job, bitch," she said, smacking my butt. "Now, get your shit together, get your pretty ass dressed, and *go. Get. Your. Man.*"

Chapter 35

Stained

Vince

"Alright, stay on him, stay on him! Skate, skate!"

I called out to our guys on the ice along with the rest of the team on the bench, chugging water and trying to catch my breath. My eyes skirted to the scoreboard, heart hammering in my chest.

We were tied two-two with less than ten minutes left in the last period.

Both of those goals were mine.

It was an explosive game for a rookie, and I knew that's all the commentators would be talking about regardless of how this one turned out. But internally, the team felt something completely different.

Everyone on that bench with me and everyone out on the ice knew something was wrong.

I didn't miss the way they'd eyed me over the last few days, how they'd tiptoed around me, avoiding all conversation. Coach didn't ask if I was okay, and my teammates didn't poke me for information, either.

Because my heart was broken and bleeding, but I was more focused on hockey than I had been all season.

I threw my all into it. I spent all my time at the rink — skating, biking, recovering, stretching, sleeping. Whatever I could do here, I did it.

And tonight, when we skated out for the first period, I lost myself in the one constant in my life.

I just wished it was enough.

Both goals I scored felt like nothing. I didn't get the zip of accomplishment I usually did. I didn't do a celly dance or chirp at the goalie or give any kind of reaction to the roar of the crowd. For the first time in my life, I felt numb on the ice.

It scared me almost as much as the thought that I'd actually lost Maven.

Watching Will at the goal, I wondered if this was how he felt, if this was why he was always so quiet, so severe and focused. I wondered if he threw himself into hockey so he wouldn't have time to think about the loss of his wife.

My stomach roiled, and I thought I might actually puke there on the bench. One of the trainers ran over to check on me when I gagged, but I waved them off, assuring them I was fine. My eyes locked on Coach's next, begging him to call the line change so I could get back in.

When we cleared the puck out of our zone, Coach nodded, and I was already jumping the boards as the other line skated over to the bench.

As soon as my skates hit the ice, I felt calmer, steadier, less like I was about to spin out of orbit and float off into space. That ice grounded me, the thrum of the crowd humming in my veins as I sprinted toward the puck. I slammed into Ryan Crosby, heaving us both into the boards where we battled for the puck until I stole it away.

Then, I was skating down the ice.

I passed to our center, running a play that I knew would get me in scoring position. As soon as I was lined up, he shot the puck back to me.

But before I could take a swing, I was tripped.

I felt the stick catch my ankle, felt how my feet were pulled up from under me without a chance in hell of me saving it. I slammed down to the ice, my breath knocked out of me to the roaring disapproval of the crowd.

The *boos* intensified when the ref didn't call the foul.

I jumped up, gritting my teeth before I laid into him. "Need to borrow my cell, ref? You got a few missed calls."

He ignored me, which was par for the course, and normally I would have shaken it off.

But nothing about tonight was normal.

Before sense could set in, I skated hard and fast down the ice toward the player who had tripped me, and I shoved him into the glass so hard the entire stadium let out a collective, "*Oh!*"

Crosby was the first one to swing at me when he saw his teammate knocked to the ice, and then we were all fighting, the crowd cheering as we whaled on each other until the refs peeled us apart.

When they did, I was being steered toward the penalty box.

Coach gave me a stern look when they tossed me in, and I kicked the side of the boards before slamming my stick against the glass so hard I wondered if I'd cracked it.

I sat down furious, stewing, glancing at the clock and cursing when I saw we only had six minutes left. Two of those minutes would be a power play for our opponents now.

I cracked my neck as the puck was dropped and the power play began. Our fans chanted and cheered, giving their support to the four players we had on the ice trying to defend the post. Daddy P was an absolute weapon, blocking every shot that came close.

I watched from the sin bin with my eyes losing focus, brain fuzzy and in a daze. I wasn't on the ice, and I felt that numbness creeping in again, threatening to drown me, to take me under and never let me up for air.

I glanced up at the clock, and then down at the bench across the ice, hoping to lock eyes with one of my teammates and get the reinforcement I needed to pull me back to the game.

Instead, I found Maven.

Time slugged to a stop like an old train, every noise that made the collective roar of the arena fading out piece by piece. First it was the screams, and then the sticks hitting the ice, the skates, the chirps, until nothing existed but my heartbeat.

It was unsteady and loud in my ears, my ribcage restricting every breath as I blinked, wondering if I was imagining her there. When she hadn't shown by the second period, I was so sure she wouldn't show at all.

But here she was — eyes red and swollen under the makeup she'd tried to cover them with. Even still, she was breathtaking.

She stood at the end of the bench, half-hidden behind the thick glass that led back to our locker room. Her hair was tied at the nape of her neck, an Ospreys hat pulled over top. Even from across the ice I noted the freckles on her cheeks, the ones I had mapped out at this point from all the mornings I'd traced the lines between them as she slept next to me.

And she was wearing my jersey.

It wasn't *just* my jersey, either — it was *the* jersey, the one still marked by my clay handprints.

Possession ripped through my chest at the sight, at my team's logo sprawled across her chest and my number stitched onto the sleeves. I knew without seeing her turn around that it was my name across the top of her back, too.

It was a declaration without a word being said. It was her telling me what I was sure I'd never hear. It was every gut-wrenching hour of the past few days erased in a single second.

My eyes skated over that jersey, over her chest and shoulders and the exposed skin of her collarbone, too. I took my time, gaze lingering on her lips until I found her eyes once more.

Her smile was soft and tentative, and she shrugged, looking down at the jersey before she caught my eyes again.

She was here.

She was *mine*.

I knew it like I knew ice was cold. I knew just by her presence, by her wearing that jersey, by the way her brows bent together as she watched me from across the rink.

Now, my sole focus was on ending this game and getting her in my arms.

Time and sound and energy snapped back all at once, like I had just kicked my way above the treacherous waves and sucked in my first breath. There were eight seconds left in the power play, and as soon as they ticked down to zero, the crowd erupted.

We'd killed the penalty.

I kicked through the box door and flew out onto the ice, joining my team as they battled against our opponents' advance. And I wasted no time, stealing the puck and sending it down to the other side of the rink as we all chased after it.

The numbness was gone. Every cell in my body buzzed to life with Maven in that arena, with her eyes on me, with my jersey hanging off her shoulders. Through all the noise, I heard her scream my name, heard her cheers rising out above the rest.

My legs burned as I skated fast and furious down the ice. The two-minute rest had me feeling stronger than I had all game, and I blocked any player who tried to check me or steal the puck. I was laser-focused — a pass, a shot attempt, a steal, a pass. We wreaked havoc on their goalie after two minutes of them doing the same to us.

And in a slow-motion moment of clarity, I saw an opening.

I dangled players on my team and theirs, passing the puck to Carter long enough for me to skate through their defense. He sent it back to me with perfect timing for a beautiful slap shot.

I wound up and slammed it home, the puck zipping right past the goalie's helmet and into the top right of the net.

The explosion from the crowd was deafening. The buzzer didn't just sound and cut off, it rang on, like someone in traffic trying to make a point by laying on their horn for a full minute. It made my ears ring as my teammates tackled me, all of us screaming and jumping and clinging to each other. In the next breath, hats rained down on the ice.

It was my first hat trick in the NHL.

They flew from the rafters and from behind the glass, too. Some fans even threw their stuffed animal fishes, a signal to the other team that even though there were minutes left to play, our fans were sure we'd win. It was all we could do to sidestep the toys and the hats as we celebrated.

But I smiled the more they rained down, because that meant more to clean up.

And that meant play would stop.

Breaking out of the huddle of my teammates, I made a beeline for the bench as the crowd roared their thunderous approval. I dodged hats every step of the way, my eyes locked on Maven, who was still jumping and screaming and celebrating, too.

I jumped the boards with my teammates still on the bench clapping me on the shoulders, but I shoved past them, past coach, past the trainers and everyone else. I dropped my stick and ripped off my helmet just in time to slide up in front of Maven.

"I'll take that," I said, swiping the hat off her head. I placed it backward on my own, and then I swept her into my arms and kissed her.

It was the deepest breath I'd taken in days, my lungs filling themselves greedily as I held my lips to hers. Maven threaded her arms around my neck, holding me to her as if I was ever letting go now, and the crowd grew to a decibel that could permanently damage ear drums. I fisted my hands in her jersey, kissing her deeper, my heart slowly melding back together.

I was whole again.

"You're here," I whispered against her lips, breaking the kiss only long enough to say them before I was claiming her again.

"I'm here." She gripped my damp hair in her hands, pressing her forehead to mine. "I'm so sorry, Vince. I'm sorry I ran. I'm sorry I'm like this."

"Stop." I shook my head, kissing her silent. "It's not your fault. And for the record, I still want to murder that piece of shit for making you feel this way."

"Don't worry, I beat you to it."

I cocked a brow, pulling back to look down at her. "You killed him? Shit," I said, looking around and holding her head to my chest. "Maybe we shouldn't pull stunts that will have you all over national television right now."

She laughed against my chest, swatting at it before her glossy eyes were peering up at me. "I killed the hold he still had on me," she said. "I killed the fear."

"I'm a little scared, too, you know."

"Wrap it up, Tanev!" I heard Coach yell, and I didn't turn around, but I guessed they were close to done with the hat cleanup on the ice. I also didn't have to glance up to know that every phone in that arena was pointed right at where I held Maven, where she held me.

"You?" She laughed. "Why?"

"Because I've never felt this way for anyone," I confessed, thumbing her jaw. "I've been fucking sick, Mave. I've been numb. You see these marks?" I asked her, gripping the clay-covered spots of her jersey. "This is how you've stained me. You're everywhere. Do you know how terrifying it is that you have that much power over me, that without you, not even hockey makes me feel alive?"

"I do. I do know what that feels like. That's the whole reason I ran." She swallowed. "What if we fuck it all up?"

"We won't."

"What if we do?"

I shrugged. "Well, then I guess there's no one I'd rather let ruin me for anyone else." I framed her face in my hands, thumbing away a tear when it slid down her cheek. "Give me your heart."

"It's already yours," she said, climbing me, crushing me to her. "*Please,* don't break it."

"Never," I promised.

I kissed her again to another chorus of whistles and cheers from the crowd, both of us inhaling the other and holding on for dear life. I could have stayed there forever.

But there were still three minutes left to play.

"*NOW*, FORTY-ONE," Coach said, and the sternness in his voice told me that — hat trick or not — my ass was going to be grass if I didn't comply.

"Go," Maven told me, pushing against my chest.

"That was for you, by the way," I said, pulling the hat off my head and tugging it down on hers again. I backed up with a wink as she shook her head at me, and then someone handed me my helmet and my stick, and I joined my teammates on the bench just in time for the puck to drop.

Coach stared at me like he was going to end my life, but then he smirked, shaking his head before folding his arms over his chest as he turned his attention to the ice. I knew I'd be paying for my stunt, but every drill, every lap, every minute of pain would be worth it.

My knees bounced, eyes on the ice but focus completely obliterated now. I just needed my team to hold for a few more minutes. I needed this game to be over.

I needed Maven back in my arms, in my bed.

Coach called for a line change with sixty seconds left, just as our opponents pulled their goalie. It was all hands on deck to defend against them. Will batted every shot attempt away, and the rest of us served as a first and second line of defense, doing everything we could to hold the score.

And we did.

They tried with their last shred of desperation to hit us at the final buzzer, but Daddy P dropped his knees together and covered the puck with his glove.

And that was it.

We won.

I swept Maven back into my arms the moment the final buzzer sounded.

Chapter 36

Kaleidoscope

Maven

I could stare at that man's hands for the rest of my life, and it would still not be long enough.

Those hands, the ones that scored three goals tonight, the ones that held me to him in a crowd of twenty-thousand people, the ones that turned clay into art, that transformed me from hard and guarded to soft and surrendering — they were a drug.

And right now, those hands were holding a photo of me and Livia after her graduation from dental school, his thumb smoothing over the glass as a wide smile spread on his lips.

"I bet you two were hell on wheels," he said.

"Still are."

He chuckled, his head bobbing side to side like he knew that all too well. When he set the photograph down, he tucked his hands into his pockets and kept walking, taking in the surroundings.

It was the first time I'd had him in my home, and it felt almost more intimate than when I had him inside me. I stood at the door with my keys clutched in my hands, nervously fidgeting with the rings as I watched him.

My phone was in my pocket, buzzing like crazy with notifications I wasn't sure I'd want to see. After what happened at the arena, I could only imagine how we were blowing up. Strangers had been making assumptions about us for months, ever since that night Vince posted the photo of us in Baltimore. Now, they had those assumptions proven right.

The only texts I'd read were the ones from my parents, Livia, and my bosses.

Mom was excited, though still a bit wary — which was fair, all things considered.

Dad was demanding a full background check and a one-on-one talk with Vince. Poor guy.

Livia popped a bottle of champagne and sent me a video of her sipping the bubblies in my honor.

And Reya and Camilla sent so many emojis, my phone nearly broke trying to process them all. They were excited, to say the least, and the last text I saw from Camilla stated that Vince and I were all over the Internet.

I decided that, at least for tonight, I just wanted it to be us.

So, I pulled my phone from my pocket and powered it down completely before turning my attention back to Vince.

He was quiet as he studied the surroundings, studied *me*. He paced my living and dining area before disappearing down the hall, and I followed him back to my bedroom, where his smile doubled. He ran his fingertips over one of the crocheted plant holders I'd made, brushing the leaves of the pothos before he moved over to the bed. He flopped down onto it, the mattress bouncing with his weight as he inhaled a deep breath.

"God, everything smells like you."

"I hope that's a good thing," I said, finally relinquishing my hold on the keys. I placed them on top of my dresser and carefully sat on the corner of the bed.

Vince was sprawled out like a starfish. He crooked a grin at where I sat with an arched brow. "Scared I'll bite?"

"Maybe."

I couldn't explain it, but I was nervous — as if I hadn't been in a bed with Vince dozens of times before this. My heart was racing, my breaths shallow, head light.

As if he could sense it, he snagged me by the wrists and tugged me into the middle of the bed with him. His legs wrapped around me, his arms holding me to his chest until I was completely enveloped and laughing, the nerves dissipating.

"You love when I bite," he murmured in my ear, and chills raced from where his breath touched my skin all the way down to my toes.

I rolled as best I could in his vise grip, threading my arms around his neck and tangling my fingers in his hair. I loved that touch, that familiarity of the silky strands still a bit damp from his post-game shower.

"I'm so sorry, Vince," I breathed, closing my eyes on another zap of pain as it shot through me.

He leaned up on one elbow, enough to brush my hair out of my face. "Okay, I'll let that one slide, but no more apologies."

"But—"

"I understand, Maven," he said, cutting me off. "I get it. I'm not mad. Not even close." He sighed, pulling me into him. "I'm just so fucking happy you're giving me the chance to show you I'm not like him, and that I'm not going anywhere."

He kissed me as anxiety spiked in my chest, but it was quieter now, more subdued. I realized it was okay to be scared, as long as that fear didn't stand in our way.

"What are we going to do now?"

"I can think of a few things," he mused, kissing me with more intent.

I pressed a hand to his chest on a laugh. "I mean after tonight."

Vince balanced his chin in his hands, watching me. "What do you want to happen?"

"I don't want to give up my job."

He frowned. "Of course not. Why would you?"

"Well, I just didn't want you to think I was going to quit and like... follow you around."

I waved my hand with that, and he caught it before kissing my knuckles.

"That wouldn't be my girl," he said, holding my hand there at his chest. His brow furrowed. "But are you going to be okay not traveling with me? Do you trust me?"

I swallowed. "As much as it freaks me out... yes."

"Good. I swear, I'll keep it to two bunnies a trip. Maybe three. Just some good luck blowjobs before the game, you know? Nothing too—*oof!*"

I cut him off with a knee to the gut, and he laughed, wrapping me up in a straitjacket of arms and legs again.

"Don't even joke like that," I warned, but it was through a smile, because I *knew* it was a joke. And that was the most beautiful relief, the most incredible feeling — to know he was mine and no one else was a threat.

"But I like to push your buttons."

"Find more creative ways to push them."

"Oh, I like the sound of that game," he said, and then I was flipped onto my back, and he was pressing me into the sheets, opening my legs with his thighs.

He was still smiling against my lips as we kissed, as I sighed and opened for him. But that smile faded the more we tangled ourselves together, and he pressed his forehead against mine, shaking his head like he didn't deserve to be there, with me, in my bed.

"I can't believe what you've done to me." His hands gripped me harder, and I gasped, writhing under his touch. "Everything before you was black and white, a monochromatic existence."

"And now?"

"Now, it's a kaleidoscope of color," he said with a kiss. "Dizzying and maddening and beautiful."

Words were gone after that, and once again, I found myself paying homage to his hands. His hands that undressed me, piece by piece, that splayed me out in the sheets beneath him as he rid himself of his own clothing next. His hands that pulled me into his lap, that palmed my ass and guided me until I was sinking down and he was filling me. His hands that fucked up my hair and my makeup and my very way of life.

Vince wrapped those hands around my shoulders and pulled me down onto him, flexing his hips like he couldn't fill me enough. He rocked in and out, holding me to him, kissing and fucking me in an unrelenting rhythm of need. It was just like that night at the pottery wheel, but somehow even more.

He was claiming me, marking me, erasing any trace of anyone who came before him.

It was a sacred union of souls, a burning hot shotgun wedding.

"I love you," I whispered against his lips.

Vince froze, his hands holding my hips and my weight suspended just above him. He locked his eyes on mine, searching, and then one hand snaked behind my neck to bring me into him.

"I love you," he echoed.

His next kiss was bruising, and he pressed inside me deep and strong. He held me there, fucking me with small, precise little flexes of his hips as his lips took their time nipping and sucking and kissing mine.

I rocked against him, finding the friction I needed to release. My legs quaked, moans suffocated by his mouth as he devoured every single one.

As he devoured *me*.

The last of who I was before Vince Tanev vanished in a puff of smoke that night, and I emerged on the other side, a phoenix rising. The past couldn't control me anymore, and the future couldn't paralyze me with its claws.

I was free.

Free to choose, free to fall, free to love and to *be* loved.

My assignment was over. The job was done.

But I knew I'd make a career out of loving that man and his magic hands, and I'd only just begun.

Chapter 37

We'll See About That

Vince

May

I should have been used to the glare Maven's father loved to pin me with, but it still shook me to my core.

Bernard King was a tall man, broad and stern with everyone except his baby girl. For her, he'd smile wide and bright, his blue eyes crinkling at the edges. But with me, they were always hidden beneath bent brows and a suspicious gaze.

I couldn't blame him, not after how James had broken Maven. I knew I'd have to earn his trust just as much as I had to earn Maven's, and I was fine with that. I was here to put in the time.

Where Bernie looked at me like a mangy dog he wasn't sure he wanted to keep around, his wife, Leah, fawned over me like a brand-new puppy. She and my mom had become fast friends, and I was pretty sure they were planning a wedding regardless of the fact that I hadn't given Maven a ring.

Yet.

Where Bernie was tall, Leah was a slight little thing, and I loved to sit back and watch the two of them when they were together — especially with their daughter and doing what they loved most. It was fascinating to me, how selfless they were, how they gave their time and energy and money without a second thought.

Leah had ink-black hair that she wore short and curly more times than not, her skin a rich brown. Bernie was pale white and had more gray than any other color on what was left of his hair. But what I loved most was that I could see a little of each of them in Maven — the shape of her father's eyes, the color of her mother's, a blend of both their smiles and noses and laughs.

Today, they were supporting and celebrating their only daughter as she officially launched her new initiative — the Tampa Bay Babes Compassion Project. She'd flipped the Vince Tanev channel, using the followers and traction she'd gained to steer everyone's attention toward Tampa community heroes and ways for locals and tourists alike to give back.

Her parents weren't the only ones here to support. The entire Ospreys team was sweating in the Florida heat, fresh off a season and ready to get their hands dirty. We were helping build houses with Habitat for Humanity, where Maven's father still worked. Not making the playoffs meant these bastards had plenty of time on their hands, and Maven made sure it was put to good use.

Bernie handed me a pole digger, nodding toward the mailbox that needed to be handled near the end of the unfinished driveway. I saluted him with a smirk, but before I could make it to my new job on the site, Maven popped up in front of me with her phone right in my face.

"The people are demanding to know which is better — scoring a goal, or scoring a date with the remarkable, beautiful, bedazzling Maven King?"

I grinned at the camera. "The people, or you?"

"Answer the question, Mr. Tanev."

"Mister?" I let my eyes run salaciously over her body, marveling at how even in a pair of dirty overalls and old sneakers, she turned me on like a fucking light switch. "I like that," I mused, pulling her into my arms. "We should try that in a different setting."

She laughed as I pulled her in for a kiss, but she pushed me away quickly, flushing as she looked back at where her father was watching us like he was one step closer to drop-kicking me across the yard.

The last five months had passed in a blur. I was wrapped up in hockey for most of it, and any time I wasn't on the ice, I was with Maven. Whether she was in my bed downtown, or I was in hers by the beach, we soaked up every minute we could get together — which wasn't nearly enough when the season was in full swing.

The Ospreys had a winning season through January, but we choked in the playoff race, missing the clench in a gut-wrenching loss to Ottawa. It never felt good to lose, but it had a particularly sharp sting when we were so close to something we'd worked hard for all season. Now, we were watching other teams battle it out for the Cup, all the while planning for next season, when we'd have to start all over again.

As much as I couldn't wait for next season to start, for our chance to do even better and make the playoffs — I was more excited for the next few months with Maven.

The offseason was short, and we still had expectations to stay in playing shape. But with a much less demanding travel schedule, I'd have more time to take Maven out, to lose mornings and afternoons and nights with her.

When she wasn't too busy running the world, at least.

"How are you doing?" I asked her.

She smiled, shaking her head and looking around at all the work being done. "Amazing. I thought for sure we'd start to lose followers when I changed over all the logos and branding images, but we've retained most of them. *And* we're already pulling in new followers. Probably has something to do with all the shirtless, sweating Ospreys' players I've been posting on our stories."

I barked out a laugh. "Why do I have a feeling this won't be the last of us being roped in to help?"

"Don't act like you all don't love it. Look at them," she said, gesturing to my teammates. Even Coach McCabe was helping, bent down and hammering lattice into place around the porch of one of the houses. Jaxson was on the roof laying shingles. Will was working on the floors. The entire *team* was hard at work — in-between horsing around, of course.

My chest tightened a bit when I noted Carter talking to Maven's mom across the yard. He was mid-laugh, and he looked so carefree I might have believed he really was if I didn't know the truth.

"I can't believe Carter got sent down," I said.

Maven frowned, following my gaze. "I can't either. But he said this is par for the course with rookies. And who knows, he could come back, right?"

"He'll be back," I said with conviction I truly felt.

Carter had been sent down to the AHL in March, just in time to help them with their playoffs. For now, that's where he was staying. Just because he wasn't knocking socks off here in the NHL didn't mean he wasn't a great center. It was just hard to compete with the veterans, and he needed a little more work to level up. I knew he'd take the time to get better, but it didn't make my chest hurt any less at the thought of him not being around. We'd gone through rookie camp together, our rookie party, and the first decent season Tampa had secured in more than a decade.

He was like my annoying little brother and one of my best friends rolled into one. It wasn't going to be the same without him.

But he'd be back.

And we'd welcome him with open arms and a long night at Boomer's when the time came.

Shaking the thought off, I pulled Maven back into my arms, smiling as she squinted up at me with one hand shielding her eyes from the sun.

"I'm proud of you," I said.

She beamed, standing a little taller. "Thank you."

"And I'm excited for tonight."

"What's tonight?"

"Our first real date."

She laughed. "Is that so? What, you don't count the yacht in Baltimore?"

"No more than the dinner date I crashed when you were with that real estate prick."

"Hey, he was nice," she said on a laugh.

"Oh, is that what you want?" I asked, tickling her ribs as I nibbled at her ear. "A *nice guy*?"

"If I did, I wouldn't be with you."

"Ouch," I said, covering my chest like she'd wounded me. But then I smirked and pulled her in again. "I'll show you just how *nice* I can be tonight."

"Hmm... you might have to wait."

"Why is that?"

She pressed up on her toes so she could whisper in my ear, the feel of it making me wish we were alone.

"I don't put out on the first date."

I bit my lip on a grin, making sure no one was watching before I smacked her ass. "We'll see about that."

Chapter 38

We Make the Rules

Maven

June

We boarded the party bus to the roar of two-dozen rowdy teammates, all of them chanting Vince's name as he hoisted the Calder Trophy high over his head in victory. I laughed as he propped his foot on the first bus seat and did a ridiculous twerk and body roll with the trophy, but it only made his teammates get even crazier.

The NHL Awards had been hosted in Austin, Texas, and the entire team had flown out with Vince on the nominee list for the Rookie of the Year. When he'd won, we'd blown the roof off the place, and Jaxson revealed that he'd already booked us an afterparty.

A bus with a stripper pole that would take us around to all the bars and clubs in the city until we shut it down.

Vince's family had flown in for the ceremony, as well, but while his parents had retreated to their hotel, his sister held fast to my arm as we boarded the bus behind Vince.

"It's so loud!" she screamed over the noise.

I laughed, squeezing her arm. We paused by the driver at the front of the bus as Vince held his trophy up proudly.

"I've dreamed about this moment since I was in high school," he said, and by some miracle, the guys on the bus calmed enough so they could hear him. "Back then, I saw it as a solo award, as one I would earn all on my own. But now that I'm holding this," he said, looking at the trophy and then back at his team. "I know I couldn't have earned it without all of you. I'm honored to be a part of this team, of this organization, and I can't wait for us to hang another banner on our rafters when we win the Stanley Cup together."

There was a mixture of cheers and teammates making fun of him for being a mushy princess — both of which made me and Grace chuckle.

"Alright, enough of that shit," he said, hoisting the trophy up again. "LET'S FUCKING PARTY!"

Carter had flown in for the celebrations even though he wasn't technically on the team anymore, and he was the first to throw a cold can of beer to Vince. He caught it with one hand, cracked the top, and poured it straight into the cup of the trophy.

Grace and I stared in half amusement, half horror as he crushed the empty can and tossed it to the floor before guzzling the beer out of the trophy to the wild approval from all his teammates.

"I hope you're ready for a long night out," I told Grace.

Her eyes were wide, mouth parted, and it reminded me a little of how I'd been the first time I'd traveled with the team. It really was such a spectacle.

"Come here."

I was still half holding onto Grace when my wrist was wrapped up, and a strong set of hands tugged me into a warm lap. Vince planted a wet, beer-scented kiss on me to the tune of whistles and catcalls, the trophy in the seat closest to the window.

"Um, your sister," I said, blushing as I pressed against his chest until there was some distance.

"Oh, shit, here, Gracie," he said, moving the trophy and scooting over so she could sit next to us. But she scoffed, flicking her long blonde hair over her shoulder.

"Please. I'll pass on the third wheel." She turned to the bus full of Ospreys next. "Who's got an open seat next to them?"

It was silent for two seconds.

And then the bus erupted into chatter, every guy yelling for her attention while they shoved teammates out of seats to make room.

I threw my head back in a laugh, but Vince's jaw was tight as he stood up and pointed a death finger at every single one of them.

"Don't you fuckers even think about it." He snapped at Jaxson in the very back. "Jax, let her sit next to you. You're the only one I can trust."

"Hey!" Carter said in mock offense.

Vince ignored him, turning to his sister next. "If any of them lay a hand on you—"

"Oh, my God. *Relax,*" she told him, and then she skipped to the back of the bus.

Vince was pulled into a conversation with Daddy P and one of their defensemen as the driver started us toward our first destination. I held onto the stripper pole in the middle and leaned against the seat, half-listening to them and half-watching where Grace had just slid into the seat next to Jaxson in the back.

I swore I could see him gulp even from here, his eyes like that of a deer caught in headlights as someone handed

Grace a beer and she chugged half of it, wiping the suds from her lips when she was done. She pinned him with that beautiful smile of hers next, and I didn't miss how his eyes raked over her. Grace was stunning — it was impossible not to notice.

If she wasn't Vince's baby sister, I'd say Jaxson might actually have a chance.

Then again, she did confide in me earlier at the hotel bar that she was seeing someone, so maybe it didn't matter.

Still, I found it hard not to watch them as the night's entertainment, especially when we went out to the first bar and Grace grabbed Jaxson by the hand, dragging him onto the dance floor. The look she gave me over her shoulder as she passed told me what my job was, and I pulled Vince to the opposite side of the crowded place, making sure to distract him.

It wasn't much of a favor, if I was being honest.

Distracting Vince Tanev was my favorite thing to do.

***

"I don't know how y'all do this during the season," I groaned as Vince held the passenger side door open for me to crawl inside his Maserati. I never grew tired of the way that engine purred to life beneath me when he took his place in the driver's seat.

"Stamina, baby," he said with a wink, leaning over the console to kiss me. His hand slid over my thigh, and he kept it there after he broke the kiss, driving with one hand as he usually did when I was beside him.

It had been a fun weekend in Austin, but I was glad to be home, the lights of Tampa welcoming us as I smiled and watched the palm trees pass out the window. I was so exhausted from the long hours partying all weekend that I was in a daze, and I didn't notice we were heading toward the beach until we were halfway across the Courtney Campbell bridge.

"Vince, you're going the wrong way," I said on a frown.

"Am I?"

His mischievous smile was all he left me with as he continued driving, and we crossed into Clearwater until we were right on the beach, pulling up to a massive, beautiful home guarded by a large metal gate. It swung open with the tap of a card Vince swiped out the window, and he drove the Maserati up the stone driveway to park in front of the beautiful home.

"What is this?" I asked, my fatigue fading under the excitement. "Did you rent us this place for the night or something?"

"Or something," he said, cryptic as ever, and then he rounded the car and helped me out of it.

It was dark, but even still I gasped when we walked through the grand foyer, the layout of the house steering us right toward the expansive windows that provided an uninterrupted view of the Gulf of Mexico. The sand was white as snow, reflecting the moonlight above.

There was no furniture in the home, and it seemed brand new, the marble floors glossy and smooth. My heels clicked on them as I crossed the space and went straight out the back doors, inhaling the scent of the ocean, breathing in the salt air as the waves lapped at the shoreline.

"Do you like it?" Vince asked, wrapping me up from behind.

"It's unbelievable," I breathed, turning in his arms. "And very empty."

"Well, that's because I thought we should pick out furniture together."

My heart galloped before sliding to a halt.

Vince took my silence as shock, which it was, and he held my hair out of my eyes as the wind battled against him. "I bought this house," he said. "For us."

"You... *what*?"

"Move in with me," he whispered, just loud enough that I could hear him over the waves. "Let's make a home together. Let's make a *life* together. Right here, on the beach where you love to be, in a house where we make the rules." He smoothed his thumb over my jaw, smiling. "No more driving back and forth. No more half of my stuff at your place and half of yours at mine. I want to wake up next to you every morning, Maven. I want to listen to you snore when you fall asleep."

I swatted at his chest, but my eyes still glossed with tears, my cheeks burning from how big my smile was.

"Whatever plants you want, whatever garden you want to create — it's yours."

"Is there a space for your pottery wheel?"

He chuckled. "Yes. It's *ours*, Maven. We can make it whatever we want."

"Oh, does that mean we can have a kinky sex room?"

His eyebrows shot up. "If that's what you want."

"I mean, I *have* been daydreaming about that toy you used on me a few weeks ago..."

He groaned, capturing my lips as he pressed his hips against mine. I felt him growing hard already, likely at the same memory.

"Tell me that's a yes," he said. "So I can take you inside and christen every room of our house."

"Our house," I said, wrapping my arms around his neck. I jumped, knowing he'd catch me, my legs winding around him next. "It does have a nice ring to it."

"Woman," he growled, nipping at my bottom lip.

"Yes," I breathed, and I barely got the word out before he was hauling me inside, pressing me against the sliding glass door as soon as we shut it behind us.

I clawed at his shirt until he dropped me long enough to rid himself of it, allowing me to do the same with my dress. I peeled it overhead, making quick work of my heels, panties, and bra while Vince watched with an amused smirk at me hopping around, the layers flying like confetti in every direction.

I skipped toward the kitchen island when I was bare, hopping up and sitting my naked ass right down on the cool, brand-new granite. I slid back until my feet were propped on the counter, too, leaning on my palms and letting my legs fall open with a wicked grin.

Vince groaned, quickly finishing his disrobing before he was palming himself and stalking toward me like a predator. His fist rolled over his cock in slow pumps until he was standing at the edge of the island.

His hands wrapped around my ankles, tugging me to the edge until my ass hung off it. He spread my legs wide, kissing down the insides of my thighs until his tongue was right where I wanted it.

I arched off the granite with a moan, legs already shaking as he licked and sucked and teased. He knew me more intimately than anyone ever had, knew all the right places to touch, the right pressure to lick, the right words to say to make me come undone.

Sometimes, Vince took his time with me. I'd had mornings where he'd prayed at the altar of my body until well after noon. Some nights were nothing but hours and hours of foreplay, of kissing and touching and learning new ways to make me come.

But other times, like tonight, Vince was an impatient, starved man.

He flipped me, smacking my ass once my feet hit the floor. I was bent over the island now, breasts pressed against it, and he grabbed my wrists and held them at my lower back in a vise grip. I was already panting when he slid inside me, filling me as we both hissed out a curse. I couldn't move, pinned by his hands and his hips, and I reveled in the surrender of control as he slid out of me and then all the way back in.

"Look at you," he said, slowing his pace. "Dripping wet, hugging my cock like such a good girl."

I squeezed around him with the praise, smiling over my shoulder as I did.

"This perfect pussy was made for me," he groaned, flexing in deep with a slap of his hips against my ass. "*You* were made for me."

"Yes," I breathed, moaning as he pulled on my wrists until I had no choice but to bow off the island.

Then, something cool and hard was slipped over a very specific finger of mine.

My heart stopped, along with our lovemaking, and Vince tentatively released my hands. One palmed my breast as the other wrapped around my throat.

He held me there with the perfect pressure, somehow twisting me so he could claim my mouth while he found a toe-curling pace behind me. Each time he thrust inside, I chased the burning stars dancing at the edges of my vision.

I would never get tired of this — this man, this home, these fucking *hands*.

"Vince," I said, more of a question than anything as he flexed inside me.

"It's a ring, Maven," he said, answering what I hadn't yet asked. His lips were right by my ear, his breath warm against my skin. "A big, expensive, shiny fucking ring."

"You didn't properly ask me."

"You want me on my knee for you?" he teased, licking the skin at the back of my neck. Then, he twisted me, my back hitting the edge of the island as he knelt before me, holding my hand in his.

My hand that now sported a very large, marquise-shaped diamond ring.

"Marry me," he rasped, his throat bobbing with the words — as if he was actually nervous, as if I could ever say anything but yes.

"That's not a question."

"And I didn't stutter, did I?"

I bit my lip against a smile, pulling him back to his feet and finding his mouth with mine. I left my answer there on his lips, kissing him so deeply he groaned before I was being carried to whatever the next room on his list was.

We fucked in every corner of that house until the sun started to rise, and then, he pulled me out onto our private beach, and we went one more round for good measure.

When we were both so exhausted and sore we could barely move, Vince wrapped me up in his arms, our eyes on the water as the sun transformed it from dark blue to a turquoise masterpiece.

With my head against his chest, I held out my hand, the diamond glittering in the light, and I laughed to myself. Flashes of the last nine months hit me like a film reel. It felt like another lifetime, that first night I met him at the gala, but I smiled at how I could still remember the way he set butterflies free in my stomach and made me mad with rage at the same time.

I could still remember how light my chest was that first morning I showed up at his place, how I felt when I saw his pottery corner, saw *him* drinking coffee without a shirt on. I could still close my eyes and feel the heat from when he cornered me outside Boomer's, how he kissed me even before I could admit that was all I wanted him to do. I hoped I'd never lose those memories. I hoped I'd always remember how it felt to fall in love with Vince Tanev against my will.

"What's got you smiling like that?" he asked, kissing behind my ear.

I turned in his arms, framing his face as he wrangled my hair in his hands.

"You know how much I hate to say this, but I think you were right."

He bit his lip on a moan. "*God,* that is such a turn on. Say it again."

I poked his ribs, and he laughed, kissing my nose before he pulled back to watch me. The blue of the water played with the green in his hazel eyes, bringing it to life more than I'd ever seen before. Those eyes were mine to stare at now for as long as I wanted.

"What was I right about?" he asked.

I leaned into him, planting a kiss to his chin. "I really did meet my match."

The laugh that barreled out of him was my favorite sound in the world.

And *he* was my favorite person.

The End

Epilogue

We Ride at Dusk

Jaxson

She blew back into my life not like a storm, but like the sun – hidden behind a dark cloud but still shining all the same.

There wasn't a day that had passed where I hadn't thought about Grace Tanev, about the night I spent with her. It was just a party bus and a rowdy night out with the team celebrating Vince winning the Calder Trophy, and yet, it had been like an awakening.

My whole life, I'd been waking in a fog, in a dense and heavy cloud that I thought would stay with me forever.

But one night with her had brought in the sun.

Of course, I'd spent the better half of the last two weeks doing my level best to erase her and that night from my mind. Because it didn't matter how easily the conversation came, how heartily she'd made me laugh, or how my body had hummed to life with her hips in my hands as we danced in a crowded club.

Grace was off limits.

Not only was she already in a relationship, but she was also eight years younger than me.

She was also my teammate's little sister.

That was a hurdle not even I could jump.

I'd done a somewhat decent job of letting the idea of her go. I had resisted the urge to look her up on social media, had ignored the fact that she'd given me her number, that she'd put it in my phone before we said our goodbye.

Because that was exactly what it was – a goodbye.

Until it wasn't.

"You really want to lose your money that badly?" Vince asked Carter with a whistle, shaking his head. We were at his new place on the beach, half of it still littered with boxes, waiting for Will to show up so we could hit our tee time. "You know my game puts yours to shame."

"I've been practicing. Besides, you've been so busy crawling up Maven's ass, my bet is you'll be too distracted to play."

"Hey, leave my ass out of this," Maven called from the kitchen where she was organizing glassware in the cabinets.

"But it's the best one I've ever seen," Carter said with a pout, which earned him a slug on the arm from Vince.

"Gotta say I agree on that one," I piped in, ducking before Vince had the chance to pull me into a chokehold. "I still dream about that yellow dress..."

Vince shoved Carter out of the way and started chasing me, and I dodged the coffee table and hopped over the couch, staying just out of reach. Carter started humming the *Benny Hill* theme song, clapping his thighs in time with the bazooka sounds he was making with his mouth like we were Tom & Jerry.

I was sliding on my socks around the kitchen island, half-hiding behind a laughing, red-faced Maven, when a figure appeared in the foyer. I thought it was Daddy P at first, so I kept up the charade. But when a suitcase was dropped to the marble floor and a soft cry followed behind it, we all stopped, our heads snapping in that direction.

And there she was.

Staring right at me.

Those green eyes I'd fallen so easily into that night in Austin were glossy and red, her button-nose the same rosy shade. The bags under her eyes were a terrible shade of purple and gray, her shoulders slumped, bottom lip trembling the longer she stood there without anyone saying a word. She was petite, even in heels, but standing there in flip flops, she was so slight, so small, like a little mouse.

Her long, straight blonde hair that had blurred my vision the night I twirled her around on the dance floor in Austin was a tangled mess, dirty and greasy and dull. She'd covered it with a ripped-up ball cap that said Asshole on it.

But even with her lips in a flat line, I could remember her smile.

I could remember her laugh, her ridiculous dance moves, her even more ridiculous questions.

I remembered everything.

As put out as she looked, her bronze skin still blazed against the white t-shirt she wore, against the tiny jean shorts she paired it with, like she had been at the beach for weeks. Her shirt had a cartoon of an opossum wielding a gun like a cowboy, and the text under it said we ride at dusk.

I would have laughed, if the sight of her didn't make my chest spark with something possessive and feral.

She looked like hell, like she'd been through hell, and yet she was still the most beautiful thing I'd ever seen.

Before I could think better of it, I started toward her — at the very same time Vince did. He gave me a strange look before I stopped in my tracks and he continued on, rushing to his sister and wrapping her in a fierce hug.

Maven turned back to unpacking, giving them privacy, and Carter pretended to be on his phone.

I, on the other hand, couldn't look away.

Vince pulled back after a moment, holding Grace's shoulders in his hands as he spoke in a hushed voice to her. She said something back, and then Vince hugged her again, and grabbed her suitcase. They walked down the hall and up the stairs, and when they were gone, Maven blew out a breath.

"That didn't look good," she said.

Carter's mouth pulled to the side as he looked up the stairs and then back at me. His eyes narrowed a bit then, but before he could say a word, Vince was back, running a hand over his head.

"She okay?" Maven asked.

"No," he said. "But she will be. I told her she could stay here with us."

"Of course," Maven said, rounding the kitchen island until she was slipping her arms around Vince's waist. "For as long as she needs."

Vince nodded, blowing out a breath and kissing Maven's forehead. He seemed to relax with her embracing him, but my muscles were coiled tight.

Carter tried to lighten the mood with a joke, and then Will walked in, breaking the tension of the moment as he grumped about it being too hot to play golf. I mumbled something about needing to use the bathroom before we left, excusing myself down the hall.

Then, I glanced over my shoulder to make sure no one was watching, and I made my way up the stairs two at a time.

Vince's new place was massive, with so many rooms I wasn't sure which one he would have put Grace in. But I heard her sniffling through a cracked door toward the middle, and I paused just outside it, rapping my knuckles lightly on the wood.

"Come in," she said softly, pathetically, her voice hoarse.

I pushed the door open just enough to see her, for her to see me, and then we both froze.

I wasn't sure what I expected. Maybe it was for her to tell me to fuck off and leave her alone, because when she lit up with a smile, it twisted my gut — like I didn't deserve that, like it was dangerous for me to want every smile she ever had to give. Her cheeks lifted, eyes crinkling, and two more tears slid down in perfect unison, like the smile had set them free.

"Hey," she said, and it was just one word, just a greeting. But that smile, the way she watched me, it made me feel like I had the power to make everything okay.

"Who do I have to kill?"

She choked on something between a sob and a laugh, wiping her nose with a bunched-up tissue in her hands. She swiped the tears away next. "He's not worth the jail time."

My chest ignited then, the spark turning to flame.

He.

That confirmed my suspicion.

That night in Austin, she'd told me in the most adorable but firm way that she was taken, dating some guy she'd met camping. Judging by her tear-stained face, the guy had blown it.

Idiot.

"You okay?"

Her smile waned. "Yeah, yeah," she said quickly, waving her hand in the air like she was swatting a gnat away. "It's his loss. And probably good I found out now before..." She shook her head, her voice fading. "Nothing a little sunshine and salt water can't fix."

She forced another smile, and I frowned, stepping more fully into the room.

"You don't have to do that."

"Do what?"

"Pretend to be fine. Pretend like you're not hurting. Pretend like the bright side is all you're thinking of."

Her eyebrows slid together, but then she looked down at where her hands still clutched the balled-up tissue, and she shrugged.

"It's easier than admitting the truth."

Carter called my name from downstairs, and I cursed, stepping out of the room and down the hall a bit before yelling, "Be right there!"

Then, I slid back into the doorway, chest aching at the sight of Grace so small on that large four-post bed.

"Go," she said with a weak smile. "I'm fine."

But her eyes said differently.

"What are you doing tonight?"

She arched a brow. "Hosting a ball. Isn't it obvious?" She splayed her hands, waving them out over herself and the room.

The corner of my mouth twitched up. This girl was heartbroken, and yet she was making jokes.

"What if we drove?"

"Drove?"

I nodded.

"Where?"

"Anywhere."

She folded her arms. "And my brother?"

A warning flared in my gut, but I ignored it. "Do you tell your brother everything?"

Mischief bloomed to life in her sea green eyes, the first real smile I'd seen since Austin curling on her light pink lips.

I should have walked away. I should have shook my head and said nevermind and bolted out of that room. This was a girl with a broken heart, fresh out of a relationship that clearly hurt her. This was a girl, period — one far too young for me.

This was Grace Tanev, my teammate and one of my best friend's little sister.

Walk away, common sense begged me. This is not your place.

But I stood tall, rooted in place, watching her and waiting for her to be the stronger one because I damn sure couldn't be.

Grace popped off the bed. "Road trip?"

My eyebrows shot up. I had more of a drive along the beach in mind, or maybe a long winding road in the country. But that didn't stop me from opening my stupid mouth and replying, "If that's what you need."

Her eyes narrowed a bit, like she didn't quite believe I was serious. "What about practice?"

"Off-season," I explained.

Her eyes sparkled like diamonds.

"Anywhere?" she asked, echoing my earlier sentiment.

"Anywhere."

Her smile climbed even more, and she crossed the room in two strides, holding out her hand for mine.

"We ride at dusk," she said, referencing her shirt. I ignored the sirens in my mind when I took her hand and she shook it like we'd just done a multi-million-dollar business deal. Then, she backed away in a moonwalk, making finger guns and a pew pew sound that made me snort out a laugh through my nose.

I was pretty sure I'd just taken a wrong turn and steered myself right toward Disasterville.

But I couldn't find it in me to change course.

What happens when the Ospreys' star defensemen ends up on a road trip with his teammate's hot little sister? Find out in *Watch Your Mouth* (https://amzn.to/43CeSJj).

Can't get enough of Vince and Maven? Here's a bonus scene to make you swoon! (https://kandisteiner.com/bonus-content)

While you wait for *Watch Your Mouth,* you'll love Kandi Steiner's Red Zone Rivals series. College football with ALL the spice! Keep reading for a sneak peek inside book one: Fair Catch (https://amzn.to/3OHcFIc)!

More from Kandi Steiner

The Red Zone Rivals Series

Fair Catch

As if being the only girl on the college football team wasn't hard enough, Coach had to go and assign my brother's best friend — and *my* number one enemy — as my roommate.

Blind Side

The hottest college football safety in the nation just asked me to be his fake girlfriend.

And I just asked him to take my virginity.

Quarterback Sneak

Quarterback Holden Moore can have any girl he wants.

Except me: the coach's daughter.

Hail Mary (an Amazon #1 Bestseller!)

Leo F*cking Hernandez.

North Boston University's star running back, notorious bachelor, and number one on my people I would murder if I could get away with it list.

And now?

My new roommate.

The Becker Brothers Series

On the Rocks (book 1)

Neat (book 2)

Manhattan (book 3)

Old Fashioned (book 4)

Four brothers finding love in a small Tennessee town that revolves around a whiskey distillery with a dark past — including the mysterious death of their father.

The Best Kept Secrets Series
(AN AMAZON TOP 10 BESTSELLER)
What He Doesn't Know (book 1)
What He Always Knew (book 2)
What He Never Knew (book 3)
Charlie's marriage is dying. She's perfectly content to go down in the flames, until her first love shows back up and reminds her the other way love can burn.

Close Quarters
A summer yachting the Mediterranean sounded like heaven to Jasmine after finishing her undergrad degree. But her boyfriend's billionaire boss always gets what he wants. And this time, he wants her.

Make Me Hate You
Jasmine has been avoiding her best friend's brother for years, but when they're both in the same house for a wedding, she can't resist him — no matter how she tries.

The Wrong Game
(AN AMAZON TOP 5 BESTSELLER)
Gemma's plan is simple: invite a new guy to each home game using her season tickets for the Chicago Bears. It's the perfect way to avoid getting emotionally attached and also get some action. But after Zach gets his chance to be her practice round, he decides one game just isn't enough. A sexy, fun sports romance.

The Right Player
She's avoiding love at all costs. He wants nothing more than to lock her down. Sexy, hilarious and swoon-worthy, The Right Player is the perfect read for sports romance lovers.

On the Way to You

It was only supposed to be a road trip, but when Cooper discovers the journal of the boy driving the getaway car, everything changes. An emotional, angsty road trip romance.

A Love Letter to Whiskey
(AN AMAZON TOP 10 BESTSELLER)

An angsty, emotional romance between two lovers fighting the curse of bad timing.

Read Love, Whiskey – Jamie's side of the story and an extended epilogue – in the new Fifth Anniversary Edition!

Weightless

Young Natalie finds self-love and romance with her personal trainer, along with a slew of secrets that tie them together in ways she never thought possible.

Revelry

Recently divorced, Wren searches for clarity in a summer cabin outside of Seattle, where she makes an unforgettable connection with the broody, small town recluse next door.

Say Yes

Harley is studying art abroad in Florence, Italy. Trying to break free of her perfectionism, she steps outside one night determined to Say Yes to anything that comes her way. Of course, she didn't expect to run into Liam Benson...

Washed Up

Gregory Weston, the boy I once knew as my son's best friend, now a man I don't know at all. No, not just a man. A doctor. And he wants me...

The Christmas Blanket

Stuck in a cabin with my ex-husband waiting out a blizzard? Not exactly what I had pictured when I planned a surprise visit home for the holidays...

Black Number Four

A college, Greek-life romance of a hot young poker star and the boy sent to take her down.

The Palm South University Series

Rush (book 1) FREE if you sign up for my newsletter!
Anchor, PSU #2
Pledge, PSU #3
Legacy, PSU #4
Ritual, PSU #5
Hazed, PSU #6
Greek, PSU #7

#1 NYT Bestselling Author Rachel Van Dyken says, "If Gossip Girl and Riverdale had a love child, it would be PSU." This angsty college series will be your next guilty addiction.

Tag Chaser

She made a bet that she could stop chasing military men, which seemed easy – until her knight in shining armor and latest client at work showed up in Army ACUs.

Song Chaser

Tanner and Kellee are perfect for each other. They frequent the same bars, love the same music, and have the same desire to rip each other's clothes off. Only problem? Tanner is still in love with his best friend.

Acknowledgements

Kicking off a brand new series after having the best success of my career was harder than I ever expected. There's always a bit of anxiety mixed with excitement, and I wanted to make sure I did justice to the sport I love so much while also having fun with the spice and romance. I could not have achieved that without the large team of friends who helped me!

My first acknowledgement is to Rhiannon Gwynne and her husband, Josh Brittain. When I asked you for an interview, I meant something quick and painless. Instead, you indulged me for THREE HOURS while I peppered you with endless questions about hockey, life as a player as well as a WAG, and so much more. You helped shape so much of this book and this series, and I truly could never thank you enough. Hopefully, bringing your gym scene fantasy to life and naming a character after you showed a little of my appreciation. ;)

To my husband, Jack, my ever-steady force – thank you for loving me and for pushing me to be better, always. When I stepped up to the plate for this series, you rubbed my shoulders and told me you knew I'd hit it out of the park even when my knees were shaking and my hands were sweating. I can't thank you enough for believing in me and for watching playoff hockey with me peppering you with questions every second of it.

To my momma, Lavon, and my bestie, Sasha – I can never get through acknowledgements without telling you both how much I love and appreciate you. Thank you for always supporting my dreams.

To Tina Stokes, my Executive Assistant and more importantly my FRIEND – thank you for loving me and fighting for this dream as if it were your own. You are such a huge part of Kandi Steiner, LLC and of my life. I can't imagine this world without you.

To my Spicy Sprint Slutz, Lena Hendrix and Elsie Silver, thank you for always being there to write (and cry) together. My best days are when we blow off our focus timers to gab and laugh, and my worst days are when you're both busy or on vacation. It's hard to find a tribe in this writing world. I'm so glad I've found y'all.

In that same thread, I couldn't have done this without two of my best friends – Karla Sorensen and Brittainy C. Cherry. On all the hard days, we pushed together. On all the easy days, we celebrated one another and our little (or big) successes. Our group chat is my favorite thing in the world. I love you both!

Laura Pavlov, thank GOD you swung into my life last year! I know we have talked online for much longer than that, but I'm so glad our relationship has bloomed into a beautiful friendship. I look forward to hearing your voice every day, and I love how we are always there to push one another and cheer each other on. Let's do it forever. Love you!

Shout out to Hannah Chiclana, not only for working with your hot husband to bring my audiobooks to life, but for sending me the TikTok video that planted the seed for Vince's pottery hobby. HOT HANDS. We love to see it. And I am so thankful for your friendship, talent, and inspiration.

Maggie Ehrgott, thank you for pumping me up about my first hockey series, and for giving me all the inspiration when it came your way. And thank you for just being the most wonderful friend. I'm so thankful you came into my life!

To my incredible team of sensitivity readers – Tiffanie Shipp, Chelé Walker, and Imani Blake – thank you so much for your time, effort, and consideration on this project. Writing diverse romance has always been important to me, and it's thanks to women like you that I can learn each and every time I do. I am so appreciative of all your feedback and help in making this book the best it could be.

I had a BIG team of beta readers for this book, because I wanted to ensure it was as polished as possible by the time the final draft was finished. This might have been my most productive feedback from any group before, and I'm so thankful to everyone who helped. A huge and heartfelt thanks to Frances O'Brien, Patricia Lebowitz QUEEN MINTNESS!, Allison Cheshire, Kellee Fabre, Sarah Green, Meagan Reynoso, Marie-Pierre D'Auteuil, Janett Corona, Jayce Cruz, Gabriela Vivas, Carly Wilson, Danielle Lagasse, Nicole Westmoreland, and Jewel Carusoa. Without you, this would have been a mess. All my love!

To the team who helps bring my vision to life: Elaine York with Allusion Publishing, Nicole McCurdy with Emerald Edits, Nina Grinstead, Kim Cermak, and the whole team at Valentine PR, Ren Saliba, and Staci Hart with Quirky Bird Cover Design – THANK YOU. From editing and formatting to photography and promotion, it truly takes a village. I'm so thankful for each and every one of you.

And finally, to YOU, the reader – if you've read this far, all the way into the acknowledgements? Kudos, babe. And I just want you to know that none of this would be possible without you. There isn't a day that goes by that I take any of this for granted, that I don't pinch myself and send gratitude bombs into the universe. Thank you for reading my books, for posting about them on social media, for leaving reviews, and for reading indie, period. You are the wind beneath my wings, and I appreciate you more than I could ever convey.

About the Author

Kandi Steiner is a #1 Amazon Bestselling Author and whiskey connoisseur living in Tampa, FL. Best known for writing "emotional rollercoaster" stories, she loves bringing flawed characters to life and writing about real, raw romance — in all its forms. No two Kandi Steiner books are the same, and if you're a lover of angsty, emotional, and inspirational reads, she's your gal.

An alumna of the University of Central Florida, Kandi graduated with a double major in Creative Writing and Advertising/PR with a minor in Women's Studies. Her love for writing started at the ripe age of 10, and in 6th grade, she wrote and edited her own newspaper and distributed to her classmates. Eventually, the principal caught on and the newspaper was quickly halted, though Kandi tried fighting for her "freedom of press."

She took particular interest in writing romance after college, as she has always been a die hard hopeless romantic, and likes to highlight all the challenges of love as well as the triumphs.

When Kandi isn't writing, you can find her reading books of all kinds, planning her next adventure, or pole dancing (yes, you read that right). She enjoys live music, traveling, hiking, yoga, playing with her fur babies and soaking up the sweetness of life.

Connect with Kandi:

NEWSLETTER: kandisteiner.com/newsletter
FACEBOOK: facebook.com/kandisteiner
FACEBOOK READER GROUP (Kandiland):
facebook.com/groups/kandilandks
INSTAGRAM: Instagram.com/kandisteiner
TIKTOK: tiktok.com/@authorkandisteiner
TWITTER: twitter.com/kandisteiner
PINTEREST: pinterest.com/authorkandisteiner
WEBSITE: www.kandisteiner.com
Kandi Steiner may be coming to a city near you! C
heck out her "events" tab to see all the signings
she's attending in the near future:
www.kandisteiner.com/events